CONTENTS

PROLOGUE   Pg 1

Chapter One   Pg 3

Chapter Two   Pg 25

Chapter Three   Pg 36

Chapter Four   Pg 50

Chapter Five   Pg 64

Chapter Six   Pg 78

Chapter Seven   Pg 87

Chapter Eight   Pg 100

Chapter Nine   Pg 117

Chapter Ten   Pg 141

Chapter Eleven   Pg 159

Chapter Twelve   Pg 172

Chapter Thirteen Pg 195

Chapter Fourteen   Pg 206

Chapter Fifteen   Pg 220

Chapter Sixteen   Pg 233

Chapter Seventeen   Pg 257

Chapter Eighteen   Pg 272

Chapter Nineteen   Pg 287

Chapter Twenty   Pg 298

Chapter Twenty-One   Pg 316

Chapter Twenty-Two   Pg 333

Chapter Twenty-Three   Pg 345

EPILOGUE   Pg 367

PROLOGUE

Von Vadim Estate
Hixton, Wisconsin

In the dark confines of the basement, Corin watched over Angelique as she endured her transformation. Having his own mental connection since they had joined by blood, he was privy to a message she'd telepathically sent to her brother.

"Angelique." He watched her awaken. "You've eased Tomes's mind. Mine as well."

She smiled at him. "You heard?"

"We are tied by blood, but we can control who hears and doesn't. However, with twins, the connection is much stronger. And high emotion can sometimes interfere with our ability to control our thought transference," he explained. "How do you feel?"

"Like you said, the monster is with me. I feel it. But I also feel strong. Powerful."

"It will take time to adjust to the changes."

"I'd imagined much worse, but the hunger—"

"It is tormenting," Corin finished. "You feel as though you need to hunt, kill, anything to stop the pangs." He held his wrist out in front of her. "Drink."

She hesitated.

"You'll need this. It's hours till nightfall." He cut a vertical slit along his left wrist, knowing the sight of fresh blood would compel her to action.

Her hazel irises, rimmed in sangria, transitioned to a widened black border as her fangs emerged, but she fought her hunger, struggling to maintain control.

"I know you're starving. Don't fight it."

Needing no further persuasion, she took his offering, consuming the fluid as if she'd never drink again.

"That's enough." He pulled his wrist away, tearing his flesh in the process.

"What am I doing? I couldn't stop."

"It's okay." Corin brushed his fingers over the wound and healed the minor injury. "It takes time to learn to control the urges. You'll feel better once we feed tonight." He wrapped her in his arms. "Regrets?" He stroked her long, dark hair.

"I told you before, I could never regret you, but I am afraid of what comes next."

"We'll face it together."

Holding her close, he could hardly believe that she was immortal. He would never lose her to time or illness...mortality. Now, walking as one, they would share the night. To have and to hold for all time.

1

Six months later
Von Vadim Estate
Hixton, Wisconsin

En route to the foyer, Dusk and Dawn—two spotted servals—leapt past Corin's feet. Reaching the mansion's tall entrance, the felines hyperactively paced, casting their lanky shadows along the mixed ivory and slate floor.

"Jax." Corin was happy to see his friend, giving him a warm welcome, with an accompanying slap to his shoulder. "You've brought someone." His sight settled on an unexpected female guest.

"This is Kara. A friend."

The young woman dusted snow from her hip-length vinyl jacket. "I hope you don't mind that I tagged along."

"We're glad to have you," Corin welcomed her. "Come on inside."

Passing through the doorway, Jax handed Corin a long, white envelope. "This was pinned to the door." He removed his overcoat. "I'm glad to be rid of this thing for a while. I know you're partial to the look, Corin, but I don't like being weighed down."

"When we're in public, we have to blend in with the mortals." Kara slipped off her jacket. "We don't want to draw attention."

"True," Jax said, "but here, among friends, we're thankfully free to be ourselves."

Corin, taking a closer look at the envelope, was suddenly shot with a rush of unease when he saw the addressee—Luca. His heart rate accelerated as he peered back out the open doorway, wondering who had made the delivery. Only a minute number of individuals knew his given name, and of those still living, he was referred to as Corin, never Luca.

"Is something wrong?" Jax reclaimed Corin's attention. "Do you sense something?"

"This—" Corin started to respond, but deferred the topic when Angelique entered the room. "Later." He shoved the envelope in his pocket, shut the door, and maneuvered Jax in her direction. "My love." He wrapped his arm around her waist. "This is my good friend, Jax."

"The famous Angelique." Jax kissed her hand.

"Famous?" Her brow rose. "I don't understand."

"To those who have known Corin—a nightwalker who has never taken an immortal companion, until you—it must be fate."

"I see." Angelique's mouth drew upward. "She who has tamed the beast."

"Precisely." Jax gestured toward Angelique. "Beauty." He then turned and tossed Corin a smirk. "And the beast."

"Couldn't resist, could you? Always managing to find

amusement at my expense," Corin said with a scowl. "But you're right about one thing, Jax, it is without a doubt, fate." He freely admitted his firm belief in the mystic goddesses.

"She is stunning, Corin. You're a lucky man."

Corin pulled Angelique close. "Very lucky."

"You've brought someone with you." Angelique eyed Jax's friend who was preoccupied with Dusk and Dawn.

"Forgive me. This is Kara," Jax introduced the immortal.

Angelique kindly greeted her. "Dusk and Dawn are certainly accepting of you."

Thick flaxen strands parted, revealing soft blue eyes, as Kara peered up. "They are beautiful animals. Not your typical housecats." She ran her hand along one feline's back. "African servals, aren't they?"

"Yes. They're not always so affectionate," Angelique told her. "They are quite intuitive. Their reaction to you tells me a lot about you and your character."

"Then they probably won't come near me," Jax joked.

"That's not a lie," Corin corroborated with a laugh, and Angelique playfully elbowed him.

Kara rose as Dusk sauntered over to Angelique.

Corin reached down and rubbed the animal's head. "They're protective of Angelique, especially this one."

"They're not full-grown." Kara observed the size of the cats.

"No. They're six months old, a gift from Corin when I moved to the estate." Angelique smiled at her partner. "One of many."

"As well as that engagement ring." Kara admired the diamond adorning Angelique's ring finger. "It's beautiful."

"Thank you." Angelique adjusted the band that had slid somewhat askew.

"With Corin, I'm surprised you're not lugging around a rock the size of a golf ball," Jax blurted smartly.

Angelique laughed. "No. This is flashy enough. I'm not that flamboyant a person." She looked at Corin, and their gaze momentarily locked as she spoke to him telepathically. "Something is troubling you. What is it?"

He should have known she'd sense his unease. "Everything's fine," he silently responded, catching Jax's curious stare. "Ladies," he spoke aloud. "I don't mean to be rude, but it's been a while since I've seen my good friend Jax. Would you mind if he and I take a moment to catch up? We won't be long."

"Keeping secrets already?" Angelique needled.

"Could I keep anything from you, my love?" Corin referred to their strong connection since being tied by blood.

For nightwalkers, certain relations, strong blood ties, and intense emotion heightened telepathy. Especially twin connections; however, all thought transference could be blocked at will, even the stronger ties.

"Go ahead." Angelique waved a hand. "We'll be fine."

With a departing kiss, Corin exited the house with Jax, and stepped past his friend's gray Boxster. At 3 degrees below zero, the ground was blanketed white, but it was no bother to Corin. Nightwalkers didn't feel the cold the same as humans.

"What's this all about?" Jax asked.

"Let's walk a little further." Corin stopped when he'd reached a distance he surmised no one inside would intercept their conversation. Looking back at the house he was weighed down by guilt for secretly blocking his telepathic connection with Angelique, but it couldn't be helped. Being the eve of their wedding, he didn't want anything to overshadow the occasion, and he sensed trouble.

"Did you detect any immortals near the estate when arriving?" Corin visually scoured their surroundings while pulling out the envelope that dominated his thoughts.

"None in range. But you well know that's not foolproof. Someone skillful enough could be close...watching." Jax glanced at the envelope gripped in Corin's hand. "You apparently didn't sense whoever delivered that message. What is this all about? Who is Luca?"

Corin cut his eyes at him. "I am Luca." He pressed his fingers to his chest. "My given name from centuries ago. A name that very few know."

"You think this means trouble?"

"I'm not sure, but I'd feel better if we swept the perimeter. See if we pick up anything."

"Okay. I'll take this direction." Jax indicated north and east. "Cover this side, say two or three miles out, and meet you back here." He shape-shifted, feathers replacing skin as he transformed into a hawk, and leapt into flight.

Corin tucked the envelope back in his pocket and took the form of his favorite nocturnal predator—a Great Horned Owl. He set out in the opposite direction and thoroughly combed the winter-worn area, returning nearly ten minutes later to find Jax impatiently waiting.

"I was getting worried."

"I had to be sure they're gone."

"So, you take the message as a threat?" Jax interpreted his meaning.

"Whoever delivered this letter has gone to great lengths to conceal their identity, and that doesn't set well with me."

"What does the note say?"

"I haven't read it yet"

"What are you waiting for? We could be worrying over nothing."

Corin reached for the envelope, ripped open the end, and slid out an off-white sheet of paper. A look of disbelief melted his expression as he silently glanced over the handwritten letter. "This can't be."

"What is it, Corin?"

"The person who sent this is claiming to be Jozsef. My brother. But that isn't possible." Corin held a distant stare. "Jozsef was killed in Serbia five hundred years ago."

Jax's eyes locked on Corin. "You know that for fact?"

"The family received word that his party had been attacked and that no one had survived. With him being so far from home, we never found out what became of his remains."

"A body was never produced?" Jax popped his knuckles. A nervous habit.

"No." Corin's voice was distant. "It wasn't."

"So, this could very well be him, alive, and apparently changed."

"Or someone is playing games." Corin found it hard to accept the idea of Jozsef being alive...immortal. If it were true, why would his brother have waited so long to find him? "It's been hundreds of years."

"Nothing's impossible. We're living proof of that."

"It's written in old Hungarian, my language when I was mortal."

"The name on the envelope is in English," Jax pointed out.

"I assume in case someone else found it."

"What does it say? Is it threatening?"

Corin read the words aloud: "Score, Luca, worthy of the shield. Jozsef."

"Not much of a message. But I take it you know exactly what it means."

"Yes. It's something Jozsef and I used to say as boys, after a match. Score, worthy of the shield. Our whole life was centered on knighthood, from page, to squire, to being dubbed a knight representing the honor of our family coat of arms."

"Funny picturing you as a knight."

"Many lifetimes ago."

"Well, it seems your brother is alive and letting you know he's here. But why the mystery? Did you part on bad terms?"

"Not at all. And I'm not convinced this is from Jozsef." Corin folded the letter and slid it in the envelope. "I'm not sure what someone's trying to pull, but it'll have to wait till after tomorrow night." He gestured toward the house. "This is Angelique's time."

"And yours." Jax strode alongside. "Eternal union is the greatest vow two immortals can make to each other. You're already companions, so why marriage? Something she wanted?"

"No. Something I wanted," Corin made clear.

"I see." Jax grinned, his teeth gleaming bright white in contrast to his straight red hair that framed his face. "Everything has to be honorable with you. Must be morals stemming from your knighthood heritage."

"One day, when you find the right partner, you'll understand."

"God, I hope not." Jax slapped Corin's back. "I couldn't imagine being tied down to one woman, or to one place. I'm free as a bird and plan to stay that way. Of course, you did always prefer the solitary, quiet life. So, for you, this fits."

"Angelique loves Hixton as much as I do. Her family farm and this estate land mean the world to her, as it does to me."

"Sounds like you've found your perfect match. Are you going to tell her about the letter?"

"Not until I know more." Corin stopped short of the door. "Let's keep this between us for the time being."

Jax agreed. "About Angelique, it seems she's fared quite well for a pup...with her conversion."

"I don't care for that expression."

"Sorry. A newly-born nightwalker then," Jax rephrased.

"She's learning to deal with the hunger, but yes, she's adjusted well."

"She's lucky. Most newborns take much longer finding balance, learning to control their monsters and discovering their gifts."

Corin reached for the door handle. "She has me."

"Of course." Jax laughed. "That must be it."

Corin opened the entry door, catching Angelique's awaiting stare from the sofa, where she and Kara leisurely conversed. He knew she'd detected his return even before he'd reached the door.

"Talking nice about us, I hope," Jax teased.

"Kara was just about to tell me how the two of you met," Angelique shared.

"I'd better sit in on this, for accuracy." Jax plopped down next to Kara and winked at her. "See if we share the same version."

"Well, we met a year ago in a jazz club in New Hampshire," Kara began. "The band was playing *My Funny Valentine* when I sensed him, sitting in a dark corner, watching me from over the top of a menu. He thought he was so suave...debonair."

"Sounds about right." Corin scooted next to Angelique.

"Hold on, now." Jax held up a hand. "I am very *debonair*." He spoke with a French accent. "I think we can all agree on that."

Kara continued. "He finally came over and asked if I'd like to join him for a drink. I asked: 'What kind of a drink?' He said: 'How about we start with a couple Bloody Marys, or Elizabeths, or Jims?'"

"Smooth." Corin chuckled. "You sure put a lot of thought into that pickup."

Jax leaned toward Corin. "It's not the line, Corin, but how one delivers it. And Kara, she appreciates my sense of humor."

"I really do." She brushed his pale cheek. "You're one of a kind, my dear."

"Now the real story starts." Jax settled back. "We'd spent several nights together in my nearby home, getting acquainted, when early one morning—around 3 a.m.—a nightwalker named Luke Shaw paid us an unwelcome call."

"My clan leader. Powerful and controlling," Kara enlightened.

"He'd tried to coerce her into his little harem, but she'd refused his every attempt." Jax laid his arm over her shoulders. "Still, bound by blood, she was tied to him and his clan."

"A harem? You mean more than one wife?" Angelique clarified.

"Precisely." Kara looked at her. "He had five at last count and could care less for any of them."

Angelique grimaced. "No wonder you wanted out."

Kara nodded. "The more I fought him, the harder he pursued. But luckily, I found Jax."

"I bet Shaw didn't take that too well," Corin said.

"No." Kara's lips tightened. "He wasn't too happy."

Jax audibly exhaled. "That's an understatement. "But the resourceful guy I am, I managed to turn a slaying into a wager."

"A wager?" Corin couldn't resist winding a section of Angelique's long, silky hair through his fingers. "With a clan behind him, I'm surprised he didn't take you out right then."

"I was prepared. Kara had told me a lot about Shaw and his interests. To say that he was a real archery enthusiast is putting it mildly. He'd set game loose in nearby woods and hunt the animals down for sport. So, armed with that knowledge, I channeled his competitive side and challenged him to a match. If he won, I'd leave town and walk away from Kara forever, but if I won, he'd relinquish his hold on her—give her freedom."

"Knowing his thrill for the game, you were sure he'd take the wager, unable to resist your challenge." Angelique was thoroughly immersed.

"Let's say ninety percent sure." Jax straightened in his seat, leaving a gap of several inches between him and Kara. "I'd already come to care for Kara. There was no way, at that point, I could just walk away."

Angelique smiled. "I see why Corin thinks so highly of you. And since Kara is here with you now, I assume you won the match."

Jax grinned. "By the skin of my teeth."

"A narrow win, huh?" Corin said.

"You have no idea." Jax popped his knuckles. "Thankfully, luck was on my side. Shaw was on his sixth buck when several wolves moved in on his chase and interfered with what would have otherwise been a timely kill, affording me crucial seconds I desperately needed to beat him to the seventh count...and win."

"Beware, Kara, Jax has always been good at managing to land himself in impossible situations," Corin warned.

"I can't argue," Jax agreed. "It is the truth."

Kara reached for Jax's hand. "So far, for me, your presence in my life has been nothing but a good thing."

"Everybody loves me." Jax played the clown.

Laughing, Angelique repositioned, preparing to stand. "It's so great having you here for the week." She looked at Corin. "I'm anxious to show off the new addition."

"Angelique's brother, Tomes, just completed a special project for us. Underground living quarters." Corin stood up. "Let me give you a tour. I'm sure you'd like to get settled in."

"I should grab our luggage from the car." Jax aimed for the door.

Corin followed. "I'll give you a hand."

Returning, luggage in tow, Corin led their guests to a door that opened to a descending stairwell. Going down the steps, he continued through another door and into a large, circular multi-functional room. A long bar with eight swivel stools took up most of one side, and opposite the bar, a flat screen TV hung on a forest green wall near a sofa, chairs, and several tall cases filled with books.

"This is outstanding. I like the open, circular design. Very modern," Jax complimented. "A wedding gift?"

"Tomes wanted Angelique to be comfortable during the daylight hours. I've said it more than once, he's a man full of talents." Corin admired his closest friend's handiwork. "Angelique calls it saven, for safe and haven."

"Kara, I think you'll like this room." Angelique opened one of six doors that branched off the main room, revealing a furnished bedroom with a dusty-raspberry color scheme. "There's an adjoining bath." She pointed out the room. "I'd initially chosen the room next door for Jax, but I think this one better suits you."

"I could definitely grow accustomed to this." Kara moved toward an antique-finished poster bed, running her hand up one of the intricately carved posts. "I may never leave."

"Nice setup." Jax gave the room a quick once-over as he and Corin set the suitcases inside the door. "But I still sleep in a crypt."

"Being human, I think it bothers Tomes to think of his sister in a crypt, plus, I believe he's trying to modernize me. But it's hard to leave the old ways behind," Corin told him. "So, I made sure we had a choice." He pressed a button next to the light switch that set the back wall of the room into motion, sliding to the right, revealing a crypt forged into a casing of rock.

Jax whistled. "Genius."

"How about a drink?" Corin headed out of the room and toward the bar.

"Sure." Jax followed and sat in one of the eight stools. "I could do with a little something."

Corin pulled out a highball glass and set it in front of Jax along with a bottle of Jack Daniels. "I stocked up."

"I appreciate that." Jax reached for the whiskey bottle and poured a generous measure, swallowing it down in one gulp. "Appropriate décor." He observed two swords hanging on the wall behind the bar.

"You never know when they might come in handy."

Angelique and Kara emerged from the bedroom and took seats on the sofa.

"I hope you don't mind sharing the main room," Angelique said. "We're expecting more company."

Jax swiveled in his chair and faced them. "Not at all."

"Angelique and I will be staying in the basement while you're here." Corin emerged from behind the bar and claimed a chair adjacent the sofa.

"We don't want to displace you." Jax remained at the bar.

"No one's being displaced," Corin assured them.

"Tomes just finished this project. We'll be moving in here later, but for now, we want you to enjoy your stay."

Angelique suddenly stood. "Someone else is here."

Corin rose as the doorbell rang out and straightway headed upstairs with Angelique, Jax, and Kara trailing him to the foyer. Opening the door, he greeted their third guest with a firm handshake. "It's good to see you, Jordon." He pulled him inside. "Still masquerading as a marshal, I see."

"Yep. I'm still at it." Jordon dropped his bag next to the door. "Angelique. You look wonderful...stunning." He immediately took note of her. "You've adapted well to your new life."

"With Corin's guidance." She accepted a friendly hug from the daywalker. "I have my moments, but it gets easier every day."

Corin eyed the 9mm strapped to his shoulder. "You can set that gun aside for a few days."

Jordon patted the holster. "Happy to."

"I'd like you to meet Jax and Kara. They've come for the wedding," Corin introduced his guests. "Jax is an old and trusted friend."

Jax shook Jordon's hand. "A marshal, huh? Jeans, gator-skin boots...ponytail. You don't exactly fit the profile of a lawman."

"He defies the stereotype," Corin told Jax. "Jordon was an ally six months back against Boldor," he explained their connection.

Angelique motioned to the living room. "Let's sit."

Jordon leaned into Corin. "Do they know about me?"

"I'd never break your confidence," Corin assured him. "Your secrets aren't mine to tell."

"You're nightwalker?" Jax asked. "With secrets?" He'd caught their exchange.

"You'll have to forgive Jax for being so meddlesome," Kara apologized on Jax's behalf.

"Meddlesome?" Jax scoffed. "I'm just trying to get to know the guy."

"No, it's okay," Jordon said. "I'm not a nightwalker, but I am immortal. I'm a daywalker. Unlike you, the sun doesn't harm me, and I don't drink blood."

"I've heard of your kind, but you're the first I've met." Jax continued to size him up. "You have the best of both worlds."

"Yes, he certainly does." Corin cut his eyes at Jordon, amused by the irony of Jax's words.

Jordon—an Indith immortal from the Eleventh Dimension—actually was from another world. But that information wasn't Corin's to divulge.

Jax held a perplexed expression. "I feel as though I've missed something."

"An associate of Jordon's, a nightwalker named Galvar, will be performing the ceremony." Corin diverted the conversation. "He, too, has become a good friend."

Jax pointed a finger at Corin. "You're a changed man. You have never been so sociable in all the years I've known you."

Angelique leaned forward. "I like to think I had a little to do with that."

"Without a doubt." Jax grinned. "Lured him right out of his shell."

"When is Galvar arriving, Jordon?" Angelique inquired.

"He's traveling with another nightwalker. His name is Vynce. They have business nearby. They'll be here tomorrow night."

"He's cutting it close." Corin was concerned, wanting a perfect ceremony. "The transference of vows has to take place precisely at midnight."

"He'll be here," Jordon guaranteed. "It would have to be a matter of life or death for him not to show."

Corin was honored that the hierarch of the clythguard had agreed to officiate his and Angelique's union, but he wasn't comfortable with the commander's delay. In addition to the mystery of the letter, he was further troubled by a dark foreboding that something bad teetered on the horizon, the message claiming to be from Jozsef the primary indication.

Angelique intertwined her fingers with his. "You're so on edge." She communicated through thought transference. "Don't worry. It's going to be a night to remember." She shifted her focus to Jordon and spoke aloud. "I thought you'd like to stay with the others in our new underground quarters. You'll be able to spend more time with Galvar when he arrives. There are plenty of rooms."

"If you don't mind, I'd rather stay in the house," Jordon declined. "I was very comfortable in the room I occupied on my last stay. Someone should keep an eye on things."

This added to Corin's apprehension. Why was Jordon being guarded?

After a lengthy visitation, Jax and Kara retired to their room in the saven to settle in while Corin and Angelique made their way to the basement to go over a few final details before the upcoming ceremony.

"I can't wait to see you in that." Corin eased up behind Angelique who stood at the dresser admiring looking over the dress she'd special-ordered for the occasion—white satin, adorned with pale silver lace.

"You shouldn't be seeing it now." She tucked it out of sight.

He placed a hand on the small of her back, and she turned to face him. Unable to resist, he pulled her into a passionate kiss. He could never get enough of her, she was his sustenance, his reason for living.

Shedding their clothes, he swooped her off her feet and carried her to their crypt forged into the back wall.

"I hope you'll always want me this much," she whispered.

"Forever is not long enough."

His hands traveled over her entirety as he took possession of her lips, breathing her in. Slowly drawing back, he gazed into her hazel eyes that glittered with flecks of violet in their moment of passion and couldn't believe how lucky he was.

She was his angel. His savior.

"You are everything to me, Corin." Her long, dark tresses pooled around her face as she looked up at him with a loving expression, her want and desire matching his own.

"I believe you have that backward. It is you, my love, that is everything to me."

He kissed her again with a deeper intensity, heat between them rising to a raging furnace as their bodies melded.

Lying in the blissful aftermath, he held her naked body against him. "I never want to let you go."

"Right now, you have to. I have a few more things to look over before morning." She pulled away and crawled out of the crypt.

He sat up and watched her dress.

"It's still a while till sunrise." He got up and pulled on his pants. "I think I'll go back upstairs, unless you need me here."

"You want to spend a little more time with Jordon?" she presumed. "I'm not sure what's troubling you, but maybe talking with him will help."

"Everything is fine. Just nerves."

"Not having second thoughts, are you?"

"To the contrary." He stepped up to her and brushed the back of his fingers along her cheek. "I want it to be perfect. Eternal union. It's an important night. And now Galvar has been delayed."

"I have faith in him. But Jordon can better assure you. Go ahead. I have things to do here."

Corin finished dressing and left Angelique in the basement, eager to have a private talk with Jordon. Flooded with déjà vu, the house felt unsettled, as it had when Boldor had been a threat six months earlier.

Jordon opened his door before Corin knocked. "I sensed you coming."

"Angelique shares your talent." Corin referred to her precognitive ability. "Care to join me downstairs for a drink?"

"Sure." Jordon stepped into the hall and pulled the door shut behind him. "Were you wandering the house earlier?"

"No. It was probably Jax or Kara. They still have some time till daybreak."

Descending to the first floor, Corin poured two brandies, and they stepped onto the lanai, taking a seat at a wrought iron patio table. The scene was painted silver under the cascading light of the moon.

Jordon looked toward the woods. Several wolves' forlorn howls echoed in the near distance. "Persistent animals. They never back off."

"As long as we're here, they will be too." Corin continually turned his glass in short rotations as he talked. "Jordon, I want to know if something's happening that I should know about. What's delayed Galvar?"

"I didn't want to spoil the occasion with negative news."

"What news?"

"Several things are plaguing our lives at present. The

most alarming is the Passage of Dimensions. Something has disabled it. No one has been able to cross worlds for over a week. We can only pray that things are okay in the Eleventh Dimension." Jordon took a drink. "I'll have to return to the Order immediately after the ceremony."

"You have no idea what's caused the disruption?"

"I can only imagine the worst of scenarios," Jordon groaned. "But the thing keeping Galvar from joining us tonight is another matter—the Body of the Clyth. The Order has reason to believe it's still here."

"I thought Lehndra took the charm."

"She's now back in the custody of the Order, and she wasn't in possession of it. From what I understand, one of the clythguard posing as a spy, overheard contact made between someone here, in Hixton, and a member of a highly organized clan known as Örök Vér, located in The Dalles, Oregon—a nightwalker called Meical Evon. It's been reported that over the years he's compiled a book he calls the *Trove Chan Allu*—Welsh meaning gathering or trove of power. It discloses secrets that could destroy worlds by revealing the existence and powers of several protected charms and talismans, his most recent installment—the Clyth. He somehow gained knowledge of the Order and has now set out to expose the clythguard."

"Lehndra?"

"There's been internal turmoil for some time, spurred by her ideals of Delghorlin dominion, but as much as I distrust her, I don't think she's the leak."

"There are others like me that know about the Order." Corin leaned forward on the table.

"I suspect sabotage from within. Only members would have the detailed knowledge that Meical has managed to obtain. Looks like we have a traitor among us."

"If the Body of the Clyth didn't leave the graveyard with Lehndra the night we faced Boldor, who did it leave with?"

"That's a question we'd all like an answer to. The only name our informant caught before they grew suspicious was the town—Black River Falls. We also now know that Meical is on his way here."

"I take it Galvar is setting a few things in place," Corin figured. "Meical should lead him to whoever has the charm."

"I'm not entirely certain of his plan, but as experience has proven, nothing is ever that easy. He'll enlighten me when he arrives."

"I think I'll take a run before dawn. Clear my mind."

"Galvar promised to be here, Corin, despite the circumstances. Only, like I said, our stay will be short."

"I understand."

Corin left through the lanai door, transformed, and took to the woods to expel his tension. In the form of a large, white wolf with slight brown detailing, he moved through the thick span of land at a high rate of speed, knowing every inch of the terrain so well he could traverse it with eyes closed if need be. It was home and had been for five hundred years.

Stopping near the creek that bordered Jaffler Farm, he stopped, reclaimed his human form, and reflected awhile. He recalled an encounter he'd had there with Angelique six months prior and smiled, never imagining, at that time, that things would turn out the way they had. Jax was right, he was a changed man, because of Angelique.

Returning to the mansion, Corin poured another drink and sat alone on the lanai, listening to the wolves. Pulling out the letter he still carried with him, he read the message again.

It's not possible.

He couldn't accept that Jozsef was alive. But who else would know such an intimate detail from his past life?

Seeing that dawn was ushering in the light of a new day, he finished his drink and aimed for the basement. Pausing at the door, he decided to make one last sweep through the house before going below and went about the task, meeting up with Jax in a long corridor lined with portraits.

"Bored with the lair already?" Corin spoke first.

"No. It's Kara. She's watching the History channel. Like we haven't seen enough history." Jax huffed.

"My sympathies." Corin found Jax's plight comical. "But you'd better get below. The sun's on the horizon."

"I know. I'm heading back down. Hopefully she's moved on to something else."

Corin gave his friend a slap to the upper arm for encouragement. "I'll see you this evening." He parted way and strode on to the basement.

Angelique was in the crypt, peacefully sleeping, with Dusk lying at her feet. The other serval, Dawn, watched from a position above them, following Corin's movement as he settled in a corner of the room and looked over the letter yet again, tormented by the mystery.

His memories took him back to a specific day when he was mortal, the age of twenty. He'd returned home from training to mourn the loss of an uncle who'd been killed by a Turkish prince over a woman both men had favored. A barbaric race, the Turks proved their savage nature by nearly wiped out the Hungarians several years later.

Being a squire at that time, in apprenticeship to a knight that lived more than a day away, Corin had resided with his master's family and hadn't returned home often. He recalled standing beside his uncle's coffin, his brother next to him, staring down at the cloaked body wrapped in winding sheets sewn at his head and feet. Glancing at Jozsef, a look of mortification plagued his brother's face. He'd figured the thought of sealing their uncle within the coffin must had dredged up repressed terror that stemmed from an unfortunate occurrence a couple of years prior to that day, when he and Jozsef had been victims of a collapse on the north side of the castle, a terrible event that had trapped them within a ground-level room and buried for several hours beneath a mountain of debris.

How did that room not collapse?

That was a question Corin had been asking himself for five hundred years. He'd once thought that he and Jozsef had been spared for a greater purpose, but when Jozsef was killed, and he was damned to darkness less than a month later, that belief proved false, for there was no greater good in their outcomes.

He recalled their rescue from the rubble by their father, Count Ramone von Vadim, along with several servants. He and Jozsef had survived without physical injury, but not fully unscathed. The incident had mentally traumatized Jozsef, leaving him with a continuing fear of tight spaces—severe claustrophobia.

Shifting his thoughts to the night following his uncle's funeral, a time forever etched in his mind with it being the last time he'd seen Jozsef, he had retired early for the evening with plans to bid his family a proper goodbye the coming morning. But before sunrise, a messenger had arrived with an urgent call from his master's home to return immediately. Fearing for his teacher and friend, he'd left without delay, leaving a letter explaining his unexpected departure. Days later, overseeing his master's estate while the nobleman lay bedridden from a life-threatening sword wound, Corin had learnt Jozsef was being dubbed into knighthood. However, due to his mentor's deteriorating condition, he wasn't able to attend the ceremony, and pushing his own aspirations of knighthood aside, he'd continued to manage his master's affairs and estate since there were no sons or immediate male relations to take on the duty.

After two long years, the nobleman fully recovered, and Corin's day for knighthood finally returned him to von Vadim Castle to prepare for the grand occasion. Expecting to find Jozsef home, he was disappointed to learn that his brother had been sent on a goodwill mission to deliver a chest of opals from his families' mine to a King in Serbia. A trip he'd never returned from.

"Jozsef." Corin laid his head back and shut his eyes. A tear traced his cheek as he conjured to mind a message that had arrived announcing that Jozsef had been killed, words he'd never forget, cutting so deep that he still felt the ache to present day.

"Time heals all wounds," he muttered, having wished on more than one occasion that the idiom was true.

But the heartache he carried with him proved that sometimes there is no cure for the pain, and one must simply learn to endure. And over the years, he had endured more than his share. But now he had Angelique, and she had renewed his zest for life.

He glanced at the crypt, then he looked back at the letter.

I have to protect you from this.

He refolded the paper and returned it to his pocket.

I don't know who you are, claiming to be my brother. But come after us and you'll share Boldor's fate.

Above all else, he had to keep Angelique safe.

2

A white wolf transformed from animal to man at the edge of dense woods surrounding the local cemetery. Wind whipping through thick, entangled branches moaned as the individual moved toward an aboveground family vault marked *Chesterson* and entered its cold, dark confines. He glanced over the caskets of the silent inhabitants resting within, immediately taking notice of a figure slumped against the back wall. Several grinding pops sprang out from the shadow-shroud form, giving away the individual's identity.

"Beloved Mother." Jozsef's hand grazed the coffins as he ambled past each one. "Father. Sister." He slapped his hand down with an accompanying grunt. "Brother." His vision locked on a cloudy epitaph.

"So, you've let von Vadim know you're here." The dark form straightened, now presenting the obvious image of a man, and stepped his way.

"I've got him wondering." Jozsef looked over the

coffin where his hand still pressed against its cold surface. *Yes. Beloved brother.* He could see who the deceased had been in life, like a movie playing before him.

"I guess there's no turning back now. You sure he'll believe it's you?"

"I've got something else to follow that message." He held out his hand revealing a large opal ring adorning his middle finger. "This won't fail." His gaze readjusted on the immortal who'd progressed to the door. "Is there something more?" The individual gawked, making him uneasy.

"Sorry. I can't help staring. It's hard to get used to."

"You just keep up with things on your end. You do your job, and I'll do mine."

Nothing more to say, the immortal exited the crypt and vanished into the night.

Jozsef broke the lid off a casket and cleaned out its human remains. He climbed in and lay back, shutting himself in. His body needed rest, but his mind was working overtime.

"Score, Corin, worthy of the shield. It's been a long time coming, but now it's time to face the past...brother."

* * * *

Tomes arrived at the mansion at precisely 9:25 a.m. and made his way to the back lawn where he intended to make some final touchups on a gazebo he'd built for the wedding.

Darn. I left my drill in the underground quarters yesterday.

He knew guests had arrived, but needing the tool, he figured he could quietly slip into the saven and grab it without disturbing their sleep.

I'll be quick.

He hurried inside and eased down the stairs, into the lair, and dashed stealthily toward the bar, the last place he remembered having it.

"What the—" A figure suddenly lunged at him, and in one swift maneuver, restrained him in a headlock from behind.

"Who are you?" The female immortal's breath struck his ear in a gruff whisper.

"Take it easy." Tomes's face contorted in discomfort. "I'm Angelique's brother, Tomes."

The immortal's grip softened, and she released him. "Sorry. Can't be too careful." She stepped back and introduced herself while thoroughly scanning him. "I'm here with Jax."

Tomes straightened the collar of his brown military jacket as he turned and faced her. "Who...." He momentarily lost focus when he saw her striking face. "Um, I...I don't know him."

"I think we should rectify that right now." A redheaded man approached. Slightly shorter than himself, the immortal wasn't too imposing, except for his penetrating forest-green eyes, which Tomes avoided looking directly into.

"I'm Jax. A friend of Corin's." The immortal extended a hand. "So, you're the mastermind behind this underground retreat. Genius."

"I want Angel to be comfortable, day and night."

Jax aimed for the sofa, cracking his knuckles as he walked. "Corin said as much, and I think you've achieved your goal."

"You call your sister Angel. I love that." Kara glided behind Jax.

"I always have." Tomes caught a strange exchange between the two immortals as he followed, wondering what the look meant.

"So, I hear you and Corin have become very good friends as well." Jax got comfortable. "I heard about your face-off with Boldor."

"I wouldn't be here today if it weren't for Corin." Tomes chose to remain standing. "He kept me from making some hasty moves. I wasn't myself then, after losing Louisa, my wife."

"Yes. I heard about that too. But in the end," Jax held up a finger, "the devil got what was coming to him."

"Again, thanks to Corin. But not before managing to inflict some damage."

"A madman's fixation." Jax shook his head. "But thankfully you made it through alive, and Corin and Angelique seem very happy."

Kara sat down across from Jax, her lively, blue eyes peeled on Tomes's every move. "I am a little envious."

Tomes shifted position, not sure what to make of the female immortal's intense stare, thinking she might be reading him as the morning menu. And with that thought, it was time to go.

"I'm sorry to have disturbed you. I was looking for a drill I left down here yesterday." He moved toward the bar and searched behind it, spotting the tool on one of the shelves. "Voilà." He held it up. "I'll get out of your hair now."

"Will we see you tonight?" Kara accompanied him to the door, hovering close. "At the ceremony?"

With her leaning so near, mere inches from him, Tomes was tempted to pull back, but he held his position. Was it possible she was attracted to him? "Brother of the bride. I'm obligated."

Jax stood. "Back off, Kara. You're making the poor guy nervous."

Tomes hated admitting it, but Jax was right, he was intimidated by Kara. She had easily overpowered him.

Strong. Fast. Immortal. And he had no idea what she had in mind, crowding his personal space. Was it hunger, or attraction?

"We'll see you at sundown." Jax waved.

Tomes hurried out and up the stairs, not stopping till he stood safely in the living room. He yanked the drapes back and allowed the light of day to flood the dim room. Collapsing in a chair, he took several deep breaths to calm his nerves.

"Kara." He exhaled her name.

In six months, since Louisa's death, he'd never even looked at another woman. But today, something about Kara stirred him. She was beautiful...intense...seductive. Possibly hungry.

"Get a grip, Tomes. She's immortal, not to mention the girlfriend of someone who could rip your head right off your shoulders. Get her out of your head. It can never happen."

He pushed himself up and went outside to the gazebo. Flipping on a portable radio tuned to a local classic rock station, he positioned a ladder and climbed to a comfortable height to work on the top of the structure. AC/DC's "Back in Black" transitioned into a news report announcing a murder that had occurred overnight. The body of a man had been found at an intersection just outside of Hixton.

"Drained of blood. No. Not again."

He glanced back at the house where four nightwalkers rested within the mansion's concealing walls.

"You're still struggling." His thoughts fell on Angelique. "No." He shook his head. "Corin would know. She feeds on animals with him. Just animals."

Jax and Kara, however, were strangers to him. Maybe they fed on humans. Or maybe one, or both of them, had killed that poor man.

"The first murder in six months the same night two nightwalkers come into town? That can't be coincidence."

But being Corin's guests, he would give them the benefit of the doubt, trusting his brother-in-law to be.

* * * *

"Meical Evon. He'll be here tonight with the *Trove Chan Allu*." Sheriff Pierson shut the top of a small, hinged jewel case protecting a locket-like charm.

"I'm not sure this is such a good idea," Patricia fretted. "Can you trust this guy? Him being a vampire?" She sat a cup of steaming black coffee on the kitchen table in front of Pierson.

"I'll watch my back." Sheriff Pierson took the last drag of a Marlboro, stubbed it out in the ashtray, and pulled out a weapon.

"What on earth is that?"

"When everything happened six months back with the Jackson County killings, and that vampire, Boldor, Tomes Jaffler used one of these for defense against the immortal. He had it custom-made. A re-engineered nail gun. He calls it a staker. He told me where he had it made, and I paid the fellow a visit. For a nominal fee he put this one together for me. The nails are made of blackthorn. Tormenting to vampires. This should be pretty good protection if things happen to take a bad turn."

"The guy who built it, does he know about the vampires?"

"He asked why I wanted the weapon, seeming very curious, so I don't think Tomes ever revealed anything to him. But being the sheriff, he didn't press for answers." Allen coughed and took a sip of coffee to sooth his irritated throat. Leaning back, he tapped out another cigarette, and lit it.

"You ought to cut down on those." Her brown eyes held concern.

"After I figure out how to use this charm—the Body—disease won't mean anything to us."

"I pray you're right, Allen. I hate the knots this puts in my stomach. You're risking your life. In your quest to achieve immortality, you could die."

"I'm doing this for us, Patricia. And I'm convinced this charm is the key to making it happen." He held up the jewel case. "We're too close to turn back now."

"Where are you meeting him?"

"There's a farm for sale off of State Road 121; lots of land with several large barns."

"McCall Farms."

"That's right. I'm to meet him there at midnight."

"You chose the spot?"

Allen shook his head. "No. A man named Miller, a middleman that Jerry from the bookstore put me in touch with, chose the place. I met with Miller three nights ago at his home, a large, old house on about fifty acres, east of Hixton." He rubbed the back of his neck. "The moment I got there; things didn't feel right."

"You're lucky it wasn't a trap."

"True. There's no telling who's after this—the Body of the Clyth." Sheriff Pierson studied the charm. "He questioned me about my knowledge of it. I told him I had worked a case that led me to the discovery of the Order of the Clythguard and the charm. I didn't give any specifics." He brushed a hand through his reddish-blond hair, lingering at the area above his left ear. "That twinge I get behind this ear," he tapped the spot, "signaling when something isn't quite right, never fails. And that night it kicked into full mode. I made it clear that I suspected him of being immortal. A vampire. He neither confirmed nor denied."

"You're too brave for your own good, Allen. How much do you know about the one you're meeting tonight?"

"Meical Evon. Author of the *Trove Chan Allu*. Vampires. He lives over seventeen hundred miles away. You have to ask yourself why he'd go to such lengths, declining my offer to travel to where he is. After all, I was the one seeking information. I figure they now assume the charm never left Hixton."

"And that you have it, since you're suddenly inquiring about it."

"Like I said, I claimed to have heard of the charm through a case. I pretended to be writing a book on unusual cases I've encountered over the years. Plausible as it sounds, yes, I'm sure he's come all this way with the assumption that I have it, or that I know more than I've admitted and can lead him to it. Also, I dared to stress a specific interest in immortality and wanting particular information on what power the charm possesses. Pretty incriminating. He'd be a fool not to be suspicious of my motives. I wouldn't be surprised if they were already watching me."

"They?"

"There were quite a few immortals present at the cemetery the night we had that standoff with Boldor."

"You've mentioned the Order of the Clythguard."

Pierson rubbed his neck again. "What I've done isn't right, I know that, but it's necessary."

"Give it a little more thought, Allen. Is it worth all of this? Besides, you won't stand a chance against immortals."

"I plan to offer a deal." Pierson leaned back. "I have a feeling Meical Evon will accept. All I want is for him to show me how to use this charm to gain immortality for you...for me. When we have that, I'll gladly give it up."

"What if he doesn't know how to use it?"

"Miller assured me that he has extensive knowledge of it documented in the *Trove Chan Allu*. And even if the charm won't grant immortality, don't forget what he is...that he has the ability. So, either way, there's a deal to be made."

Patricia's breath caught in her throat. "I have such a bad feeling about all of this. We're playing with fire."

"I have to take this risk." Allen reached for her. "This is our chance." He buried his fingers in her dusky strands.

She clutched his hand. "I'm afraid you might not come back."

"Don't worry. I told you, I have the staker." He looked into her warm eyes. "I hate to ask this of you, Patricia, but I need you to keep the charm safe while I go out tonight." He passed her the jewel case. "This immortal, Meical Evon, might sense it. I wish I didn't have to involve you, but you're the only one I can trust."

"I know what this means to you, Allen." She paused. "I'll do it for you...for us. I just wish it could be done another way. Vampires. Creatures that require drinking blood in order to survive. Is that really what we want to become?" She looked down.

"I have done a lot of research...you right there with me. This is the only way I know of to cheat death." He lifted her chin. "I know you're afraid, but look at Corin von Vadim, he's no monster. He and Angelique Jaffler seem to manage just fine. So will we."

"Did you ever consider just asking von Vadim for immortality? He trusts you enough to keep their secret."

"I discovered what von Vadim was on my own, through investigation. He never would have revealed his secret otherwise. And I did speak to Tomes Jaffler on several occasions, slipping in a few inquiries in regard to von Vadim, and it seems he's rather adverse to granting immortality. According to Tomes, and what I saw for myself, it took a lot of convincing for him to change Angelique. If she hadn't been on the brink of death, he may have never changed her."

"He must have his reasons. Something we don't know."

Pierson pulled back. "There is something. I was waiting for the right time, but there will never be a right time."

"What is it?"

"Nightwalkers carry a presence within them that has to be controlled. I figure it's what causes their hunger for blood."

Patricia sat the case on the table. "A presence?"

"I won't lie to you, Patricia. I want you to know what we're facing...nothing held back. What I saw when von Vadim fought Boldor was frightening. A monster emerged from him, like he was possessed by—"

"A demon?"

"Yes. But he controlled it. Angelique controls it." Pierson gripped her hands. "And so will we."

"All the research we did and you're just now telling me this?" Patricia pulled her hand back. "That's why he's so adverse to changing anyone. He sees it as a curse. And you hid that from me?"

"I didn't want this one thing to scare you away. It's but a small part of the whole picture."

"This isn't a small thing, Allen." Patricia walked to the sink with her back turned to him. "The walking dead. Immortals possessing demons who survive on blood of the living. You'd have to be blind not to see that clearly painted picture."

"It's a small price for immortality. Von Vadim and Angelique Jaffler, they—"

Patricia stopped him. "I understand that others live

as vampires. I understand the pros and cons. What we'd be gaining...and losing." She turned around. "Just give me a little time."

Pierson went to her. "Forgive me, Patricia. I should have told you sooner."

"I love you, Allen. But we can't keep things from each other. Nothing good will ever come of it."

He touched her cheek. "What good is immortality if you hate me forever?"

She looked into his eyes. "I could never hate you."

"It's your decision to accept immortality. Only yours. But I'm selfish. I want you with me."

Patricia tenderly kissed him. "I feel the same. I just wish I had more time to come to terms with it."

Light streaming through the branches of a tree outside the window cast shadows along the beige wall.

"It's nearly sunset. I should go." He stepped toward the table and put out his cigarette burning in a brown ashtray.

Patricia reached for his coat and hat and followed him to the door. "Be careful."

Pierson slipped on his coat. "Don't try to reach me. I'll get in touch with you when it's safe."

With a parting kiss, he aimed for his SUV and set a course for the station. As he drove, their conversation dominated his thoughts.

"For immortality." He reminded himself what they had to gain. Why he was risking his life...her life. "We can have it, Patricia. It's in our reach. Immortality."

Noticing the time, he pushed the speed limit, desperate to put a safe distance between him and Patricia before nightfall, because that's when nightwalkers crawl forth from their dark sanctuaries—after the fall of night.

3

Corin rushed outside to the sight of Galvar dropping out of the passenger seat of a roadster that had screeched to a halt in front of the mansion.

"Get Jordon." He called to Angelique who stood in the doorway.

An unnecessary order with Jordon already barreling out the door.

"I heard from upstairs." Jordon aimed for Corin and Vynce. "Galvar." He squatted next to the commander.

"He's hurt. Bad." Corin examined a horrific wound on the side of Galvar's neck that spanned from his chin to the nape of his neck.

"Vynce, what happened?" Jordon sought an explanation.

"Meical Evon. We were ambushed. Walked right into his trap. It was six against two." Vynce's royal-blue stare froze on Corin. "You are the brother. He was a perfect copy of you in age and appearance."

"Jozsef," Corin said. "My twin brother. But I don't

know how it's possible."

"Yes. Exactly who he claimed to be." Vynce's fit body leaned over Galvar.

"You have a brother?" Angelique and Jordon simultaneously voiced their surprise.

Corin felt Angelique's dissatisfaction in her bombarding array of questions bouncing about her mind, but he chose to delay the subject and refocused on attending Galvar. "A good attempt at decapitation."

"He nearly succeeded. The blade went deep. I thought I had lost him, but he's managed to hold on. I healed him as much as I could." Vynce gripped Galvar's hand. "Meical's blades must contain nytum."

"What is nytum?" Corin had never heard of it.

"It's an extremely rare metal found in the Eleventh Dimension, the color of Earth's silver," Jordon answered. "It is deadly to immortals."

"Smuggled out of the Eleventh Dimension. It is illegal to bring it here," Vynce added. "I wonder how Evon even knows about it, much less got his hands on any."

"Let's get him inside." Corin helped lift Galvar, who groaned in pain.

At the doorway, Angelique gestured toward the sofa before hustling away, returning a moment later with a large bowl of water, towels, and a medical kit.

Jax and Kara surfaced from the saven.

"What is all the commotion?" Jax inquired.

"Galvar is injured," Corin answered. "He and Vynce were attacked."

Kara stood behind Jax, silently watching.

"The cut's deep, Galvar." Jordon helped Angelique clean and dress the wound. "There's no doubt this was done with nytum. It's going to take some time to heal."

Corin bent next to Galvar. "We're going to have to move you again, to the saven—underground quarters.

You need a quiet place to rest...heal."

Proceeding with the task, they settled Galvar in a room and then gathered in the circle where Corin, with Jordon's approval, revealed to Jax and Kara the secret of the Order of the Clythguard.

Vynce, distraught, couldn't keep still. "We have had a mole in the Örök Vér, knowing of their interest in the Clyth. Receiving a message from Tarik, to meet him just after sunset behind an antique store off 95, we found the store had closed at five, and the lot was empty. We drove to the back of the building and got out of the car. I sensed a presence, thinking it was Tarik, but when the individual stepped into view, I saw it was Evon." He wrung his gloved hands while pacing. "Three other immortals advanced and took positions around us." He paused and looked at Corin. "Galvar was taken aback by something I didn't understand at the time, intently scoping one of the nightwalkers. Seeing you now, I see what gave rise to his shock."

He recounted the incident in detail.

"'Corin von Vadim, you have turned on us?' Galvar accused while studying the individual. 'No.' He shook his head. 'You are not Corin.' He was not fooled by the likeness.

'Corin, or I should say Luca, is my brother from long ago, Clythguard.' The nightwalker emphasized his aversion of the Order.

'An identical brother, or are you deceiving us in his form?' Galvar was skeptical.

'He is my twin,' the immortal disclosed.

Meical reclaimed our attention. 'We've caught your spy.'

Galvar demanded to know what they'd done with Tarik just as a black van raced onto the scene, stopping just short of Meical. Two more immortals dragged a bound and hooded captive out of the vehicle. I immediately recognized a tattoo on the prisoner's left hand, confirming he was Tarik, and pointed it out to Galvar.

'What do you want in exchange for his life, Meical?' Galvar called out.

I watched as Meical's ring adorned hands crossed at his abdomen while reaching for two daggers with pronged handles, one belted at each side. The weapons resembled sai weapons, only they had wider, double-edged blades in place of the sai's rounded shaft.

Standing at a stance, I was sure he was about to advance, but instead, he motioned to one of the nightwalkers who responded by forcing Tarik to his knees. Then, before we could react, Meical flew into a samurai move and severed Tarik's head that hurled from his shoulders and rolled to our feet before disintegrating."

"He intended to kill you all," Jordon said. "How did you get away?"

"There was no getting out of there without a fight. We met them head-on, and I was able to take out two of the immortals while Galvar held his own against the other four. I barely made it to him in time. Meical almost had his head in addition to Tarik's."

"You must be some fighter," Corin surmised.

Jordon nodded. "Vynce is a skilled shinobi."

Corin glimpsed Vynce's torn and bloodied shirt. "Did you manage to kill them all? My brother, Jozsef, did you—"

"No," Vynce quickly replied. "But I confess, it was not for lack of trying. He got away with Meical. He has unfortunately teamed with our opponents. What is your present standing with him? What has placed you on opposing sides?"

"Until last night, I had no idea he was alive." Corin told him about the message Jax had found pinned to the mansion door. "I'm still not convinced it is Jozsef."

"How were you able to keep this from me? A brother? A twin?" Angelique spoke to Corin telepathically. "And the letter. That explains what was bothering you."

"Forgive me, my love." Corin had a lot of explaining to do.

"For your sake, Corin, I hope it's not. Every member of that group needs to be eradicated. Since they know about the Order and the Clyth, they are a major threat." Jordon went to the bar and reached for a glass. "I wonder what Meical's agenda is?"

"The Örök Vér want control. To be the supreme Earth clan. A hierarchy with them at the top of the pyramid. Other clans would become mere satellites under their rule." Vynce looked at Jordon who scanned the liquor choices. "The clythguard stand in the way of that goal."

Corin sat on the sofa next to Angelique. "Similar to Lehndra's crazy ideals of world dominion."

"Except this unfathomable conspiracy is more possible than you would think," Vynce said. "They are a large clan of five hundred, and very organized."

"Five hundred in one place?" Corin wondered how they stayed under the radar. "How do they find enough blood to feed so many nightwalkers?"

"Tarik earlier revealed that they have cattle ranches for keeping plenty of ready blood. He had also discovered that they run a research facility as a cover for storing human blood and laundering money." Vynce leaned against the wall near Jordon. "We had not heard from Tarik in weeks when he finally made contact, stating he had learned something significant. Only he was never able to deliver the information. He said they had grown suspicious, and he was getting out. Only not soon enough."

"Knowing about the *Trove Chan Allu* and of Meical's interest in exposing the clythguard, I knew he would come after the Clyth. That was a given. But I had no idea of the extent of the threat," Jordon expressed annoyance. "Why wasn't I informed before now?"

"Galvar wanted to give you a rest after chasing down Lehndra." Vynce stepped toward the bar. "Then, being in charge of overseeing the search for the Body of the Clyth, he thought you had enough on your plate. But he was planning to fill you in tonight."

Corin joined them at the bar and poured a brandy. "Care for one?" he offered Vynce.

Vynce declined. "I am going to check on Galvar." He aimed for the bedroom and disappeared beyond the door.

Jax strode to the bar. "I'll take one of those."

Corin slid him a drink while addressing Jordon. "Besides all of this, you're worried about your world."

Jax tossed back his drink and looked blankly into the empty glass. Corin observed he showed no reaction to the mention of another world.

"I keep trying, without success. I can't help wondering if this sudden uprising might be connected with the passage malfunction." He glanced at Jax. "I should explain, I am from a world called the Eleventh Dimension."

"Eleventh Dimension," Jax repeated. "I feel I should be more surprised, but I sensed something different about you."

Corin raised the bottle. "You want another?"

Jax held up a hand, palm out. He'd had enough.

Angelique arose from the sofa and walked up behind Corin, wrapping her arms around his waist.

He turned and faced her. "The ceremony isn't going to happen tonight."

She smiled. "Just a postponement."

Jordon and Jax withdrew to the sofa where Kara quietly sat.

"Today. Tomorrow. A hundred years. I'll love you always." Corin pressed his lips to Angelique's. "About Jozsef, I'm—"

She hushed him. "It's okay. We'll discuss it later."

Corin was enraptured by her hazel gaze—eyes lit with speckles of yellow ocher—a face he could stare into forever. He brushed her cheek. "Always."

* * * *

Leaning against a rail, Sheriff Pierson checked his watch.

Midnight. Where are you, Evon?

A sound outside the barn startled him, and he cautiously eased in the direction of the open door, coming face-to-face with a wolf that instantly transformed into a man. Early twenties, tall with straight white hair, he was dressed in all black.

"Meical Evon?" Sheriff Pierson took a step back.

"Sheriff Pierson. A bit out of your element?"

"I'm not in the habit of meeting vampires in dark, abandoned buildings." Pierson stared into the immortal's shadowed face. "You've brought the *Trove Chan Allu*?"

The immortal removed a backpack and pulled out a large, worn book. "Going to these lengths, information on the Clyth means a great deal to you. I suspect you know more than you'd like me to believe."

"If I say I do?" Pierson noticed the immortal was armed with two silver-colored daggers.

"You'd be a fool to meet me at this desolate location without taking precautions. I figure, if you have the Body, it's stashed someplace safe. Far from the likes of me."

"I want a deal. A trade for the Body." Pierson didn't want to drag the matter out. "If you kill me now, you'll never see the charm."

Meical laughed. "A deal." His words trailed as he considered the proposition. "Trade for what?"

"Immortality for myself and another."

"You're asking me to change you, and a friend, in exchange for the Body?"

"If the charm doesn't have that power, then yes. Agree to make us immortal, and the charm is yours. You have my word."

The immortal opened the *Trove Chan Allu* and showed Pierson a particular page. He pointed out an ink sketch of the Body, drawn beneath a passage written in an unknown language. "Just so we're certain, is this what you have?"

"Yeah. That's it."

"Lucky for you, I won't have to change you. The Body is very powerful. One of its powers is calling forth supreme beings from other worlds, beings possessing unimaginable powers. In your case, Carhalli. With the right offering, Carhalli has been known to change the genetics of a being. Animal to man. Mortal to immortal."

"And you know how?"

"I do. The spell requires an earth pentacle, a portion of ibex horn, feather of a griffin, Thyine sap, talon of a raptor, and the blood of a gray wolf."

"You've got to be kidding. Sounds more like a pagan ritual." Pierson rubbed his left ear, bothered by a twitch.

"An ancient evocation...she who will grant you immortality. These offerings, through the power of the charm, will summon her."

"Can I trust you?" The immortal's penetrating stare sent a chill up his spine.

"We each have something the other wants, so trust goes both ways."

"Okay. If the spell brings her to us, then what more, besides the ritual, will I have to give in return for immortality?"

"Immortality in exchange for your soul."

"My soul," Pierson said.

"Something you would lose anyway," Meical told him. "But I don't have the spell with me. We'll have to meet again tomorrow night. You bring the Body and your friend. I'll bring the spell to summon Carhalli."

Pierson agreed to the same time and place, and Meical transformed and departed into the night. Pierson hoped he wasn't in over his head, but with matters set in motion, he was in too far to turn back now.

* * * *

A white wolf stepped out of the tree line. A farrago of night sounds played around him as he looked on the skyscraping mansion before him, consuming the intensity of the structure that seemed to possess a life of its own. With two feet of snow covering the ground, he shed his fur for feathers and flew to the front entry where he claimed human form, instantly met by an opening door.

"Jozsef." Corin had exited in a blink. "Is it really you?"

"You sensed me this time." Jozsef kept his emotions in check. "Now that you know I'm alive, our connection will only grow stronger."

"I don't know what to believe."

Jozsef pulled off his opal ring and handed it to Corin. "Our eighteenth birthday gifts. This perfect stone, chosen by our mother from the family mine.

There's only one other like it."

"Yes." Corin studied the ring. "How? When were you changed?"

"I was taking a chest of opals to Serbia when my company was attacked. But the assailants weren't human. And they were after more than jewels."

Corin handed his ring back. "So, you didn't die in that attack."

"Gedeon, my immortal father, spared my life...changed me. He's now known as Andras Metellus."

"Gedeon? My maker?" Corin snarled.

"One and the same." Jozsef could feel Corin's agitation, proving that being reunited was rekindling their twin connection. "You won't recognize him. He's changed his appearance three times since then."

"Why haven't you contacted me in five hundred years?"

"I didn't know about you, Luca. Just as you didn't know about me. He just recently told me."

"It was no coincidence that he seeked me out less than a month after changing you. Why? What was his motive? And why tell you now?"

"I've just discovered things about him I never knew. Things he intentionally kept from me. But he did spare my life and guided me all of these years."

"He's done you no favor's, Jozsef. He cursed you." Corin's eyes flashed red. "And me."

"The way you cursed Angelique."

"That's different. She was dying and wanted to be changed. To be with me." Corin bridled his temper. "How do you know about Angelique?"

"Informants. Be careful who you trust. Andras's influence is far-reaching." Jozsef didn't offer any names. "I was changed against my will, but Andras, he didn't abandon me. Unfortunately, conversion didn't eliminate my claustrophobia."

"After receiving your message, I thought about that day—the collapse on the north side of the castle that had trapped us—remembering how it had affected you. It must have been hard for you, being forced to retreat underground during the day?"

"At first, I kept to caves and caverns. As you know, I could not tolerate being confined in tight spaces. It was a fear that took a long time to conquer, but Andras saw me through the nightmare. I can't say I haven't seen his malevolent side, but I owe him, no matter what he's done."

A growl rose in Corin's throat. "You owe him nothing."

Jozsef ignored the outburst and attempted to divert their conversation in a different direction. "Enough ode to Jozsef. Tell me about this estate. You've done quite well for yourself."

"You said you've discovered things you never knew. What have you learned?" Corin wasn't swayed. "Does he have some ultimate plan? Should I fear for my family?" He pressed for answers.

"I understand you know about the Eleventh Dimension. Well, Andras is from there as well. He's waited hundreds of years for a comet to pass in that world, something that's finally happening. It's apparently wreaking havoc. A week of pure hell."

"That is why the Passage of Dimensions has been down. Jordon needs to know, and Galvar, when he awakens. He almost died at the hands of your clan."

"Meical is ruthless. Watch out for him," Jozsef warned. "About the comet, they'll know soon enough. It's the end of their world as they know it."

"How does Andras know what's happening there?"

"From what I've put together, an informant made it through just before the Passage of Dimensions shut down on the second day. He saw the beginning of the end."

"Wait," Corin spoke aloud, but not to Jozsef. He pressed his hand against the door.

"You should introduce us." Jozsef presumed it was Angelique. "We are, after all, family."

"Her safety comes first." Corin's voice was stern. "Brother or not."

"Understood."

Corin pulled the door open to Angelique who stood in jeans and a simple white blouse. Astonishment showed on her face.

"Angelique," Corin protectively reached for her hand, "this is Jozsef. My brother."

"This must come as quite a surprise to you," Jozsef said.

Angelique's voice momentarily muted.

Corin felt her shock. "We didn't know about each other being changed. That's why he never made contact."

"I...I can't believe this. You...you're identical," she finally found her voice. "I knew you would look alike, but I wasn't as prepared as I'd thought." She brushed her fingertips along her left cheek. "You even have the same dimple."

Jozsef grinned. "Now that's the real curse."

Angelique looked at Corin. "This explains why you always understood my connection with Tomes so well. You've shared that same twin connection with Jozsef. I can only imagine what else I don't know about you." She turned her gaze back to Jozsef. "What happened to Galvar, you were there. How could you be part of that?"

"I'm glad he survived," Jozsef told her, and said nothing more.

"Jozsef and I are going to take a walk." Corin guided Jozsef away from the door. "Stay inside. I'll be back shortly, and we'll feed."

"My brother's a lucky man, Angelique. I hope we meet again."

Angelique stood expressionless, without responding. She then stepped back inside the house.

Corin grabbed Jozsef's arm. "I don't want you getting too close to her," he warned.

"You don't trust me." Jozsef broke his grip.

"You may be my brother, but I don't know you, or what your intentions are."

"You're very protective...loyal. That hasn't changed about you, Luca."

"I go by Corin now. I left Luca in Hungary long ago."

"You'll always be Luca to me. But changing identities is necessary when you live in one place too long." Jozsef caught Corin's inquisitive look. "As you have here."

"You've done your research."

"It's obvious what you've had to do to maintain your life here. I imagine you've mastered the art of pretense."

"The first centuries were quiet, but as more people settled in the area, I was forced to protect my secret. With the illusion of aging, I raise no suspicion, other than being considered a recluse. And when the time comes to fake my death, I return as an heir—some form of estranged relative."

"You've done a superb job of pulling it off. This is a sizable estate; a centuries-old estate."

"Is it money you're after?" Corin asked.

"You insult me." Jozsef pretended a stake had just pierced his heart. "But you can't deny your wealth."

"No. I set roots and grew."

"Flourished. And I'm happy for you. That's the truth."

"You mentioned Andras being from the Eleventh

Dimension. Because he fathered us, we're not only immortal, but possess alien blood."

"That's true. We are far from ordinary." Jozsef stopped and leered toward the woods as several howls echoed. "I should go."

Corin grabbed his shoulder. "You're going back? You don't have to go back to that life."

Jozsef avoided eye contact. "It's my clan. Where I belong."

"I am your brother."

Jozsef turned his back to Corin. "Too much time has passed...separated us. We each have our obligations. We have no other choice but to live up to them."

"There's always a choice."

"Not in my case." Jozsef knew Andras wouldn't let him go. "Watch your back, brother." He rotated. "Andras is using me, and others, to extract information about a charm."

"The Clyth."

"Yes. He knows it's here, and he'll stop at nothing to get it. Even pitting brother against brother. The next we meet will likely be on unpleasant terms."

Having said all he came to say, Jozsef took the form of a spotted owl and leaped into flight, ignoring Corin's trailing call to stay. Quickly putting distance between them, he entered a thick area of woods and shape-shifted into a wolf. He needed to run and shake his ode to Jozsef, self-pitying state of mind, and the woods brought comfort and release.

4

Jordon slapped both hands down on the table. "The comet prophesied to bring about the end of my world. Apocalypse. The Eleventh Dimension is falling apart, and I'm trapped here."

"Jozsef warned me to watch my back." Corin shared what he'd learnt, with the exception of Andras being his immortal maker. That shock was still fresh, and he wasn't ready to reveal that connection with the others. "He knew a lot about what happened six months back with Boldor. He mentioned informants."

"Sounds like he was warning you of someone?" Vynce said. "Any indication who it might be?"

"He gave no name." Corin paced. "Andras's influence is far-reaching." He paused and looked at Jordon. "That's what he said."

"He is head of the Örök Vér." Vynce sat opposite Jordon who was standing. "The Örök Vér is powerful."

"Andras Metellus." Corin resumed motion. "Jozsef said he's from the Eleventh Dimension. How much do

50

you know about him?"

"I've never met him," Vynce answered. "Only his henchmen. He's remained behind the scenes, sending Meical and others to handle his business."

"I had no idea he was from my world." Jordon leaned on the table with his hands planted firmly before him, supporting the weight of his tense body.

Corin pulled out a chair and sat down. "You have to wonder why he's planned this for so long."

"I can't image how he's tied to the end time prophesy," Vynce said, "but something tells me we'll find out soon enough."

Corin couldn't sit still and stood back up. "Jozsef mentioned he's changed his appearance several times."

Jordon stared at the tabletop. "To keep from being recognized by those from the Eleventh Dimension."

"If he's after the charm, we have to beat him to it," Corin stressed. "Failure isn't an option."

"When it comes to the Clyth, it never is." Jordon's gaze rose and settled on Corin. "Strange that you never knew about your brother being immortal. Had the Örök Vér not come looking for the Clyth, you may have never known."

Corin nodded, not ready to confide the truth of Andras being his maker. He needed more time to contemplate all that Jozsef had told him, and to weed out any deception.

"Are you sure now that it's him?" Jordon asked.

"He is my brother," Corin said, "but I'm not sure what to expect from him after five hundred years."

"A tough situation, him being a member of the Örök Vér," Vynce sympathized.

Corin sighed under the strain of his own deception of not sharing all of what he knew with his friends. It was indeed a tough situation.

* * * *

Overcast and cold, the gloomy day crawled. Tomes, mentally probed by Angelique with a call to come to the saven with Jordon, immediately responded to her summon. Even though he was human, being Angelique's twin, they shared a special connection that allowed them to communicate telepathically since her change.

"Shouldn't you be resting?" Tomes took a seat in the circle, amongst the immortals. "Some of us could use a little sleep."

"I'm with Tomes." Jordon leaned back with fingers locked behind his head. "For those of us not nightwalker, our schedules are a mess."

"I've been reviewing the timeline of events from our final standoff with Boldor six months back," Corin said, "trying to narrow the list of candidates, those who had access to the charm."

"Lehndra was the last one I saw it with." Tomes sat across from Corin. "She had both halves of the charm and was attempting to connect them."

"Yes, the Heart and the Body," Jordon said. "That was a close call. If she'd succeeded to obtain the full power of the Clyth, she may have been unstoppable."

"When I shot three blackthorn nails into her back, she flew into a frenzy. Both pieces went flying." Tomes recalled his moment of justice.

"Blackthorn." Jax whistled. "Ouch."

"That's when Jordon showed up," Tomes continued. "With Lehndra fighting the effects of the blackthorn, I called him over to help me with Angelique who'd been stabbed by Lehndra. I don't remember seeing it after that."

"That's right," Jordon corroborated. "Our attention was focused on Angelique. Also, Corin's possession. No one saw it after that."

"So, whoever took the charm must have seen it thrown from Lehndra's hold," Corin presumed. "That was before the Order of the Clythguard arrived, which leaves me, Angelique, Tomes, Jordon, Lehndra and Boldor."

Tomes raised a finger. "Don't forget the sheriff."

Corin cut his eyes at Tomes. "Sheriff Pierson. The good ol' boy who trailed our every move. You don't suppose—"

"What is that?" Kara cut him off, motioning toward an anomaly manifesting before them.

Vynce, who'd been leaning against the bar, quietly listening, scrambled toward Jordon who'd jumped to his feet.

"Looks like a portal. But different from the wormhole we use." Jordon motioned for the others to back away.

Within seconds, the manifestation had expanded and formed a doorway, giving passage to a misty presence that emerged wrapped in white flames. Without speaking, the spirit-like entity glided toward Tomes.

"How do we fight an apparition?" Tomes looked to Jordon for instruction, unsure what to do.

Corin pulled Angelique behind him and signaled to Kara, who stood beside Jax, to join her.

"The Circle of the Morpar Kingdom." Jordon pointed out a symbol marking the entities ivory robe. "He's Indith."

"I am Piiric." The spirit's hollow tone resonated. "Once diurnal. Now deity."

The white flames extinguished as the portal closed.

"What do you want from us?" Corin held a defensive stance next to Jax.

"I come for the dir cyohr." The spirit's gaze was fixed

on Tomes.

"Piiric." Jordon dropped onto one knee in unison with Vynce.

"What?" Corin's brow furrowed.

"I can't believe this." Jordon looked at Tomes. "You are the dir cyohr." He was overawed. "An age-old prophecy states that when our world suffers the wrath of the heavens, a half-demon prince will return as a great deity. Wearing a crown of two kingdoms, he will be transformed, becoming our savior in our day of cataclysm. He will dwell within a host—the dir cyohr."

Tomes rejected the idea. "No. Not me." He attempted to back away from Piiric, but with uncooperative limbs, he was held in place by an unseen force.

"You were chosen, even before birth." Piiric's voice held steady and calm.

"It's an honor, Tomes," Jordon told him. "A phenomenal destiny. There have been many signs, since ancient times, leading us to this moment. War. The Rise of Gaun. All signs. And you, Tomes, are the last. This is your destiny."

"I'm not even from your world. How could it be my destiny?" Tomes refused to accept the possibility. "This is a mistake."

"The prophecy describes the chosen one as a son of man, an outlander who will possess strong blood and an inherent wisdom and understanding. Resurrected from loss, he will be a great peacemaker. And though born of day, and a light of life, he will walk with the night, where a part of him forever dwells." Jordon spoke with enthusiasm. "It all fits. You've experienced loss. A part of you dwells in darkness—Angelique. And look where you're standing right now, Tomes, amongst a room full of nightwalkers. Accept who you are."

"The day of joining has come." Piiric stood several

feet in front of Tomes. "Fate has carved its course and chosen us to become savior to a suffering world, to mediate their troubles and offer new hope."

"With the Passage of Dimensions disabled, is it possible for me to use your portal to reach the Eleventh Dimension?" Jordon asked.

"This doorway leads to Zarmeva. The Plane of Supreme Beings. It is forbidden to cross from other worlds into Zarmeva, which is why the portals connecting dimensions were blocked long ago and secured by supreme guardians. We can cross into your worlds, but you cannot cross into ours."

Jordon understood. "Some supreme beings and guardians have the power to travel between the dimensions without the need of the Passage, even to other universes, as you have proven by crossing here."

"Only a small number of us have that power." Mist danced around Piiric's incorporeal form. "Keep trying the Passage. When the time is right, it will be restored." He returned his focus to Tomes. "A legacy awaits you in the Eleventh Dimension. Rightful ruler of Indithian territory."

"I'm no ruler." Tomes found it hard to conceive.

"Tomes." Angelique moved to his side. "It's not that you're afraid. You don't feel worthy."

"I'm no one. How can I be a vessel to a deity? Save a world?" Finding motion again, he clasped her hand.

"You think too little of yourself. I always believed you were destined for great things." She faced him. "We've crossed many hurdles together, Tomes. You are the strongest person I know. And if this is your predestined fate, you must accept what you were born to be, just as I have."

Tomes scanned the room of immortals and then looked back at Angelique. "Our lives have turned out nothing like I'd imagined."

Angelique smiled. "No. It's so much more."

Tomes released her hand and stepped before Piiric. "If this is my calling, I'll accept what I'm meant to do."

"You'll feel no pain." Piiric assured him. "Our merge will be similar to the nightwalkers with their monsters. You'll know I'm with you, but you'll remain in control."

Tomes nodded. "I'm ready." He took a deep breath and closed his eyes. Freeing his mind, a presence overcame him, and several foreign words broke his lips. All consciousness momentarily left him as Piiric stepped into his body.

A moment later, Tomes opened his eyes and looked at the others. "He's with me."

"How do you feel?" Corin asked.

"Different. Yet the same." Tomes clenched his fists, experiencing a strength he didn't have before the merge. "I feel strong. And I can sense you."

"You've inherited Piiric's immortality and powers," Jordon said. "Piiric was diurnal, Indith Immortal, as now, you are."

"I'm picking up on some of his memories." Tomes saw flashes in his mind.

"To be expected. In time you'll encounter all of who he was, including the knowledge of all he knew," Jordon enlightened before dropping onto one knee again, this time pressing a fist to his chest. "I pledge my loyalty and life to you. Full allegiance."

"Get up." Tomes gestured. "That's just too weird. I'm still me."

"You're immortal." Angelique's bottom lip quivered. "I didn't think—" Her eyes swelled with tears. "We won't lose each other."

"There is more." Vynce looked at Tomes. "Piiric was—"

Jordon interrupted him. "Piiric will show him things as he's ready to learn them."

Vynce nodded.

"What don't I know?"

"It's just about your powers." Jordon cut his eyes at Vynce. "But you'll learn soon enough."

"The way you're acting, it must be *some* power." Tomes's pursed lips drew to one side.

Kara stepped forth from the backdrop, eyes locked on Tomes, her expression showing deep emotion.

Tomes caught her stare. *You care for me.*

Then catching Jax's piercing glare, he realized the immortal had apparently noticed. And having the distinct impression the nightwalker wanted him dead, he cut his eyes at Jordon.

"Your loyalty and life, huh?" he said. "That's good to know."

* * * *

An obscured twilight sky shadowed Hixton as Meical Evon emerged from a farmhouse, accompanied by a tall, thin-framed immortal. Flipping a cell phone shut, distant lightening setting the clouds aglow captured his attention.

"Just my kind of night," Meical told Jitters, who's head twitched to his right, one of several ticks afflicting the lip-ringed immortal.

Replacing skin with feathers, they took to the air, aimed for the cemetery. Landing ten minutes later, they intercepted Jozsef and Jax, who were exiting the Chesterson crypt.

"It's time you join us at the farmhouse," Meical confronted Jozsef. He restrained a rearing of jealousy, never having understood Andras's favoritism toward Jozsef. "I hope you're not contemplating anything rash, like bailing on us."

Jozsef ignored his remark. "I was on my way to see

you. Jax has major news."

"A deity came to Tomes Jaffler and named him the dir cyohr," Jax reported.

Meical groaned. "This is certainly an unexpected turn of events. The dir cyohr, right here under our noses, in this little know-nothing town."

Jitters rocked from right foot to left, unable to stand still. "Andras needs to know." His words came in a nervous rush.

"Jax, get back to your post," Meical instructed. "Keep watching and informing."

As Jax departed, he pulled out his cell phone and called Andras's number, keeping a watchful eye on Jozsef who meandered through the cemetery, distancing himself from Jitters.

I don't trust you. Meical narrowed his eyes. *Andras may view you as a son, but you are no brother of mine.*

He fantasized the thought of Jozsef turning on them and Andras finally casting the invertebrate from his fold. It was only a matter of time.

* * * *

Jozsef put some space between himself and Jitters and walked the cemetery, looking on the gravesites, thinking back on his meeting with Corin.

You have a right to know all of who you are.

Jozsef hadn't known for long that Andras was from an ancient bloodline called Delghorlin. He'd since learned that only highborns—individuals with a unique component to their blood—could have a successful Delghorlin transformation. Something he and Corin were born with.

You're right, brother. He settled his gaze on Meical. *Andras is after the Clyth for more than just Earth domination. He wants his home world, and he'll stop at nothing to get it.*

Pressing a hand against ridged bark of an old, gnarled tree, a repressed memory surfaced of a time long ago, when he and Corin were boys living in Hungary.

Hiking woods beyond the thresholds of the castle grounds, they caught sight of a cloaked figure darting into a dense understory, the individual too shadowed to make out his identity. Spurred by Corin to follow, maintaining a safe distance, they trailed the swiftly moving form deeper into the dark, tangled terrain.

Jozsef caught a glimpse of the man's face as they dared to push closer. "It is father."

Corin hushed him. "We are in the sacred territory." He recognized the area. "We are not supposed to be here."

Jozsef squatted next to Corin, watching wide-eyed as their father talked to the spirits of the Tree of Lelkek—an ancient, disfigured oak. He tried to make out the conversation, but from their position, the words were faint and unclear. Finally, after several paralyzing minutes, the count departed, passing mere feet from Jozsef and Corin who hunkered under thick undergrowth. Holding his breath, Jozsef dared no movement, fearing detection...punishment.

"He's gone." Corin arose from hiding. "Do you hear that?"

A hollow voice beckoned from the old oak.

"It knows we are here." Corin moved toward the haunting tree.

Jozsef hesitantly followed, leerier than Corin, experiencing a suffocating dread. Jumping back as a face suddenly appeared on the algae-ridden trunk, the entity's eyes were penetrating, intently peering into his inner being. Standing at a distance he estimated thirty feet from the tree, he gaped at the manifestation.

"Remember what Father told us about the tree?" Corin said. "It will someday hold our souls."

"I hate this, Corin. I want to go." Jozsef backed away.

"What did it say?" Corin looked back at the tree. "Could you tell?"

Jozsef shook his head. "We should not be here."

Corin maintained his position. "I wish I knew more...how many souls it holds."

"Or has trapped. The thought gives me nightmares."

Corin cocked his head, seeming to ponder the thought, then, to Jozsef's relief, reversed course. "Father said he would tell us more when the time was right." He began backtracking through the woods.

"I would rather not know. I sure hope I am given a choice." Jozsef shuddered, knowing he would never be ready to face such a dark fate.

"Whatever comes, at least we have each other."

Emerging from the memory, he repeated those eight words that lingered in his mind. "Whatever comes, at least we have each other."

* * * *

Andras slapped his phone shut. He'd been expecting the dir cyohr to surface, he just wished the chosen one had been someone less associated with immortals, especially Jordon and the Order.

"Regardless. Their protection won't be enough," Andras growled under his breath. "I'll just have to expedite things. Clythguard, you won't know what hit you."

Andras had waited a long time for this chance to

take back what the Delghorlins had lost—control of the Eleventh Dimension. His goal—reinstating the sovereignty of his lineage. Delghorlins were the oldest of their species, but their numbers grew at a very slow rate, only able to convert mortals containing a rare blood mutation—highborns. Faced with wars, struggles against higher powers, and altered lines that followed, eventually, the Delghorlins were vastly outnumbered and thrown from power.

He had been away from the Eleventh Dimension for six hundred years, building a Delghorlin army to a number of five hundred under the cover of his clan, the Örök Vér. Residing in The Dalles, Oregon, he provided for his clan through several means: cattle ranches, a large research facility as a cover for laundering human blood and funds for their association, and bought power. And although he'd been away from his home world for centuries, he'd followed the signs of prophecy, even having returned briefly during the Rise of Gaun. His hope had been to seize control during that time of upheaval, but realizing the power of Gaun, who wielded the Clyth, he'd withdrew back to Earth, confident prophecy would continue and give him another chance when the end time apocalypse came to pass.

"How lucky was I that Morpar sent the Clyth to Earth?" He laughed.

He had been watching the Order since its inception, keeping track of the Clyth, biding his time. A time now come.

It had been mere months since Meical came to him with information regarding a fugitive he'd stumbled upon. Lehndra. Her story and dilemma had piqued Meical's interest, explaining how she was pursued by an order of immortals that believed she possessed a stolen charm. Wanting to earn her trust and learn more, he offered her protection by bringing her into the Örök Vér, sharing his compilation—the *Trove Chan Allu*—that act prompting her to open up to him about a cloak-and-dagger order and a treasure they guarded—the Clyth.

Meical, loyal to Andras, communicated all he'd discovered, only to be shocked to learn that Andras already new about the Clyth. Andras then summoned Jozsef and divulged to both immortals a long-kept secret, that he and some of the other clan members were actually from another world called the Eleventh Dimension. He disclosed the truth of his lineage—being Delghorlin—a secret those of his race had religiously guarded for their protection, even from their own Earth-born clan members. He told how he'd come to Earth from the Eleventh Dimension six hundred years ago, building his clan while awaiting prophecy, a time when the forces of the world would be weakened by apocalypse, allowing the Delghorlins to rise from obscurity and take their rightful supremacy. Positions due them and their children of superior bloodline. A triumph to be further ensured by possessing the Clyth, a power that will defeat the only thing standing in their way.

The dir cyohr. The one who must die for more than one reason.

"The Order has no idea who they're dealing with. How long I've been watching. Who I am."

Lehndra, showing up when she had, was a lucky happenstance. He'd had a spy—Umorius—in the Order for the last two years, keeping him informed of the charm's whereabouts, so when he was ready to make a move, he would have an inside advantage.

Through Umorius's reports, Andras was very familiar with Lehndra's name, having followed her previous theft of the Heart of the Clyth—outwitting the sentry, Jordon, for over two years—followed by her involvement with the disappearance of the Body. However, having discovered that she was not in possession of the Body, nor privy to its location, he was disappointed, but still deemed her an asset and accepted her into the clan. She was beautiful, resourceful, Delghorlin, and what made her most attractive was her connections to the Order.

Deducing that the end drew near in his world, he required the Clyth to seize control when the end time prophecy came to pass. He knew that one half of the charm was guarded by the Order, and determined to succeed, he set a plan in motion, of which Lehndra would play a large part.

Lehndra. Do not let me down.

He recalled the moment he'd conveyed his bloodline and objective to her, which had come as a surprise. Until that moment, she had believed herself to possibly be the last of her lineage.

You are definitely not the last Delghorlin.

Sharing a common goal, it took little coaxing to persuade her to join his cause and agree to his devised plot that required her being purposely captured by Jordon in order to place her back within the Order of the Clythguard where she would aid Umorius in setting the stage for infiltration. A well-devised scheme.

Ready. Set. Action. Andras was ready to make his longstanding dream reality.

Pleased with his current position, he marched from the room and ordered his company to prepare for departure. "It's time to move."

5

Lehndra nodded to Umorius and headed down a long corridor for their rendezvous. The Order of the Clythguard compound, nestled amid a large tract of woodland and disguised as a religious organization, felt empty and unusually quiet as she slid into a dark, well-concealed corner.

Umorius's voice, barely audible, whispered in her ear. "It's time for your performance." He dropped a key in her pocket. "With several of the council presently absent, the time could not be better."

Lehndra lingered several minutes, taking precaution not to draw any suspicion should someone happen to be watching. Then, moving swiftly, with the use of the master key Umorius had slipper her, she covertly skulked through several doors and exited the west side of the building. Having reached her point of intent, she cocked her head and scanned the outdoors, mimicking the motion of a bird. Short, quick turns. A habitual movement of hers.

This is it. She purposely drew attention to herself. *Come and get me.*

She claimed animal form and led several immortals on a wild chase, managing to evade capture until reaching the back wall of the grounds. Surrendering to her captors, she took back human form and was immediately seized and searched, displaying a smug grin when they uncovered the key.

"Someone helped you escape." One clythguard shook the key at her. "Who?"

Before she could respond, a blast captured their attention. Lehndra cocked her head, knowing it had originated from the main gate leading into the compound. The Örök Vér had arrived, and they weren't asking for an invitation.

"This was a decoy. Get her back inside." The higher ranking clythguard motioned to the immortal gripping her arm. "The rest of you, come with me."

A distant commotion offered Lehndra a mental visual of the incursion. Clangs of striking blades. Cries of battle. Massacre. She fought the guard as he dragged her back to the keep, freed by Andras as they entered the central building.

"The clan won't keep the clythguard detained long. Let's move. Take me to the Heart." Gripping an agate-trimmed handle of a sword, Andras pointed toward a hall.

Following Lehndra's direction, Andras cut down anyone who stood in his way, finally meeting up with Umorius near the repository chamber.

"There will be two at the vault," Umorius informed. "Emergency procedure in the instance of an attack."

"I don't think that'll be a problem." Andras's mouth curved upward. "They think you're one of them."

Deceiving the guards, Umorius moved in first and viciously turned on the unsuspecting immortals.

Andras stepped over the disintegrating bodies. "How do we open this door?" He looked to Lehndra for guidance. "You've opened it before."

"They'd never trust that same code."

"I know the combination." Umorius flipped up the cover of a keypad mounted on the wall next to the door. "I planted a camera...there." He pointed out a design on the ceiling. "Small as a pea, but very effective. It caught Galvar inputting the code."

"Good work," Andras praised.

The heavy door swung open, and Andras flipped a switch on a partial wall just inside the room. Glancing over the space, he zoomed in on a decorative gold box resting upon a pedestal along the back wall. He opened the lid of the chest and pulled out his prize.

"The Heart." Andras admired the black diamond that was suspended from a chain. "Mission accomplished." He put it on. "Now, time to go." He looked at Umorius. "Except for you. The Order won't know of your involvement."

"What more can I do here?" Umorius was anxious to leave.

"The Order is powerful, and you are my eyes and ears within their inner sanctum." Andras made his wishes clear. "Pretend to be in pursuit as we flee."

"Understood." Umorius gave no further argument.

Sounding the signal to depart, Lehndra fled the compound with Andras, feeling a pang of remorse for so cruelly betraying the nightwalkers she'd lived among for so long. She had deceived the Order before, but her past disloyalties were a far cry from this bloodbath. But there was no way to change what had been done or the part she'd played in this merciless infiltration.

Andras gathered his gang in a field several miles away. "We're heading to Hixton, Wisconsin to meet up with Meical. The other half of the Clyth is there." He gripped the Heart hanging around his neck. "There is also the matter of the dir cyohr. To prevent him from fulfilling his part in the prophecy, he must be killed."

* * * *

McCall Farms
Midnight

Patricia snapped the collar of her coat and rubbed a chill from her arms. "I hate being out here so late at night." Her breath fogged. "It's freezing, and this place is deserted. Spooky."

Sheriff Pierson nervously messaged his left ear, trying to shake a fired-up quiver. "He should be here any minute."

A black mist floated through the barn door and materialized into Meical Evon. The immortal sauntered toward them, carrying a leather bag in his right hand. "You have the Body?"

"When the ritual's done, it's yours." Pierson displayed the Body, along with the staker, which he aimed at the immortal's chest. "Blackthorn."

"Nicely done." Meical's lips stretched as if amused.

"Are you prepared?"

Meical opened his bag. "I have everything I'll need."

The nightwalker pulled out eight candles and arranged them in a circle. He then lit them and proceeded to exhibit several odd items, identifying the pieces as he positioned them within the circle. In all, they consisted of: An earth pentacle, a portion of ibex horn, feather of a griffin, Thyine sap, talon of a raptor, and the blood of a gray wolf.

"Are you sure about this?" Patricia grabbed Pierson's arm.

"Second thoughts?" Meical slowly raised his gaze.

"Immortality always comes at a cost." His tone was sinister and lacking emotion.

Pierson gripped Patricia's hand and claimed her focus. "This is our chance, likely the only one we'll ever have."

"I'm scared, Allen."

"I know, but I'm right here with you," Pierson calmed her down, then determined to continue, looked back at Meical. "Keep going."

"Step inside the circle." Meical motioned and smeared a dab of oily substance on their forehead, pouring the remainder around the perimeter of the circle.

A chant rolled from his lips; foreign words Pierson didn't understand. With eyes shut, Meical repeated the chant over and again. Mist rose from the border, and Pierson attempted to step outside the circle, but the perimeter was locked.

"What is this?" Pierson bellowed as a rumble filled the barn, and a magnetizing force drew him and Patricia on all fours.

Meical's menacing laughter rang out, and Pierson knew they'd been double-crossed. Unable to escape, Pierson's heart revved.

Meical then uttered a second spell and a misty anomaly appeared and expanded into a portal.

"Carhalli." An entity emerged in a tunnel of white fire, a transparent being dressed in flowing garments that waved about her form as if she stood amid a storm.

"Why do you summon me?"

"I ask for immortality and transformation." He motioned to Pierson and Patricia. "A melding of seven from dusk to dawn. Reverted back, dawn to dusk."

"What are you doing?" Pierson yelled out. "Please. All we wanted was immortality."

"Why?" Carhalli circled the captives.

Pierson paused. "To never die." He didn't have any other answer.

"When not born of immortality, it always comes at a cost." She stared at Patricia who clung to Pierson. Carhalli then turned to Meical. "Why transformation?"

"They wronged me." Meical sneered at Pierson.

"That is a lie," Pierson denied. "I have a—"

Meical cut him off. "I offer this in exchange for the favor." Meical presented a gold mask. "A treasure of ancient earth."

You don't want me mentioning the charm. Pierson got that distinct impression. *She would want it.*

He was glad Meical had stopped him from revealing the Body. And at that moment, he made a personal declaration. *No matter what you do to me, you'll never get your hands on it. Neither of you.*

Carhalli glanced at the mask, then back at the captives, as if deciding on a course of action.

"It is done." She waved a hand, and a blanket of mist materialized and fell over Pierson and Patricia. "Dusk till dawn, immortal seven. Dawn till dusk, immortal one."

"No." Pierson pulled Patricia close as the thick, smothering energy consumed them.

With the deed done, Carhalli claimed her mask and withdrew into the portal, disappearing amid a swell of white flames.

Patricia moaned and doubled up.

"Patricia." Pierson bent to look into her face, stumbling back at the sight of her facial features contorting, morphing into what appeared to be a snout. Realizing he, too, was changing, he attempted to cry out, but the sound he conjured was no longer human.

Patricia roared as hands became claws and horns protruded from her head. Her flesh shed, replaced by bark and fur, and colossal wings ripped through her clothes and broke the barrier as they outstretched beyond the circle and hurled the candles out of position.

Patricia. She was no longer recognizable. *What have I done?*

"Beasts, dusk to dawn. Human form, dawn to dusk. Enjoy your immortality." Meical laughed. "You should never have bartered with a nightwalker. Certainly not this nightwalker." He pressed his thumb to his chest.

The Body fell from Pierson's hold and Meical attempted to claim it, but Pierson attacked, tearing into his enemy with raptor talons, forcing the nightwalker to pull back.

"You are fast." Meical examined his wound while zeroing in on the charm.

Without hesitation, Pierson scooped up the Body in his mouth and bolted for the open door of the barn with Patricia following, tearing out a portion of the wall in their haste to escape. And extending their massive wings, instinct urged them into flight, a means of escape Pierson surmised their inflictor hadn't considered by the barks of rage spewing from Evon, who shifted and pursued them.

Doubling back in attack, Pierson charged the night bird mid-air, slamming him with such force that the immortal fell from flight.

Devil, it seems your creations turned out to be more than you'd bargained for.

* * * *

The first rays of sunlight brought release. Pierson and Patricia's bestial forms melted away, and they regained their human bodies.

"What has he done to us?" Patricia had nothing to cover her nakedness. "Are we going to change into those monsters every night?" She collapsed in the knee-high grass.

Pierson knelt next to her, offering what consolation he could. "He's cursed us. And he'll pay."

"We're the ones paying." Her eyes filled with tears. "Immortality like this...I'd rather be dead."

Pierson pulled her into his arms and held her for a long, silent moment. "I'll find a way to break it. I won't rest until I do," he declared, gripping the Body that he'd managed to hold onto.

"Where are we?"

Pierson stood up. "I know this area. We're not far from Jaffler Farm." He pointed out the direction and they made their way to the edge of the woods and behind the barn, where they spotted Tomes tending the horses.

"He'll help us." Pierson assured Patricia.

Tomes looked in their direction as if detecting them and dropped two buckets he was carrying.

"Who's there?" He eased toward them.

"He knows we're here. How?" Pierson mumbled, then stepped into view.

"What the devil." Tomes held up a hand to block his line of vision when he saw that Pierson was naked. "What on earth are you doing? What happened to your clothes?"

"A nightwalker named Meical Evon. A deal gone wrong," Pierson told him. "Can you get us something to cover up with?"

"Us?"

"Patricia is with me." Pierson motioned to an area of brush concealing her.

"Wait here. I'll get some clothes from the house." Tomes darted away. Several minutes later, he returned. "This should fit." He handed Patricia a floral-patterned dress. "But you, Pierson, you'll have to make do with these."

"Pajamas? Superman pajamas?" Pierson's face drew into a scowl. "This is all you have?"

"Sorry." Tomes's mouth tipped upward. "I don't think my jeans will fit. And it's just one small logo. Hardly noticeable."

Pierson grabbed the pajama bottoms and white T-shirt with annoyance and pulled on the elastic waist pants, careful to keep the Body out of sight. "I need to see von Vadim. Hopefully, he can help us."

"I'll give you a lift." Tomes pointed toward his truck.

Pierson had little to say as they rode. He clutched Patricia's hand and stared dead ahead, hardly moving until they pulled through the gates of von Vadim Estate.

"Corin won't be up, but under the circumstances, we can wake him." Tomes aimed for the door, met by Jordon who'd sensed them.

"Black, I'm glad to find you here?" Pierson was surprised to see him.

"That's something I never thought I'd hear from the likes of you." Jordon looked down at the sheriff's bare feet.

"This is Patricia." Pierson held her close.

"Nice to meet you, Patricia. I'm Jordon." He extended a hand.

Patricia reluctantly shook it.

Pierson felt her tremble. "We're safe here."

"Come inside." Jordon stepped aside. "It looks like you've been through some ordeal. What's happened?"

"A nightwalker," Pierson said. "Meical Evon."

"I know him." Jordon followed them to the sofa. "He's no one to mess with."

"A little late for the warning." Pierson sat Patricia down. "He performed a ritual last night. Transformed us into some sort of beasts. Then, at sunrise, we changed back. Unless you can help us, I'm afraid this is our immortality."

"I'd rather die." Patricia broke into tears.

"Angelique wants us to come to the saven." Tomes suddenly informed them. "She knows I'm here and that something's wrong."

Pierson pulled Patricia back up, and they trailed Tomes to a door that led down a flight of stairs, to another door below.

"Wait." Patricia hesitated to enter.

"You're perfectly safe," Jordon, who followed, assured her.

Tomes pushed the door open, and Pierson glanced over the room that was dimly lit with several candles.

"I thought you would be in the basement." Tomes spoke as he entered the room.

"With all of the turn of events, we thought we should stay together." Corin glided toward them from the shadows.

"Well, you can add another event to that list," Tomes said. "Sheriff Pierson and his lady friend, Patricia, have a bit of a problem."

"What has happened?" Angelique stepped toward her brother.

Pierson felt exposed as the immortals visually scanned him. Standing in his bare feet and wearing nothing but pajama bottoms and a T-shirt that was much too snug was humiliating...emasculating.

Corin caught his stare. "What is this all about?"

"It seems Meical Evon has put a curse on them." Jordon leaned against the bar. "Beasts at night. Human form during the day."

"He summoned a being called Carhalli," Pierson said.

Vynce appeared in the doorway of his room. "He evoked a very dark and power demon."

"Like Piiric, she is a supreme being, having the ability to travel between the dimensions and universes without the need of the Passage." Jordon poured a drink. "In her case, summoned by Meical."

"Is there anything you can do?" Pierson searched their expressions for any sign of hope. "I may deserve this, but not Patricia."

"Black magic." Vynce moved toward them. "Galvar may be able to help, when he awakens."

"Wake him," Pierson urged.

"At the moment, that's not possible," Corin told him. "He's in a deep sleep, healing from an injury."

"An injury inflicted by none other than your tormentor, Meical Evon." Vynce spoke with contempt for the immortal.

Tomes drew everyone's attention. "I believe Sheriff Pierson has something more to tell us. To confess about the charm...the Body."

Pierson's forehead rippled as he cut his eyes at Tomes. "How did you know?"

Tomes didn't offer an explanation.

Jordon slapped his hand down on the bar. "You took it? You sly dog." His mouth formed a grin as he marched toward Pierson. "Mr. do-right sheriff? He who does everything by the book?"

"I made a terrible mistake." Pierson relinquished the Body to him, ready to be rid of it. "This needs to be placed back in the right hands."

"You brought it to the right place," Vynce told him.

Pierson looked Jordon in the eyes. "I wasn't even suspected, was I?"

"We only recently considered you a possible suspect. Until now, none of us ever guessed you the thief." Jordon seemed to be the most taken aback. "I'm typically a good judge of character. Sure hope I'm not losing my touch."

A thief. Pierson didn't care for the label. He felt like a louse. A criminal.

Jordon passed the charm to Vynce.

"Galvar will be glad to see this." Vynce thanked Pierson.

"Don't thank me. I basically stole it." Pierson was ashamed of his actions. "If things had gone differently, it would be in Evon's hands right now. I have a lot to atone for."

"Many of us do," Corin sympathized. "No one here is perfect."

"You should probably have someone cover your position for a while, Sheriff, until you get your situation resolved," Jordon suggested.

Pierson nodded. "Rudy, my second in command can take over for the time being. I'll come up with something for a cover. I've done it before. You're not without influence, Black."

"I sure would like to get my hands on your final report on the Jackson County killer." Jordon cast a wide grin. "I bet you got a little more creative than you'd like to admit."

"I'm afraid it would disappoint. I kept it simple," Pierson said. "Would you mind if Patricia stays here while I settle things at the station? With matters what they are, I'd best not delay."

"No," Patricia disputed. "Allen, don't—"

"He's right." Angelique's interruption broke her argument. "You should stay here for your own protection. At least for now."

"Our band of misfits is ever expanding," Tomes said. "Soon, this house won't be big enough."

"I'll need a lift into town," Pierson looked at Tomes. "Would you mind driving me?"

"I don't mind. Let's go." Tomes thumbed toward the door.

Pierson, Patricia, Tomes, and Jordon exited the saven and returned upstairs.

Pierson kissed Patricia on the forehead. "I won't be gone long."

Jordon offered her an arm. "I'll show you to a room where you can rest."

Pierson hated leaving her. "Keep an eye on her, Black."

"She'll be fine," Jordon assured him. "I'll stay right here till you get back."

Pierson thanked him and headed out the front door with Tomes. He climbed into the cab of the blue work truck.

"Straight to the station?" Tomes started the engine.

"No. Head for State Road 121. McCall Farms. I'm hoping my SUV is still there."

"I know it." Tomes pulled out.

As they rode, Pierson silently cursed himself for the predicament he'd put himself and Patricia in, rewinding his thoughts to the moment they'd been cursed. *An earth pentacle, a portion of ibex horn, feather of a griffin, Thyine sap, talon of a raptor, and the blood of a gray wolf.* He would never forget those items, the things making up the beasts they became.

Reaching McCall Farms, Pierson was relieved to find his vehicle where he'd left it, and even happier that his gun, keys, wallet, and badge remained where the spell had been cast.

"I guess he had no use for these." He retrieved his belongings. "But he took the objects he used to cast the spell." He rubbed his eyes. "This is killing Patricia. There has to be a way to break this curse."

"At least you're alive. Sometimes we just have to accept what we've been dealt in life and learn to live with it."

"Don't tell me to count my blessings, Jaffler. In this

case, being alive is worse than death. Patricia, she won't be able to live with this curse, turning into beasts every night, for God knows how much time to come. I'm afraid of what she'll do." Pierson's stare locked on his gun.

"If she's now immortal, it'll take more than that gun to do the job," Tomes told him.

Pierson nodded, understanding that it took certain methods to kill immortals. A task his Glock .45 wasn't equipped for.

"I guess you wish now you'd never followed me into that cemetery six months back."

"You have no idea how right you are. Before Boldor, I was happily ignorant. Since discovering immortals, I've become obsessed with immortality. I've surprised myself by my actions." He sighed. "I guess you can say I got what was coming to me. I got what I was after—immortality—but not in the manner I had planned, and at a terrible cost."

6

After sunset, at von Vadim Estate, Tomes walked the back grounds, still coming to terms with what he had become—the dir cyohr.

Looking up, an image moved toward him from the side of the house. *Angelique.*

"Thought I'd join you." She carried Dusk, a task that would have proved challenging if she were still mortal.

"I'm just thinking on some things."

"I know." She stroked the oversized feline. "Your merge with Piiric."

"And whatever it is that Jordon's not telling me."

Angelique put the cat down. "If it were anything terrible, he wouldn't keep it from you."

"He said it was about my powers. But I'm not convinced that was the truth." Tomes slid off his brown jacket. "I don't feel the cold anymore." He tossed it on the ground. "What does this make me?" He was agonized by his thoughts.

"I ask myself that same question every night. But I

know I'm still me. Just as you are still you. Only now immortal."

"No. I'm more than just me, Angel, and we both know that. And you're more than just you. We carry things within us. Things not of this world." He groaned. "How did we get to this place?"

"There is only one answer to that. Fate." Angelique nodded toward Kara who approached. Leaning toward him, she whispered, "She could be your fate as well."

Kara smiled. "I thought I'd take a run." She gave a fleeting look toward the woods. "Care to join me?"

"Not this time," Angelique declined. "I have business inside. But have a good run."

Angelique walked away with Dusk at her heels, leaving Tomes and Kara alone.

"Where is Jax?" Tomes's gaze was drawn to a small pendant resting in the hollow of her throat—a gold dove.

"He took off. Probably feeding. He goes off alone a lot. I don't ask."

"I didn't see you earlier...in the saven."

"I was there, but Jax didn't want to get involved. Instead, he eavesdropped on your conversation from inside the room."

"Strange. He's supposed to be a close friend of Corin's. Why would he do that?" Tomes was spellbound by Kara's blue gaze.

"He has...issues." Kara stepped closer. "Enough about Jax. Have you tried transforming since your merge?"

"No. I feel I should know how, but I'm not sure."

"Would you like to try? Take a run with me?"

"I suppose I could give it a shot." Tomes wasn't opposed to trying.

"There's not a whole lot to it. Simply envision the animal of your choosing and will yourself to become it.

In this case, let's make it a wolf. An animal you'll find yourself choosing often."

"Will I know what I'm doing when I'm in animal form?"

"We're always in control of our actions no matter what form we're in."

Kara shifted to canine form first, showing him the transformation.

"Okay. I can do this." Tomes closed his eyes and pictured a wolf. *Make me a wolf. Make me a wolf. I am a wolf.*

He felt his body morphing and hesitated to open his eyes, until he felt a nuzzle. Realizing he was in wolf form, he pursued Kara who instigated a chase, feeling wild, exhilarated by the wildness stirring within.

After several minutes, Kara took back human form.

Make me human. I am human. Tomes repeated the words in his mind, and he returned to his human form, met by a passionate kiss.

Tomes wanted her, but he pulled away. "Wait. This can't happen."

"I know you feel it," Kara told him, "the magnetism between us."

"I do. But this isn't right. You're with Jax."

"I'm not drawn to him the way I'm drawn to you, Tomes. I can't stop thinking about you."

Frustrated, Tomes turned away. "I'm going to pass on the run. You go ahead." He headed for his truck, glancing back as she took animal form and ran for the tree line.

"If only things were different. If you weren't with Jax."

He climbed in his truck and drove home to his neighboring farm. He parked in front of the house and started inside but whirled with surprise when Kara appeared on the porch behind him.

"What are you doing here?" He held the key in the door lock.

"I followed along the road," she confessed, her blush-pink blouse shimmering in the moonlight.

"Damn it. You're not making this easy."

"Don't reject me, Tomes." She leaned against him and wrapped her arms around his neck.

Her touch was electrifying. He'd never wanted someone so much. Filled with hunger, he pulled her into a passionate kiss. He could fight his urges no longer. The chemistry was too intense to ignore.

Pushing the door open, he led her inside and to his bedroom. Pulling her into bed, he peeled away her clothes and suckled every inch of her creamy flesh.

"You're the first woman I've been with since Louisa, my late wife." He ran his fingers through her blond strands as she explored his toned upper body.

"Is this hard for you, being with me now, because of her?"

"I didn't think I'd ever be ready, then you show up and awaken a part of me I thought was dead. I can't resist you, Kara. You're intoxicating." Tomes kissed her again.

Kara wrapped her legs around his waist, and in her arousal, her animal side emerged, causing Tomes to draw back.

"I'm sorry." She averted his stare and attempted to sit up. "I lost control."

"Lie back." He halted her action. "You're beautiful."

"The monster, it's a problem."

"Just unexpected." He gave her a tender kiss. "This is a first for me, being with a nightwalker." He brushed his lips along her neck and trailed to her breasts, where he suckled with teasing exploration.

"I want you so much." Kara's words rode on heavy breaths. "It's hard to control the impulse...the thrill.

But I'd never hurt you, Tomes."

Tomes paused. "Don't forget I'm immortal now." He ran his index finger along the chain draping her neck, stopping on the dove, a symbol of peace, love, and the renewal of life. "You just caught me off guard." His fingers traveled to her jaw; he brushed a thumb over her fangs. "I want to know all of you." He claimed her mouth again, yearning for her, tongues dancing to a symphony played only for two. Rolling her over, he took a moment to admire her fit, feminine body. "You really are beautiful." He returned to exploring as she guided his movements with hands buried in his light-brown mane.

Finally, assuming a position to enter her beckoning cavern, he plunged, sending her arching with pleasure, bringing her closer to fulfillment with each intensifying stroke. And when he knew she'd peaked, he sought his own climax.

"I could do that a hundred more times...a thousand." Lying against him, she traced the contours of his chest.

"Not in one night, I hope." He reached for her hand and kissed it.

"I don't want this to end."

"What about Jax?"

"It's over with him. I haven't told him yet. But I will."

"I didn't intend to come between you."

"The feelings I have for you, Tomes, are so strong. What's happening between us now is something I've never experienced before, and I can't walk away from it...from you."

Tomes laid her back and serenaded her with kisses, arousing their sexual energy for a second term. Taking his time, he savored her before bringing them each to a simultaneous climax.

"Ah. Not now." Tomes messaged his temples.

"What is it?"

"Since the merge I've been getting flashes. Piiric's memories."

Kara leaned up. "Do you feel him with you?"

"Yes. I feel him. His memories are building. I'm afraid that a time might come when I won't know the difference between his memories and my own."

"You'll learn to separate them. But I can only image what you're experiencing. It is different with the monster I carry as a nightwalker. The only memories I have are my own." Kara rested her head on his chest. "I love being here with you, but I'll have to go before morning."

"I know." Tomes brushed her hair back. "Ironic isn't it? Two immortals, but not enough time."

* * * *

Pierson entered the bedroom, set his gun and wallet on the nightstand, and walked to the window where Patricia stood with arms crossed, staring out at the stark treetops bobbing in the morning sun.

"I can't accept this." She didn't look at him. "Changing into that monster every night."

"I'll find a way to break the spell."

"Don't promise something you can't give. Be honest. No one can help us, can they?"

"I'm hoping that Galvar can do something when he wakes up."

"If you hadn't pushed, Allen, given me more time to decide. I was happy living a normal, human life."

"I don't expect forgiveness. I promised you immortality and look what I got us. I hate myself for what I've done."

"I can't get the image of what I saw you become last night out of my mind." Tears swelled in her eyes.

Pierson pulled her into his arms. "Don't give up on me. I'll make this right."

"I don't fit into this world you want so much to be a part of, Allen."

"It shouldn't have been this way. If things had turned out like I'd planned—"

"We still would have been cursed." She stopped him from finishing. "Just in a different way." She stepped past him and sat on the bed. "I could use a drink. Something strong."

"I saw some bottles downstairs. I'll be right back."

Pierson was halfway down the stairs when a gunshot rang out. Reversing course, he flew back up to their room, fearing the worst.

"What have you done?" He watched as she slid to the floor with his .45 hanging loosely in her hand.

"I can't die, Allen." Blood trailed down her face from her temple. "Nothing will end this nightmare."

Jordon appeared in the door as Pierson took the gun from her. "Not this way, Patricia. Please, you can't give up on me." He pulled her into his arms, cradling her in his hold. "Don't lose hope."

Jordon hurried over and inspected her wound. "Amazing."

"What?" Pierson knew he'd noticed something unusual.

"Her rate of healing is phenomenal. Immortals usually heal quickly, but not at this speed."

"Like Galvar, healing from his injury?"

"His is a different circumstance, being injured by nytum and nearly decapitated with it. Nytum is a metal that's deadly to immortals, but luckily, it's hard to come by." Jordon stood up. "I'll leave you two alone to sort things out." He squeezed Pierson's shoulder before leaving the room.

"I'm sorry, Allen." Patricia's voice quivered.

"You tried to kill yourself, Patricia." Pierson held her tight. "I've brought you to this."

"I don't want to hurt you," Patricia sobbed. "I just want to end the madness."

"There's something I want to tell you." Pierson released his hold and looked into her face. "Why I wanted immortality so badly. The real reason."

"To not grow old?"

"No. I'm sick, Patricia. Cancer. This was the only way I knew to beat it."

Her gaze locked with his. "How long have you known?"

"For a while." He laid his forehead against hers. "I wasn't ready to die. I'm not ready for either of us to die."

"You should have told me. Now I understand why you went to the lengths you did. You're trying to save your life."

"Immortality was the solution. The only solution. The doctors gave me a year with treatment, a lot less without. I chose without."

"Because you were counting on immortality. To cheat death."

Pierson gripped her hands. "I'll find a way to break this curse and give you back your life. Please, give me that chance. No more suicide attempts. I can't lose you that way."

"It was a useless attempt. We apparently can't die. Not with a gun anyway."

"We're immortal."

"About you, Allen, if the curse is broken, without immortality you will die."

"Yes. But to save you, I would be happy to die this very minute."

"Immortality. Beasts at night. But it's the only solution," Patricia said and pushed herself up. "No more self-pity. From this moment on, I'm with you, no matter what. Till the end."

<h1 style="text-align:center">7</h1>

Remaining vigil at Galvar's bedside, Vynce fidgeted with a black leather glove covering his right hand. "Do you think something has gone wrong with his healing? Another night and day have passed, and he still hasn't awakened."

"From what you've said about nytum, his healing is just slow." Corin inspected Galvar's neck. "The wound is hardly detectable now. I expect he'll wake up anytime."

Corin exited the room finding Angelique waiting outside the door. He breathed in her lavender scent and ran his lips over the top of her head. "We should feed. How about a drive tonight in the 'Vette? It's been awhile."

"I'd like that."

Corin turned in the open doorway and looked back at Vynce. "We'll be back shortly. You should feed yourself. Keep up your strength."

"I will have Jordon sit with Galvar while I feed. You

two go and enjoy your evening."

Corin and Angelique departed in the 'Vette, and upon arriving at one of their feeding spots, they slipped into a pasture and took nourishment from grazing cattle. After satisfying their hunger, Corin drove on to Jaffler Farm, suggesting a moonlight stroll to their special place—a shallow creek that connected their properties.

Walking a snow-laden path, Angelique asked about Jozsef. "Do you think he'll contact you again?"

"I hope he will, but he's loyal to his clan, and to his maker, Andras. Jozsef feels he owes him. Although, he did warn me to watch my back, that Andras was after the Clyth."

"You're on opposite sides. This has to be hard for you. He's your brother. Family."

Corin still hadn't told her about Andras being his immortal father, and it was time to share that truth.

"There's something I need to tell you about Jozsef. About me." He stopped and faced her.

"What is it? Has he done something? Have you?" Angelique intertwined her fingers with his.

"No. It's about our past. I've just found out that he and I were changed by the same nightwalker, an immortal known long ago as Gedeon, known now as Andras Metellus."

"Andras, head of the Örök Vér, made you immortal? And Jozsef? Both of you changed by the same nightwalker?"

"A long time ago."

"Why target both of you? With you and Jozsef being identical, he knew you were brothers."

"I don't have that answer."

"So much has happened lately, I'm afraid to know what we might find out next."

Corin resumed a slow gait. "I can't help wondering

how differently things might have turned out for me had I chosen to stay in Hungary the way Jozsef had, instead of escaping to America.”

“Don’t give up on him. He’s your flesh and blood.”

“It’s been so long, I’m not sure I know him anymore. I certainly don’t trust him.”

Minutes later, the creek came into view, a beautiful, frozen wonder.

“I want you now. Right here.” Corin drew Angelique to him and lifted her chin.

Needing no convincing, she unbuttoned his shirt and kissed his chiseled chest.

He captured her mouth as fire raged through his veins. Quaking under her caressing touch, she was his strength, and weakness, moving him like no other woman ever had. She would move him forever.

Corin swept her off of her feet, and finding higher ground, laid her back in the shallow snow. Driven by desire, they shed their clothes, two cold, nocturnal creatures building their own heat, soaring to heavenly rapture in the symphony of the night.

* * * *

“That is no accidental happening.” Jordon reacted with surprise to Corin’s news. “Andras was either intrigued by the conquest of changing identical twins, or something more.”

“The idea of something more is what bothers me.” Corin stood up. “I’m sorry I didn’t tell you right away. I needed time to think, and Angelique had to be told first.”

“I understand. You’ve had a lot to absorb. Where is Angelique?”

“Downstairs. We just got back from feeding.”

“With so many immortals in the house, it’s hard to

tell who's coming and going."

After several more minutes of conversation, Corin left the library, and Jordon sat pondering his friend's situation. "What is Andras up to?"

Reaching for a book, he suddenly straightened when he sensed someone outside the door. Waiting several seconds, his body tensed, wondering why the individual hadn't announced themselves. Rising from his chair, he aimed for the door, but stopped midway as it swung open.

"Kara." His tightened muscles relaxed. "I wasn't sure who was at the door. With Meical around, we all have to be extra cautious."

"I couldn't agree more." Kara stepped into the room and shut the door. "I was waiting for Corin to leave. We need to talk."

"Where is Jax?" Jordon returned to his seat where he had dropped his book and picked it up.

"That's what I want to talk to you about. There's something you should know."

"Sounds serious. What is it?"

"Andras. He's en route to Hixton. He'll probably arrive tomorrow night."

"How do you know?"

Kara lowered her gaze. "Jax. He's working with the Örök Vér. Spying for Andras."

"What? Jax? A spy?" *Could it be true?*

"I know. It's the last thing you expected. Which made it the perfect cover."

Jordon groaned. "Corin's not going to take this well. I understand they've been friends a long time."

"Jax's hand was forced. He had little choice."

"How did he manage to get mixed up with the Örök Vér? How are you involved with the Örök Vér?"

"First, let me confess that a story we told Corin and Angelique when first arriving here, at the estate, was a lie. There was never any wager. No archery match. No Luke Shaw. As you now know, my clan leader is Andras Metellus. But I wanted out of the Örök Vér and Jax tried to help me."

"And got caught?" Jordon surmised.

Kara nodded. "Andras gives no one the option of walking away, and he is certainly not the forgiving kind. But he spared our lives with the understanding that there would be no second chance."

"Why the whole made-up story?"

"Albeit somewhat outlandish, we couldn't tell the truth. And outlandish fits Jax."

"So, Jax is now controlled by Andras?" Jordon narrowed his eyes. "How do I know I can trust you? Why are you admitting all of this now?"

"Because of Tomes. I won't let anything happen to him."

"Ah. You and Tomes?" Jordon grasped what was happening.

Kara walked the room. "Jax and I had a good time, but it was never anything more than that."

"Are you sure he sees it the same way?"

"By his reaction when I told him I was ending our relationship, I could see he feels more for me than I feel for him." She browsed books lining the wall, running her fingers along the dusty spines. "But there is nothing lasting on my part. Not with Jax."

"But there is with Tomes?"

Kara pulled out a book and flipped through the pages, dispersing dry particles into the air. "When I met Tomes, it didn't matter that he was mortal. I felt an instant connection." She shut the book and put it back on the shelf. "He felt it too."

"Tomes is now immortal. The dir cyohr."

"Born to play a very important role in the Eleventh Dimension. I know all about the Eleventh Dimension. I know what he is and what that means." Kara faced Jordon.

"You know a lot."

"And there's so much you don't know."

"What else don't I know?" Jordon's stare locked with hers.

"Andras," she hesitated. "He is Delghorlin."

"Delghorlin?" Jordon stood. "A whole new clan of the demons? How is that possible when they were believed to be nearly extinct?"

"I can only tell you what I know. He recently disclosed his secret lineage to the clan. He told us about the Eleventh Dimension, preparing us for what is to come. He has big plans."

"Then you are Delghorlin." Jordon's hatred of the lineage rode on his words. "And Corin's brother. Jozsef. He is too."

"Yes. We are."

"I can't believe this." Jordon was livid. "He's been rebuilding his line all this time, right under our noses. Andras never wanted control of Earth. He wants control of the Eleventh Dimension. He wants the Clyth to make that happen, and he'll eliminate anything standing in his way, with his biggest threat being the dir cyohr—Tomes."

"We can't let that happen." Tears stung her eyes.

"You really do love him." Jordon saw her sincerity.

"Yes. I love him. I know he'll probably never forgive me for my deception, but together or not, I want him safe."

"I have pledged loyalty and life to the dir cyohr," Jordon assured her. "What about your safety? You've spent your second chance."

"I can't go back. That's a given."

"Stick with us. You have protection here," Jordon told her.

"Tomes's safety is all that matters."

"As soon as the Passage of Dimensions is operable, I'll get him to the Eleventh Dimension." Jordon moved toward the door. "For now, all we can do is prepare for an attack. Everyone needs to know what's happening. What we're facing—Delghorlins." Grabbing the door handle, he paused, struck by a sudden realization, and whirled back to face Kara. "Corin just told me that he and Jozsef were both changed by Andras. That means Corin...."

"Changed by Andras, yes, he is Delghorlin."

Jordon spun and charged out the door, and Kara rushed to keep up as he flew downstairs, finding Tomes, Corin, and Angelique in the living room.

"Where are Pierson and Patricia?" Jordon inquired.

"In the woods, I believe," Corin answered.

"Emergency meeting." Jordon ushered them all to the saven where Vynce relaxed in front of the TV, remaining close to Galvar who still hadn't awakened.

"What is going on?" Vynce turned off the television.

"Kara just informed me that Andras is expected in Hixton tomorrow night." Jordon looked at Tomes. "In addition to the Body, he's coming after you. I believe he wants to eliminate the dir cyohr."

Jordon's gaze drifted to Corin, wondering if he knew about his true bloodline and was hiding that truth. *Did you tell me everything, or are you clueless to your true lineage? How will you react to the news of Andras being Delghorlin?*

"Kara, how do you know this?" Corin asked.

"Jax." Jordon answered for her. "He's been spying for them."

"No. I don't believe that." Corin rejected the accusation.

"It's true." Kara explained Jax's secret association with Andras. "For what it's worth, Jax didn't want to do this. Betraying you was not easy for him."

Corin cursed. "How did Andras find out about my connection with Jax?"

"Jax made the mistake of befriending Jitters, a nervous SOB closely tied to Meical. When it became known that the Body was thought to be in Hixton, Jitters ratted to Meical that Jax knew you, having seen an email he'd received from you. The invitation to attend your eternal union. Armed with that information, Meical went straight to Andras, who forced Jax to spy and report on your activity, hoping to track down the Body."

Corin ambled to the bar. "I had complete trust in him, and all the while he's been feeding the wolves." He cursed again and slammed his hand down in a jarring slam. "There's no going back. He knows I'll kill, even him, to protect my family."

Tomes stepped in front of Kara and stared into her eyes. "You knew what he was up to all along? Playing us all?"

"Yes, at first." She didn't deny it. "But then things changed. I got to know you. All of you." She looked sincerely at the others.

"She's telling us now, Tomes," Jordon spoke up for Kara. "Cut a little slack. This isn't easy for her."

"Unlike Jax, you've chosen to make things right," Angelique told her. "You're putting your own life on the line for our sake. That counts for a lot in my book."

Tomes shook his head. "I'm sorry, Kara, but I can't overlook what you've done that easy." His voice was filled with anger...with hurt. "You should have told me. You'll never have my trust again. This destroys anything we might have had."

"Tomes, please. I've confessed all of this for you. I only want you safe. I love you."

"The way you loved Jax?" Tomes snapped at her.

"How long would it have taken for you to stab me in the back for the next man? I wish I'd never met you."

With those sharp words, Kara broke into tears and fled the saven.

"Tomes, that wasn't fair. Go after her," Angelique demanded. "She betrayed her clan for you. They will kill her for helping us. She loves you, and I know you love her."

"She's put her life on the line. She's made it clear why," Jordon said.

"I can't trust her now." Tomes wasn't yielding. "The most important quality to me, and she failed."

"I think her actions tonight have more than proven her devotion to you. You're just too bullheaded to see it." Angelique headed for the door.

"Where are you going?" Corin blocked her path. "I don't want you wandering off alone."

"Wait. We have more to discuss," Jordon stopped them. "Things everyone here should know."

"I have to stop her...bring her back." Angelique was determined.

Jordon waved a hand. "Go. Get her. Then we'll finish this talk."

Corin opened the door. "I'm coming with you."

"Jordon, you should come too." Angelique motioned to him. "You're the one she chose to confide in."

Jordon glanced at Tomes as he aimed for the door, glimpsing a look he interpreted as jealousy. "No one leave. Like I said, we have more to discuss." He followed Angelique and Corin outside.

Finding Kara leaning against Tomes's truck, Angelique approached her. "Tomes is just angry right now."

Kara straightened and brushed back tears.

"Give him some time." Angelique stepped next to her. "He'll come to see what you've done for him. For us all."

"All I saw was hatred in his eyes," Kara said through sniffles.

"What you saw was hurt and disappointment," Angelique corrected. "He loves you. And he's lucky to have you, even if he doesn't see it right now."

"You can't leave, Kara," Jordon told her. "By now, Andras must know what you've done—switching sides—and that puts not only you, but all of us in danger. Your relationship with Tomes makes you a valuable asset, something he could use to get to Tomes." He looked at Corin and Angelique. "A road we've been down before."

"Please, Kara." Angelique touched her arm, offering support. "Here, you have allies ready to stand against him."

Kara looked at her. "I'll stay, if for no other reason than to help protect Tomes. Even prepared, you'll find the Örök Vér a force to be reckoned with. You have no idea what you're facing. Few that oppose them walk away alive."

"They don't know yet," Jordon told her and cut his eyes at Corin. "The Örök Vér, they —"

"Someone's coming," Angelique interrupted and turned with a jerk.

Jordon scanned their dim surroundings. "It could be Pierson and Patricia."

"There." Angelique pointed out figures swiftly approaching, at least ten immortals in animal forms—wolves and other carnivorous creatures.

"Get inside," Jordon barked.

"I didn't think they'd attack before the clan arrived, or without Andras," Kara said as they scrambled for the entry and back inside.

"Jax must have warned him of you switching sides," Corin presumed. "Cause for acting sooner, to catch us unprepared. Thanks to him, they know how many are here to fend off an attack."

"This is better for us," Kara told him. "With an entire clan of five hundred on their way to Hixton, at least with Meical's small group, we stand a chance."

Corin's dark eyes widened. "Five hundred? God help us."

"His intent is to get the Clyth, and when he has it, to cross his clan over to the Eleventh Dimension. To carry out his plan there." Jordon held a strong stance twenty feet from the door, ready for attack.

With his next heartbeat, a vicious-looking lion burst through the mansion door. The creature roared and took human form—Meical Evon with daggers drawn.

"Attack!" Evon bellowed as the rest of his gang poured in behind him.

Jordon spotted Tomes and rushed to protect him. "Meical is attacking."

A hellish wail encompassed the room as Pierson and Patricia arrived, the beasts tearing through the entry and ripping out the frame as they stormed the Örök Vér, sending the immortals scrambling from the wild things' limb-dismembering jaws.

Corin blocked Meical's charge, cautious of the nightwalker's blades. "They want Tomes. Get him out of here," he shouted to Jordon.

"Where is Vynce?" Jordon scanned the room.

"Below." Tomes motioned.

"Let's go." Jordon urged Tomes toward the saven door.

Tomes refused. "I'm not leaving them to fight alone."

"Andras is intent on assassinating the dir cyohr, and Meical is here to carry out that act."

"I don't care. My sister is in danger. And Kara."

"An entire world is depending on you, Tomes."

Jordon reminded him. "With Pierson and Patricia, they can hold their own."

Jordon steered him toward the door leading below and descended the stairs to the underground lair.

"It's Meical. He has attacked," Jordon informed Vynce who peered out of Galvar's room. "We have to protect Tomes."

"Try the disc." Tomes's voice had changed, possessing a deeper tone. "It is time."

"Piiric?" Jordon sought confirmation.

"Yes," the deity spoke through Tomes. "The Eleventh Dimension awaits."

"You are able to take control?" Jordon asked.

"Until my presence fades, and he learns to master his abilities," Piiric answered.

Jordon reached for his shalym disc pierced at his lower abdomen and pulled it free. "The Passage...strange that it should suddenly became operable at this particular moment. But I'm not questioning it."

Placing the quarter-sized disc in his palm, it melted into his skin, the top still visible, marked with ten interlinking circles surrounding a larger circle, representing the ten portals that connect the main world to the other ten dimensions.

Outstretching his hand, he turned his palm outward as if halting someone from passing and said, "Ta marof beegha," meaning "take me home" in the ancient language of his ancestors. And with those words a wormhole appeared providing a passage to the Eleventh Dimension.

"Wait." Vynce darted into Galvar's room, returning with the Body.

Jordon looked up as several thundering bangs jarred the walls. "I hate leaving you, Vynce, but they could use your shinobi skills right now."

"Go. Keep Tomes, and this, safe. We will take care of the Örök Vér." He handed Piiric the Body. "The Clyth belongs with you."

"Vynce. The Örök Vér, they are Delghorlins," Jordon revealed. "I just found out. From Kara."

"This is unexpected." Vynce held a fixed stare. "Not good news."

"No. Be careful."

"Something else. This news may have a particular impact on Corin. But with the present situation what it is, I leave it in your hands," Jordon added.

Piiric touched the charm to his lips. "We have a higher purpose. To save the Eleventh Dimension."

"Good luck, my friend," Jordon said as Vynce dashed away. *A higher purpose.*

He couldn't help being distressed by sounds of battle drifting from above, fearing lives would be lost. But knowing his duty, he stepped into the passage with Piiric and passed into the Eleventh Dimension.

8

Corin's heart skipped a beat when he caught sight of Angelique intercepting a charge on Kara, but her fighting skills were impressive as she held nothing back, managing quite well in battle.

Vynce surfaced from the saven near Corin, fangs and talons extended. Gripping a sword in each hand, he pursued an immortal who scarcely escaped his swing. "See if you can handle this." He tossed Corin a weapon.

Corin executed a move on an oncoming immortal, severing his head. "Another one down." The remains crumbled, and he smeared a foot in the ashes. "Where is Tomes?"

"He has the Body, and he and Jordon have crossed to the Eleventh Dimension. The nightwalker I was after...there." He pointed him out. "He was spying from the stairwell."

"At least Tomes is safe."

"And the Body, for now." Vynce spotted Kara and summoned her to his and Corin's position. He then spotted Meical advancing. "Watch the saven door. Protect Galvar."

Another immortal trailed Meical, whom Corin presumed to be Jitters, but noticing Jax targeting Angelique, she was his greater concern. "Angelique's in trouble."

"Go," Vynce told him. "I will take care of these two."

Midway across the room, Jozsef blocked Corin's heroic rescue. "I wouldn't worry about her. Not against Jax anyway."

"I don't want to fight you, Jozsef." Corin was frustrated by his inability to get to Angelique. "But I will do whatever it takes to save Angelique."

"She's a superb fighter. Her Delghorlin blood gives her a superior strength."

"What are you talking about?"

"Pretend to take me down," Jozsef spoke under his breath. "While everyone's engaged," he pressed. "Just do it."

It took little convincing for Corin to slam him to the ground. "Say your piece. You have one minute, no more." He kept an eye on Angelique who held a defensive position against Jax.

"We're more than just alien blood, you and me. We are highborns." Jozsef talked through gnashed teeth, pretending to fight, keeping his voice low.

"Highborns?"

"That is what Andras calls individuals who possess a rare blood mutation that is required for a Delghorlin change to be successful. Highborns. Those fated for greatness. That is why he chose us. Because of our blood. Blood that creates Delghorlins whose demons make the most powerful nightwalkers."

"That means Angelique has the component." Corin faked a move. "What were the odds of her having the blood mutation?"

"And most likely her brother. Possibly necessary for his purpose in becoming the dir cyohr. But that's just a guess."

Corin released a roar as Jozsef's talons ripped through two layers of material and into his side.

"Just makin' it real." Jozsef knocked him into the next room.

Corin's eyes narrowed into a wince as he pressed a hand over the stinging wounds. "When I changed her, I made her Delghorlin." He soaked in the information.

"Just as Andras made us Delghorlin." Jozsef shoved Corin against the wall.

"Retreat!" Meical's cry rang out. "Örök Vér, depart!"

"My cue." Jozsef leaned close. "Score, Luca, worthy of the shield." He released his grip and retreated with the others.

"Angelique." Corin called out, having lost sight of her.

"I'm here." She rushed toward him from across the room.

He wrapped her in his arms, then checked her for injuries. "Jax. Did he hurt you?"

"No, I'm fine. But you're not." She noticed his side.

"It's nothing." Corin ran his fingers over the gashes and healed the ripped flesh.

"Jax didn't fight me, Corin. For your sake. Kara was right, betraying you was not easy for him."

"I would never trust him again. There's no going back."

"He knows that."

Vynce rounded the corner. "They took Kara. I could not get to her."

Angelique gasped. "What will they do to her?"

"They won't kill her. Not yet. She's too valuable to Andras. You can count on him using her relationship with Tomes to its full advantage. Those closest to us are always our greatest weaknesses." A tormenting memory of Boldor's filthy hands on Angelique resurfaced. "How about everyone else? Any injuries?" He strode toward Pierson and Patricia and looked them over, noticing cuts they'd incurred during the fight were quickly fading. "We wouldn't have survived without you two."

Angelique looked around. "What about Tomes. Where is he? I don't sense him."

"He is with Jordon. They left for the Eleventh Dimension...with the Body." Vynce explained how Piiric took control of Tomes. "One of the Örök Vér overheard, which I am sure is why they retreated. When Andras is informed, you can count on him going after Tomes again."

"He will try to use Kara to force his hand." Corin hated that the past was repeating itself.

"Tomes will do whatever he can to save her." Angelique knew her brother better than anyone. "Tomes was angry, but he loves her."

"They won't cross over till tomorrow night," Vynce said. "That gives Tomes and Jordon a good head start."

"Are you sure Andras has access to the Passage?" Angelique asked.

"He's been planning this uprising for a long time, waiting for the end time apocalypse. There is no doubt he has a shalym disc. He will definitely follow," Vynce told her. "Jordon and Tomes do have one advantage. Being diurnal, they can travel day and night. There are ten portals scattered about the world. One is in the Morpar Kingdom, where Jordon and Tomes have gone, but Andras will not risk entering there. The next portal is hours away, and the nightwalkers will need plenty of night to travel once they cross over."

"How do you control where you'll arrive when you cross over?" Corin wondered.

Jordon had told him quite a lot about the portals in the other world after first meeting the daywalker six months earlier, but he hadn't told him everything.

"We tell the passage where to take us with what we refer to as a calling. Then, before we completely pass through, we are able to see what awaits us. However, when going back to the Eleventh Dimension from another world, like Earth, we must return through one of the ten portals."

"Complex, yet simple." Corin expressed his satisfaction. "How different is time there?"

"It coincides with Earth. When it is day here, it is day there; night here, night there. Moving in synch with the Eleventh Dimension makes Earth a perfect alternate world. Nightwalkers can travel between the two worlds with certainty of their safe arrival."

"Can you take us there?" Angelique asked. "Tomes may need us."

Vynce shook his head. "Not without Galvar's approval."

Corin noticed Vynce's talons retract with no damage to the leather gloves he wore. "Amazing you haven't gone through hundreds of those."

"It is a talent," Vynce said.

"Tomes is in good hands with Jordon," Corin assured Angelique, hearing her troubled thoughts.

Vynce suddenly straightened and cocked his head. "Galvar. He is awake." A smile curled his lip, and he darted for the saven door and down to the lair below, finding the commander exiting his room.

Corin and Angelique followed.

"What have I missed?" Galvar grabbed ahold of Vynce for support, still lacking strength.

"The Örök Vér attacked. Meical and his gang." Vynce guided him to the sofa. "We have learned a lot since your injury, what Tarik was unable to disclose. Andras.

He is not just after the Clyth for Earth domination, but control of the Eleventh Dimension. The end time prophecy, it is happening now. Why the passage was down."

Angelique took that moment to slip into one of the rooms.

"The comet?" Galvar's expression froze. "The end time apocalypse?"

"Yes." Vynce hovered close. "The Eleventh Dimension is suffering, but the dir cyohr has been named."

Galvar leaned forward. "Who was the chosen?"

"My brother, Tomes." Angelique reappeared, toting a striped shirt, which she handed to Corin. "Something we sure never expected."

Corin removed his torn clothing and slipped on the clean shirt.

"I witnessed the merge. Piiric is with him," Vynce confirmed, then cut his eyes at Corin. "Jordon revealed something unexpected, that the Örök Vér are Delghorlins. He had a particular concern for you, Corin."

Angelique took in a quick breath. "Delghorlins." She looked at Corin with widened eyes. "Is it true?"

"It's true," Corin corroborated. "Jozsef just told me the same thing...warned me."

Angelique spoke to him telepathically. "What does that mean for us? Andras changed you. Are we—"

"Give us a minute," Corin told the others and pulled Angelique into a room. "It means just that. You and I, we are of his bloodline," he communicated with Angelique through thought.

"We're like him?"

Corin felt her disillusionment as he stared into her worried eyes. "We may have Delghorlin blood, but we're nothing like Andras." He scooped up her hands.

"What we do have is the superior strength that comes with being Delghorlin, and we'll use it against them."

"My change went so smoothly, better than you'd expected. I've adapted so quickly to my transformation. Is this why? Because I'm Delghorlin?"

"I believe so." Corin had already come to that conclusion. "Delghorlins are the strongest vampires. The most powerful of our kind."

"That's what scares me."

"I have managed for five hundred years, and so will you." Corin peered through the cracked door, observing the others silently waiting. "Knowing we could soon come into contact with Andras, our friends should be warned of my connection with him, that we are Delghorlin."

Rejoining the others in the circle, Corin revealed his lineage.

"My only question is: Can we trust you?" Galvar said. "Learning that your brother is alive will impact your life in some respect. How much impact? Can we rely on you?"

"Angelique and I, we are no different today than we were yesterday. I never knew I was Delghorlin. I never knew my brother was alive and immortal. None of this changes who I am, and it will not change me now," Corin told him. "I admit, I wish I could help Jozsef break free from Andras, but I would never risk the safety of friends and family. Besides, Jozsef has made it clear that his loyalty resides with Andras."

"He did warn you. He must be conflicted," Galvar pointed out. "Being Delghorlin, it explains a lot about you, Corin. Now we know why your demon was so strong when you faced Boldor those months back. A Delghorlin demon. Yet, still one of the strongest I have encountered."

"Lucky me," Corin spoke under his breath.

"Andras leading a Delghorlin clan. That must have been the information Tarik planned to reveal," Galvar assumed. "All of this, staggering news to awaken to, but considering the interest they had in the Clyth, I suppose I should not be so surprised to find they are Delghorlins."

"He intends to rise up and claim control during this time of cataclysm," Jordon said, "when the divisions are at their weakest. He will go after Tomes not only to end his life, but to get the Body. With the attack tonight, I sent the charm with him...with Piiric. I figured it was safest with him."

"You did the right thing," Galvar told him.

"Andras knows he has it. One of the Örök Vér overhead what transpired when he and Jordon departed," Vynce added. "With Meical here, and Andras on his way, we believe they will cross over tomorrow night."

"The Body is in the right hands. It belongs with the dir cyohr." Galvar stood up, testing his strength. "We will cross tomorrow night as well. That will give Jordon and Tomes time to evaluate the condition of the territories. I do not believe Andras would dare enter at Morpar without certainty of what he would be facing. That puts time on our side."

"I said as much," Vynce agreed.

"I want to go with you, to the Eleventh Dimension." Dark strands of hair fell across Angelique's right shoulder. "Tomes is my brother. I should be there for him."

"Do I have a say in this matter?" Corin considered the dangers. In addition to the threat Andras posed, there would likely be all forms of disasters in a time of apocalypse. "We don't know what condition the world is in."

"Corin." Angelique whirled. "It's Tomes. I have to

go."

Corin, struck by the intensity of her emotion, relinquished his argument knowing he was fighting a losing battle.

A loud bang captured the immortals' attention.

Galvar looked up. "Is someone else in the house?"

"Beasts." The word drew back Galvar's stare. "Meical Evon's creations."

"Beasts?" Galvar sought an explanation.

Corin explained what had occurred between Sheriff Pierson and Evon.

"I want to see them." Galvar moved toward the door. Making it upstairs, he approached Pierson without fear. "Ancient dark arts," he deduced.

"Yes. Carhalli," Vynce told him.

Galvar knew the name. "The one possessing the power of transformation."

Corin viewed the condition of the mansion, finding it a wreck in the wake of Meical's attack. Wind brushed his face as it whipped through two large holes in the front wall, openings large enough to accommodate Pierson and Patricia in their bestial forms. "They're hoping you can help them," he told Galvar. "They're beasts at night and human during the day."

"A cruel curse." Galvar laid his hand against Pierson's shoulder. "I am afraid there is nothing I can do. If there is any hope, it will be found in the Eleventh Dimension."

Pierson snorted and stomped a massive claw, shaking the foundation.

"Their strength is astounding." Galvar studied Pierson. "With your situation it is best that you cross to the Eleventh Dimension. Remaining here, it is just a matter of time till someone spots you." He considered their options. "Acting ruler, Regent Fehre, will have a place for you, possibly as guards at Morpar Palace. I'll make arrangements."

"They will be useful against Andras." Vynce stood to his right. "They are powerful."

Galvar nodded. "Animal. Nature. Magic. How could they not be? Meical did not think his actions through."

"They were a real asset against him tonight," Vynce said. "I can imagine he is cursing himself right about now."

"Kara mentioned the size and strength of our opposition at five hundred. That's a large clan, enough to establish a small army." Corin blew out a heavy breath. "I guess we'd better prepare."

Galvar looked at him. "I wish you had not been drawn into our plight, but I see now that we have all been brought together for the purpose of fulfilling prophecy. We are each destined to carry out our part."

Corin knew the commander was right. Learning that he and Angelique were Delghorlins just further substantiated that they had all been brought together for a greater purpose—to fulfill prophecy that would now carry them to another world.

* * * *

There were no words to express Jordon's disillusionment as he stood at the edge of a large crater, staring down into a smoldering pit. "It must be a thousand meters across."

Tomes laid a hand on Jordon's shoulder from behind while visually trailing a meteorite that streaked across the dark sky, rocking the ground as it crashed a few miles away. "I've never seen anything like this." The sky glowed red in the aftermath.

"In those days, fire will fall from the heavens, and the land will tremble and burn. Mountains will divide and fall into the earth, bringing woe unto all inhabitants." Jordon's despair sounded in his voice. "The prophecy. Foretelling the comet's debris. Large, earth-shaking meteorites, as well as earthquakes."

"The loss of life from these strikes must be staggering."

"Yes. Enormous Loss." Jordon faced east. "The western division is hardly recognizable." He brushed back pooling tears, striving to contain his emotion. "Morpar Palace isn't far from here."

"I know the palace. From Piiric's memories. It's strange, recalling two pasts."

"Are you angry that he took control?"

"I was aware of everything that was happening, but he overpowered me." Tomes's focus caught a large, translucent globe in the sky, its light scantily breaking through the hazy atmosphere. "I never would have left Angelique, or Kara, during an attack. He knew that."

"We just have to trust that they survived."

"I heard what you said about the Örök Vér being Delghorlins. That it may have a particular impact on Corin. What did you mean by that?"

"I found out that Corin and Tomes were changed by the same nightwalker. That nightwalker being Andras," Jordon told him.

"Corin? Delghorlin?"

"And your sister."

"It doesn't matter. They are my family and I completely trust them...with my life." Tomes pointed up. "With the sky so polluted, I can scarcely make out your moon."

"One of three. There are two smaller satellites adjacent Hiquire, but they're not visible through this haze."

"Now that I'm here, seeing the state of this world, I know this is where I'm meant to be."

"Recovery is going to be a long process," Jordon

sighed. "We should get moving."

With those words, Jordon and Tomes transformed and took flight in the dust-laden sky. Riding a current, Tomes, in the form of a red-tailed hawk, released a hoarse cry as if testing his animal vocals.

Reaching the palace, the aerial view thoroughly showcased the structure's spires and surreal magnificence. Zeroing in on a courtyard, they landed, met within seconds by three Indith immortals.

"His forearm." One immortal caught sight of Jordon's mark. "He's Indithian."

"Sentry," Jordon informed them and shape-shifted from the form he used on Earth as Marshal Black—an older version of himself—to his actual identity, appearing an age of twenty in human years. "We are here to see Regent Fehre. I have important news."

A fourth immortal approached and immediately recognized Jordon. "I hope it is encouraging news."

"Master Constable Lavor." Jordon bowed his head in respect. "It's good to see you." He was thankful for the familiar face, and one of authority. "And yes, the news is encouraging."

"Come with me." The broad-shouldered constable's knee-length cape waved in a current as he whirled and led Jordon and Tomes into the palace. Passing through an array of corridors, Jordon observed Tomes's bewilderment.

"This palace seems so familiar. It was Piiric's home, wasn't it?" Tomes followed alongside Jordon.

"Yes. You're remembering his past life."

Tomes looked at him. "Are you also from here?"

"I serve in Morpar, but my roots lie in Kordes. Jordon Day Morrain of Kordes."

"Nice title." Tomes smirked. "I feel like I've stepped hundreds of years back in time."

"Life here does closely compare to Earth's Medieval

history."

Finally reaching what the constable presented as the council room, Tomes entered, finding several high-ranking immortals awaiting them, all seated at a long, narrow table.

Constable Lavor addressed the council. "Sentry Morrain brings news."

Regent Fehre entered and acknowledged Jordon who knelt in his presence.

"What news have you brought?" The Regent gestured for him to stand.

"I've brought the dir cyohr." Jordon introduced Tomes as the prophesied one. "By the devastation, it appears we've come just in time."

Murmurs swept amongst the council.

Standing at the head of the table, Regent Fehre motioned for silence. "The dir cyohr?" His gray eyes locked on Tomes and then shifted to Jordon. "You are sure?"

"Yes. I personally witnessed the merge," Jordon assured him.

The ruler looked back at Tomes. "If this is indeed true, I welcome you to Morpar, the capital city of the Eleventh Dimension. I am Sir Aros Fehre, Regent of Morpar."

"Thank you, Regent." Tomes shifted under the councils' scrutiny.

"All signs indicated this to be the time of your arrival, with our world in calamity. All divisions are suffering, some altered by disasters of immense proportion. I just received word that the Xallon Lowland Territory in the far-east has been engulfed, struck by a tsunami and left partially submersed in the Wen Sea." Chestnut strands broke across the regent's shoulders in contrast to his royal green cape.

Jordon took in a sharp breath in reaction to the

news. "Mainly a human region."

Regent Fehre sighed. "Worldwide disasters have ravaged the mortals."

"Mirillow Traxl. His clan is also in that territory," Jordon expressed concern. "What about Traxl-1?"

"The nightwalkers' caves are flooded, leaving the world without an outgoing supply." Fehre took a seat and motioned for them to sit. "The whole world is under attack. Every disaster imaginable. Meteor storms, matching what we've experienced here, in Morpar. Quakes leveling mountains. Volcanoes that have swallowed up villages. A never-ending barrage. And the humans have no way of escaping nature's fury. Their existence is highly threatened."

One of the councilmen stood. "Forgive me, Sentry Morrain, but I need more than just your word that this is the dir cyohr." He was unconvinced.

"As I said, I personally witnessed the merge," Jordon attested.

The councilman turned to Regent Fehre. "There must be no doubt. Piiric's chamber will tell the truth."

The regent agreed, and the group proceeded to the palace temple.

"Piiric, our beloved Prince of Morpar." Regent Fehre pointed at a life-size statue of Piiric portrayed in a floor-length robe, standing partially encased in a tall, stone wall, the focal point of the temple. A medallion marked the center of the statue's chest—the Circle of the Morpar Kingdom.

"Yes. I know this." Tomes instinctively moved toward the statue and the seal spiraled open revealing a secret cavity. "It opens for no other." He reached in and pulled a lever.

Murmurs once again swept through the group as the statue regressed revealing a doorway to a hidden room.

"No one has been able to enter this chamber since

Piiric's death. The door opens for no one but him." Fehre faced Tomes. "It is true. You are the dir cyohr," he proclaimed and knelt before him, pledging his loyalty and life. "I relinquish the throne to you, Dir Cyohr, and graciously take my place as Grand Chancellor of Morpar in your service."

"I'm not ready for that, Regent. For now, I need things to stay just as they are." Tomes stepped into the room. "Piiric. He was more than just immortal. He was a sorcerer."

Memories of Piiric's life kept building, sometimes flooding him at the most inopportune moments.

Tomes cut his eyes at Jordon. "That's what you didn't tell me before. What Vynce started to tell me."

"Yes," Jordon confessed. "You were absorbing so much already, and I knew Piiric would reveal that power when the time was right."

Tomes browsed the room. "Piiric didn't always live here, in Morpar."

"No. Piiric was from Kordes." Jordon followed behind the regent. "My territory."

"When Piiric's family was slain over six hundred years ago, he spent his youth in a monastery. Although claimed by the King of Kordes as his own son, it was rumored that he was actually fathered by a demon from the plane of supreme beings—Zarmeva. A Delghorlin known as Var, bent on ending his life, led an attack on his family's territory, and with the exception of the then infant Piiric, succeeded in eradicating the remainder of royal family. Piiric was saved by a child who'd escaped and delivered him to trusted monks, where the prince was hidden until adulthood, when he resurfaced and took his place here, in Morpar." Regent Fehre told Piiric's story. "As ancient prophecy states, he has been a prince of two kingdoms. The most powerful kingdoms."

"Why didn't he go back to Kordes?" Tomes asked.

"Var destroyed that kingdom and left it in ruin, but it rose again under a new ruler," the regent said. "Piiric's destiny was here, where he was embraced by our hierarchy and soon rose in power to Prince of Morpar."

"He was not king then?"

"No." Fehre ran his hand along a narrow table that was edged with decorative etching. "Morpar had a king at that time, but with his son killed in an attack, there was no heir. Piiric became prince and heir."

Tomes looked at him. "Since you are now ruler, the king was also killed?"

"Yes." The ruler sighed. "I was Grand Chancellor of Morpar at that time, so the responsibility fell to me. The Kingdom of Morpar bears many scars and has suffered great loss...as well as Kordes."

Tomes paused in front of a small, silver mirror and stared at his reflection. "A half-demon, sorcerer prince. What kind of a person would that be? What kind of person have I become?"

"Demons in Zarmeva are supreme beings," Jordon told him, "possessing superior power."

"Dark power?" Tomes needed to know, bothered by the thought of dark forces dwelling within him.

Jordon hesitated. "Yes. But that didn't affect what Piiric was. What you are. And Piiric was royalty—Prince of Kordes." Jordon stood near the door. "Also, Prince of Morpar. Beloved by both kingdoms."

"I guess I'll gradually see more of his memories." Tomes reached for a relic sitting atop a dusty table, a golden stone encasing an eye with a strange red iris. "I know this."

"The Eye of Ephog," Regent Fehre identified the object. "Protected by Piiric. Now by you. He was tempted to destroy it, but as you see, he did not. The

Eye shows the future, and Piiric believed—"

"No one should have that foreknowledge and advantage over others," Tomes finished his sentence. "That knowledge belongs to the fates alone." He replaced the object. "Time will tell our destinies."

Jordon approached and took a closer look at the Eye. "An object containing this magnitude of power can never fall into the wrong hands. As with the Clyth."

The regent agreed. "Which is why it shall remain here, in Piiric's chamber, where no one can enter but him."

9

Tomes stared blankly at the sparse expanse of land simmering before him, dim even in the light of day from the polluted sky. "A pilgrimage of resurrection starts here, in the western division."

Constable Lavor accompanied Tomes and Jordon, turning as a soldier rushed toward them with a report that the Village of Salmari was under siege by Junch over resources, primarily access to the river. "They were peaceful before the comet," Lavor said. "Now neighbor kills neighbor for limited food and water."

"Salmari. Our first stop then," Tomes told Lavor.

"We will see to it," Lavor sent the soldier away.

Journeying by air, Tomes visually absorbed the lay of the disaster-stricken land, the world bringing to mind earlier times on Earth. No modern conveniences. Dirt roads. Thatched roofs.

Touching ground in Salmari, they arrived in the midst of a skirmish.

"Cease fighting!" Tomes cried out, his voice

resonating like thunder.

"Lower your weapons," Lavor seconded the command.

With outstretched arms, palms out, Tomes rotated clockwise, scanning the people who'd halted their actions and lowered their weapons consisting of bows, knives, axes, spears, and various farming tools. "Killing each other accomplishes nothing. Who is in charge here?"

Two men stepped forward, both battered and bloody.

"Sire," one of the men addressed Lavor. "We fight to survive."

"This is not the way," Tomes told him. "Our fight is to save lives. Save this world."

The other man observed their manner of dress. "You are not from this world."

Tomes glanced at Jordon who stood to his left, equipped with a sword, but dressed in jeans and his trademark cowboy boots, out of place apparel for the world's common class era of simple woolen tunics and leather ankle boots with front laces.

Jordon leaned toward him. "With so much happening, I forgot about our clothes."

"You stand before the dir cyohr." Lavor's cape draped behind him as he gripped the handle of a short-bladed sword hanging at his left side. "We've come to help."

With that introduction, murmurs swept through the crowd.

"You have finally come." One man threw down his weapon and dropped onto one knee. "Our savior."

The remainder of the men followed his lead and did the same.

Tomes felt Piiric guiding him, looking down as one man reached out and touched his foot. "The fighting must stop." He motioned for them to rise. "In order to survive, you have to join together."

He observed women and children emerging from hiding. Weary, frightened individuals.

"Temperatures plummet at night, food is scarce, and now the river has run dry in many areas." A man pointed toward a waterway. "This oxbow basin is a prime example."

Tomes, surrounded by the multitude, walked to the steep bank, bent, and pressed his palms against the ground. Uttering a passage in a foreign tongue, the ground rumbled, and water bubbled up from the muddy depths.

The people, in awe of the miracle, cheered and swarmed the river.

"I cannot believe I just raised water from the earth." Tomes stood beside Jordon, watching the event. "It's just sinking in...what I've become."

"You possess phenomenal power now, Tomes," Jordon told him. "But you cannot correct every problem."

Tomes nodded, knowing he had limitations. "I gave them water, but I can't conjure food...create life." He turned and scanned the village. "I don't understand why those of you who travel between worlds haven't brought back technology?"

"It's against the law. Code dictates that worlds must evolve at a natural pace," Jordon explained. "Advancement will come when it's meant to come." He gestured toward Lavor who had climbed onto a boulder. "I believe the constable has something to say."

"Remember what you have seen today and spread the word," Lavor called out to the people. "The dir cyohr is with us, and his name is Tomes."

* * * *

Corin had been awake for hours, waiting for the unforgiving day to end, anxious for nightfall, when they'd cross over to the Eleventh Dimension.

"Another world." He sat down, hoping Angelique was prepared, having told her all he knew about the Passage.

His thoughts then rewound to six months earlier, recalling the night Jordon had first told him about the Passage of Dimensions. He'd been sitting on the lanai at von Vadim Estate when Jordon joined him, delving into a conversation he would never forget.

Leaning back, the scene played in his mind.

"There's an ancient passage called the Passage of Dimensions. It's been used since sorcerers ruled the divisions."

"Sorcerers? That must have been something."

"Sadly, today, only one sorcerer remains."

"You travel through this passage?"

Jordon nodded. "The Eleventh Dimension has ten portals that lead to ten other dimensions, with each of those other worlds connected to us by a single portal," he divulged. "We use those portals."

"So, each of the other worlds has just one portal that leads back to the Eleventh Dimension?"

"That's right. The Eleventh Dimension is the main world that all the others are tied to."

"Eleven dimensions. That says it all. Why your world is called the Eleventh Dimension." Not knowing Jordon, and being told of the existence of other worlds, Corin couldn't help being skeptical. "Amazing to think about. Multiple dimensions. And having the ability to travel between them."

"Not anymore. The portals in the other ten dimensions have been blocked since the time of our ancient sorcerers and kept under the watch of

supreme guardians."

"Why are they blocked?"

"In the beginning of our world, a supreme being, old as time, resided in the Eleventh Dimension. He favored the sorcerers, granting them discs that allowed them to travel through the portals to the other ten dimensions. It is believed that this supreme was actually the creator of the portals, and possibly the other dimensions as well," Jordon expanded the story.

Corin wasn't sure he believed any of the daywalker's tale, but being a broad-minded individual, he kept listening.

"He gave the sorcerers knowledge of great things," Jordon continued, "but as they evolved, they became vain and unruly, placing themselves above all other beings, with the belief that they should rule over the other dimensions. Even daring to challenge him. So, in his wrath, the supreme destroyed all discs he had created and left the Eleventh Dimension to reside in one of the alternate dimensions known as Zarmeva—the Plane of Supreme Beings."

"That is some story."

"Not just a story. Our history."

"But if he destroyed all of the discs, how do you travel now? How did you come here, to Earth?" Corin held an inquisitive stare. "You also said that the portals were blocked."

"The portals are only blocked entering the other ten worlds," Jordon explained.

"But without the discs...."

"The sorcerers put all of their effort into recreating them and eventually succeeded. But when the supreme discovered their achievement, that's when he blocked the portals in the other dimensions and ensured their security by assigning supreme guardians, preventing anyone from entering the worlds. But the sorcerers *didn't stop there and kept advancing the power of the discs, inadvertently developing a way of tapping into the wormholes to create new pathways capable of reaching other universes. Other worlds."*

"Wormholes?"

"Yes, the portals are wormholes, but the Passage is partly engineered, controlled through a melding of science and magic. Discovering inhabitable worlds, the sorcerers were able to save the coordinates, enabling them to return by means of something they called a shalym disc, a sort of calling card. What we use now. The discs activate the passage for leaving and returning. They are our only means of getting back, so we guard them with our lives. Only those authorized to cross worlds are issued a disc. It is a great honor to be entrusted with one."

Roused from the memory, Corin stood up, knowing night had finally fallen, and he and Angelique joined Galvar and Vynce in the living room where Pierson and Patricia had just transformed to bestial form.

"Thank you for finding someone to see to these repairs." Corin motioned toward the damaged walls. "And to look after the farm." He stepped in front of Pierson and showed him an envelope before placing it on a side table. "This is a list of instructions Angelique jotted down, along with a nice incentive to give the man you hired. Let him know that is only half, and he'll get the rest when we get back."

"Can we trust this guy?" Angelique worried.

"Pierson told him we had a family emergency and had to leave town in a hurry. Besides, when he sees the money—and I was generous—I don't think there will be any questions."

"Are you ready?" Galvar was eager to go.

"Ready as we'll ever be." Angelique held tight to Dusk.

"Dusk and Dawn will be fine," Corin assured her while adjusting his Stetson. "They have food and water to last several days, and access outside." His front-button shirt fell loosely over dark, snug-fit pants. He turned back toward Pierson who stood several feet from him. "Keep out of sight."

Galvar seconded that instruction. "We'll make arrangements and come back for you as soon as possible."

Pierson bent his head in acknowledgment.

Angelique put Dusk down and cuddled Dawn, reluctant to leave them. "I can't help worrying." Bending between them, she communicated a message. "If anything should happen and none of us return, go to the woods."

Dusk responded with chatter.

"It seems they understand you," Vynce said. "A rare gift." He moved toward Galvar who placed a shalym disc in his palm and opened a passage. "It is time to go."

"We'll see you soon," Corin told Pierson and stepped toward the wormhole. "This is it." He gripped Angelique's hand.

With Galvar leading the way, he, Vynce, and Angelique followed through the portal and entered the Eleventh Dimension. Emerging, they stood in a state of shock and gaped on the ravaged land.

"I can hardly believe this is Morpar." Vynce looked upward. "Meteorites."

Corin pulled his gaze from a massive crater to the dark heights above him. "The sky is filled with smoke. Dust...diffusing the light.

"With three moons, the Eleventh Dimension has never been so dark." Galvar was disillusioned. "Hiquire, our largest moon, is the glow you see."

"Three moons." Angelique was amazed.

"I hope the palace escaped a direct hit." Vynce feared the worst.

"This is all prophecy," Galvar said. "In those days, fire will fall from the heavens, and the land will tremble and burn. Mountains will divide and fall into the earth, bringing woe unto all inhabitants."

"Where will we find Tomes?" Angelique asked.

"He and Jordon would have headed for the palace," Galvar told her. "Let's go." He took the form of a hawk and leapt into flight, with Corin, Angelique, and Vynce following. Landing at the palace, he needed no introduction, taken straightaway to Regent Fehre. "Forgive me for crossing others over without permission from Council. With circumstances what—"

"Commander Mikhail, I have been expecting you," the regent interrupted. "All of you."

Corin felt uneasy, subjected to an intense visual scan.

"In this time of prophecy, apostles of the dir cyohr will cross worlds," Fehre cited.

Galvar related all that had occurred leading up to that point.

"Tomes? He arrived safely?" Angelique sought confirmation.

"Yes. He and Jordon left this morning on what the dir cyohr called a Pilgrimage of Resurrection," Regent Fehre apprised them. "They headed southeast. Master Constable Lavor is accompanying them."

"We need to get to him before a Delghorlin named Andras does." Vynce explained the urgency to the regent.

"They're hours ahead." Corin knew it wouldn't be easy catching up with them.

"Yes, but they will be making a lot of stops." Vynce pointed out. "Still, we should not delay."

Galvar grabbed ahold of a pillar to steady his

balance.

"You are not fully recovered." Vynce maneuvered to his side. "You cannot make this quest."

Corin adjusted his Stetson and pulled Angelique in front of him. "I want you to stay here, with Galvar. There's no telling what we'll encounter out there."

"I know you worry, but I can handle myself," she said.

Corin guided her outside the door. "You see the state of this world. And Andras, he's an ancient. I don't want you caught in the crossfire. Let me go with peace of mind knowing you're safe."

Angelique wrapped her arms around his neck. "You know I would do anything for you, but this is Tomes."

"I know what he means to you...to both of us. But I can't lose you. Please, Angelique, do this for me." He reached for her hands and transferred their interlocked clasp to his chest. "Just this once."

Angelique released his hands, stretched up, and tipped his hat back. "For you." She pressed her lips against his. "Find him. Then come back to me."

"Nothing can separate us." Corin embraced her. "Neither life, nor death."

Rejoining the others, Angelique was approached by Galvar.

"We share the same worries," he told her. "My mind is a barrage of foreboding fears, imagining the worst of obstacles and dangers. But I have faith in Vynce's abilities, having entrusted my life to him on more than one occasion. There is no better partner to be had."

"Look after her, Galvar." Corin caught the commander's stare. "I'm counting on you."

Galvar nodded. "We will be safe in the palace."

"We had better get moving." Vynce urged and moved toward the door.

"Wait." Regent Fehre halted them, calling for an

assistant to retrieve some weapons. "You will need these." He offered two swords.

Corin chose one and secured it at his waist.

"Be careful." Angelique stood between the regent and Galvar. "I love you," she added through thought.

Heading out the door, Corin looked back at her. "Always, my love," he communicated telepathically, then departed.

* * * *

Vynce and Corin trailed Tomes and Jordon southeast, across the western division, finding stories circulating like wildfire throughout remaining villages, telling of the dir cyohr's pilgrimage and miracles he'd performed.

Half the night was spent before they finally caught up with them resting near Jordon's home territory of Kordes.

"You had us a little worried, especially Angelique." Corin looked into Tomes's face, swept by a wave of relief.

"Master Constable Lavor," Jordon greeted the head of the Indithian Army and proceeded to inform him of their perils. "With Andras Metellus pursuing, Tomes will need more protection. We should return to the palace."

"No," Tomes refused. "I have to keep going. This is my purpose."

Corin couldn't believe the change in Tomes. "A miracle worker. Savior of an entire world. You've come a long way in six months."

"I think I've succeeded at surprising everyone." Tomes laughed. "Leave it to me to outdo the whole kit and caboodle."

Corin slapped his shoulder. "It's good to know you're still in there." He pulled Tomes aside. "Pierson found someone to look after the farm until we return. I thought knowing that might ease your mind."

"It does. Thanks for taking care of that." Tomes looked at Corin's hat. "Couldn't travel without the Stetson, huh? Some sort of *Indiana Jones* obsession?"

Corin removed his hat and bushed it off. "It's lucky."

"I'm not sure it's working for you, with all of the trouble we've had lately."

"But we always manage to come out on top," Corin reminded him.

"Is Angel okay?"

"She's at the palace with Galvar."

"And Kara?"

Vynce, Jordon, and Lavor stood close enough to overhear.

"He should know." Vynce stepped toward them.

"What? Is something wrong with Angel?" Tomes looked to Corin for an answer.

"No, not Angelique. It's Kara. She was abducted during the attack at the estate." Corin recognized Tomes's anger, the same anger and helplessness he'd felt when Boldor had held Angelique hostage six months earlier. "Andras will most likely use her as leverage against you."

"He has a vision—the rise of the Delghorlins. In this time of apocalypse, even without the Clyth he would stand a good chance of seizing power, if not for the dir cyohr. As much as you may love Kara, one life is nothing compared to divisions." Vynce averted his eyes. "Sometimes hard choices have to be made."

"A choice no man should be forced to make," Corin said. "You know what I would do, Tomes, and have done for Angelique, but your circumstance is much more complex. You carry the weight of a world. You are no longer just you, but the dir cyohr."

Tomes had been assigned a very heavy lot, a destiny

Corin would never wish to shoulder.

****

Jax leaned against a tombstone, tuned in on Meical's interaction with Andras, whose party had just arrived in Hixton. Guarding Kara a short distance away, Jax's position was close enough to overhear their conversation.

"I heard you were overpowered by two beasts?" Andras waited for an explanation. "Black magic...."

"I didn't think they'd be so powerful," Meical fessed up.

Jax couldn't hold back a laugh, finding Meical's reprimand amusing.

"Please Jax. Let me go." Kara's gleaming blue gaze bore through him.

"I can't do that." Jax walked toward her, casting a cold glare. "Why him?"

"It just happened." Kara wriggled her hands to reposition the rope cutting into her wrists. "I can't tell you why."

"I thought we were good together. I gave up freedom for you."

"I'm sorry if I hurt you, Jax. But some things just aren't meant to be."

"But they are with him?" Jax barked with contempt. "He'll soon be dead. Andras will see to that."

Needing distance from Kara, Jax enlisted another immortal to take over his watch and stormed away. Agitated, he laid low in the backdrop of the clan until he calmed down, then slipped up behind Jozsef who stood at the outermost edge of the congregation, listening to Meical's report.

"The dir cyohr has taken the Body to the Eleventh Dimension." Meical reached the end of his recount.

Jax suddenly straightened as a wormhole appeared near the group, igniting the immortals into defensive mode.

"Xylor." Andras acknowledged the man who emerged, and the clan eased.

"The dir cyohr is in the Eleventh Dimension. He's already making an impact on the western division, restoring hope through miracles and a promise of resurrection. If you plan on stopping him, you'd best act soon," Xylor advised.

Andras expelled a devilish growl. "I cannot allow this chance to escape me." He held his composure. "Go back to your post under Master Constable Lavor and keep me informed."

Xylor cleared out and Andras ordered that the group prepare to depart.

Jax glanced at Kara with one thought. *The dir cyohr, Tomes, must die.*

It was all a matter of pride.

* * * *

In the witching hour, Angelique strolled the sleepy palace corridors with Galvar.

"I've noticed people here speak formal," she said. "No contractions."

"Just like on Earth, language dialects vary depending on location. The real difference between here and Earth is that the three main species, regardless of region, all speak the same language."

"Just one language? For the whole world?"

"There are ancient languages rarely used anymore, and a few other species with their own languages, but primarily, yes. I am always amazed how worlds are connected by common threads."

"It is mind-boggling, learning that there are other

worlds."

"We are not alone."

"You mentioned dialect changes depending on location. I guess that explains Jordon."

"With Jordon, it comes from Earth. For those of us that have been living there for many years, your manners and styles have been adopted."

"But you've been on Earth a long time, yourself, haven't you?"

"I am vigil in my duties to the Order, so I have not ventured out much among the people, usually only leaving the compound when there is business to attend to. However, with the manner of speech changing around me, within the Order, I have been somewhat affected, having caught myself slipping on occasion."

"You make it sound like a bad thing." Angelique laughed. "What about Vynce? He talks like you. He hasn't been out in the world?"

"Some. But he spends most of his time with me, at the Order, unlike Jordon, who lives and works among Earthlings."

"Being a marshal and chasing fugitives."

"Yes. He has to fit in."

Entering a small hall, Angelique paused to admire a grand seal on the wall. "This place is so regal. Very old I suspect."

"It has a long history."

"Indith immortals reside here. Daywalkers. So, being nightwalker, where are you from?" Angelique was curious.

"Some humans and Krivros live here as well."

"Krivros?"

"My line. The most prominent line of nightwalkers in the Eleventh Dimension. But there are others, all somewhat different."

"You're not like the Delghorlins...Andras."

"No. The Krivros are much more humane and sympathetic toward other species and races, traits the Delghorlins deem as weaknesses."

"You have heart." Angelique smiled. "Knowing that I carry Andras's blood, I hope I never lose my humanity."

"As Corin has proven, your bloodline does not have to define who you are."

"Yes. He is nothing like Andras. That's for sure." Angelique looked at Galvar and smiled. "Thank you for the reassurance."

Galvar returned her smile with a nod, his expression suddenly reversing when a tremor rocked the foundation on the palace.

Angelique lost her balance. "What's happening? Did a meteorite hit the palace?"

"I think it is an earthquake. One of significant magnitude."

Cries rang out from distant chambers as Galvar steered her to a doorway, dodging stone raining from the ceiling.

Angelique grasped his hand. "The humans won't survive this."

Galvar observed an expanding fissure snaking along the ceiling, spanning the full length of the passageway. "Topside is caving." He pulled her into a room just as the ceiling collapsed and shielded her from the impact.

Several more seconds of intense seismic activity followed before finally dying down.

"I think the worst is over." Galvar let her go. "Are you alright?"

"I'm fine." Angelique brushed dust from her clothes. "I can't see very well."

"We have night vision, but we cannot see in total darkness." Galvar ran his hands along the wall. "The doorway is blocked, but there is a small amount of light seeping through the cracks. Fire. A torch is still burning in the corridor. We are lucky this wall held."

"We're trapped. We'll have to transform to get out of here."

"We cannot transform inside the palace, a safeguard put into place long ago to prevent saboteurs from entering unseen."

"What do we do?"

"We tunnel." Galvar pushed through the rubble and started maneuvering along what remained of the corridor, taking possession of the torch burning in an iron sconce near the doorway, oddly unaffected by the disaster. "Buried underground, we will need this." He passed the torch to Angelique.

Making good headway, Angelique suddenly halted Galvar. "Someone is close. Ahead of us."

Galvar resumed tunneling while calling out to any survivors, pausing when he caught a young man's voice responding to his call.

"Here. We are here."

Galvar pinpointed their location.

"It is Sergeant Bren Lavor," the man identified himself. "My mother and I are trapped."

"Staca?" Galvar knew the constable's wife. "It is Commander Mikhail. Galvar."

"Galvar, yes, it is Staca," she responded. "I am glad you found us."

"What is your situation on that side?" Galvar searched for an opening.

"It is dark. From the sounds, I am sure the supports will soon give way. This portion of the room will not hold much longer." Bren guided them to a position that forced Galvar and Angelique to backtrack several feet. "Taking into account the sounds indicating areas of stress, I started digging here, where I felt was safest."

Galvar pinpointed the best course of entry. "Keep digging; we will work from this side," he instructed and tore into the barrier of debris that contained massive sections of stone.

"You're overdoing it," Angelique said when he leaned back with a groan.

"I just need to regain my strength."

"Let me take over for a while." She took his place and continued burrowing through the wreckage, meeting up with Bren several minutes later.

With a clear tunnel, Angelique backed out, and Bren and his mother followed.

"Are either of you hurt?" Galvar examined Staca, who brushed her fingers over a shoulder wound.

"Nothing that will not heal." Staca's chestnut-brown gaze rose, her youthful face framed by strawberry strands, looking only slightly older than her son. "An earthquake?"

Galvar nodded. "A fierce one."

"I had a dream two nights past of large stones raining from the highest reaches of the palace," Staca said. "Do you think the whole palace is in this same condition?"

"I would not be surprised." Galvar felt a lingering tremor in the earth, building to a rumble. "It is not over yet. Brace yourselves."

The four huddled as an aftershock displaced more stone, collapsing the tunnel they had just cleared in order to free Bren and Staca.

"That was a close call." Bren combed a hand up and over the top of his head. "We are lucky you came along when you did. It sounds like the whole room caved in."

"This tremor was much less intense than the initial quake." Galvar was glad their area of the tunnel had held. "I believe the worst is behind us."

Angelique scooted next to Staca in the crowded space. "Bren is your son?"

Staca nodded.

"I didn't think immortals could have children." Angelique was thrown by the revelation.

"I'm daywalker, not nightwalker." Staca's expression revealed her inquiring thoughts before she spoke them. "You're not from here."

"She is from Earth," Galvar informed her. "Angelique is the dir cyohr's sister."

"The dir cyohr's sister." Staca looked into Angelique's face. "It is an honor. I only wish you were seeing our world under different circumstances."

"It is an honor," Bren reiterated.

"About Bren, he is my one and only child. Female daywalkers can bear a child the same as humans, but we only conceive once," Staca explained.

"Just once?"

"Since we are immortal and could quickly overpopulate a world, it is nature's way of keeping things in proper balance," Staca clarified. "There are also very few female daywalkers, compared to the number of men."

"Very few and far between." Bren placed emphasis on that fact.

"What about relations with mortals?" Angelique asked. "Is that possible?"

"It is against the law." Galvar focused on tunneling head. "For the very reason of overpopulating the world. But that does not mean the law has never been broken."

"Daywalkers are so much more connected with humans than nightwalkers," Angelique said. "Even moreso than those of us who were once human ourselves."

"Yes." Galvar pushed aside a heavy joist. "They are the blessed immortals."

"We are born mortal, but eventually become full immortals with powers and gifts matching nightwalkers," Staca related, "only without requiring blood to survive or being bound by the sun."

"Like I said," Galvar talked while working, "the blessed ones."

"It is amazing, the differences between you." Angelique was fully absorbed.

"Even in our deaths," Staca told her. "When daywalkers fall to their death, energy within us is released in what we call a dispersal, because it dissipates back into the atmosphere, becoming part of every living thing around us."

"That is beautiful." Angelique moved toward Galvar. "Certainly a nicer ending than just disintegrating to dust." She looked at Staca. "I assume you have a soul."

"Yes. Being born as humans are born, we have a soul. But there is a difference between our energy and our soul," Staca said. "One is our source of power, and the other is our spirit. So, during dispersal, while our energy is dispersed, at the same instant, our soul is crossed into another plane of existence," she explained.

"There must be others trapped." Bren guided the conversation back to their crisis at hand.

"Officials who know about the underground tunnels will no doubt aim for that escape." Galvar broke through another section.

"Tunnels?" Angelique cut her eyes at him. "How do we get to them?"

"There are three accesses. The closest one is in the council room," Galvar motioned, "the direction we are headed."

Bren continued plowing through the rubble. "It may take some time."

"Listen." Angelique halted their work. "Do you hear that? Others are digging."

"Go toward the council room," Galvar called out to the other survivors, catching a faint response—a desperate plea for help.

"They're trapped," Angelique said. "We have to help them."

Galvar altered their course and navigated toward an impassable hall that branched to their right.

"We will not get far through this." Bren heaved a large beam from their path.

A man's voice called out, "The hall is blocked."

"They are close." Galvar sought a detour around a mountain of debris sealing their path. "This is not going to be easy."

"Let me see what I can do." Bren managed to advance an estimated twenty feet more before reaching an impenetrable blockade of stone. "We have gone as far as we can. We are not getting past this."

"Can you hear us?" Galvar called out to the survivors.

Several people responded.

"They are just a few feet ahead. There has to be a way around this blockade. Or over it," Galvar said, spotting a gap in the rock above them. "There," he pointed. "An opening. That may be our means of reaching them."

Bren leapt into action, crawling over the wreckage like a spider up a wall, and disappeared into the breach.

Galvar, feeling a sudden rumble beneath him, spun and faced Angelique and Staca. "It is another aftershock."

"Bren!" Staca's frantic call rent the air, and she started for the gap in a desperate attempt to reach her son, but Galvar intercepted her endeavor and pulled her against the wall.

Stone and rubble dislodged and fell from the ceiling, the displacements filling the passage with thick, drifting dust. But the aftershock was short-lived, and in seconds, all was calm.

"Bren." Staca rushed for the breach, receiving his response as she entered the crevice.

Angelique released a heavy breath, relieved he was safe. She then heard the other survivors crying out for help.

"Bren, can you reach them?" Galvar called to him.

"I am nearly there," he answered.

"It is stable," Staca called down to Galvar and Angelique.

"Good. We are coming up." Galvar aimed for the gap.

Reaching Bren and Staca, they descended the opposite side of the blockade, finding three human survivors desperate to escape their entrapment.

"You work to escape one confinement, only to enter another." Bren jumped several feet to the floor.

Galvar, Staca, and Angelique entered the space behind him, with Angelique taking precaution with the torch.

"At least you have light." Galvar surveyed the survivors—a man and two women.

Angelique scanned the condition of the hall that appeared clear a good 10 meters, observing two burning torches secured in sconces on the wall. Her gaze then fell on a partially exposed corpse crushed beneath a slab of stone, reminding her just how fragile human life was.

"You are lucky we heard your call." Galvar stepped toward the man. "How does it look in the other direction?"

"No better." The man sighed. "There is no easy exit."

"Come with us." Galvar motioned for the people to follow. "There are tunnels beneath the palace. We were headed for them when we heard your call." He retrieved both torches burning in the hall and put one out before passing them to the man. "Immortals can manage in the dark depths of the tunnels with our heightened senses, but humans would be lost without light, so gather all of the torches and lamps you come across."

"We will help you," Staca assured the people and assisted the women into the gap and over the barrier.

Bren followed last and lowered the women to the ground on the opposite side. "Now, the tunnels."

Continuing toward the council room, they soon came upon the remains of a corridor littered with human corpses.

"This corridor led to the human quarters. It was lined with large statues." Galvar stepped over a shattered face of a fallen stone figure.

"There is light ahead." Staca indicated by pointing an index finger. "There are more survivors."

With growing numbers, Galvar led the group on to the council room, relieved to find the entrance accessible. Entering the space, he approached a long table that occupied the room and reached for a circular stone object embedded in its center—the Circle of the Morpar Kingdom. Surrounded by eleven symbols, the dial clicked as he forced it clockwise, counterclockwise, then clockwise again. Pulling his hand away, the table jolted as the floor beneath it rose and slid westerly, revealing a secret passage hidden beneath the table.

"You want us to go deeper into the earth?" One of the men voiced reluctance. "Can we not keep tunneling?"

"This is our best chance of escape," Galvar told the humans, seeing their apprehension as they gaped into the dark abyss. "The torches. You will want to conserve them. Put that one out." He motioned. "Burn only one at a time."

"Galvar, someone if following," Angelique alerted.

Bren quickly backtracked, spotting Regent Fehre

accompanied by his assistant, Engll, trailing their course.

"Are the tunnels reachable?" The regent moved swiftly.

"We just opened the passage." Bren led the way.

"Commander Mikhail," Fehre acknowledge upon entering the council room. "Have you assessed the situation?"

Galvar stepped aside for the regent. "Not yet. We just opened the passage."

"The access appears intact." Fehre descended a stone staircase leading down into the dark recess, and the group followed.

"Can we change form below the palace?" Angelique stayed close to Staca.

"No." Regent Fehre glanced back. "We cannot change form until we exit the tunnels, and some of them run for miles."

"There sure are a lot of precautions set in place," Angelique said.

"Necessary precautions," Galvar told her. "The capital city has always been a target for enemy attack."

"So, a spell prevents transformation within the tunnels?" she presumed.

"No, the spell only affects the palace and directly beneath it. Once we distance ourselves, the cause preventing us from changing form underground is a mineral called morvormanite," Galvar explained. "It not only prevents transformation, but completely blocks our powers, including any form of mental communication and detecting the presence of others."

"High levels of morvormanite run through this region, continuing a great distance north to the Sih Range, and south to Zarchia," the regent added.

"We should go north," Galvar suggested. "The tunnel is clear and leads to higher ground. The underground lake has likely flooded the south tunnel."

"I agree." Regent Fehre signaled the go ahead.

"How far does this tunnel run?" a man called out.

Galvar turned and addressed the people. "There is a cavern several miles ahead. The tunnel exits there."

Resuming their pace, Angelique ran her hand along the smooth tunnel wall. "The rock, it glitters...changes."

"The green flecks in morvormanite are unique, appearing to shift and change pattern, but what appears to be movement is merely a play on the eye," Galvar educated her as he brushed cobwebs from their path.

Continuing amid intermittent aftershocks that kept the humans in a constant state of unease, they finally reached the cavern one to two hours later, finding it partially collapsed.

"The entire east side of the cavern has caved in," the regent stood dismayed, his broad shoulders slumped, "taking our exit with it."

"If we could reach the staircase, maybe we could break through." Bren examined the situation alongside Galvar.

"No," Fehre told him. "We are too far underground. We will have to find another way out."

"Watch out," Galvar alerted the humans of a falling stalactite, missing one man by inches.

"What do we do now?" Another man asked.

"We search for another exit, and if we do not find one, we turn back," Galvar answered. "That is our only option."

10

Jordon stood on a hillside, staring across a dark field. "The last I saw this field, it was covered in saffron. Kenijor. It's sad that a land so bright and beautiful is remembered by its scourge of war."

He envisioned the great battle in his mind as he bent and touched the ground, absorbing its energy, knowing countless dispersals had occurred there. What part of this valley had his father, Denlor Day Morrain, fallen to his death? His half-brother, Lake? Where had he taken his last breath?

"Damn you, Gaun." Jordon hated what the warlord had done to not only his family, but his world, dividing species and races, annihilating every living thing in his path.

"Earth has had its share of wars," Corin noted, "a few of those events so incomprehensible that people look back today wondering how we ever allowed such heinous acts to happen."

Making an about-face, Tomes cut his eyes at Corin.

"Do you feel that?"

"Angelique." Corin shared the experience.

"I feel fear from my family," Constable Lavor alerted. "Something has happened at the palace."

Jordon's heart rate suddenly accelerated. "The craters. A meteorite?"

"The number of strikes has lessened considerably," Constable Lavor said, "but that is my fear as well."

"We need to move," Corin stressed the urgency. "Now."

"Galvar will look after Angelique," Vynce assured him.

"If they are together." Corin found little comfort in his words. "We have no idea what's happened."

"Corin, you and Vynce will need shelter before sunset," Jordon reminded the nightwalkers. "We may not be able to reach Morpar before morning."

"We can't wait that long." Corin's frustration rode on his words. "Vynce and I will go as far as the night will permit, then, if sunrise catches us, we'll seek shelter while you three continue on."

"You should not abandon your pilgrimage. As you said, this is your purpose." Jordon offered to continue with Tomes despite the increased threat posed by their Delghorlin opposition.

Jordon was sworn to serve and protect Morpar and their leaders, but since the arrival of the dir cyohr, his first loyalty was now to Tomes.

"Angel is my sister," Tomes said. "Besides, something tells me it's time to return to Morpar."

In accordance, the five immortals took flight.

The dir cyohr had only just begun his work, but Jordon trusted the eminence of what the others were experiencing, and the capital city was a crucial landmark in the Eleventh Dimension. He also felt certain that word of the dir cyohr would continue spreading throughout the regions from the miracles Tomes had already performed. The effects of the dir cyohr's power and influence had made a drastic impact in a short time, and soon the world would know of his wonders, that their savior had come.

* * * *

"At least there is water." Angelique watched the mortals huddle around a small pool of crystal-clear water.

She observed a stream veining along a narrow crevice that filled the basin with a continual supply of water.

"It is beautiful down here." She glanced up at stalactites glistening several feet above her, hanging from the roof of the cavern. "I've been in a cavern like this one before, on Earth, but I don't remember feeling so at ease."

"You are a nightwalker now and comfortable in the earth," Galvar told her. "If not for the aftershocks, it would be very peaceful."

"I, personally, would rather be above ground." Staca overheard.

"You are not alone," Regent Fehre concurred. "Daywalkers are not meant to be underground."

"When was anyone from the palace last down here?" Galvar veered toward the regent and his assistant, Engll, a quiet, reserved daywalker who never said much.

"I am not certain." Fehre paused. "But there has been no need for the escape in many years."

"I have found something," Bren alerted. "A hidden passage. Behind here." He motioned toward a line of stalactites that reached from roof to floor in the farthest depths of the cave.

"This is not one of our tunnels." Regent Fehre

moved in for closer inspection. "It appears to continue north."

"I say we follow it," Galvar proposed. "It leads somewhere, and I am betting an outlet."

With everyone in agreement, they continued along the passage for miles...hours.

"The people are slowing down." Angelique leaned close to Galvar, speaking in a hushed voice. "Do you think they're getting enough oxygen?"

"I had the same concern. The levels are probably low, but for them to have made it this long, a sufficient amount must be reaching them through the tunnel, possibly seeping through cracks in the rock that extend to the surface."

"They're tired." Angelique reached for his arm. "We should stop and let them rest for a few minutes."

Galvar patted her hand. He then turned and halted the group. "We will take a short break. Rest. We do not know how much further we have to go."

"It must be nearly morning." Angelique slumped against the wall, her breathing heavier than usual. "We have been down here for hours. Maybe we should have turned back."

Regent Fehre shook his head. "It was no easy feat digging this tunnel. There was a purpose for it. I am sure it will lead to an exit."

"This is difficult for the humans, but we have been fortunate in finding water," Bren said. "I hope our luck holds out."

Galvar nodded. "For their sake, it is imperative we find an exit, and soon."

"I have another concern." Angelique stared at the people resting amid the shadowy tunnel, entranced by play of light dancing along the walls from the flame of a single torch. "Don't forget I'm a newborn," she reminded Galvar, fighting increasing pangs of hunger.

"I haven't mastered my restraint. If I don't feed soon, I'm afraid of what I might do."

Galvar reached for her hands. "Look at me." He pulled her gaze from the humans. "I understand your hunger, but you are strong. Do not allow the monster to rise."

"Can that happen down here? With the morvormanite?"

"The monster is part of you; it's something that is always with you. It is not a power."

"So, it can rise," she understood. "I wish I could sense Corin." Her eyes showed her desperation. "I don't feel him with me."

"The morvormanite is blocking your connection." Galvar interlocked his right arm with her left. "Stay by my side. I will see you through this."

Angelique gripped his arm. "I can't lose control. I won't."

Galvar leaned toward Regent Fehre. "We need to keep moving."

"I heard." Fehre motioned to the people who talked amongst themselves several feet behind him. "We must keep moving."

Pressing onward, the tunnel gradually grew wider, with an increase in gaps and cavities lining the walls. Feeling more drained as another hour passed, Angelique had no doubt that night had transitioned to day.

"Something is not right." The regent stopped. "We have reached a dead end."

Galvar pressed a hand against the cold, solid wall facing them. "This makes no sense. There has to be a way out. Why would a tunnel lead to a dead end?"

Angelique whirled as several immortals suddenly appeared in the tunnel behind them. She stumbled back as Regent Fehre, Galvar, Engll, and Bren quickly placed themselves between the assailants and the mortals. "Where did they come from?"

Staca ushered the people against the wall marking the end of the tunnel. "The walls," she looked at her. "They came right out of the walls."

Angelique, fighting intense pangs of hunger, moved as far as she could away from the people. Being so close to warm, blood-filled bodies was torment, and she wasn't sure how much longer she could maintain control.

"Who are you?" One of the assailants stepped forward, gripping a sword, a portion of his face revealed in the dim light of the tunnel.

"We are from the palace." Fehre's gray eyes scoped the strangers. "I am Sir Aros Fehre, Regent of Morpar."

The stranger released his sword and moved toward the ruler. "Yes. I see that now. Forgive me, Regent Fehre. What has brought you into our underground?"

"An earthquake struck the palace forcing us into the tunnels. We followed the northern tunnel but found our exit destroyed. Then, discovering this tunnel, we hoped it would lead to another exit," Fehre explained. "We have humans with us. They have been through a great ordeal."

The immortal motioned to his comrades to lower their weapons. "We have felt the tremors." A slender hand extended a welcome. "I am Torq." His focus settled on Angelique. "That one does not look well. Her eyes...the red."

"She needs to feed." Galvar hurried to her aid. "Hold on," he whispered.

"We can help. Come with us." Torq backtracked a good ten yards to a path hidden along the tunnel wall by an optical illusion.

"Concealed between two overlapping walls." Bren examined the opening. "With attention drawn to the visible gaps in this area of the tunnel, this passage is virtually undetectable."

Angelique clung to Galvar, fighting her emerging monster as they followed the strangers through the gap and along a narrow, zigzagging course that merged into a broader tunnel. Continuing for what felt to be a good quarter mile, they soon reached the tunnel's exit and emerged into a large cavern. The space was meagerly illuminated by torches, oil lamps, and candles supported on various wall mountings.

"Donian, bring some Traxl-1. Quickly." Torq called out.

A moment later, Angelique observed a dark-haired immortal's fast approach, watching as he delivered a brown cloth bag to Torq.

"This will do it." Torq opened the bag that was closed with a drawstring. "Get one of these in her." He gave Galvar a mottled blue pill.

"Here. Take this." Galvar made sure Angelique swallowed the pill. "You will feel much better in a few minutes." He looked at the bag. "Can you spare several more of those? I will need one soon."

"Take what you need." Torq handed him the bag. Then, considering the needs of the mortals, he sent for food and water.

Within minutes, Angelique regained control and thanked Torq. "I'm feeling human again, thanks to you. But I don't understand how that pill satisfied my hunger."

Standing near a lamp, Torq's short, white hair held a lambent glow. "Traxl-1 is the greatest discovery of our time, created by a nightwalker—Mirillow Traxl. This substitution for bloodfeeding makes a nightwalker's existence much simpler. Unfortunately, disasters have halted supply, which I am sure you are aware of, Regent."

"Yes." Regent Fehre visually scoured the cavern and the people occupying the space. "What is this operation?"

"A fellowship of tomorrow. We are a mixture of all species from various regions, brought together by a common goal. We await our savior—the dir cyohr. Being supporters of the prophecy, when he appears in these latter days, we will rise from obscurity to witness the advent of a new world order."

"I have heard of your organization...many human followers." The regent leaned against a naturally formed column of rock. "This territory makes a perfect hideout. A subterranean camp concealed by morvormanite, where those opposing the prophecy cannot detect you."

Angelique observed figures coming and going from other vicinities of branching caverns. She watched as they vanished into dark recesses amid rock and stalactites. "The dir cyohr is here." She turned her focus to Torq. "My brother, Tomes. He is the dir cyohr. I've come from Earth to find him."

Torq looked to Regent Fehre for affirmation.

"It is true. He is here and has proven himself the chosen one," Regent Fehre confirmed. "Piiric walks with her brother."

"The dir cyohr." Torq was riveted by the news. "I will send Donian and another scout out immediately to confirm what you have declared. No disrespect, Regent Fehre, but the supporters will require verification from within."

"I would desire the same." Fehre took no offense.

"I will see if Neil is available." Donian darted away.

"The cavern, I see it interconnects with other caverns," Angelique said. "It's a maze down here."

"We appreciate the formation and have taken full advantage of the location, reaching deeper caverns through a network of tunnels. Immortals occupy those inner alcoves while the humans reside in this main cavern, using cubicles divided by use of any material at our disposal: cloth, wood, stone, furs...." Torq pointed out several items. "It is not as private as one might like, but it is important we keep things transitory should we suddenly be forced to evacuate."

"How long have you been down here?" Regent Fehre asked.

"About a year," Torq told him. "We took heed of the latter-day signs and reserved necessary resources accordingly."

"You have succeeded in creating a well-organized secret society." Galvar was impressed.

"I hope it will remain secret." Torq's stare froze on Regent Fehre. "The Delghorlins would destroy us should they locate our camp. Can we rely on your silence?"

"Yes. You have my word," the regent swore. "Your camp is now in our protection. We fight the same fight, and standing with the dir cyohr, we will prevail."

Torq was relieved. "Yes. We will."

Galvar cut his eyes at Torq. "How do you know about the Delghorlin uprising? We only just discovered Andras Metellus's intent to seize control...that he had created a Delghorlin clan."

"Prophecy tells of opposition," Torq said, "but until Donian, we could only speculate as to the identity of our enemy."

"Donian?" Galvar's brow furrowed.

"Donian was a spy for Andras Metellus," Torq disclosed.

"Was?" Galvar sought clarification.

"Yes. Donian is one of us now," Torq vouched for him. "He has converted to our cause."

Galvar held a fixed stare. "I would be skeptical."

"I fully trust Donian," Torq declared. "Here, with us, he has found a purpose. Something he did not have before."

"Heading out in the day, he is not nightwalker," Galvar stated.

"No," Torq confirmed. "He is Indith. Daywalker."

"Strange that he would be tied to the Delghorlins." Galvar looked at Regent Fehre.

"How did he come to be here?" Fehre asked.

"Guards keeping watch over the base entrance spotted him trailing several humans into camp and captured him." Torq replaced a torch he saw was completely burnt. "After remaining with us for several weeks, he adopted our purpose. Up until the comet, he had continued reporting to another spy at the palace, secretly gathering information for us."

"A double agent," Angelique said.

Torq rejoined them, gripping the burnt-out torch. "Yes. But now, since contact has stopped, they will most likely believe him to be dead."

Bren stepped toward Regent Fehre. "We should get to the palace. We do not know the extent of damage from the earthquake."

Fehre nodded. "Torq, if you will show us to the exit," he stressed urgency.

"Give me a few minutes to brief my scouts, and they will see you out." Torq disappeared into the unseen reaches of the cavern.

"I realize it is imperative to assess the damage in Morpar, but Angelique and I cannot go above till nightfall," Galvar reminded the regent. "We can manage on our own." He straightened as Torq returned with Donian and a second, smaller-framed immortal. "We will meet up with you after sunset."

Angelique surveyed Donian, hoping he could be trusted.

"Donian and Neil will see you to the surface." Torq indicated the direction.

Supporters gawked as the scouts led Regent Fehre, Engll, Bren, and Staca away.

"Allow me to show you around our camp," Torq extended an offer to Angelique and Galvar and led them through the caverns.

"There are children." Angelique was surprised. "Do they ever go above?" She observed their pale complexions.

"Not as often as they would like." Torq returned a wave to a wide-eyed boy. "We have to be cautious."

"I take it that the Delghorlins are aware of your operation," Galvar said, "your support of the dir cyohr."

"Yes. And should they locate our camp, we would not stand much of a chance."

"The kids, at least they have room to play." Angelique smiled at the sight of several children kicking a red ball back-and-forth between them.

Sweet laughter reverberated, a very pleasing sound in an otherwise somber dwelling.

"The arrival of the dir cyohr brings hope that their lives will soon change," Torq said. "We gladly endure all that we have for the prophesied future—the new world order."

Angelique admired his faith.

A new world order. She looked forward to watching her brother's incredible destiny unfold.

* * * *

Tomes gaped on Morpar Palace, floored by the decimation. "Angel. You have to be okay."

Constable Lavor moved into action, taking over command of search and rescue. "We need to move these pillars." He slapped his hand against one of two massive stone columns, that prior to the quake, had marked the stately entrance to the palace. "It will take several men."

Tomes instinctively raised his hands, knowing what to do. "Stand back." Energy emitted from his palms and engulfed one of the columns, and levitating the pillar, he guided it several feet away.

With the exit cleared, immortals trapped within the rubble broke through the remaining debris and crawled out of confinement.

Lavor rushed toward one particular man. "What is the situation inside?"

It was obvious that the man was a friend.

"The Great Hall is accessible," the Indith answered. "There are a lot of human casualties."

"Staca and Bren? The dir cyohr's sister? Have you seen them?" Lavor was desperate for word.

"No, I have not seen them. They must not have been able to reach the Great Hall."

Angel, where are you? You're alive. I know you're alive. Tomes entered the ruins and gaped at the despairing sight.

Jordon stepped next to him. "There's only one way to find them." He chose a direction and started clearing debris.

Working for several hours in full rescue mode, progress was slow, finding the extent of devastation widespread.

Jordon paused. "If only you could use your power to locate them," he told Tomes.

"I've tried. I don't know how to do anything more...what I'm capable of doing. I have no control over when that knowledge will strike me." Tomes wiped dust from his eyes. "Why can't we sense them? I'm getting—"

"Wait," Constable Lavor interrupted him, coming to

a sudden realization. "I should have thought of this before. The tunnels. Tunnels run beneath the palace. We would not be able to sense them because of the morvormanite."

"A mineral in the earth," Jordon enlightened Tomes. "It blocks detection, use of all powers, including transformation."

"Staca knows about the tunnels," Lavor said. "Galvar would know as well."

Tomes felt a wave of hope. "Can we reach them from here?"

Lavor's mouth drew tight on one side. "Not quickly at this pace."

"There is another option." Jordon dusted off his left shoulder. "We can meet them at the exit."

"There is no way of knowing which tunnel they would have taken," Lavor pointed out. "North or south. Morvormanite reaches to mountains in both directions."

Jordon pulled a quarter from his pocket. "Heads, south. Tails, north." He flipped the coin, caught it in his fist, and slapped it down on the top of his free hand. "Heads."

Withdrawing from the ruins, they set a course southward, combing the land from the sky as they traveled. Following Lavor's direction, they found the tunnel's exit point, but to their dismay, the cave was inaccessible.

"It's flooded." Tomes's agitation heightened, but he told himself that Angelique was alive. *I would know if she wasn't. Morvormanite or not.*

"With the earthquake, I should have anticipated this flooding from the underground lake." Lavor slapped his hand against a slab of rock. "I have wasted precious time."

"We'll head back north," Jordon said and started to

change form.

"Wait." Constable Lavor caught his shoulder. "Staca." He expelled a sigh of relief. "I sense her. And Bren."

"I'm getting nothing from Angel." Tomes shut his eyes, attempting to detect her, but without success.

"Staca and Bren will head for the palace." Lavor was anxious to go. "They may have information about your sister and Galvar."

"Corin must be going crazy." Tomes fidgeted, too upset to stand still. "I hope he doesn't try anything rash."

"He'll wait till sunset," Jordon said with confidence. "He knows he's no good to Angelique dead. And he trusts that we'll do all we can to find her."

Tomes nodded. "Let's move."

Taking the form of birds, they leapt into flight and returned to Morpar, met by Staca, Bren, and Regent Fehre at the palace ruins.

"I am glad to see you," Jordon greeted the regent.

"Galvar and my sister, Angelique, a female immortal with long, dark hair. Have you seen them?" Tomes's inquiry broke Staca and Lavor's embrace.

"They are safe," Staca assured him.

"Where are they?" he sought more information.

"Come close." Fehre drew the immortals into a huddle, taking a moment to scan for anyone who might be in hearing distance. "Commander Mikhail and your sister are at Jach Lagon Canyon," he told Tomes, speaking in a hushed voice. "We stumbled upon an underground camp there—supporters of the prophecy." He gave detailed instruction on locating the entrance to the camp—a passage west of Soaring Tower, facing south, between two gorges at the base of the lowest peak. "I promised to keep their location secret, but you, Dir Cyohr, are their purpose, the one they are waiting for."

"I know the way," Jordon told Tomes.

Tomes looked around. "What about the wounded? They need medical treatment."

"Plameth, a human physician who resides here, is tending the humans." Regent Fehre spotted the man and pointed him out.

"The palace is in ruin. What a sad loss," Bren said.

The regent's eyes held sadness. "The history it held. Lost in an instant."

"It will be rebuilt." A fragment of engraved stone caught Tomes's attention, and he bent and scooped it up for closer inspection. "A new birth. The beginning of a new age." He envisioned the future palace in his mind.

"Constable Lavor will oversee recovery," Fehre told Tomes. "Go with Jordon to Jach Lagon Canyon. Find your sister. Meet your supporters."

"The Indithian Army will continue searching for survivors, but I doubt many more humans survived," Lavor said. "It will soon become a recovery effort."

Confident that Regent Fehre and Lavor had matters well in hand, Tomes and Jordon departed, flying nearly forty-five minutes before reaching Jach Lagon Canyon. Transforming on a rocky slope near the eastern gorge marking their destination, they scanned the scene.

"Sih Range." Jordon peered up at the hazy mountains.

"This canyon reminds me of Earth's Grand Canyon. Phenomenal."

"We'll find the entrance there." Jordon gestured toward a "V" formation where two gorges merged at the base of the mountain looming before them. "We're not alone. Stay alert."

Tomes felt the earth vibrate. "An aftershock."

"We're quite a distance from Morpar, but I suspect

the quake affected the whole region."

The tremor quickly passed.

"You're right about not being alone. Look. We have company." Tomes eyed two large fork-tailed hawks that emerged from surrounding rock.

"Guards."

The immortals landed on a nearby ledge and claimed human form, keeping a safe distance, but close enough to communicate.

"I am Indithian, Sentry Jordon Day Morrain of Kordes," Jordon identified himself. "This," he said and pointed at Tomes, "is the dir cyohr. We were told his sister is taking refuge here, with supporters of the prophecy."

They reclaimed hawk form and swooped toward Jordon and Tomes, touching ground several feet in front of them.

"The dir cyohr?" one of the men said, scanning Tomes up and down. "How did you find our location?"

"Regent Fehre," Jordon answered.

Tomes saw skepticism in their eyes. "You don't trust that I'm who I claim to be—the dir cyohr."

"That will be for Torq to determine," the other man responded. "Follow us."

The guards showed them to the entrance of a passage and into a twisting course that led to a deeper tunnel. Reaching its end, they entered a well-concealed cavern, where they found Angelique and Galvar in the accompaniment of the daywalker in charge.

"Tomes." Angelique threw her arms around him. "I'm so glad to see you."

"This is Torq," Galvar introduced the leader.

"The dir cyohr." Torq approached Tomes, overawed by his presence. "I saw your face in a dream." He dropped onto one knee, and the two guards, trusting Torq, knelt as well.

"The gift of future sight," Jordon said.

"Yes. But foreseen events are not always a hundred percent accurate." Torq rose and motioned for the guards to return to their post. "I have scouts out seeking your whereabouts, and you walk right into our camp."

"Where is Corin?" Angelique stood shoulder-to-shoulder with Tomes, clutching his arm.

"We separated when he and Vynce were forced to seek shelter for the day," Jordon told her. "We'll meet up with them after nightfall."

"He has no idea what's happened to you." Tomes hugged her again. "I hope he waits till sunset."

"As soon as I'm able, I'll go above, so he can sense me," Angelique said.

Jordon looked at Galvar. "You both must need to feed."

"All taken care of." Galvar showcased a Traxl-1. "Traxl-1. Dinner."

"It's amazing, Tomes." Angelique's enthusiasm was apparent. "No bloodfeeding."

Tomes's brow rose. "It satisfies the hunger?"

"Completely," Galvar said. "A real breakthrough."

"Why haven't you shared this knowledge?" Tomes held the Traxl-1 in front of him, getting a close-up look at the mottled pill.

"Law prohibits interference in the natural advancement of other worlds," Torq explained. "We cannot bring technology back from Earth, nor carry our discoveries—such as Traxl-1—to you."

"A world must evolve on its own," Galvar added.

"Earth may never make this discovery." Angelique brushed back a wisp of hair. "There's so much we could do to help each other."

Tomes noticed individuals crowding their vicinity of the cavern, with all eyes locked on him.

"They've vowed their lives to you," Torq told Tomes.

Tomes made a slow 360° turn while holding up three spread out fingers—index, middle, and ring fingers—bending his thumb across his palm and overlapping the tip of his pinky.

The supporters responded to his gesture by lowering onto one knee, each with a fist pressed to their mid-chest.

"Three fingers...what does it mean?" Angelique looked to Galvar for an explanation.

"Trinity of the three main species of our world: daywalkers, nightwalkers, and humans. There are other species, but these three are the core, the foundation from which all else was built, or has evolved."

"They're bowing as if he's king," Angelique said.

Galvar looked at her. "He is more than king. The dir cyohr is our prophesied savior."

Our lives will never be the same, Angelique thought to herself.

Tomes heard her thought. "No. Our lives changed six months ago when Boldor invaded our home," he spoke to her telepathically through their twin connection. "Now, we are both immortal, only I carry an alien deity within me."

"A deity that sets you apart...a cut above the rest of us," she silently communicated.

Tomes faced her and made eye contact.

"I always knew you were meant for great things." She smiled at him. "I just never imagined this."

Tomes felt her pride...and fear. And looking back at the supporters, he grappled with his own anxiety, for he bore a monumental weight...the fate of a dying world.

11

Corin and Vynce emerged from their shelter to a caravan of freaks setting up camp for the night. In the dim, hazy surroundings, several small fires burned in various locations near covered buggies and makeshift tents painted with sideshow artwork.

"Nomads." Vynce nodded toward an approaching individual.

"The name is Semmi," the mutant introduced himself.

Corin was taken aback by the man's appearance—four perfect golden eyes set equally spaced from ear to ear across his wide, pale face—an oddity unlike anything Corin had seen before. "You're a traveling carnival?"

"Till the comet." Semmi told how his sideshow was moving west, hoping to find relief from the disasters.

Corin's gaze wandered past the stranger to a sharp-toothed woman covered from stark head to bare feet with leopard-like spotted skin. Wearing a tunic, the hem of her garment hung midway down her patterned calf.

"Bema." The man noticed Corin gawking. "She was found as an infant, abandoned along a secluded riverbank. She comes from a lost species rarely seen anymore. Others, here, are either mixed breeds, or like me, were simply born a mutant, having no explanation for why they are different."

Corin apologized for staring.

The man waved a hand. "We are used to it. What others may see as abnormalities or deformities, we view as gifts. We appreciate our unique attributes."

"A band of misfits. But it works. I've said those words before. You're not alone in that department." Corin's focus transferred to three men conversing nearby, sensing immortal presence. "You have immortals traveling with you?"

"A few. But those, there, talking with Ander," he indicated with an inconspicuous motion, "they are not with our group. They arrived just before you, inquiring if we had encountered the dir cyohr."

"Have you?" Corin's voice rose with interest.

"Ander was lucky enough to chance upon him while scouting ahead. He has not stopped talking about how he managed to touch the chosen one, experiencing a feeling of ultimate peace."

"Was that today?" Corin's words flew from his lips.

Semmi shook his head. "No. He joined back with us yesterday. Like I told those men, you can get particulars from him."

"That was before Kordes," Vynce told Corin.

"Did you happen to come through Morpar?" Corin asked Semmi.

"What's left of it." Semmi's dark, choppy hair fell around his squared face. "A quake leveled the palace."

"Angelique." Corin's breath caught in his throat.

Vynce pressed a hand on his shoulder. "I know Galvar is looking after her."

"Let's get moving." Corin wouldn't rest till he knew she was safe.

"Wait, I want to have a quick chat with these immortals before we go and find out why they're so interested in the dir cyohr." Vynce strode toward the men with Corin trailing him.

The immortals, observing their approach, took immediate defensive positions.

"You can put your weapons away." Vynce caught sight of a mark the taller daywalker bore on his right forearm, an earlier rendition of Morpar's current marking, before it had been redesigned to exclude a symbol representing sorcerers. "I recognize that mark. You are Indithian. A seal on your chest would probably prove you to be the old militia."

"Yes, the Sol Krigare. A very long time ago."

"Now, simply the Indithian Army," Vynce said. "I am not daywalker, but I am in service of Morpar, as are other nightwalkers."

"There have always been a few. I am Donian, and this is Neil." He nodded toward his consort.

Vynce reciprocated introduction.

"Why are you pursuing the dir cyohr?" Corin sized them up, eyeing Ander as he fled the danger zone, no doubt sensing an ensuing altercation.

"Our only intent is to substantiate his existence. Have you met him in your travels?" Donian asked.

"He's family," Corin stated. "And I am highly protective of family," he warned.

Neil's eyes narrowed. "You are not the first to make that claim."

Corin caught the man's stare. "Only one other person *can* make that claim."

"His sister," Neil said.

"Angelique." Corin's heart sped. "What do you know of her? She is my partner."

Corin fought back his emerging monster as the immortals deliberated. Overhearing their conversation, he was glad they believed him.

"She is in our camp," Neil disclosed.

"Is she safe?" Corin needed answers. "We just learned that there was an earthquake, and I haven't been able to sense her."

"Morvormanite. It blocks detection," Donian said. "Jach Lagon Canyon." He gave up the location. "You will find her there. We would escort you, but as I said, we are tracking the dir cyohr."

"The Sih Range." Vynce knew the place. "It is not far."

"About the dir cyohr, he reversed course, to return to Morpar," Corin informed the Indithians. "He went back to find his sister, whom ironically, you have."

Donian looked at Neil, then back at Corin and Vynce. "With that being the case, we will escort you after all." He swung his sheathed sword behind him.

Corin suddenly cocked his head, finally connecting with Angelique. *I feel you.*

Such sweet relief.

"Semmi." Corin caught the ringleader's attention, who stood nearby. "Good luck to you."

Semmi waved, and the four immortals transformed, wings beating air, aimed for Jach Lagon Canyon.

Reaching their destination, they touched ground in a narrow pass where two gorges met at the foot of a mountain.

"I have lost my connection with Angelique." Corin scanned the location.

"She must have gone below," Donian told him.

Several mounds made of small stones caught Corin's attention outside the mouth of a cave, an area concealed by a maze of cliffs. "Are those graves?"

Donian nodded. "Humans."

Corin went to the nearest mound and pressed a hand on the grave, experiencing the last year of the inhabitant's life. Possessing a gift that allowed him to visit the past lives of the deceased just by touching the sacred ground where dust and bone rested, he saw the supporters' camp and felt the deceased woman's passion for their cause.

Pulling his hand away, Corin followed the others into the cave and along a dark and winding passage. He sensed no one as he skimmed a hand along the tunnel's glistening walls. "This is morvormanite?"

"Yes," Vynce answered. "It blocks our powers."

Departing that tunnel for another, he soon picked up on faint voices and saw a flickering light ahead. The voices grew louder, the light brighter, as they entered a cavern where they were met by several supporters.

Corin searched for any sign of Angelique. *Where are you?*

"Get Torq," Donian ordered. "Tell him we have visitors—family of the dir cyohr."

The man rushed away, returning momentarily with the leader, along with Tomes, Jordon, Galvar, and Angelique.

"Corin." Angelique threw herself into his arms. "I went above after sunset. I felt you."

Corin kissed the top of her head. "We were lucky enough to cross paths with these two outriders who were tracking Tomes." He gestured toward Donian.

"I'm glad you learned that the dir cyohr was here before traveling further," Torq told Donian and Neil. "Our savior has found *us*," he presented Tomes to them. "The dir cyohr."

With that introduction, Donian and Neil knelt before Tomes and pledged loyalty and life.

* * * *

"I had a talk with Tomes a few minutes ago. He already knew about Angelique and I being Delghorlin." Corin leaned against a pillar of stone in an obscured corner of the cavern.

"Yes," Jordon said. "He had overheard something I said to Vynce. I had to tell him. I hope you're not upset."

"No. He needed to know."

"He said it doesn't matter. That he completely trusts you."

Corin nodded. "What about you? Knowing I'm Delghorlin, where does our friendship stand?"

"I can't say I'm happy about it. You know where I stand on the matter of that lineage. My question to you is: Where do you stand?"

"I carry Delghorlin blood, but I am not one of them. And never will be."

"But Jozsef is, and he *is* your brother."

"We've chosen different paths. I wish it were different, but it's not." Corin shifted his weight. "I consider you a close friend. I don't want that to change because of this."

"I feel no differently toward you and Angelique now than I did yesterday. I just hope she can control it as well as you have."

"Just something more she has to cope with while still coming to terms with her new existence. But she has handled her conversion well."

"You've had no worries with her control?"

"No. None."

"Would you tell me if you had?" Jordon asked outright.

"Probably not. But it happens to be true," Corin

swore. "She's exhibited remarkable control."

"Good."

"Knowing what I now know, her extraordinary strength should have been an indication of something unusual, but we each have our unique gifts, so I figured...."

"You and your brother. Angelique and Tomes. You all possess the blood mutation," Jordon said. "When you fought Boldor, and your monster consumed you, I had never seen such a demon."

"Galvar has said as much." Corin knew he had to keep his Delghorlin monster buried. "Delghorlin blood. The root of the evil." He knew Jordon was thinking the same thing.

"Like I said before, you and Jozsef, both of you changed by Andras five hundred years ago, that is no accidental happening." Jordon expelled a heavy breath. "It appears he's been building an army for a long time."

"Jozsef said he'd been waiting for the prophecy."

"He wants resurrection of Delghorlin rule in the Eleventh Dimension. I'd like nothing more than for that ruthless line to be wiped out. I had hoped Lehndra was the last." Jordon looked at Corin. "No offense."

"After meeting her six months back, I completely understand. I may share her lineage, but I don't share her venomous nature."

"No. There is something different with you and Angelique. Being tied to the end time prophecy, to the dir cyohr, it was meant to be. The fact that we were all brought together six months ago was fate. Every event. Every happening. Every encounter. Everything has been centered around Tomes and what he was destined to become. From the murder of his wife by Boldor, to now, it's all been predetermined. To save a world."

"What about the Clyth?"

"In those days the dir cyohr will claim the great dark

power," Jordon quoted. "According to the prophecy."

"Half of it has found its way to where it belongs, with its keeper—Tomes."

"Yes," Jordon said. "It's the dawn of a new day. And when Tomes has the Clyth, the Order will be free to return to what's left of the Eleventh Dimension—their home."

* * * *

"We have each come with news." Constable Lavor said upon taking human form.

"Umorius," Galvar addressed a clythguard who'd accompanied Lavor to Jach Lagon Canyon. "Has something happened at the Order?"

Jordon, Tomes, Vynce, Corin, Angelique, and Torq gathered around.

"We were attacked by the Örök Vér. They had Lehndra's help. Many were slain," Umorius sadly reported. "They got away with the Heart."

"Lehndra." Galvar looked at Jordon. "We should have heeded your ojections to our lenient methods of dealing with her."

"You were pressured to protect her," Jordon reminded him.

"Because of her, lives have been lost. Our brethren. And now, our enemy has the Heart." Galvar's fingers clenched into his palms. "How many clythguards remain? How many council?"

"In all, we lost a third of our men, but most of the council survived," Umorius told him.

"The dead are to be honored for having lost their lives in the line of duty." Galvar spoke with a heavy heart.

"I have brought these. We lost the Heart, but the ten amber stones were saved." He relinquished a black pouch to Galvar.

Galvar poured out the stones, each one containing a trapped insect. "These should be under guard at the Order."

"With the code to the vault compromised, the council has temporarily placed them in my custody," Umorius explained. "You are the only one still alive authorized to change the code."

"There is one other." Galvar pointed a finger at Vynce. "But neither of us can return at the moment."

"I will keep them safe, at the Order, until you do," Umorius assured him. "They are certainly interesting. Have you ever figured out how to use them?"

"No." Galvar brushed a hand over the gems. "They are a mystery."

Jordon picked one up and handed it to Tomes. "Being a sorcerer, maybe you can tell us something about them."

"Sorcerer?" Angelique didn't understand.

"Piiric was a sorcerer," Jordon told her. "Tomes is learning his powers as he gains Piiric's memories."

Tomes saw Angelique's surprise in her wide-eyed expression. "That was what Jordon had stopped Vynce from telling me, right after my merge with Piiric."

"Yes," she recalled. "He said it was about your powers. But who would have imagined a sorcerer?"

"It's taking time, and I don't know much." Tomes handed the stone back to Galvar. "I can't tell you how to use them."

Galvar dropped the stones back in the pouch. "Boldor's secret died with him—a spell needed to make the required connection with the insects to call them from the stones. Without that spell, they are useless."

"Probably for the best." Jordon stood next to Galvar. "If they're ever stolen, it's not likely anyone else will figure out how to use them either."

Galvar handed the pouch back to Umorius. "Return to Earth and have the council plan a memorial to honor those that have fallen."

Umorius tucked the pouch into his pocket. "With the grave situation here, the Order will most likely want to return home."

"Not yet. I will send word when that time comes," Galvar instructed.

Umorius nodded. "I will let them know." He wished the group luck and took his leave to return to Earth.

"Andras has the Heart, and now, nothing will stop him from coming after the dir cyohr," Vynce said.

"That is the news I brought. He is already here," Lavor informed them. "Regent Fehre just received word that our enemy has congregated in Sloe Forest at Samuar Quarries, led by a nightwalker—Andras Metellus.

"They'll have Kara." Tomes had agonized over her capture since receiving the news, feeling guilty for the manner in which he'd treated her when learning of her deception.

"I would expect Andras to use your love for her to his advantage, just as Boldor used Angelique to get to me," Corin reminded Tomes. "When Boldor proposed a trade, it was only one life I risked—my own. But you have much more to consider. The fate of an entire world is at stake."

"I suspect he has revealed his position purposely in an attempt to flush us out," Jordon presumed. "With his spies scattered about the regions, I'm sure he has been well-informed."

"If we attack, we'll be playing right into his hands," Corin stated the obvious.

"He knows we will go after Kara. And the Heart of the Clyth," Galvar said.

"Regardless of the danger," Vynce added. "And he

has chosen a dark and deadly location."

"Very deadly," Lavor concurred. "I hate that territory. Treacherous pits full of carnivorous gabrans."

"With five hundred on his side, we don't stand much of a chance without reinforcements." Corin removed his hat and brushed back his wavy ash-blond hair.

"He may have five hundred men, but we have a wizard," Galvar pointed out.

Tomes cut his eyes at Galvar. "I'm not ready. I have no control over my abilities."

"I trust Piiric," Galvar told him. "A sneak attack with a hundred soldiers should suffice."

"They will be on guard, expecting an attack." Vynce's brow tightened over his bold, blue eyes. "I suggest we cross over Pierson and Patricia. Now that would be a surprise. In their bestial forms they would give us a much-needed edge against the Delghorlins."

"Yes," Galvar agreed. "Jordon, go with Vynce. See if Pierson and Patricia are willing to come and fight. Make sure they are aware of the danger."

"I will accompany them as far as Morpar and assemble a troop," Lavor said.

"Should I gather my soldiers in preparation for the Great Battle?" Torq looked to Tomes for instruction. "The men have been well-trained."

"The end time battle mentioned in the prophecy," Constable Lavor elaborated.

"It's not that time yet." Tomes somehow knew. The last thing the suffering world needed at this point was more loss, but the end time battle had been prewritten by a higher power, something Tomes wasn't able to change. But when the time came, he knew he would stand with the inhabitants of the Eleventh Dimension, now being one of them, and growing more connected with each passing day.

Vynce, Jordon, and Lavor departed, and Tomes

mingled with the supporters. The overwhelming belief they had in the prophecy inspired him. Faith was all they required.

Soon, Lavor returned to the secret sect with a troop of soldiers, arriving mere minutes ahead of Jordon and Vynce and their escorted secret weapons—Pierson and Patricia in bestial form.

"What are they?" The constable marveled.

"They are unfortunate victims of an ancient magic," Galvar told him. "Unless the curse can be broken, they are doomed to continue in this cruel existence, changing into these creatures every night, reverting to human form in the day."

"Even in bestial form, they maintain their intelligence. They know what we are saying, everything that's happening." Tomes pointed out how Pierson and Patricia's focus shifted to whoever was talking and how they interacted if spoken to.

"I believe they will greatly improve our odds." Constable Lavor circled Pierson.

"Constable, if you need to return to the palace, to your family, I understand," Tomes told him.

"Regent Fehre ordered that I guard you. Especially now, with the rise of the Delghorlins," Lavor said. "No one will be safe until the Delghorlins are eradicated."

"I couldn't agree more." Jordon shared his views. "With the exception of Corin and Angelique."

"And Kara," Tomes said. He then laid a hand on Pierson's side, against his wing. "By standing with us, you and Patricia put your lives on the line."

Pierson tipped his head in acknowledgement.

Tomes glanced at the others. All of their lives were on the line. He then zeroed in on Galvar. "We have a few hours till sunrise."

Galvar nodded. "We should not waste a minute. It will be a long flight."

"Around five hours from this point," Jordon estimated.

"If we leave immediately, heading northwest, we can reach the caves at Destin Cove before sunrise," Galvar suggested. "There, we can wait out the daylight hours and organize a plan of attack for next nightfall. We would be about an hour from Samuar Quarries at that point, where the Örök Vér will be forced to seek shelter."

Torq stepped toward Tomes. "What should we do?"

"For now, remain here...hidden." Tomes lowered his head. "A few miracles are all I've done. It's not enough. The victims of these disasters deserve more."

"Right now, your divine presence alone offers hope in this time of apocalypse. This is merely the beginning of your destiny," Galvar said. "You are shepherd to the lost. The mere mention of your name restores belief in the prophecy, and the new reign to come."

Tomes felt Piiric's energy stir within him, a phenomenal power. *Shepherd. Savior. Dir cyohr. Why me? Why was I chosen?*

Questions he knew he'd probably never find answers to.

12

Pierson, reverted to human form, accepted Lavor's offering and quickly wrapped himself in the constable's knee-length cape. Seeing the men averting their eyes, he glanced at Patricia who stood stark-naked, receiving assistance from Angelique.

"Hurry." Angelique spurred Corin's process of removing his front-button shirt, reducing his apparel to a gray undershirt, dark pants, and boots. "Don't give up hope," she consoled Patricia who brushed away tears of embarrassment.

Pierson took Angelique's place, pulling Patricia into his arms, sharing her curse and pain. "We will find a way to end this curse."

"I hope you're right." She buried her face in his shoulder.

Pierson turned to Jordon. "Is the cove safe?" He thought a walk on the beach might help calm Patricia.

"You may find it safer out there, with the soldiers, than in here," Jordon said. "We're not alone."

172

Pierson navigated Patricia toward their point of entry as three immortals emerged from the unascertained depths of the cave, apparently having entered the large spread of interconnecting cavities through another access.

"We want no trouble." Lavor faced the strangers. "We just need cover till nightfall."

Pierson could see bloodlust in the trios' wild eyes.

"Get outside," Jordon yelled at Pierson as he and the others blocked the nightwalkers who aimed for prey, unable to control their rising monsters.

Escaping the wide-mouthed cave, Pierson looked over the Indithian troop camped along the beach, knowing that they were safe outside. He knew the blood feeders would not dare exiting the caves. Even though the hazy sky dimmed the sunlight, they would not risk the penetrating rays.

"There is some trouble inside," Pierson informed a soldier. He then led Patricia toward a grouping of trees. "All we can do is wait."

"Do you think they're okay inside?"

"Those nightwalkers are on the run." Pierson glanced toward the cave, unable to hear anything over waves crashing onto the rocky shore. His gaze then trailed to the water. "It's a large lake." He could barely make out a distant shoreline on the opposite side. "I wonder if the caves encircle the entire lake."

"Look at this, Allen." Patricia plucked a round purple fruit from one of the trees. "Looks like plums. Do you think they're edible?"

Pierson examined the fruit. "There's only one way to find out." He took a bite. "I don't think killing us would be that easy."

"No. I've proven that."

Pierson recalled her suicide attempt. "You can never do anything like that again."

"I couldn't stand the thought of turning into a monster every night."

"We'll find a way to reverse this curse. There has to be someone in this world with the power to help us."

Patricia's attention was drawn to the mouth of the cave. "It's Jordon. I hope the others are okay."

Pierson straightened as Black strode toward them. He had never cared much for the marshal, but right now, the daywalker was a welcome sight.

"The nightwalkers retreated into the caves once they realized our number," Jordon reported. "I don't think we'll see them again, but the soldiers will keep watch, just in case."

"They're hungry," Patricia said.

"Yes, but we couldn't give up what few Traxl-1 we have with us, otherwise, our group of nightwalkers would soon be in the same shape." Jordon picked fruit from the nearest tree. "I see you've found some tograra plums."

"They're safe to eat?" Patricia asked.

"Perfectly." Jordon bit into the fruit before reaching for his *Camels* and tapping one out. "Care for one?" he offered Pierson.

"I don't think so," Pierson declined, watching as Jordon lit the cigarette and took a drag. "I've set my mind to quitting. If we ever break this curse, I'd like to live as long a life as possible."

"Sorry. I'm not helping your goal." Jordon respectfully tossed down his cigarette and rubbed it out. "We should find some food." Jordon searched for dried wood to start a fire. "Crab. Clams. Speel roots—"

"Speel roots?" Pierson interrupted.

Jordon pointed out an area of fernlike plants growing in the shade of the trees. "Cook them right over a fire."

"Hmm." Pierson cocked an eyebrow. "Guess I can

give it a go."

"Thank you, Jordon," Patricia said while helping to gather branches.

"I can't get over how young you are." Pierson couldn't help staring at Jordon.

"Only in appearance." Jordon chose a spot for the fire and started arranging the wood.

Patricia dropped an armful of sticks next to Jordon. "I'm going to pick a few plums."

"Stay close," Pierson said as she walked away.

"She's leaving so we can talk." Jordon pulled a lighter from his pocket.

"Yeah," Pierson said. "There is something I'd like to say." He squatted and attempted to block the breeze from blowing out the flame Jordon worked to achieve. "I know we didn't start out on the best of terms six months back."

"Water under the bridge, Sheriff. I'm just glad we're now on the same page; although, I would have preferred more favorable circumstances."

"U.S. Marshal Black and Sheriff Pierson. We are neither what we seem. I sure wish I could turn back the clock, having learnt the hard way that the short road leads to perdition. I tried to make a deal with the devil, and I got burned, dragging Patricia down with me."

"She seems to be coping."

"She shouldn't have to cope. I did this to her." Pierson's gaze froze on her position. "She was happy living a normal human life. Knowing she's suffering on account of me. I cannot bear that existence." He stood up.

"We've all made mistakes, Pierson. Ease up on yourself a little."

"I deserve all the punishment hell has to offer."

"No, you made a mistake. Hell is reserved for the likes of Andras, or that gremlin who cursed you—

Meical Evon. You are not the first mortal to be lured by the promise of immortality, and I think I can safely predict, you won't be the last."

Pierson collected himself. "Don't think this little talk makes us buddies, Marshal."

Jordon laughed. "I wouldn't dare presume, Sheriff."

Despite everything that had gone wrong for Pierson, he knew how fortunate he was to be allied with Jordon, Corin, Tomes, and Angelique. In that respect, he was a very lucky man.

* * * *

Outside the caves at Destin Cove, the immortals watched as two large forms came into view over the dark water, shadowed by a group of soldiers.

"I was beginning to worry." Lavor rushed toward Pierson and Patricia, who landed on the beach.

"It took a little longer than expected." Jordon slid off of Pierson's back. "I nearly cut the task too close to nightfall. We spotted Andras and his party emerging from the pits, but we kept a safe distance. They didn't know we were there."

"Pierson and Patricia," Corin motioned, "you're lucky they didn't spot them."

"We had already taken to hiding when I heard the nightwalkers moving around underground," Jordon told him. "Then, seeing they were leaving the quarries, I had Pierson, Patricia, and the men wait while I followed them to a clearing a few miles into the forest."

"They distance themselves from the gabrans at night, yet remain close to the pits for daytime shelter," Galvar said.

"Since gabrans live in colonies and typically populate a specific area of the deep, depleted pits, the Örök Vér have to be cautious in scouting out a location," Vynce explained. "Coming upon gabrans can prove deadly. Jordon and the other men took a real risk getting close enough, the endeavor requiring swift movement without uttering a sound, in order to pick a few off to provide us with the means needed to safely travel the area."

"We caught as many as we could before the sun set. It should be enough." He sent the other men to distribute their catch among the troop. He then presented his catch—a number of small, slaughtered animals, tied in pairs by long, ratlike tails. "They are nocturnal," he looked at Corin. "You have to catch them sleeping."

"They don't look all that threatening," Corin said.

"But they sure do stink." Angelique's nose wrinkled as her face scrunched in aversion. "They resemble Earth's opossum, except for their longer, thinner tails. The tails on those things must be at least two feet long for them to be tied together like that."

Jordon tossed the gabrans down on the ground. "You haven't seen their teeth." He squatted and showed the rodents' large, razor-sharp teeth. "They swarm like ants." He pulled his knife and started dismembering the animals. "Devouring their prey in a matter of seconds. If you fail to escape a swarm, you're in real trouble. They do not leave a bone. Not a scrap."

"Andras will not want to remain at Samuar Quarries long, being forced to utilize the pits." Constable Lavor collected several chunks of raw meat and passed them to Corin. "Carry these on your person at all times while we are in the territory."

Corin grimaced. "It really does stink."

"It's potent all right, which is why you don't need much to do the job." Jordon continued sectioning the remains. "This is the only means of tricking the gabrans. The creatures are blind and rely on their sense of smell to search out food. By covering our scent with their stink, we prevent them from detecting what we are."

"They won't detect the smell of blood from cutting them up?" Corin pointed out several Earth animals that were known to turn on injured prey, even the weak of their own species.

"Gabrans secrete a fluid that gives off the same smell as their blood, so they are easily fooled," Jordon assured him.

"This is so disgusting." Angelique followed Corin's lead and stashed small pieces of meat wherever she could fit them.

"But necessary." Corin made sure she was well covered. Stepping back, he took in her appearance. "It's strange looking at you with this face. Nothing compares to the original; however, I wouldn't complain."

"Don't get too excited." Angelique playfully pressed a finger against his chin, sliding it up his jaw line, to a dimple marking his left cheek. "It's temporary." She reached for his hat. "Shouldn't this go?"

"It's lucky."

"I've heard that before," Tomes razzed. "But she's right, Jax might recognize it."

"I'll take it off before we move in." Corin repositioned his sword. "This takes some getting used to."

Jordon laughed. "This is a whole other world, Corin. Here, we carry swords."

"I know how to handle one. It's just been a long time." Looking at Jordon, Corin pointed out a very visible tattoo—a half-skull, half-human design with a moon replacing the eye of the skull, and a sun replacing the eye of the man. "That will certainly give us away."

"When changing form, I always keep them—a matter of honor and pride. But this is a special circumstance."

Jordon shape-shifted and reformed with clear, unmarked skin. "I'm not about to add additional risk. I'm not ready for dispersal."

"Dispersal?" Corin's brow furrowed, unclear of his meaning.

"Nightwalkers fall to dust. Daywalkers disperse." Jordon gave a vague response.

"Staca told me about dispersal." Angelique shared what she'd learned, giving a brief explanation of how a daywalker's energy and soul was released in a flash of light, with the energy dispersing, and the soul crossing to a new plane of existence. "A beautiful way to go."

"What do you think of my new look? I figured tall, dark, and regal was fitting." Tomes's declaration prompted the others to laugh.

"Still the same ol' Tomes," Corin was happy to say. "About these identities...." He moved to a more serious note. "It's a good plan, going in ahead of the soldiers to throw off the enemy, but I'm not convinced these disguises will work?" He couldn't help being leery. "If Jozsef gets close enough, he'll know me regardless of my appearance. And they'll be suspicious."

"Knowing they are expecting a sneak attack, this is our best course of action. Your connection with Jozsef does pose a problem, but do not forget, we have a wizard on our side." Galvar looked at Tomes. "The dir cyohr—Piiric. I would not attempt this mission otherwise."

"Keeping the Örök Vér distracted is what will allow our men the time needed to move into place. If they fail to fall for our cover, then Corin, you may be just the diversion we will need," Lavor pointed out.

Corin sucked in his top lip and released it with his next breath. "Why don't I feel good about that?"

"You're not the only one under pressure," Tomes said. "I hope I know what to do when the time comes."

"Trust Piiric," Galvar told Tomes. "And remember, we also have Pierson and Patricia on the sidelines, along with a troop of a hundred men."

"My bigger concern is your connection with Andras," Jordon addressed Corin. "His control, should you be unable to avoid contact with him."

"It's been five hundred years," Corin reminded him.

"Hopefully our disguises will fool them long enough for our plan to work," Galvar said. "Corin, just do your best to avoid your brother and Andras."

"Here." Jordon slapped another gabran chunk in Corin's hand. "Maybe the stink will help."

Corin shoved the raw meat out of sight and brushed off his hand. "I'll do my best to keep a distance from them both."

Galvar looked over the crew. "Remember, we are supposed to be a nightwalker clan, and I am your leader, Hythor. I will give no second name. We are scouting for a new dwelling after our territory was destroyed by meteorites?"

"You think Andras will fall for this?" Vynce shared Corin's skepticism over their disguises.

"Our small number will not threaten him," Galvar said with confidence. "However, once we make our move—"

"Disguises will be the least of our worries," Jordon finished. "With five hundred Delghorlin, it won't be an easy fight, even with Pierson and Patricia."

"Meical will be one to watch out for, having those nytum daggers," Vynce told Corin. "You saw what it can do to immortals."

"Noted." Corin looked at Angelique. "Remember that."

Galvar stepped next to Lavor who tied gabran parts to Pierson and Patricia's long lengths of mane using strips of cloth torn from several immortals' clothes.

"We will stop before reaching the Örök Vér's camp, close enough for you to hear a signal—three consecutive eagle cries. That will be your cue to emerge in full attack mode."

Pierson bent his head in acknowledgement.

"What about the soldiers?" Lavor glanced toward the troop. "When should they move in?"

"As close as we are, ten minutes should be long enough," Galvar answered. "Then, with the Delghorlins distracted by our arrival, they can take that opportunity to encircle the camp."

Jordon stepped toward the water's edge. "As soon as Andras realizes a real threat has infiltrated his camp, all hell will break loose." He rinsed his hands and the others followed suit. "Be prepared for a fight."

"Night passes quickly. We should move out," Galvar said. "We have already lost well over an hour of night, and it will take us an hour to reach the quarries."

Shape-shifting, the troop set a course for Samuar Quarries, stopping at the edge of Sloe Forest, just short of reaching the Delghorlins' camp. Hiquire was somewhat brighter than the previous night, still the only orb viewable in the night sky.

"The pits are enormous," Corin remarked on the quarries they'd just viewed from above.

"Tsurrana mines," Jordon responded. "Similar to iron ore. Gaun depleted these mines during his reign, leaving this unsightly scar on the territory. It was in high demand for production of weaponry, shields, and armor."

"When the iron ore was combined with nytum, the weapons created were unrivaled," Galvar added, "and he had somehow managed to obtain a small supply at that time."

"So, you use nytum weapons here?"

"After Gaun was defeated, any nytum weapons

found were destroyed," Galvar said. "But with so many made at that time, there are still some that still exist today. It only takes a little nytum to do the job, and there is always the chance of more nytum being discovered."

Corin brushed a hand along the ashen bark of a tree, rocking its twisted branches, dispersing a swarm of undetectable insects that were perfectly blended on the upper limbs. Jerking back with a start, his face contorted in reaction to unbearable pain ripping through his hand, realizing a large splinter had pierced his palm. Only this was no ordinary sliver of wood. "What the devil." He violently shook his hand that felt as if it had been set on fire.

Jordon rushed to his aid. "Blackthorn. It has to come out." He gripped Corin's wrist and quickly removed the splinter.

"Blackthorn is the predominant tree in Sloe Forest," Lavor apprised him.

Corin growled. "Not the safest place for nightwalkers."

"Just remember, there's no harm to you unless it breaks your skin," Jordon said. "So be careful."

Tomes looked at Corin. "A forest of blackthorn. Imagine the number of nails Gordy could have made six months back if he'd had this kind of supply—a lifetime reserve for the staker."

"A nightwalker's nightmare." Corin examined his hand. "Watch yourself," he told Angelique. "You do not want to experience that pain."

Angelique eyed Vynce's sheathed digits. "I'm beginning to understand why you always wear gloves."

"I never travel without them." Vynce swatted at black insects swarming their path.

"There must be hundreds." Angelique protected her face. "What are they?"

"December moths. They are no danger," Constable Lavor assured her. "They rely on the bark of blackthorn trees this time of year. We have disturbed their nesting. Stay still and they will settle down."

Within a minute, the moths had retreated back into the trees, once again camouflaged on the dark, twisted limbs.

"The Delghorlins' site isn't far from here." Jordon pulled everyone's attention back to the matter at hand. "We should continue in wolf form to a quarter mile or so of the camp. I wouldn't trust taking Pierson and Patricia any closer."

"Lead the way." Tomes gave Jordon the go-ahead.

Forming a pack, Jordon led them to a point he approximated to be a quarter mile from the clearing.

"This is as far as you go," Galvar told Pierson and Patricia. "Listen for your signal—three consecutive eagle cries."

"Give us ten minutes," Lavor instructed the Indithians, "then move in and encircle the camp. If you hear the signal before getting into position, then attack. You know our mission."

With everything in place, the seven immortals continued in human form toward the Örök Vér's camp, coming upon a large clearing littered with jagged blackthorn limbs. It was an environment Corin viewed as potentially hazardous, having experienced the pain that even a sliver of the wood could inflict on nightwalkers.

"We're surrounded," Jordon alerted the others seconds before a number of Delghorlins appeared.

A tall, dark-clothed immortal with straight, white hair stepped forward, clutching silver daggers. "Who are you?" he demanded.

"We are just passing through," Galvar spoke out. "My name is Hythor. This is my clan." He immersed himself in his character—bald, tattooed, and unkempt—a complete opposite of his true self. "Our territory was destroyed by meteorites and we are scouting for a new dwelling."

"Meical. Bring them to me." A voice rang out from the distant darkness.

"The boss wants a word." The Delghorlins ordered the group into the clearing.

Corin, bringing up the rear, remembered his hat and quickly ditched it in the underbrush bordering the clearing, chancing nothing that might give his true identity away.

"We are just passing through," Galvar reiterated as he neared the leader—Andras.

Corin stayed in close proximity to Angelique while scanning their opposition, shifting his line of sight when he spotted Jax and Jozsef in the crowd. Remaining calm and alert while passing several feet from them, he avoided his brother's direction, but caught a double take from Jozsef—an intense stare—knowing he suspected something.

Looking at Andras, he recalled what Jozsef had said about the leader changing his appearance, something not uncommon in a nightwalker's long existence. He then experienced a magnetizing pull and maneuvered behind Jordon in an attempt to mask the connection.

Gedeon. All doubt was gone. This Delghorlin leader was, without question, his immortal father.

"You travel by land?" Andras's tone was skeptical.

Lehndra. Corin's gaze fell on a face he remembered well as the female nightwalker stepped from the shadows and planted herself at Andras's side. Then, looking past her at movement in the backdrop, he spotted Kara. *Careful, Tomes.* He caught Tomes's sudden change of expression, hoping none of their enemies had noticed.

"We have used up our supply of Traxl-1 and were combing the woods for food," Galvar gave a plausible explanation while maintaining a steady voice. "We had just reverted to human form when your men surrounded us. We did not mean to encroach on your territory."

One Delghorlin nightwalker rocked nervously, uttering a chattering cackle. A red lip ring dangling from the fiend's bottom lip caught Corin's attention.

Stop eyeballing me. Corin tried to avoid eye contact with Jozsef who maintained a relentless stare.

"Wait," Jozsef disrupted Andras's interrogation. "They're not who they claim to be." He zeroed in on Corin, exposing the imposters. "Show your true self, brother. You can't hide from me."

In that instant, Galvar expelled three piercing cries, sounding Pierson and Patricia's signal. In a blink, the nightwalkers' monsters emerged, and the Örök Vér assailed.

Corin scanned their surroundings, releasing a held breath when Indithian soldiers sprang from the surrounding woods. He then aimed for Jozsef, but he stopped and altered course when he saw Tomes intercepted by Jax, Andras, Meical, and Lehndra.

"Corin," Angelique's voice rang out.

Corin glimpsed her over his right shoulder. "Get to Kara." He motioned. "I'll help Tomes." He drew his sword and whirled into action.

As the scene played around him in slow motion, Corin observed his comrades' positions. Lavor, directly ahead of him, fought like a master while Galvar and Vynce joined forces with Jordon who had snatched up sections of blackthorn in place of his sword, striking with lightning speed. Galvar fought admirably alongside his shinobi partner, incapacitating several less-skilled opponents, but not yet fully healed, Corin knew the commander couldn't hold out for long. Even with a hundred Indithian soldiers, none of them would last long, being outnumbered five to one.

At that moment, two thundering roars ripped through the air as Pierson and Patricia lunged from the darkness and ripped into the enemy.

"Pierson," Galvar yelled. "Protect Tomes!"

Corin pulled back as Pierson responded to the commander's summon, watching as he charged the four immortals cornering Tomes, scattering the nightwalkers.

Angelique. Corin turned and saw her with Kara, joining the fight approximately fifty feet away.

"Look out! Behind you!" Angelique's words sounded in his mind at the precise moment Jozsef blindsided him, his brother's tackle carrying his weight several feet before thundering to the ground.

Rebounding, Corin glimpsed Andras targeting Tomes and fought to get past Jozsef, who wasn't offering easy passage. "I don't want to hurt you, Jozsef."

"You shouldn't be so sure of yourself."

A deep bellow claimed Corin's attention as Pierson fought to expel Meical and Lehndra who hung to his coat. Thrashing mindlessly, Pierson barreled between Corin and Jozsef, clearing a path that enabled Corin to escape his brother and pursue Andras. Moving fast, he managed to intercept the Delghorlin leader.

"You have no idea who you challenge." Andras chuckled as if amused.

"You have taken a new appearance, but I know you...Gedeon." Corin glared. "The devil who cursed me."

"You should be thankful for the gift of eternal life."

"Five hundred years of hell. It was no gift."

"You've allotted immortality for special

circumstance. Your companion, for instance, proving we are no different." Andras suddenly shape-shifted, shedding his false façade for the image he had when living as Gedeon. "You are strong, blocking our connection. Being my blood, I should have detected you...have more effect on you." He sniffed the air. "But your special blood now calls to me. Blood I claimed as Delghorlin long ago."

"A past I wish I could erase." Corin saw Tomes's swift approach.

"You and I are not the only ones with a shared past." Andras shifted again, settling on an image unfamiliar to Corin—long, dark hair, piercing eyes, and a wide jaw.

Tomes, now planted at Corin's side, stood face-to-face with his adversary.

"A vision has plagued me for centuries of the half-breed prince, returned as the dir cyohr, ending my life." Andras's gaze bore into Tomes. "But I won't let that happen."

"So, your plan is to terminate his life before he can terminate yours?" Corin grasped his intention, glancing at Tomes who stood strangely expressionless.

"Var." Another voice suddenly spoke through Tomes. "You murdered my family, not even knowing for certain that I was the half-demon child."

"Piiric," Andras sneered, facing him in the image of Var. "Rumors told, but it was a wasted effort, since you somehow managed to escape that attack.

If I could have taken your life then and stopped you from rising in Morpar, I could have altered fate, and possibly prevented the dir cyohr."

"Taking my life would have set your life on a new path," Piiric understood. "But the dir cyohr has come. You have failed. And if your vision is true...you *will* die."

"It's not too late." Andras gnashed his teeth. "The

Clyth will be my weapon against you." He took back his present-day persona and reached for the Heart hanging from a chain around his neck.

Corin glimpsed Galvar signaling Vynce, and the two endeavoring to reach them through strong opposition. Andras, aware of their actions, tucked the Heart beneath his shirt and made a sweep for a pouch falling at Tomes's side.

Delayed in his attempt to intercept the charge, Corin was relieved Tomes had dodged the onrush, but Andras had managed to cut through a strap that diagonally crossed from Tomes's right shoulder to his left waist. And with the narrow strip of material that held the pouch severed, the bag propelled several feet, landing with the Body partially exposed.

Andras, daring another move, dove for the charm, but before reaching it, a hawk swooped in and claimed the prize.

"No!" Andras roared as his talons managed to graze the bird's body, dispersing a shower of feathers, but the hawk escaped unharmed.

"Bren." Lavor rushed to his son who touched ground several feet from him and took human form. "Protect that with your life."

Corin stepped protectively in front of Tomes and locked stares with his maker. Feeling the effects of Andras's hypnotizing pull, he was thankful when Piiric—who currently operated Tomes's body—cast a spell by calling out "gheallo habrith," two words that conjured a blast of energy that ejected from his palms and struck Andras mid-chest, hurling him several feet backward in a stir of dust.

Andras quickly found his footing. "Sorcery...Piiric's power. But you're not the only sorcerer in the Eleventh Dimension. We'll see how well you stand against Nordriss," he threatened. "Since turning to the dark side, his power is unmatched."

"Gabrans!" Meical frantic alert ripped through the air.

Corin whirled as thousands of the carnivorous creatures swarmed the camp, targeting several Delghorlins who'd lost their animal parts during battle. Astonished by the speed of the gabrans, he grimaced at the sight of one unfortunate immortal being devoured, the Delghorlin having been caught off guard and too slow in his attempt to transform.

"This isn't over," Andras declared and yelled an order to his men to disperse.

Within seconds, the Örök Vér had fled into Sloe forest, ending the skirmish.

"Patricia's in trouble," Angelique yelled.

Corin saw Pierson attempting to protect her from attacking gabrans.

Jordon rushed to assist them. "She has lost most of her gabran pieces...not enough left to fool them."

The immortals scrambled to expel the parasites.

"We need to get some pieces on her." Galvar snatched up one of the rodents, receiving a nasty bite to the top of his hand as he broke its neck. Dropping the dead animal, he focused on healing his injury, seeing that the swarm had detected his blood.

"I will get it." Lavor swept up the carcass, pulled his sword, and quickly sectioned the rodent. He tossed the pieces to Jordon. "Get these on her."

Galvar, having eluded the gabrans targeting him by shifting to mist, drifted to Jordon's position and reclaimed his form. "There's only one way to save her." He grabbed several gabran chunks from Jordon and jumped onto her back. "Take flight," he called out, sustaining numerous bites as he fought off the attacking animals. "Pierson, we must get her in the air."

Corin and the others backed away as Pierson spread

his large wings and prompted her into action by pushing her into a run. Stumbling, she nearly fell, but managed to lift her weight and rise just above the treetops.

The troop followed, watching as Galvar cast off the remaining gabrans.

She's too weak. Corin saw she was losing momentum and making a rapid descent. *She can't stay in the air.*

Galvar transformed to mist a moment before she crashed in the woods and reclaimed his form next to her.

Upon landing, Constable Lavor signaled silence, and the troop stood still as statues while he ascertained if they'd gone far enough to escape the gabran swarm. "I believe all is clear," he called out.

"How is she?" Corin rushed toward Patricia.

"She is unconscious." Galvar squatted next to her, examining her condition. "She needs a place to rest and recover."

"As well as ourselves. Before sunrise," Vynce added. "Those of us nightwalker."

Tomes moved toward Kara and reached for her hands, expressing an outpouring of regret over his past behavior. "You have no idea how worried I was. Forgive me, Kara. I was unfair and—"

Kara pressed a vertical finger to his lips. "Let's just start over."

"I'd like that." Tomes pulled her into his arms.

"I'm glad you're back to yourself. Piiric was with us. He emerged and took a stand against Andras," Corin told him.

"I know." Tomes nodded. "I regained control when Andras fled."

"How are we going to get Patricia back to Morpar?" Angelique stepped beside Galvar. "We can't wait till morning."

"Look at this." Galvar pointed out her regeneration process. "She is healing amazingly fast for this amount of injury. At this rate, I think she will be back on her feet in a matter of minutes."

"Bren. I am surprised to see you here. Has something happened in Morpar?" Constable Lavor asked.

"Regent Fehre sent me. He wanted you to be aware that earlier today the last sign came to pass. Morpar's western dunes turned to blood, marking the location of the Great Battle." Bren turned the Body over to Tomes.

"Prophecy never gave us a precise location, but Regent Fehre predicted that the final battle would be fought in Morpar," Lavor said.

"With word of the final sign, a number of supporters from Jach Lagon Canyon are being led to the palace ruins to await your arrival, along with others who have traveled from distant regions," Bren reported.

Lavor groaned. "That is not in our favor. In the heat of battle, we need to be focused on defeating the enemy, not saving humans who stand no chance against the Delghorlins."

"We'll decide what to do when we return," Tomes told him. "Right now, I'm more concerned with what we'll be facing if Andras allies with Nordriss."

"Who exactly is Nordriss?" Corin asked.

"I gained Piiric's memories of the sorcerer when Andras mentioned his name." Tomes shared his experience. "Nordriss was once very close to Piiric, but he has since turned to the dark side."

"Let's hope he fails to enlist him." Corin glanced at Pierson who stood protectively over Patricia. "The Delghorlins inflict enough injury on their own."

"Andras is determined to gain control, at any cost." Galvar's lips drew tight in a tense display of concern.

"Prophecy not only speaks of opposition, but of a powerful evil arising during the Great Battle. I believe that powerful evil may very well be Nordriss."

"Before the Delghorlins fled, Andras claimed to be someone else associated with Piiric." Corin looked at Tomes. "Var."

The name captured the constable's full attention. "The nightwalker who slaughtered Piiric's family long ago?"

"Yes," Tomes confirmed the identity. "Having the gift of precognition, he claims to be plagued by a vision of the dir cyohr ending his life. He killed Piiric's family hoping to alter his fate."

"He's gone to great lengths, stopping at nothing to succeed." Jordon repositioned a stray strand of hair that escaped the strap tying back his unruly mane. "Now his plan is to ally with Nordriss."

"We have our own sorcerer." Corin slapped Tomes's shoulder. "I can hardly believe I just said that. When will the list end? Sorcerer. Immortal deity. Dir cyohr. Prince."

"Half demon," Tomes added. "Being dir cyohr, that has been proven."

"It's only a small part." Corin caught Tomes's exchange with Kara who did not know.

Angelique reached for her brother's arm. "You have to make peace with that. Corin's right, that part you're so concerned about is only a small part of who you are."

"I know you're right, Angel, but that small part is a big thing to overcome," Tomes said. "There's so much about Piiric I still don't know. For some reason he's kept the memory of his father blocked, and not knowing why bothers me. All I know is that there was secrecy among the monks and hierarchy in regard to his origin."

"Regent Fehre explained that the monks hid him

away until adulthood...protecting him," Jordon reminded him.

Tomes remembered. "Yes. Knowing he was the prophesied half-demon deity."

"We all have pasts, and monsters, to overcome." Corin could relate, carrying his own demons. "On top of everything else, we share an enemy. Piiric knew him as Var. I knew him as Gedeon—my maker. And now, we all know him as Andras."

"Everything in our lives, leading up to this point, has been fate setting the stage for prophecy," Galvar said.

"Hundreds of years in the making." Corin knew that better than anyone; too much intertwined to be coincidence.

"We failed to get the Heart." Vynce sighed.

"We have to trust that fate will place it where it is intended to be. At least we are not leaving empty-handed." Galvar motioned toward Kara. "She is back with Tomes, and we are walking away with a little more information about our opponent."

Knowledge is power. The words popped into Corin's mind.

Patricia suddenly awoke to Pierson's nuzzling. Rising, she uttered a deep, droning purr.

"She is going to be fine." Galvar combed his fingers through his disheveled black strands. "She should have no trouble traveling."

"Let's get moving then." Tomes gestured. "Our job in Sloe Forest is done. We need to be in Morpar."

"Wait." Corin darted away to retrieve something he couldn't leave without, finding his black Stetson right where he'd dropped it. Bending, he picked it up, brushed it off, and flipped it on his head.

Angelique, who'd followed, smiled. "I have to admit, it truly suits you."

Corin draped an arm across her shoulders, and they

rejoined the group. Looking into her face, he pondered their future. How had life brought them to this point? He wasn't sure what fate the Great Battle held for them, but whatever their destiny, they'd confront it together. Always together.

13

The Kingdom of Shudrorah—a large sheeted plane—
its cracked surface stretched for miles. Enormous
rock formations eerily towered into misty heights, their
peaks unseen in a dismal abyss. In the far-reaching
distance, Nordriss's castle loomed, dark and doomful.

Coming upon its outer gates, Andras and his party
were met by two large gargoyles guarding the castle
entrance.

"They're moving." Jozsef watched as the gargoyles
rose from their stone perches and expelled a shrieking
warning as if they were living beings.

With large, outstretched wings touching tip-to-tip,
the creatures blocked any further passage.

"What is it you seek in Shudrorah?" One of the
gargoyles spoke in a deep, amplified voice.

"My name is Andras Metellus. I've come to see
Nordriss with hope of forming an alliance."

The Gargoyle lowered his head with a menacing,
transfixed stare, seeming to read his thoughts. "You

have another name." The creature's depth of tone rumbled.

"Yes. My true name is Var. But I haven't used that name in a very long time," Andras confessed. "I am now known as Andras Metellus, leader of the Örök Vér, a Delghorlin clan. I come with a proposition."

"A proposition?" The gargoyle sounded intrigued, then fell silent in an awkward moment of indecision. "You and one other may enter." The gargoyles lowered their wings. "Follow the silver vein over the moat of fire and beyond the terrace to the gatehouse. From there, proceed past the inner bailey to the lapis doors of the keep and rap three times. The keeper will show you to my inner sanctum."

"Meical, you're in charge till I return," Andras ordered. "Jozsef, you will come with me."

"I should accompany you, Andras, not Jozsef," Meical opposed his choice. "In case there is trouble."

"It makes no difference who goes. Nordriss's power if far superior to any of ours," Andras told him. "I need you here. In my absence, I trust the party in your hands."

Andras and Jozsef stepped past the gargoyles and to the edge of a large moat, its depths concealed by dense, rolling steam.

"Look." Jozsef stepped back as a pool of silver liquid bubbled up from the ground at their feet and branched into mid-air before them, crawling, intertwining, and expanding until fully extending across the whole width of the moat.

"It's a bridge." Jozsef tested the strength of the creation. "It's solid."

Crossing the bridge, they continued past the terrace to the gatehouse and inner bailey, finally reaching the lapis doors of the keep. Rapping three times as instructed, the doors opened to a spectral being whom

Nordriss communicated through, as he'd done with the gargoyles. Only now his voice had evolved with growing dimension and pitch.

"Follow." The specter led them to a windowless room where the sorcerer sat in a broad, jewel-encrusted chair awaiting them. Two servants hustled away as they entered.

"Nordriss." Andras bowed in respect. "I see you have servants, but where are your guards...soldiers? You haven't an army?"

"My army is close at hand." Nordriss waved a pale hand before him, and a window appeared. "This is the Realm of Dremlon. I created this small realm within our own dimension, hidden in a pocket of space, separate, yet one." He waved his hand in a second arched pass, and the scene changed, showing an immense hive. "My Dremlon army."

"An army of what?" Andras couldn't make out much in the distant view. "There must be hundreds."

"One thousand Dremlons," Nordriss informed him. "But my attempt at creation was not without flaws. The beings you see are soulless puppets and have to be controlled."

"But they're alive?" Jozsef stared in awe.

"Yes. They are alive," Nordriss confirmed.

"How are they able to survive if they have to be controlled?" Jozsef had many more questions, but he dared not ask any more.

Nordriss closed the window and his icy gaze slowly shifted. Wearing a gray floor-length cloak, his black hair broke across his shoulders in twisted sections. "Magic." The sorcerer showed no emotion, holding a dead expression. "You spoke of an alliance?"

"The day has come for Delghorlins to rise and take back their standing as rightful rulers of the Eleventh Dimension"

"The dir cyohr stands in your way," Nordriss stated. "Piiric."

"Yes. He is a sorcerer, like you. But with your help, we can beat him. Beat the prophecy." Andras noticed that the sorcerer's silver eyes had changed color, turning a noticeable emerald green.

Nordriss stood, presenting his tall and youthful stature as he moved toward Andras and Jozsef. "I have three conditions."

"Name them." Andras had expected demands.

"First, I want a signed pact that my kingdom will be excluded from Delghorlin rule. That includes the villages and inhabitants of Shudrorah."

"Done." Andras didn't hesitate.

"Secondly, I want an expansion of my kingdom to encompass the Range of Koll. I am due a larger territory, and the precious minerals that the mountains lodge will benefit my kingdom."

"The region is controlled by Krivros," Andras said. "They are completely expendable. We won't stand in your way. In fact, you'd be doing us a favor."

Nordriss slowly maneuvered the room with his fingertips pressed together before him, each digit matching its mirror opposite, and palms untouching. "Lastly, you will reward me with the Eye of Ephog. You will find it at Morpar Palace, kept in Piiric's secret chamber in the temple."

"With your unmatched power, you could just take it." Jozsef presumed.

"No. The castle is protected by a spell. I cannot use magic once within its walls. Piiric took that secret to his grave." The sorcerer's eyes had changed color once again, now golden amber.

"But he is back as the dir cyohr," Andras said. "His secrets may not be lost."

Nordriss paused as if in thought. "His chamber is

also protected by a spell. No sorcery can penetrate the field, and only Piiric can open the door."

"If no one can enter the chamber, how would we get in to steal the Eye of Ephog?" Andras considered what seemed an impossible task.

"Simple." Nordriss's eyes flickered. "Capture the dir cyohr...alive."

Andras expelled a loud breath. "Easier said than done."

"Items protected in that room are invaluable. Well worth the trouble."

Andras was intrigued. "What power does the Eye have?"

"It shows the future. It is a great power. One I want to possess. I see many things, but the Eye is never wrong."

"How will we know it?" Andras asked.

"It is a transparent, golden stone, the size of your hand." Nordriss described the relic. "Encased in its center is Ephog's eye."

Jozsef grimaced. "A real eye?"

"A demon eye." Nordriss peered at Jozsef. "It is an age-old artifact, hidden away when the sorcerers were stripped of world control by High Deity Nuthura. In the beginning, it was granted to an ancient sorcerer by a demon familiar. Now, it belongs with the last."

"I've failed to obtain the Clyth, a secret weapon I'd hoped to possess when entering the Great War. One half is not enough." Andras pulled out the Heart he wore around his neck. "The Body is with the dir cyohr."

"If you could manage the other half, capturing the dir cyohr would no longer be necessary." Nordriss shifted course. "You could take his life force, and in theory, then possess Piiric's spirit, giving you the power to open his chamber within the palace temple."

"In theory?" Andras preferred to not rely on guesses.

"Which is why every effort should be put into the dir cyohr's capture," Nordriss said. "At present, they have no greater power over us than we have over them; a level playing field." He stopped at faced Andras. "Now, if we are in agreement with my terms, I, along with my Dremlon army, will be your secret weapon."

Andras tipped his head in agreement. "I'll comply with those conditions."

"If you should succeed in acquiring both halves of the Clyth, I caution you, Andras Metellus, do not attempt to use its power against me." Nordriss gave a stern warning.

"You have nothing to fear," Andras quickly assured the sorcerer. "I'd be a fool to cross the most powerful force in the Eleventh Dimension. And I am no fool."

Nordriss uttered an incantation and conjured a written pact stipulating their agreement, and they each signed the parchment.

"To our alliance." Nordriss handed Andras a goblet.

Andras sniffed the substance, identifying the drink as wine. "Our alliance." He raised the goblet, then took a drink. "United, we shall prevail. The Indithians and their allies will fall...trampled under our power."

"You will need shelter for the day." Nordriss opened a window to the gates of his castle, seeing Meical nervously pacing, awaiting word from Andras.

"Sunrise is too near his comfort." Andras looked on the scene with concern.

"Pass through and lead your men inside," Nordriss said. "When they are settled, return here. We have details to set in place. A world to conquer."

* * * *

In the depths of the palace ruins in Morpar, Tomes found Corin in an alcove, sitting several feet from

Angelique, watching over her while she slept.

"I was beginning to doubt we'd beat sunrise," Tomes said. "Traveling as falcons, we cut it close."

"Too close," Corin spoke softly and relocated to a position where he and Tomes could talk without disturbing Angelique. "I don't like taking chances like that with Angelique's life. Even though the days here are dimmed by the dust-filled atmosphere, the dense haze is not thick enough to prevent disintegration."

"I'm glad she has you. I know I can count on you to always put her first."

"Her life comes before my own."

"You've proven that." Tomes stepped toward a rock formation that lay on exhibit a couple of feet from him and sat down.

"How is Lavor and Pierson?"

"Lavor is seeing to them...that they have food and clothing."

"Good. All of this must be hell on them. But I'm glad they're here. In bestial form, they are a real asset in battle."

"Speaking of battle, Jordon just left for Sloe Forest to gather blackthorn to use in traps. He took several men with him."

"Blackthorn traps...not a bad idea. But it's a rather long trip to take for a little wood. Leaving from here, that's five and a half to six hours of steady flight. I hope he doesn't run into any trouble."

"He's resourceful," Tomes said.

"True, but I'm worried about hungry nightwalkers out there seeking food after nightfall...any food. Without Traxl-1, I can only imagine how bad it will get."

"He can better that flight time to closer to five hours with a bit of effort. I wouldn't worry. This is Jordon we're talking about." Tomes glanced at Angelique.

"She's not entirely at ease."

"No. She's worried not only about everything happening here, but also about Dusk and Dawn. Sometimes I question ever having given her those animals. I didn't expect the strong connection—her ability to communicate with them." Corin leaned his head back. "I dread the day they pass away. But with mortality it's inevitable."

"You should be resting. You'll need your strength."

"The same goes for you. But I suspect, like me, you have too much on your mind to rest."

"I can't get my mind off what's to come. Andras and Nordriss will travel tonight. I expect they'll find shelter nearby and attack tomorrow night." Tomes took in and released an audible breath. "Andras. Var. One and the same. I never expected his connection to Piiric so long ago, when Piiric was a child."

"Andras is intent on killing the dir cyohr...you."

"The dir cyohr. I'm still absorbing the fact that I've inherited the immortality and power of a sorcerer, half-demon entity. Our lives couldn't get any more bizarre."

"Wizardry isn't so far-fetched to me. When I was mortal, my family harbored a dark secret—the practice of dark arts—a blend of ancient Magyar paganism and Black Magic." Corin shared details of his past. "Father was a táltosok and taught his children the family art. But when I was changed, I left those ways behind, trading the dark arts for the dark existence of a nightwalker." He tilted his head back. "I've tried to forget, but certain memories are etched in the recesses of my mind forever, one being my uncle's funeral, and the saving of his soul. A ritual was performed using a bowl of blood, and each family member placed a mark on a shroud that covered his chest, forming a symbol required to enter the Tree of Lelkek."

"What is the Tree of Lelkek?"

"An ancient oak. Von Vadim purgatory. The last time I saw the tree was following my change, before leaving Hungary for America. I stood before the oak, and my uncle's face appeared in one of the tree's great limbs. The spirit slid toward me, seeming at peace, but then I scrambled back when my own face appeared alongside his...something I've never understood because the Angel of Death took my soul during my conversion."

"Where does the angel take the souls he collects?"

"No one living has that answer."

"So, your soul could be in that tree, with those of your ancestors. Not knowing what became of your soul when you were changed, you can't 'one hundred percent' rule that out."

"I suppose not. But it wouldn't really matter. I could never reclaim it."

Tomes reached for the pouch holding the Body, this time secured by two straps. *The power of resurrection, to recall souls from the realm of death.*

Corin's arms rested laxly across his knees. "What do you know about Nordriss?"

"Piiric knew him well. He's more powerful than you could imagine. I'll brief you later, I don't want to wake Angel."

Corin nodded.

"I called a meeting for sunset. Everyone needs to know what to expect." Tomes glanced at Angel sleeping. "I hate knowing she's going into battle."

"There's no stopping her. But I will do all I can to keep her safe."

"I'm counting on that." Tomes pushed himself up. "You need to bring your A game, so get some rest. I'll see you at sunset."

Tomes left Corin and found Kara tucked away in her own private cubby—a partially collapsed room several chambers from where Corin and Angelique rested. Waking her as he climbed over a pile of debris, she smiled, pleased to see him.

"Can we talk?" He waited for her approval.

Kara made room next to her.

"You have no idea how scared I was when I learned you'd been taken by the Örök Vér...worried what Jax might do."

"He didn't hurt me." Kara leaned against him. "His ego's been bruised, but he'll get over it. He doesn't understand our attraction."

"I was so hard on you. They could have killed you."

"I was far from innocent. I hate the part I played in Jax's deception." Kara leaned forward and sought his gaze. "From the first moment I laid eyes on you I felt a connection. I love you, Tomes."

"I don't deserve your love." Tomes shied from her stare, full of shame and regret for his past actions. "I was unforgiving. How can you ever forgive my behavior? How I hurt you?"

"The same way you've forgiven me. You had plenty of cause for your anger."

"How do you feel knowing I'm the dir cyohr? That I have Piiric with me? Does it bother you...what I am?"

"The man with me here, now, is the man I fell in love with." Kara brushed her fingertips along his jaw. "I haven't known you long, but I know I will always love you, Tomes."

Tomes laid her back and kissed the small of her neck. "Tell me to stop, and I will."

"Never stop." Kara tangled her fingers in his smooth, light-brown strands, drawing him into a heated kiss.

Tomes peeled her clothes from her flesh, pulling away only long enough to shed his own clothes. Exploring her body, he tenderly grazed her flesh with his lips, feeling her quickened heartbeat, strong and rhythmic. Hearing her breath grow heavier as he strove to fulfill her desires, this time he was prepared when her monster emerged.

Meshing his body to hers as she clung tightly to his lean form, they generated a fiery heat that built to a savage dance, raging to a soaring climax.

Lying together in contentment, the signs of Kara's monster withdrew as Tomes held her against him.

"You are such a wonderful surprise." He stroked her shoulder. "I never thought I'd love like this again."

"You loved your wife very much."

"Yes. She was kind, beautiful...innocent. I can't help thinking of her as a casualty of my destiny, knowing everything that occurred six months back has led me to this point...to what I've become. If she hadn't been killed by Boldor, I would never have teamed with Corin and been thrown into this world of immortals. I wouldn't have met Jordon or knew anything about the Order of the Clythguard, or the Eleventh Dimension." Tomes repositioned in unease at the remembrance of Louisa, fighting back stinging emotion. "She'll always have a place in my heart. I hope that doesn't bother you."

"We've all lost people we've loved." Kara slid her fingers over his chest, stopping at his heart. "So long as I'm in here somewhere."

"Your name is branded." Tomes claimed her hand. "You mean so much to me, Kara. I never want to lose you." He propped himself up and gazed into her vivid, blue eyes. "I don't know what the future holds, but I offer you all that I have...all that I am."

Kara stretched up and kissed him. "What more could a girl ask for?"

14

Jordon tossed down a shriveled gabran, one of many carcasses strewn about the clearing in Sloe Forest that Andras's party had occupied. "Bone dry." He visually combed the area and immediately noticed that the number of blackthorn limbs earlier littering the perimeter of the clearing had drastically declined. "Let's collect what we came for and clear out." He felt uneasy.

Remaining in close proximity as they gathered blackthorn, a cry of agony suddenly rang out as a spiked boulder swung down from the treetops, striking one of the daywalkers.

"There are booby traps. Watch your footing," Jordon warned as he rushed to attend the injured party. "You have a stake lodged in your side," he told the injured man. "I'm going to remove it. Thankfully only one of the six spikes got you." With a swift yank, he pulled it free. "At least blackthorn doesn't affect us the way it does nightwalkers. This would have been hell for one of them." He helped the man to his feet, then called out, "I don't feel good about moving deeper into the woods, so stick to the perimeter. Abandon the ground search and take to the trees. But watch out for traps."

Flying into the trees at impressive speeds, the daywalkers collected an ample amount of wood in a matter of minutes, more than they could manage on their return trip.

"I wish we could carry more, but this should be enough to do the job." Jordon was confident that blackthorn traps would prove beneficial if properly placed, serving not only as alarms—announcing the arrival of the enemy—but also to slow the enemy's charge. "Prepare to move out," he ordered.

"We will not make it back by nightfall," one Indithian said.

"No," Jordon responded. "When night catches us, the hunters will emerge. With circumstances what they are, they're desperate for food."

"We will stay alert," another Indithian stated.

"There's something else." Jordon scanned the faces of the men. "I need to recruit three volunteers to accompany me to the nearby village. Discovering what we have here, that the nightwalkers have been reduced to feeding on gabrans, I don't have a good feeling about the human communities."

"I will go," one immortal stepped forward, with two others quickly following his example.

"Good," Jordon said. "The rest of you get moving. Cover as much distance as you can before night falls. We won't be far behind."

The men departed and Jordon and his recruits aimed for the human village, finding his fears a reality—a village left to vultures. Stepping over corpses, he couldn't imagine the bloodbath—a merciless massacre.

"The humans won't survive this apocalypse." He

shook his head in despair. "It's become an unrelenting land, a deadly and savage world."

* * * *

In the dark of night, fourteen immortals gathered at the rear of the palace ruins.

"Come tomorrow night, we all put our lives on the line." Tomes glanced at each immortal: Corin, Angelique, Jordon, Galvar, Vynce, Regent Fehre, Constable Lavor, Staca, Bren, Kara, Pierson and Patricia in bestial form, and Torq. "Nordriss will no doubt stand with the Örök Vér, and he is an ancient sorcerer...powerful."

Through Piiric's memories, Tomes knew that Nordriss and Piiric had once shared a close friendship. In the past, Nordriss had been one of only a few individuals to know that Piiric was a sorcerer, something no longer kept under wraps.

"What should we expect?" Corin stood between Jordon and Angelique.

"A strong opposing army. I can't say what dark forces he may conjure, but there's bound to be casualties," Tomes stressed the danger. "Some of us probably won't survive." He paused and scanned the group once more. "I understand if any of you wish to walk away."

"We all know the risk," Jordon spoke up. "We stand with you till the end. I believe I speak for us all."

"What is your position?" Tomes addressed Pierson and Patricia. "Are you with us?"

Pierson glanced at Patricia before responding with two nods and an accompanying grunt.

"None of us will turn our back on a world in crisis...friends that need our help," Corin stated.

"We are eternally indebted to those of you from

Earth who willingly risk your lives for our world." Regent Fehre stepped into the center circle. "From this day forward, we are all bound forever."

"The Indithian Army is ready," Constable Lavor informed. "I will see that the men are armed and prepared for battle before next nightfall."

Galvar took the floor. "Each side has a half of the Clyth. Andras carries the Heart. It is imperative we protect Tomes and the Body. If the Delghorlins were to obtain both halves, many other worlds would be endangered."

"We won't let that happen," Jordon asserted.

"Supporters have traveled great distances to stand with you in this final battle. Believers of the prophecy trust that the dir cyohr will triumph over our enemies. We are on the winning side." Torq's words were inspirational.

"Tomes," Jordon said, "about Pierson and Patricia's curse, since you've inherited Piiric's powers, is there anything you can do for them?"

Tomes faced Pierson and Patricia, closed his eyes, and concentrated. After a long minute, he reopened them. "Sorry. I can't help you. Not yet, anyway."

"You've performed miracles and stood against Andras." Corin pointed out how Tomes had used his power in Sloe Forest.

"I can't control when the knowledge comes to me...happening when it's needed. In this case, that's not occurring." Tomes didn't know half of who Piiric had been, and only a sliver of the power the sorcerer had possessed. "Maybe in time, as I learn more. I'm sorry, Sheriff."

Pierson's shoulders slumped as he exhaled with a groan.

"How is it that Piiric is long dead, yet Nordriss has managed to stay alive for so long?" Angelique asked.

That inquiry had awakened a memory, and Tomes saw a vivid scene in his mind. "Following Gaun's uprising nearly two hundred years ago, Piiric sacrificed himself to stop a dark sorcerer from seizing power, one of the last surviving sorcerers of this world's tumultuous past."

"Noble...brave," Angelique said. "Forced to hide what he truly was—half demon. And he gave his life for this world, leaving Nordriss as the last sorcerer."

"There were once many sorcerers," Fehre told her. "At one point in time, they ruled the divisions, but now, Nordriss and the dir cyohr are the last two sorcerers existing in this world."

"In this world?" Corin's brow arched.

"There are sorcerers in other worlds, but here, Nordriss, and now the dir cyohr, are the last," Galvar elaborated. "There has always been struggle for power over control of the Eleventh Dimension, with shifting of power primarily between sorcerers, Indithians, and Delghorlins."

"Being a sorcerer, why didn't Nordriss seize power?" Corin asked. "Does he have that power?"

"To answer that, I must tell you of High Deity Nuthura," Galvar said. "It was when one sorcerer wronged her that the sorcerers were thrown from power."

"Is Nuthura the same supreme being that was thought to have created the portals?" Corin's dark stare shifted to Jordon. "I remember the story you told me six months back about the history of the Eleventh Dimension and how the sorcerers abused their knowledge and power...why the portals in the other dimensions were blocked."

"No," Regent Fehre answered. "This was long after that time. Some supreme beings from Zarmeva, who have the power to cross dimensions, continued to make contact with the sorcerers. One of those beings was High Deity Nuthura. But when she was wronged, in her wrath, she warned the sorcerers that should they attempt to regain power, Zarmeva would wage war and destroy the Eleventh Dimension."

Jordon shook his head. "All because of one sorcerer's grave mistake."

"Who was the sorcerer? What did he do?" Angelique wanted to know more.

"His name was D'Arqua," the regent continued with the lore. "He used Nuthura to gain power and position, but all the while, he was in love with another. It was because of his deceit that the sorcerers were thrown from rule.

"It always involves a woman," Tomes couldn't resist saying, observing Kara's less-than-amused expression. "Hopefully, this won't affect me, since I am a sorcerer."

"You are much more than D'Arqua ever was. You are sorcerer, deity...prophesied savior of our world," Fehre pointed out.

"Nuthura must have gotten a little more revenge than just casting the sorcerers from power," Corin assumed. "Something a bit more personal."

"She ripped D'Arqua's heart out and fed it to a dragon." Galvar gave a blunt ending to the account.

Angelique's hazel eyes widened. "There are dragons here?"

"Not since the sorcerers ruled," Regent Fehre assured her. "It was a different world then, just as this is the beginning of a new age."

"An age of peace and prosperity under the dir cyohr." Torq faced Tomes and dropped onto one knee, pressing his fist to his chest. "Full allegiance to thee."

Being a symbol of hope and promise, savior to a dying world, Tomes had a heavy weight to bear. But he had no choice but to accept his immortal calling, for this was his destiny.

* * * *

A small group of bedraggled humans staggered toward Morpar Palace ruins—five women, several children, and three men.

"Nightwalkers attacked Junch," one of the men said as they neared Jordon and Regent Fehre. "We are the only survivors."

Fehre called for two soldiers to assist the people who were clearly traumatized and freezing in the falling night temperatures.

Jordon guided the regent out of the peoples' earshot. "The same as the village outside of Sloe Forest. If this keeps up, there'll be no humans left."

"With territories lost to the apocalypse, Traxl-1 has become scarce. Nightwalkers from other regions are searching for not only food, but new territories," Fehre said. "Survival of the fittest."

"Has anyone been in contact with Mirillow Traxl? What is being done about our lack of Traxl-1?"

"I received word from the Xallon Lowland Territory that he has begun producing Traxl-1, but any real quantity is going to take time. Weeks, I have been told, to create and then distribute supplies."

"Time. Something we don't have." Jordon sighed. "The humans have managed to survive in the past, but never under such severe conditions. Already weakened by the apocalypse, they can't stand against immortals who view them as prey to predator."

Tomes approached, and Jordon started to explain their situation, but he paused when the new arrivals gathered around them and knelt before the dir cyohr, recalling him from his earlier visit to Salmari.

"You're safe here." Tomes's presence seemed to

instantly calm their fears. "There are other humans here. They will help you."

"We stand on the eve of the Great Battle," Regent Fehre apprised them. "I will see that you are escorted north to a secret camp."

"With dwindling human numbers, the other mortals—those supporting the prophecy—should return to Jach Lagon Canyon as well," Tomes stated.

The regent and Jordon agreed.

"Some of us wish to fight." A man who stood nearby contended, having overheard. "Dreams led me to Jach Lagon Canyon, where I found the supporters' camp. We were brought together to fight. We are meant to be here."

"It's not likely humans would survive the battle," Jordon told him.

"I am willing to give my life," the man declared.

"In the wake of this apocalypse, it seems to me that your fight is against extinction. Food is scarce, making matters dangerous, especially for humans. I believe the reason you've been brought together isn't to fight, but to save your species." Tomes put their purpose into perspective. "Support me by saving humankind, and leave the Great Battle to the immortals."

The man knelt before Tomes. "I would gladly die for you."

"The point is to live." Tomes motioned for him to stand. "There are other mortals at the camp. Elders. Women and children. They need protection."

"With rogue nightwalkers out there hunting for food, they can't travel tonight." Jordon looked into the faces of the children, knowing how much they'd suffered in their short lives. "They can prepare for morning...to travel then."

Tomes nodded. "I'll talk with Torq and let him know where we stand."

Jordon saw only one promising sign in all of the cataclysm—the comet had passed, and worldwide disasters were subsiding. From what he'd pieced together through conversations with supporters who'd traveled from regions afar, he figured at least two-thirds of the world had been stricken, much of it destroyed by meteorites and fire, earthquakes and floods.

Another tremor. He felt the foundation rumble, knowing it would take a while for the earth to settle, certain there had been massive tectonic displacements triggered by the immense force of the meteorite strikes. But now, at least the worst of the destruction was past. A faint light in a dark quandary.

However, prophecy hadn't yet played out. Next would come struggle for power. War.

Prophecy foretold of good conquering evil, but that wouldn't stop the Delghorlins from pulling every trick in the book to alter that fate. And with Nordriss—the powerful evil—joining the enemy, Jordon had cause for concern.

"Look out!" One of the men yelled and pulled their terrified children close.

The sight of Pierson and Patricia in bestial form, emerging from beyond the ruins, ignited panic in the mortals.

"It's okay. They won't hurt you." Tomes assured the people. "Think of them as guardians."

The mortals were given wools and skins that had been scavenged from the wreckage and was led away to rest till morning.

"I want you to take several men and go to Junch," Regent Fehre instructed Jordon. "If the nightwalkers that attacked these people are still around, find out who they are and their intent...if we should expect any further problems."

Following the regent's orders, Jordon enlisted several soldiers from Lavor and departed for Junch. Coming to their destination, he found the inner village strewn with human remains...a horrific massacre.

"Watch yourselves. They are still here," he warned his men a moment before a band of nightwalkers surrounded them.

"You've slain an entire village," Jordon, sword drawn, threw words of anger at the immortals.

A nightwalker dressed in a blue, bloodstained cloak stepped forward. Stringy, black strands of hair fell over hooded light-blue eyes. "It is necessary to feed." The man scanned Jordon. "Your manner of dress. You are not from here. You must be a crosswalker."

"I'm Indithian...sentry." Jordon gave no additional particulars, staring at a single tattoo marking the individual's right cheek, just under his eye—an ancient symbol of life—morbid irony in these terrible times.

"Daywalkers from our capital city," the nightwalker said. "We seek only to find a new territory that offers food and protection."

Jordon maintained a defensive stance. "This massacre was necessary?"

The nightwalker scanned his surroundings, a hint of remorse showing. "Hunger took reign. We have no more Traxl-1 and food is hard to come by, not to mention competing clans."

Jordon stepped over the remains of a woman. "So, you wipe out human territories...women and children?"

"With no Traxl-1, our only alternative to human blood is animals, but with the disasters, few forests remain. And the areas that were spared are being hunted bare."

"I understand your hunger, but I'd never condone your actions, and I can't imagine the humans will ever forget these massacres, despite the circumstances. This dark history will haunt our world for centuries to come."

The nightwalker's gaze locked with Jordon's. "Daywalkers have done their share of damage to the human population. We have run across several villages overtaken by your kind."

Jordon hadn't considered rogue daywalkers in other regions, but he knew it was not only plausible, but likely. If territories weren't burning or freezing, they were flooded, and daywalkers would seek food, water, and shelter, the same as humans. And with resources scarce, it would be survival of the fittest.

"Daywalkers drive the humans from their land to the savages of an apocalyptic world to be picked off as prey. You may not be blood feeders, but you are killers. Tell me, who is the worse?"

Jordon stood in a moment of silent deliberation. "Where are you from?" He lowered his sword.

"West. We are Simleon."

The line was less notable than Delghorlin and Krivros, but Jordon knew it well. "What drove you out, sending you in our direction?"

"Fire. The region continues to burn,"

Jordon released a heavy breath. "The world is in a horrific state." He stepped around another body. "Since you've taken Junch, do you plan on remaining?"

"Till we are forced to move, in order to feed," the nightwalker said.

"Traxl-1 is being produced as we speak, but I can't say how long it will take to distribute the supplies. If you stay, I can offer a small amount...a temporary fix. Until then, feeding will have to be limited to animals, blood donors, whatever it takes to prevent further genocide of humans. These massacres must stop. Amid these worldwide disasters, they have no defenses left to stand against predators. If matters don't change, humankind in our world will soon be extinct."

"Predators," the immortal repeated the word with a snort.

Jordon wasn't sure whether he was irked or amused by the reference. "If you don't want to be swimming in vultures, you'd best clean up these bodies."

"We will see to it." The immoral was cooperative. "And we will take the Traxl-1."

"Fair enough," Jordon told him. "I'll send it back shortly. It should see you through a few days."

Leaving Junch, Jordon and his men returned to the palace ruins and informed Regent Fehre, Tomes, and Galvar of the situation.

"You will have to see Torq about the Traxl-1 supply," Fehre instructed. "It will not be much."

"They are aware of that."

"In the meantime, we should put together a task force with the sole mission of relocating human survivors," Tomes suggested. "Jach Lagon Canyon will be a perfect temporary sanctuary, but we have to consider that it'll take several years for things to turn around."

Regent Fehre concurred. "Even if the humans did somehow survive the nightwalkers, they would have the elements to contend with—bitter-cold temperatures and hunger. With sunlight filtered, they probably won't be able to grow food for some time to come."

"What are you thinking?" Jordon could tell Tomes had something in mind.

"Earth," Tomes said. "Is there any way that humans from this world could be marked so that when the time came to recall them to repopulate the Eleventh Dimension, they could be located and brought back?"

"I suppose we could equip them with shalym discs for crosswalking, along with a mark or spell. Something to identify them later." Jordon gave the matter a moment of thought. "However, I'm not sure enough discs exist, and it would take time to produce more."

"Wait," Tomes raised a hand. "There is a way." Another of Piiric's memories surfaced. "In Piiric's chamber we'll find a caller. A crossmarker," he revealed. "I see the object in my mind—a silver coin. It places a pen behind the ear, leaving a tiny metallic dot at its insertion point, and through a spell, the individual is tagged for recalling." He looked at the ruler. "This object is attached to someone Piiric kept in touch with in another world, but I can't see who it was."

Regent Fehre's brow rose. "He is blocking the memory. I guess he is entitled to a few secrets."

"It is a good plan, Tomes, but you should know, there are some differences in our humans and those of Earth," Galvar said. "Humans of this world have a second naval at the base of their head where an additional chord is attached during gestation. They also have a slightly longer spine and two hearts. But with Plameth, the relocation is doable. He will be with them to see to their medical care, so there should be no need to seek treatment outside our safe circle."

"The Order of the Clythguard compound, is it large enough to house the humans we're currently protecting?" Tomes asked.

Galvar nodded. "My concern would be drawing attention to the compound. It is secluded, and we have always made an effort to stay out of the public eye, but the locals have become meddlesome in the past. However, there are ways to work around that situation." The plan was risky, but he was favorable of the idea. "We could use the compound as a transient station—a base of operation—while overseeing placement in nearby homes. It would be best to keep them together, in the same community, till the recalling."

"I am going to leave you in charge of this." Regent Fehre passed the reins to Galvar, Tomes, and Jordon. "The Order now has a new assignment—the Human Crisis." He motioned to Jordon. "Inform Lavor of the relocation and have him assign some men with full focus on reaching the temple. We will need the crossmarker for this plan to work. The sooner, the better."

15

Jordon stood with Constable Lavor as he assigned jobs to regiments, tasks consisting of digging in the ruins to reach the temple, escorting the humans to Jach Lagon Canyon, and preparing weapons and armor for the following night's battle.

Leaving the constable to attend to the construction of blackthorn traps using the wood he'd brought back from Sloe Forest. Selecting key locations, he put men to work, engineering simple but effective contraptions ranging from staked boulders—as the one they'd encountered in Sloe Forest—covered pits, rigged trip lines that triggered spring traps, and tying down limbs, that when sprung, would thrust blackthorn spikes into unsuspecting victims.

Squatting to tie a line, he paused, feeling someone approaching. Turning as a shadow fell over him, he saw it was Galvar.

"You are intent on making them suffer," Galvar said.

Jordon tightened a knot. "There's nothing I hate

more than Delghorlins. You know that."

"Yes. Since Lehndra, you have been very transparent with your feelings. Even though I often silenced you, I always shared your views. However, with known Delghorlin supporters within the Order, I had to be cautious. But now, side by side, we will take as many Örök Vér heads as we possibly can."

"How do you think we'll fare?"

"I am counting on the prophecy being fulfilled as written."

Jordon caught sight of a lone figure, barely discernable in the backdrop. "Try not to be obvious, but we're being watched." He gestured with a slight nod. "What do you think of that guy?"

Galvar shot an inconspicuous glance. "Xylor. He is a nightwalker who claims to be from a distance region—the line of Hrazath Nal. It is a known line, but I am not convinced of his honesty. As you know, our army is primarily Indithian, with the exception of a few Krivros, but since we've been on Earth, he has somehow managed to climb the ladder to a high rank under Lavor."

"Anything else?"

Galvar shook his head. "I do not know him well. He likes his privacy...a loner."

"Something tells me we should keep an eye on that one. This isn't the first time I've caught him lurking in the shadows." Jordon continued working, pretending he hadn't noticed him, not wanting to give his suspicion away. "Over the years, chasing fugitives, I've learned one thing well...to trust my instincts."

* * * *

Spotting a large area of woods, desperate for sustenance, Andras detoured his party to the forest floor. Nordriss waited as the nightwalkers shifted to canine form and tore through the understory in search of prey.

Aided by night vision, Jozsef moved with caution, unnerved by the feel of the woods...its unusual silence.

"Something isn't right."

Lagging behind, he sensed nothing in the dark habitat.

There's no life here. No prey to be caught.

As the rest of the pack came to the same realization, they returned to Nordriss's position and reclaimed human form.

"We have to feed soon," Andras told the sorcerer. "Five hundred men, and no food to be found. Is there anything you can conjure? Animal? Traxl-1?"

"I assume there is a particular process necessary in creating Traxl-1, which is why Mirillow Traxl is the only source of supply. If given time to study the ingredients and mix, I could probably reproduce it, but time is something we do not have." Nordriss waved a hand in a curved pass. "I reluctantly offer Dremlon."

A window opened exposing his Dremlon zombies at rest in the hive he had revealed earlier. This time the view was up close, showing the creatures lying face-up in individual pods with their arms lengthened and pressed against their sides. Full body steel armor levitated above them, leaving their thick, gray-skinned forms vulnerable.

"I am going to allow you to pass through and feed. Their appearance is fearsome, but there is no danger. They possess no will of their own." Nordriss expanded the window. "I have but one stipulation—feed, but do not kill them. Take only what blood you require to survive. Creation does not happen overnight. They are not easily replaced."

Andras, knowing they had little choice, led a

hesitant clan through the window and fed on Nordriss's zombies who lay in a state of dormancy. Desperate for sustenance and frenzied by the warm, fulfilling rush of warm blood coursing his veins, he found it hard to pull away, bringing his paralyzed prey to the brink of death.

"Enough!" Nordriss was forced to intervene when his warning went unheeded.

Andras, realizing their loss of control, reached for Jozsef who fed behind him, and yanked him off his victim. "Stop! Don't kill them!" He called out to his men, rushing to dislodge the feeders from their prey, but too late to escape Nordriss's wrath.

Angered, the sorcerer cast a series of fierce energy bursts that immobilized several nightwalkers, the incident sending the others scrambling out of the pods for fear of being next.

"My men." Andras whirled and faced Nordriss who cast a second round of bursts that finished off the unfortunate few. "I could have stopped them."

Lehndra hissed and cowered against Meical, wiping blood from her mouth.

"Five hundred starving nightwalkers. You couldn't have stopped them all." Nordriss was unremorseful. "I did warn you."

Andras sought no conflict. "On Earth, we feed daily. Here, finding no prey, a day without fresh blood feels much longer."

Jozsef stepped toward Nordriss, staring at one of the zombies. "Do they feel pain?"

Andras observed the zombie's sharp, jagged teeth showing beneath drawn, thin lips. Then, cutting his eyes at Jozsef—the one he'd taken under his wing—he was disappointed by his bloodchild's sympathetic nature toward the creatures.

"The same as you and I." Nordriss laid a hand on his creation, using magic to calm the creature's convulsions. "The only thing I could not give them was a soul."

Nordriss, still visibly perturbed, ordered the nightwalkers out of the Realm of Dremlon and shut the window. Slumping, he appeared somewhat weakened by the ordeal.

"We lost control, Nordriss. It will not happen again," Andras assured the sorcerer.

"No." Nordriss shot Andras an icy glare. "It will not."

"The door to your realm." Andras gestured toward where the window had just closed. "If we can use it to pass to Dremlon, why can't we use it to travel to Morpar?"

"Crossing this many men drains energy that I will need to bring forth an army of a thousand. It will take me hours to return to my peak from this one crossing."

"When you cross the army, it will weaken you?" Andras worried about his ally's strength in battle.

"I have one black cryal crystal that will restore my power. I will use it before battle."

"Only one?"

"It is not found in our dimension. It comes from Zarmeva. And even there, it is a rare commodity."

"How did you come to possess it?" Andras dared to ask.

"I made a trade," Nordriss shared nothing more.

"Enough said." Andras asked nothing more. "Night is wasting." He urged his party into flight, not stopping again until predawn, when they came upon the remnants of a human village that had been swallowed up by a colossal fault line.

"Vultures. They feast on the land." Nordriss shooed several birds from his path.

Andras surveyed the location and zeroed in on an area of heavy debris. "It looks like we may be able to take shelter here." He indicated a gap in the debris.

"Meical, check out the situation. See if it's open below."

"One massive earthquake." Lehndra trailed Meical who forged a course into the depths.

"It's not the widest space," Meical emerged, "but it appears to run a good 200 feet."

"Hmm, a tight fit for all of us," Andras said, "but it will have to do for a day." He was relieved they had shelter. "We'll rest here, and after the fall of night, set a course for Morpar, which will be several more hours of flight."

"We'd best get below," Meical gestured. "The sun is rising."

Andras stepped over a decaying corpse. "In this apocalypse, humankind is doomed."

Nordriss glanced at him. "They will not hold out much longer."

"Humans and rodents." Meical scoffed. "There is no great loss."

Andras cut his eyes at Meical. "What do you do for food when all other life is gone?" he spoke sharply.

Nordriss shared no opinion, leaving Andras to presume his position on the subject of the human condition.

"The world you created—the Realm of Dremlon," Jax addressed the sorcerer. "With a thousand zombies, it offers plenty of ready food. With control—"

"With starving nightwalkers, there is no control," Nordriss cut him off. "You have proven that. As I said, creation takes time. More time than you have."

"Are you coming below, Nordriss?" Andras followed the others to the opening.

Nordriss shook his head. "I will stay above. Reflect on some things...the night to come."

Andras said nothing more and withdrew into the ruins where he was immediately intercepted by Meical.

"Are you sure we can trust the sorcerer not to

renege?" Meical whispered.

Andras didn't immediately respond, rubbing the Heart of the Clyth that hung at his chest. "He is hard to read, but I trust he'll honor our pact."

"I hope you're right." Meical chose a spot and sat down. "We need him to defeat the dir cyohr."

"An army of the undead. Zombies." Andras amusedly laughed, considered that was how his kind was viewed on Earth, as undead monsters.

"I find no humor in this situation."

"Funny to refer to other creatures as the undead." Andras settled next to him.

"We have no soul, but we are nothing like those controlled things he created. How is it they have no conscious intellect?"

"I think they do feel, hear, probably see everything, only Nordriss controls their every waking thought and movement."

"So, are they really undead? They walk and breath. They bleed. By all accounts they are alive. Without his magic, would they wake up free of oppression, or would they fall to death like puppets whose strings had just been cut?"

"Too deep a thought for me right now." Andras got comfortable. "But an interesting one. Something to add to the *Trove Chan Allu*?"

"No. My collection is focused on charms and talismans. Sources of power." Meical looked over the clan scattered about the hollow, and his gaze froze on Jozsef. "I have reservations about him as well. Especially since finding his brother."

"He knows where his loyalties lie."

"Does he?" Meical leaned against a smooth area of rock. "I wouldn't underestimate the bond of twins."

"I am his father. And yours," Andras said in a hushed voice. "Would you turn on me?"

"I would die for you."

"Which is why I granted you the daggers."

"The daggers." Meical reached for one. "Why did you ever part with them? You have no other weapon that matches what they're capable of."

"Being ancient, I am more than skilled in taking heads. And I was confident you would always remain close with the daggers...have my back."

"I will never leave you, Andras. Something you cannot trust with Jozsef."

"You and Jozsef, when will this rivalry end? You are both important to me."

"Jozsef and I will never see things the same way. I make no promises when it comes to him, but I will never let *you* down."

"I know."

"You wish you were as confident about Jozsef as you are about me," Meical stated. "I hope he proves me wrong. For your sake."

Andras caught their subject's gaze when Jozsef glanced their way from the far side of the hollow as if intercepting the conversation. Without responding to Meical's last remark, Andras got up and meandered through the group, bypassing Lehndra, Jitters, and Jax as he aimed for Jozsef.

"Rest while you can. We have a long night ahead," he told his clan who lay in very cramped, confined quarters.

In such close proximity to one another, too much of his conversation with Meical had been shared with eavesdroppers. He could block his thoughts, but not his voice.

Reaching Jozsef, Andras circled him once before sitting. "Any problems with recurring claustrophobia?"

"I'm doing OK."

"You've conquered the fear."

Jozsef repositioned. "Learned to cope, thanks to you."

Observing a break in the rubble, Andras investigated and discovered a small alcove. Wishing to escape prying eyes, he motioned for Jozsef to follow. "About Meical, I understand his concern," he spoke quietly. "The bond between twins can be strong. He's afraid you may be tempted to switch sides. Tell me I have nothing to worry about."

"My loyalty is to you, Andras."

"You must have feelings about your brother."

"I hardly know him. It's been five hundred years."

Andras leaned close. "What is time to blood? It binds you. In more ways than one."

"I possess your blood as well. So does Corin. We are both tied to you."

"I'd hoped the day would never come that you'd learn that fact—that I'd changed your brother."

"I don't understand why you hid Corin's immortality from me. You've kept so much secret. The Eleventh Dimension. Being Delghorlin."

"I knew your brother would likely have the special blood necessary for Delghorlin change, so I went after him."

"I told you all about my life in those first weeks. You knew right where to find him."

"Yes," Andras admitted. "My plan was for him to join our clan. How unique it would have been...identical Delghorlin twins."

"It didn't work out that way."

"No. After transformation, he fled. I never knew his location."

"You should have told me he was alive. That you'd changed him." Jozsef averted his stare.

"Yes," Andras said. "Maybe I should have."

"Water under the bridge, I guess."

"I have many immortal children, Jozsef, but you, I view as a true son."

"And Meical, he is very close to you."

"Yes. He is important to me." Andras knew Jozsef had overheard part, if not all, of his conversation with Meical. "What you overheard—"

"You gave him the daggers, to keep him safe, not me."

Andras drew close, till touching, and spoke under his breath. "He is not as levelheaded as you. He is reckless, and for that reason, I worry. I trust you to make better choices in battle. Meical acts on impulse, without considering the consequence of his actions, like creating those beasts that we now have to contend with. I don't want him hurt...killed. Neither of you."

"He believes you don't fully trust me."

"I've looked after you all this time, Jozsef. Five hundred years we've been together. Would you turn against me now? Meical believes you will, because of your brother."

"You are my father, Andras. I would not turn on you." Jozsef straightened. "I never realized how long you've existed. That you lived another life, here, in this world."

"I've been around a very long time. Var is my true name, the only name I had while living here. But when I went to Earth six hundred years ago, I assumed other names and faces, as you know, including Gedeon, the face of your maker. However, like you, not all nightwalkers find it necessary to change appearances. Still, on Earth, we are considered monsters, and forced to hide what we are."

"Tell me about the vision you mentioned of the dir cyohr killing you? Now that he's been named, aren't you afraid it might happen soon?"

"I don't know for certain when it will come to pass,

only that it will. But I'm intent on preventing it. And with the right power in my hands, I will."

* * * *

At sunrise, Jordon, Constable Lavor, and Bren assembled the humans for departure to Jach Lagon Canyon.

"It will be a long, difficult trek. Ten to eleven hours with only brief rests," Jordon prepared the people. "We will have to keep moving to ensure reaching the camp by nightfall."

Plameth stepped forward. "For those of you who do not know me, my name is Plameth, and I am a physician. Let me know if you have any problems along the way. And be sure to ration your water. Hydration is essential."

Staca approached with Pierson and Patricia.

"We will be back tonight," Constable Lavor told his wife.

"I am coming with you," Staca said. "Should something go wrong, I do not want to be separated from my family."

"Another dream?" Bren presumed.

Staca nodded. "I saw a dragon blocking your path."

"There hasn't been a dragon in the Eleventh Dimension since sorcerers ruled," Jordon reminded her.

"Her dreams are not always exact." Constable Lavor reached for her hand. "But it is a warning of danger ahead of us."

"When you need a beast, I'm human. Being mortal during the day, I will be of no help," Pierson said.

"It wouldn't matter, because you're needed here," Jordon told him. "When night falls, you need to stay close to Tomes and keep him safe."

With things in order, the outfit set out and journeyed for hours without incident, feeling confident that they would make it to Jach Lagon Canyon on time and unscathed. Reaching a large valley, Jordon, leading the train, proceeded across the rocky terrain, but was suddenly brought to a halt by cries of terror.

"A magnakyr." Constable Lavor pointed out the beast that had picked off a man who'd been lagging rearward of the group.

Screams filled the air, and the people scattered as the great lizard's tail whipped with deadly force.

"They usually avoid people. This is strange behavior for them." Lavor stood between Staca and Jordon. "Magnakyrs are omnivores. They typically eat small prey and vegetation."

"Not when they're starving." Jordon visually trailed the reptile's long, spiny neck that stretched upward from a wide body to a height of over twenty feet and supported a horned, triangular head. "And I don't think he's had enough."

Jordon shot into action, but before reaching the reptile, it struck a man with its powerful tail, hurling him through the air. It then snatched a second victim, clamping down on a woman with its massive jaws.

Staca rushed to assist the injured man as the magnakyr retreated with its meal.

Jordon pursued the creature who stopped about a hundred feet from their group, which was not nearly far enough for his comfort. "You're planning on coming back for more," he said aloud to himself.

"Guard the mortals," Lavor yelled to Bren before rushing after Jordon.

"We're going to have to kill it," Jordon told Lavor. He hated taking the magnakyr's life, but he knew with such little food to be found, the reptile would continue attacking anything in its path, until it inevitably died of starvation. "I wish I had my 9mm right now." He pulled his sword. "The large scales covering that thing are like steel armor."

"Magnakyrs have one vulnerable spot." Lavor pointed out the area on his own body. "It is where their neck joins with their body." He then shape-shifted and took to the air.

Jordon followed and watched from above as Lavor maneuver onto the magnakyr's back and reclaimed human form. Gripping the handle of his sword, he aimed for a smooth dip the size of a man's fist, located at the base of the creature's neck. Raising his blade, the constable thrust it deep into the animal's body, igniting a thundering bellow.

Lavor quickly shifted to vapor, returned to the ground, and materialized. Jordon landed at his side just as the magnakyr fell, striking the ground with an amplified bang that sent a rumble through the earth. The creature violently thrashed to-and-fro before finally growing still.

"It's not dead." Staca pointed out that the magnakyr was still breathing. "We can't leave it to suffer."

Lavor retrieved his sword still buried in the great lizard's body, and with several forceful swings, severed its head. "He could very well be the last." He regretted the act.

Bren stepped next to his father and laid a comforting hand on his shoulder. "It had to be done."

"Humans aren't the only species in danger of extinction, but they are our highest priority." Jordon looked toward the distraught group of people. "So much destruction and loss of life. The Eleventh Dimension will never be the same."

16

Upon arriving at Jach Lagon Canyon, Jordon was dismayed by the sight of steam escaping the mountain that loomed over the entrance to the camp.

"There seems to be seismic activity building deep in the earth," Donian reported. "The temperature has risen to unbearable levels, forcing us out and into the open."

"Lava, beneath the mountain, with no warning?" Jordon watched as the people they'd just escorted intermingled with the supporters who busied themselves organizing supplies.

"We felt the tremors from the quake in Morpar, but there was no warning of a problem here," Torq told him. "Morpar's quake must have triggered this activity."

"Another lingering effect of the comet." Jordon felt movement in the earth. "That fiery demon isn't going to leave any part of this world unscathed."

"There are a few nightwalkers inside," Donian

further informed them. "They are trapped till sundown."

Jordon glanced toward the entrance. "Another hour. They don't have long to wait." He then looked back at the people. "This forces us to up our schedule. We have no choice but to return to Morpar. It's the nearest portal." He turned toward the constable. "Relocation is critical. It can't wait. And Earth is the only safe place for them."

"Deployment? Now?" Bren stepped alongside his father. "I'd assumed we would have days, weeks, following the final battle."

"We are not prepared for relocation," Lavor added. "What about the crossmarker?"

"If it hasn't been retrieved, we'll have to proceed without tagging the refugees." Jordon saw no other option. "At this juncture, what matters most is saving their lives. Once crossed over, the clythguards will keep tabs on them until the crossmarker is obtained. The task of guardian will be theirs for some time to come."

"With so many people, that will not be an easy task," Lavor said.

"I know. And this is just the beginning. Galvar will likely set up some sort of taskforce with the sole mission of locating and crossing over human survivors found in other regions. Something that cannot be put off too long. With humans being the main food source, their odds of survival are quickly declining."

Staca, who'd been assisting Plameth tend to several people, joined them. "The humans we just escorted are exhausted."

"Exhausted or not, they'll have to make it back to Morpar or die," Jordon stated bluntly. "Outside these caverns, above the morvormanite, there is nothing concealing their presence. After nightfall, which is nearly here, rogue nightwalkers, hungry for food, will swarm. Our small number of immortals may not be enough to protect them." He turned to Torq. "The people need to understand that this is their only chance for survival."

"What about another area of caves?" Staca suggested. "If we could get them back below ground...."

"With the seismic activity, I wouldn't trust any caves in this area." Jordon pointed out steam rising from cracks in the ground. "And there's not enough time to reach a safe distance before nightfall."

"The people will make it," Torq assured him. "The strong will help the weak."

Jordon looked at Lavor. "It's imperative that the few daywalkers that are here remain with the survivors until we reach the portal."

"With the Delghorlins due to arrive, timing could not be worse," Lavor groaned. "We cannot return with the humans in the midst of the Great Battle."

"I'm hoping we can secretly detour around the battle site and to the portal." Jordon clutched the shalym disc pierced to his side, knowing he'd need it soon. "Right now, someone must travel ahead to Morpar and then through the Passage to Earth. Everyone—Regent Fehre, Galvar, the Order—needs to be informed of our imminent arrival."

"I will go. Being constable, my place tonight is with the dir cyohr, leading the Indithian Army into battle." Lavor faced Staca. "I want you and Bren to stay with Jordon. Assist him with the relocation."

Staca reached for his hands. "I was expecting as much."

"I should be with you, Father, fighting for Morpar," Bren disputed his request.

"You are needed here, in this fight. Lack of a battlefield makes this mission nonetheless valiant." Lavor stepped toward his son. "I am counting on you to look after your mother."

Bren gave no further argument as Lavor pulled him into a hug.

"An hour of sunlight remains," Lavor said. "When the sun goes down, the nightwalkers will be on the hunt, so stay alert."

"With the ensuing battle taking center stage, I'm hoping we'll make to Morpar without incident." Jordon tried to remain optimistic in what he knew to be a risky endeavor.

"No one knows for certain when the Delghorlins will attack," Lavor pointed out. "Be careful out there."

Jordon nodded. "The same goes for you, Constable." He caught Lavor's stare. "Now, get going. Inform Galvar. Being head of the Order, he should manage the relocation."

"I will," Lavor assured him. "And I will send reinforcements."

"Good," Jordon said, and saw Lavor off.

Turning to face the crowd, he called for their attention, informing them of the plan to relocate them to Earth. Sparing no sentiment, he bluntly stated their situation, how they had little chance of survival should they remain in the Eleventh Dimension and warning them of the danger they'd be facing while traveling after the fall of night.

"Leave our home? Our world?" One woman said with despair. "For how long?"

"As long as it takes to renew the Eleventh Dimension...possibly years." Jordon quickly reviewed a few more details of the relocation plan, including the intent to mark the people for recalling.

"We understand," a man stepped forward. "This is our only chance of survival."

"For those of us who just traveled here—hours of walking—we may not make it back," one man feared.

"We will do all we can to help you." Jordon scanned their worried faces. "Gather only what's necessary. It is a long journey."

"Bring plenty of water, and cloaks and skins," Plameth called out the most important items. "After nightfall, temperatures will plummet."

Jordon caught Torq's shoulder. "Let's form a train and get moving. Precious time is wasting."

* * * *

Corin and Tomes emerged from the ruins at sundown, catching the final seconds of Pierson and Patricia's transformation.

"That is something you don't see every day." Corin watched in awe as his friends shed their human flesh and took on beastly forms. "I don't think I could ever get used to that. I truly feel for them...what they're going through." He extended a hand to Angelique who approached with Kara. "I've always considered myself cursed. But seeing what they're enduring gives me a whole new perspective."

"I hope a cure exists for them." Kara moved close to Tomes, and he wrapped an arm around her waist.

"Maybe when your powers mature," Angelique told Tomes.

"I've tried to connect with Piiric, but he hasn't offered any guidance. His presence seems to be fading. I am less aware of him with me now. I'm hoping he doesn't let me down tonight, when I'll need him most. I don't think I can summon my powers without him."

"You and Piiric are becoming one individual. Just remember, you carry his instincts and knowledge within you. Trust it. Trust yourself," Corin encouraged him.

Tomes nodded. "I am the dir cyohr."

"Yes. The dir cyohr." Corin emphasized his title. "Who would have thought so much was possible after only learning the truth of immortals six months back?"

"That was the turning point." Angelique caught Corin's gaze. "When I discovered who you really were."

He kissed her forehead. "The fates made me wait a very long time for you."

"It's surreal, the paths our lives have taken. Immortality. Other worlds. Destinies to be met." Tomes said. "What else is life going to throw at us?"

"Whatever comes next, we'll face it together." Angelique looked at her brother. "We're a family. Maybe not the most conventional, but I don't think stronger ties exist."

"Being a writer, Tomes, imagine the story you will get out of this," Corin told him. "A sequel to our first account, showing how our lives have changed since Boldor."

"A writer's dream, to live the fantasy," Tomes said. "Only I feel as though I'm on the edge of a nightmare. I hate knowing you're all here, facing so much danger, because of me."

"We've chosen to be here," Angelique reminded him. "Whatever happens tonight, no regrets."

Several silent seconds passed as the group's attention shifted to well-armed Indithians patrolling the area, suited in uniforms trimmed in emerald green.

"The end time battle." Tomes sighed. "I wish I knew what to expect."

"According to ancient prophecy, the dir cyohr is to bring about a new world order. As I see it, you will come out the victor," Corin said with confidence.

"I will bring it about, but that doesn't mean I'll walk away from the battle in one piece." Tomes combed back his unkempt, light-brown hair. "What if I've already fulfilled my purpose here?"

"According to Jordon, prophecy states that the dir cyohr will claim the great dark power—the Clyth." Corin recalled his friend's words. "And when it is finally in your hands, no one, not even the Örök Vér, will stand a chance."

"They have Nordriss. And don't forget, I only have one half of the charm." Tomes pulled the Body from the pouch resting at his side and rubbed it between his fingers.

Corin looked at Tomes. "I don't believe there is anything unseen by the fates. I have faith that the other half will find its way to where it's prophesied to be...with you."

"I hope you're right," Tomes straightened. "The Delghorlins, with Nordriss, it couldn't get worse."

Corin scanned their surroundings for anyone in earshot and then faced Angelique. "Before we go into battle, I need to know that you forgive me for making you Delghorlin."

She grabbed his hands. "You didn't know you were Delghorlin, and if you had, would it have changed anything?"

"I couldn't watch you die." Corin would never forget the fear and agony of nearly losing her to death. "But recalling Lehndra.... There would have been more to consider."

"Knowing, then, that you are Delghorlin wouldn't have mattered. I wouldn't have done anything different, and you would have made the same choice," Tomes told him. "We are all dealing with life-altering situations. You are Delghorlin. I am part demon. Neither of us chose what we've become."

"No. We didn't." Corin thought back to Gedeon. *A unique component that's required for a Delghorlin change to be successful.* "I was sought out by Andras because of my blood. All of the mortals changed by him possess a rare blood mutation, a unique component required for a Delghorlin change to be successful. Something Jozsef stated that Andras referred to as highborns—those fated for greatness. And being Angelique's twin, Jozsef believes you carry our same mutation, believing it was necessary for you to become the dir cyohr. However, since Piiric was a daywalker, and Delghorlins are nightwalkers, I don't see how it would apply to you."

"Piiric was also half demon. It makes sense that the mutation would be needed for merging two beings—a mortal and a half-demon deity," Tomes said. "I recall Jordon saying that prophecy describes the chosen one as a son of man, an outlander who will possess strong blood."

"That's right," Corin remembered.

"I was thinking about your demon half, Tomes. Is it possible that by joining human, daywalker, and demon, that each part was divided down?" Angelique proposed.

"I wish that were the case." Tomes looked down in wishful contemplation. "But I know I have inherited all of who Piiric was, including his half-demon side. I suppose if I were to ever have a child, the demon part would be much less in my offspring, but in my situation, Piiric and I simply merged into one person, with nothing lost except my mortality—what made me human."

"There's no fighting fate. Everything that's happened up to this point has been predetermined, starting with Boldor six months back." Corin messaged his tight jaw. "That was the first link in a chain of events leading to this point. That's when we met Jordon and learned about the Order, the Clyth, and the Eleventh Dimension. Then, I find out my brother is alive after five hundred years and tied to the Örök Vér, who not only want the Clyth," he cut his eyes back at

Tomes, "but you dead. The dir cyohr. Just another link of so many."

"I'm still not certain that fate can't be altered, even manipulated by other powers, such as the Clyth," Tomes debated. "Some believe there is a difference between fate and destiny, that you can't change fate but have a small window of opportunity to alter destiny, which would then lead to a new fate. But once that window of opportunity is passed, and the course set in motion, nothing will then change the outcome."

"Alternate fates?" Corin's brow rose.

"Don't forget about the Eye of Ephog. Piiric believed it to be a threat, which is why he kept it locked away. Anyone with the power to foresee the future can change destinies, leading to alternate fates."

Corin cocked his head, pondering the thought. "I prefer to believe in one set fate, but who am I to argue with a sorcerer?"

"Theorizing now about fate? Destiny?" Angelique's words broke their discussion. "Is this really the time for that?"

"You're right Angel," Tomes apologized. "What I should be doing is telling the three of you how much you mean to me. Going into battle, we should leave nothing left unsaid, with no secrets between us on what could be our final hours together."

"There are always secrets." Corin's lip curved upward.

"True. We all have our secrets." Angelique's blurt drew instant inquiring stares from both men. "Don't act so surprised, boys."

Kara laughed.

"I like the air of mystery." Corin pulled Angelique into his arms. "Maybe I'll get those secrets out of you one day."

"Possibly," she teased. "But a little mystery never

hurts. I wouldn't want you growing bored...losing interest."

"That could never happen." Corin bent and gave her a warm kiss.

"Being Delghorlin, do you think the others question our loyalty?" Angelique asked.

"They know we would never betray Tomes," Corin said. "Jordon had misgivings...a momentary doubt. But I assured him of our position, that nothing has changed, and I believe he trusts me." He glanced toward the western dunes where the Indithian Army stretched across the distant, blood-red field, seeing no void space. Torches burned along its perimeter, blanketing the land in an eerie glow. "That is an unbelievable sight. There must be a couple thousand men."

"It's surreal." Angelique grasped his hand. "I thought gaining immortality took away fear of dying."

Corin drew her closer. "I can get you and Kara to the portal. Regent Fehre can cross you over."

"I am staying right here, with Tomes," Kara was quick to respond.

"We are both staying," Angelique said and faced Corin. "My place is here with you and Tomes. Don't ask us to leave the men we love."

"I had to try." Corin stroked her hair. "You, alone, will be the death of me."

She caught his hand. "I'm worried about Dusk and Dawn."

"How can you be thinking of those cats at a time like this?" Corin didn't share the same connection with the animals.

Angelique pressed her forehead against his chest. "I have to consider the possibility of not making it back to them."

"They have the woods to hunt. If the worst should

happen to us, they would survive." Corin lifted her chin and looked into her hazel eyes that sparkled with striking flecks the color of the sun. This was the eye color she displayed most often, and Corin's favorite. "But I plan on both of us making it back to them." Holding her right hand, he turned her palm up. "I see a very long line of life."

Angelique gave a faint smile. "Being immortal, I should hope so."

Corin did all he could to calm her fears while psychically blocking his own uncertainties, fearing what dark power Nordriss might use against them, and praying they'd still be standing in the end.

"Lavor is back," Tomes announced the constable who was accompanied by Regent Fehre.

"There is trouble," Lavor informed them of the seismic activity at Jach Lagon Canyon, and the critical situation regarding the human relocation to Earth. "I sent reinforcements."

"They will make it. Jordon will see to it." Corin had faith in his friend.

"Galvar needs to know," Lavor said. "Being head of the clythguard, he should oversee the operation."

"He and Vynce are supervising the group working to reach the temple. I'll get him." Corin darted away.

"I hope they have made significant progress." Lavor moved toward the entry of the palace ruins, where Corin had just vanished within the mass wreckage. "The crossmarker is needed for the relocation process."

"I understand they're very close." Tomes stopped at the left of the entrance and further discussed the relocation, pausing minutes later, when Corin, Galvar, and Vynce emerged from the ruins.

Lavor related what had occurred in Jach Lagon Canyon and apprised Galvar of the relocation plan. "With you being head of the Order, Jordon said you would be the one to manage the relocation."

"Yes," Galvar concurred. "Being commander, it is my duty." His expression held concern. "Do they have enough protection?"

"Like I said, I sent reinforcements. Fifty men," Lavor informed. "They will meet up with them."

"I hope it is enough," Galvar worried.

Lavor looked over the dimly lit scene that held scattered torches. "How are things progressing here?"

"The infantry is in place. The palace perimeters and western dunes are secured." The regent stood tall with his feet parted and hands linked behind him. "We have patrollers watching for any sign of the Delghorlins."

"Good." Lavor was relieved.

"I have had armor and weapons laid out for all of you to choose from." He pointed out the area. "When you are ready." He caught direct eye contact with Tomes. "The dir cyohr's position is on the front line. We will all stand with you."

Just then, a daywalker stumbled out of the ruins claiming their attention. "We have reached the temple."

"Finally, some good news." Galvar motioned to Tomes. "You are the only one who can open Piiric's chamber."

"While you see to the crossmarker, we will suit up and take our positions on the western dunes," Regent Fehre said. "We will await you on the front line." He marched away with Lavor matching pace at his side.

Entering the ruins, Tomes, Corin, Angelique, and Kara trailed Galvar and Vynce to the temple. Approaching a statue that was partially enclosed along a tall wall, Corin thought it miraculous that it stood intact in the aftermath of catastrophe. His eyes widened when a medallion marking the center of the statue's chest suddenly spiraled open. *Amazing.* He watched with interest as Tomes reached into the opening and pulled a lever that set the statue in a backward motion. When it had slid far enough to allow entry, Tomes stepped into the chamber.

"So, this is Piiric's chamber," Corin followed the others into the room.

"This is what we're here for." Tomes aimed for the crossmarker, knowing the silver coin from Piiric's memories. Picking it up, he observed four vertical symbols that reminded him of ancient Egyptian hieroglyphics, then turned and handed it to Galvar.

"Good. There is no time to waste." Galvar started to exit.

"Wait," Tomes called him back and reached for a small, wooden box. "You will need this." He opened the box. "Place one of these pins behind each individual's ear. Then, hold the crossmarker against the end of the pin and say this spell: Compitum Erebus Evoco Percur Insero Earth. The pin will melt into their body, marking them for recalling."

"There are not many here." Galvar stared at the minute supply of tiny, metal slivers.

"With each pin you use, the box will generate another in its place," Tomes told him. "You will never run out."

Vynce peered over Galvar's shoulder. "Will the spell affect the Passage in any way?"

"No. The spells for tagging and recalling affect nothing else. When it's time for those that are tagged to return home, they will be alerted through a spell, and will return to their assigned Passage. In this case, that will be the Order of the Clythguard."

"What is the recalling spell?" Galvar asked.

"The symbols you see on the crossmarker have to be pressed in sequence from top to bottom before saying: Erebus Evoco Conligo Recursus Eleventh Dimension. That spell will then activate the homing, and those tagged will hear a calling to return to their assigned Passage in whatever world they've entered, days, months, or years later."

"We had best get moving," Vynce urged. "The Order needs to prepare."

"And I need to be on the battlefield." Tomes led the group from the ruins.

At the exit, Corin drew Angelique aside. "I have to try again. You and Kara could both accompany Galvar and Vynce and help with the human relocation to Earth. The thought of you going into battle is torment."

Angelique adamantly refused. "You know how I feel, Corin. I told you, my place is here. We do this together."

"I hate it. But I understand." Corin saw that Galvar and Vynce were about to depart and moved in their direction. "Good luck to you."

"And to all of you," Galvar reciprocated, and he and Vynce changed form and took to the sky.

Tomes aimed for the armor, looked over the choices, and lifted a breastplate. "This isn't as heavy as it looks." He passed several pieces of protective covering to Kara and Angelique. "I'll feel better knowing you're wearing these." Facing Angelique, he caught her hand. "Corin only wants you safe."

"I know." She looked at Corin who browsed the armor a few feet away, knowing he was listening. "You both understand why I have to stay."

"But don't expect us to be happy about it." Tomes turned and stepped toward Corin. "Have you decided on anything?"

"I'd rather not wear any of this." Corin didn't want to feel inhibited, choosing only a shield and sword. A choice shared by Tomes.

Helping Angelique with her gear, Corin gazed into her eyes, and unspoken words passed between them—

vows of eternal love.

"It's time to take our place at the forefront." Tomes glanced at each of his loved ones. "Be careful out there."

"You too, Tomes," Corin told him.

"Angel...." Tomes held her in his line of vision. "We've been through a lot together. You've always been there for me when I needed you. I—"

"This isn't goodbye, Tomes," she said. "I plan on sticking around a long time. Both of us. All of us."

Tomes nodded and then reached for Kara. Wrapping her in his arms, she surrendered to a passionate kiss. "You know that I love you."

"I do," she whispered.

Tomes glanced once more at the three people that meant the most to him, then claiming wolf form, he set a course for the dunes.

Corin, Angelique, and Kara shape-shifted and followed him to the battlefield, met by billowing red dust as they aimed for the front line, where they reclaimed human form the moment they reached Regent Fehre and Lavor.

Corin eyed Pierson and Patricia who paced to-and-fro before the great army. He then took note of flags waving at the forefront, designs representing the Kingdom of Morpar. Admiring the display, he observed three grand banners that proudly haled the Circle of the Morpar Kingdom in rich green on ivory, flanked by smaller flags, one swaying on each side of the three main banners. To the right side of the center trio waved a simple depiction of a large, glowing sun, while on the left, the flag held a familiar symbol of a half-skull, half-human design with a moon replacing the eye of a skull, and a sun replacing the eye of a man. This rendering, Corin recognized from Jordon's arm, portraying the eternal struggle between species of day, and those of night. There is no light without dark, and no dark without light. A mutual and peaceful coexistence. But conforming to this sense of unity was repudiated by the Delghorlins who hungered for world domination.

Tomes took his place alongside Lavor. "What now?"

Lavor looked at him. "We wait. It could be minutes. Or hours. Whenever they come, we will be ready."

Anxiously anticipating attack, the next hours felt endless.

"The Delghorlins, they are getting close." Tomes, who nervously paced, suddenly paused and gaped on the distant darkness. "It won't be long now."

Corin followed his gaze. "You can sense them?"

"It's an increasing heaviness. A dark foreboding that grows stronger as they grow nearer," Tomes explained.

"How long do we have?" Corin asked.

Tomes looked at him. "Not long."

Corin's body tensed. "I wish we had some idea of what to expect."

Tomes stepped toward the regent. "I'd like to say something to the men."

Lavor pointed out a large bolder, and Tomes climbed atop its flat surface, scanning the mass of militia filling the expanse.

"What is he doing?" Angelique spoke to Corin psychically.

"My guess would be motivation." Corin was impressed by Tomes's strength of leadership...character.

"Prophecy is being fulfilled." Tomes's words echoed clear and carried far. "We stand on this field, ready to fight those who bring ideals of oppression. Those taking advantage of a world laid in ruin, when every species is at their most vulnerable. But you cannot lose hope. I, the dir cyohr, stand with you. And together, we shall prevail over our enemy."

Who is this man? Corin was stunned by Tomes's speech, turning and watching as every soldier dropped onto one knee in a surreal wave, with each striking a fist to their chest.

"Full allegiance to thee." A deafening roar rolled on a slow-moving current.

Tomes continued. "Delghorlins are strong. There will certainly be loss of life. We will likely encounter dark forces, but remember your cause, what you fight for. Find strength in that pursuit. And above all, trust the prophecy."

"Someone's coming," Angelique announced a moment before a small flock of birds came into view.

Touching ground fifty feet away, the new arrivals claimed human form. Within seconds, they were encircled by Indithian soldiers who shot into action on Lavor's bellowing command.

"We are from Jach Lagon Canyon." One of the newcomers called out, his hands raised high.

"You are from Torq's camp." Tomes recognized him. "Why aren't you with the group now?"

The nightwalker knelt before Tomes. "We did catch up with them after nightfall and accompanied them for a while, but this fight—the end time battle— is what we have prepared for...our chance to follow the dir cyohr into battle."

Corin scanned the nightwalkers, observing their dark dress and rugged appearance, struck by their eagerness to fight. These men were passionate for their cause, ready to stare death in the face for the good of their world.

"You should have remained with Jordon's group, helping to protect the humans," Lavor told them.

"The constable is right," Tomes agreed. "But you're here now, and I'm not about to turn away soldiers. Welcome to the fight."

* * * *

Galvar and Vynce passed through the Passage of Dimensions to Earth, met by Umorius at the entrance to the central building of the Order of the Clythguard compound. A black flag waved in honor of lives lost, causing Galvar to grow emotional, knowing a third of the Order had been wiped out by Andras's sneak attack.

"Your timing could not be better," Umorius said. "Two visitors just arrived, within the past hour, asking for you."

"I was not expecting anyone. Who are they?" Galvar awaited a name.

"Two women. One calls herself Hediye." Umorius opened the door and followed Galvar and Vynce inside. "She refuses to speak to anyone but you."

Galvar was short on time, but his interest was piqued, finding the timing of their arrival curious. "Show them to my office. I will meet with them before calling the Order together."

Minutes later, Galvar greeted the two women who swaying through his office door. Both fair-skinned with rich blue eyes, they were striking figures, and very similar in appearance.

"My name is Hediye," one woman said, her flaxen strands with black undertones trailing below her shoulders. "This is my sister, Suna."

"I am Galvar." He offered seats. "How is it you know about the Order?"

"We have connections." Hediye gave no details.

Galvar saw she wasn't going to elaborate. "What has brought you here, to see me?"

She turned and looked out the open door. "Can we speak alone? In private?"

Galvar saw Umorius's shadow and called out to him.

"Umorius, gather the council in the conference room. I will be there shortly."

Vynce locked his sight on Hediye. "I am not leaving," he informed her. He then turned his stare to Galvar. "We have no idea who these two are or what they are after."

Hediye's gaze burned into Vynce. "Protective." Her expression softened. "You aren't like the other. I have no problem with you staying."

"You have no choice." Vynce walked to the door and shut it. "This is as private as you are going to get."

"What is your business here?" Galvar had never seen the women before.

"I will start with the name Zachius, the nightwalker you knew as Karlot Delacruse, who was also known as Boldor Enescu." Suna paused, awaiting a response.

Galvar straightened. "What was your association with him?"

"I knew him over two hundred years ago, and I know he is now dust." Suna followed Hediye to the seat he'd offered, a sofa pushed against a side wall. "If Zachius were alive, I'm sure he'd be stunned to find me living. If it weren't for Hediye, I wouldn't be. But we are witches, with a few special talents."

"I take it you parted with him on bad terms?" Vynce wanted to be certain of her meaning.

"He stole something very precious from me. Ten amber stones." Suna leaned toward Galvar. "I know they are here, and I want them back."

"You know how to use them?" Galvar asked.

Suna chuckled. "I created them."

"How do we know you are telling the truth?" Vynce was skeptical.

"The insects will die without care. Since Zachius's death, they have been neglected. They call to me."

Vynce scoffed. "You expect us to believe that?"

"It's the truth," Hediye attested. "A potion connects the insects with a caretaker, who then controls them. But without a caretaker, they will eventually die."

"I can prove myself." Suna stood. "Allow me to call them from the stones."

"Fair enough," Galvar agreed and sent Vynce to retrieve the stones.

Upon his return, Galvar poured the gems onto a table that sat between them. He watched closely as Suna uttered a few magic words, drank from a small vial, then sprinkled the remaining potion over the stones.

"Come to me, my biraz falcıları," Suna summoned, and the insects and arachnids seeped from the stones and climbed up her arms, onto her person. "We have been separated a very long time," she spoke to them.

"As you can see, they are back where they belong," Hediye told Galvar.

He nodded. "It seems so."

"Zachius was a toad. A cruel individual. He poisoned Suna in order to steal the stones," Hediye shared a bit of their history. "Luckily, I found her soon enough to call her soul back from death."

Galvar watched in amazement as the amber stones liquefied, and the bugs returned to the gems on Suna's command. "Amazing."

"I can only imagine the evil devised by Zachius with the use of my creations." Suna's voice held contempt.

"Your story is obviously true, so I return them to you." Galvar relinquished the stones, feeling it was the right thing to do. "Now, forgive my rudeness, but if we are done here, I have pressing matters to attend to."

"The Eleventh Dimension," Hediye stated. "The world is in apocalypse."

Her words were unexpected.

Vynce cut his eyes at the witch. "How could you

possibly know about the Eleventh Dimension? You had best explain."

"I told you, we have connections," Hediye answered. "In this case, my connection was a sorcerer named Piiric."

"You knew Piiric?" Galvar was shocked by her declaration.

"In life and in death. But now, he is gone," Hediye said with strong emotion. "I assume he has been transformed to another state of being."

"Yes." Galvar was intrigued by Hediye. "The dir cyohr."

Hediye lowered her head. "Piiric told me about the prophecy. I knew this day would come."

"How did you ever connect with Piiric?" Vynce sought answers. "To have known him...can witches live two hundred years? Not to offend, but just how long have you been living?"

"A long time." Hediye smiled. "I've been around, in more ways than one."

Galvar couldn't hold back a laugh, amused by her candid remark. "I wish we had longer to talk, but like I said, we have pressing matters. We really must go." He gestured toward the door.

"To the Eleventh Dimension?" Hediye drew back Galvar's attention. "Allow Suna and I to go back with you," she requested.

"Out of the question," Galvar denied her request.

"Nordriss must be involved. What part is he playing in this end time apocalypse?" Hediye asked.

"You really are well-informed." Galvar wasn't completely sure what to make of her. "The Delghorlins have enlisted his aid. We are not certain what to expect."

"I urge you to reconsider. I can help." She caught Galvar's arm. "I know things."

Standing short of the door, Galvar transferred his gaze to Vynce, who shrugged.

"We know the danger. We place no responsibility on you for our safety," Hediye added.

"Why are you so eager?" Galvar was suspicious of her motive.

"I owe Piiric." She gave no specifics. "He and I had a very special relationship, one that crossed worlds...transcended death."

Puzzled, Galvar stared at the witch for a silent moment. "I may regret this decision, but instinct tells me to allow it. Come with us. It will be a while before we depart. We first have some things to set in place."

In the conference room, the clythguard council rose to their feet upon Galvar's entry, and one of the council vehemently objected to outside attendees.

"Wait there." Galvar motioned to a corner of the room, and Suna and Hediye moved to the point indicated to silently observe the proceedings.

"Who are they are why are they here?" the councilman demanded.

"This is a special circumstance." Galvar took his place at the head of the table. "They are guests."

"How did they find out about the Order? They could be spies."

"They are not spies," Galvar vouched.

"We are no threat," Hediye spoke out. "We are here to help."

"If your word can be trusted." The nightwalker wasn't convinced.

"Enough," Galvar barked. "We have critical matters to discuss."

"What news is there?" another clythguard asked.

"The Great Battle is to occur tonight, but that is not why we have come. The human population has been nearly wiped out, bringing about urgency for relocation, here to Earth. They are being led to the Morpar portal as we speak."

Another immortal stood. "We should be there, fighting for our world."

"With the men we lost when the Örök Vér attacked, the rest of you are needed here to direct the human relocation. We plan to mark the people for recalling later, with this." Galvar displayed the crossmarker.

"The crossmarker." Hediye instantly identified the coin, pulling all eyes in her direction.

Galvar waved a hand for her silence. The witch truly knew Piiric and knew him well.

"I believe you all know Plameth," Vynce said. "He will be attending the humans' medical needs."

"Most of the humans are from a camp headed by a daywalker named Torq," Galvar added. "He will be accompanying them here."

"Another daywalker?" An individual moaned. "Not another Jordon, I hope."

"Torq is to be welcomed and treated with respect," Galvar stated with authority. He then moved ahead with their briefing. "I have been assigned by Regent Fehre to the Human Crisis. Our sole duty, at this juncture, is preservation of the human race of our world. These individuals have been through hell, and we must make this transition as stress-free as possible."

"It will be difficult keeping such a large undertaking under wraps," an immortal said.

"We will have to be creative," Vynce responded.

Galvar laid out a plan of action, deciding the most appropriate buildings to house their tenants until more permanent housing could be arranged. He then appointed various jobs ranging from supplying food and administering medicine, to acquiring blankets and clothing. "I know time is short. Just do your best. Remember, we have friends in every sector. Now is the time to utilize those connections."

Confident most major issues had been covered, Galvar closed the meeting and hurried everyone to work. Remaining for several hours to oversee the operation, he was satisfied they would be ready to receive the refugees.

Then leaving the final details in the hands of the Order, he placed his shalym disc in his palm and said, "Ta marof beegha," opening a portal that carried him, Vynce, Suna, and Hediye to the Eleventh Dimension.

17

The Delghorlins, having descended upon Morpar, converged in what remained of a wooded area a short distance from the palace. The atmosphere, dark and ominous, exuded a befitting feel for the impending events, like death in the still of night.

Andras called his clan together. "You will wait here while I check out the opposition."

"Is that wise?" Nordriss questioned the tactical move. "The territory surrounding the palace will be heavily guarded."

"With the Heart, my presence is concealed." Andras grasped the charm. "I won't be detected."

Nordriss dropped the debate. "I will use this time to bring forth my Dremlon Army and prepare for invasion."

Andras took wolf form and dashed into the surrounding woods. When he drew near the palace, he shifted to a raven and flew deeper into enemy territory. Spotting the Indithian Army gathered on the dunes, he circled the militia, scouring the infantry in search of Xylor.

There you are. A spot of rich red caught his eye—a red helmet plume in place of Morpar's emerald-green—as previously instructed by Andras.

Touching earth, Andras uttered two caws, capturing his spy's attention. He watched as Xylor fell back from his position along the back line and faded into the backdrop.

Andras hastened toward the ruins and ducked out of sight, waiting for Xylor, who arrived a minute later.

"Is it time?" Xylor scanned their vicinity.

Andras reclaimed human form. "Nearly. Nordriss is preparing for attack. Our army is close by."

"What is the delay?"

"I want to see the temple that holds Piiric's secret chamber. I assume it is well-hidden."

"The chamber is protected by a spell. No one can enter without the dir cyohr."

"I'm aware of that."

Andras had an agreement to uphold and wanted surcurity in knowing the chamber's location in case Xylor failed to survive the battle and couldn't lead him to it later.

Xylor knew better than to question Andras's motives. "The palace ruins are guarded, but I can distract the guards while you slip along the west wall and through the entrance. Just remember, if you take another form or shift to mist, you will automatically revert to your human form once inside; however, with everyone on the dunes, the ruins should be clear."

Succeeding in their plan, Xylor led him to the temple. "There." He pointed out a partially encased statue marking the entrance to the sorcerer's inner chamber.

Standing in the flickering light of a dying torch,

Andras marveled at the sight. "So many great treasures hidden behind this wall." He pressed a hand over the medallion marking the statue's center chest. "Soon, with the power of the Clyth, they will all be mine. Including, the Eye of Ephog—my debt to Nordriss." He recalled Nordriss's warning not to attempt to use the power of the Clyth against him. "I have a pact with the sorcerer." He told Xylor about the agreement. "I must deliver what I've promised."

Both immortals' attention was captured by a faint rustle in the passage.

"Do you think someone followed?" Xylor peered into the darkness.

"I got what I came for. Let's go." Andras motioned and followed Xylor back through the tunnel but was brought to a stop just short of reaching the exit.

"Master Constable Lavor," Xylor said.

"You followed Xylor from the dunes." Andras knew he'd overheard their entire conversation.

Lavor's eyes narrowed as he glared at Xylor. "You are a filthy spy. I trusted you." He stood in a defensive position with his sword drawn. "I knew that red plume had nothing to do with honoring the Hrazath Nal lineage as you had indicated...probably not even your true lineage, but instead a way to enable the Delghorlins to pinpoint you among the ranks." His voice held both anger and disappointment. "I had to know, so I allowed the modification, despite the disrespect it shows to Morpar in this time of war."

With the constable blocking their path, Andras scanned the area for a means of escape, spotting a support a few feet from where the Indithian stood. "His loyalty is to me...to the Örök Vér," he snarled, gripping his sword. "I warn you, Constable, you will not win this fight."

"Guards!" Lavor's voice blasted out in sudden

urgency as the nightwalkers assailed.

"Get out of here," Xylor told Andras. "I will hold him off."

Andras aimed for the support, and with several forceful rams, managed to knock it loose. "Get to this side," he yelled to Xylor as debris rained down, separating them from the constable.

"Look out!" Xylor charged toward two swiftly approaching soldiers.

Andras rushed after him, meeting the guards head on, and within seconds, had skillfully taken one soldier's head. He and Xylor then maneuvered around the second guard and out the exit, shape-shifted, and took flight.

The remaining guard pursued them a short distance, but wisely turned back.

"That is unbelievable," Xylor said the moment they landed and claimed human form.

Andras gaped on the spectacular sight of Nordriss crossing his zombie army from the Realm of Dremlon through a greatly expanded window.

"Andras." Meical hurried toward him. "I'm glad you're back. Incredible, isn't it. The Indithian Army won't know what hit them."

Andras sneered. "That's the plan."

"The Indiths have set blackthorn traps," Xylor warned. "They are scattered about the outer palace grounds."

"It's good to be aware of that," Andras said. "Despite that knowledge, it will be hard to avoid them all, and we must expect some to be triggered. But what is war without casualties?" His gaze settled on Jozsef who sat alone, watching the zombie army. *You always keep to yourself.*

Compelled by lingering doubt of loyalty, Andras drifted to his position.

"I'm glad you're back," Jozsef told him.

"Meical's exact words." Andras sat next to him. "What are your feelings about tonight, knowing your brother is on the opposing side?"

Jozsef's gaze was glued on Nordriss. "I told you, Andras, you have nothing to worry about."

Andras wanted to trust his protégé, but he couldn't ignore the strength of family ties, even after five hundred years of separation. "With that army, and Nordriss backing us, we will be victorious."

"It is quite an army...a frightening legion of devils."

"Devils that are going to carry us to the thrones of this world. And you, Jozsef, will sit among the royal as my son."

Andras closely watched Jozsef's expression, seeing no enthusiasm in all he offered. "You should be more appreciative of the position I offer...what I've given you. I've showed you a kindness, a partiality, I've shown very few."

"I've asked for no favoritism."

"You've asked for no favoritism?" Andras's voice rose in irritation. "You've never spoken to me with such disregard before."

"I didn't mean any disrespect, Andras. You know I am appreciative of everything you've done for me."

Andras hoped that was true. "We started out on shaky ground five hundred years ago, but in the time since, I thought we had forged an unbreakable bond. Things have been fine, until now...until your brother. But there is nothing I can do to change the past. There is no going back in time to reverse the choices I made so long ago." Andras pressed a palm against the side of Jozsef's face. "He may have been your brother for a short while in the distant past, Tomes, but I have been your father for centuries. Don't forget that."

* * * *

"It's worse than I'd imagined." Hediye stood motionless, soaking in the dismal sight of Morpar.

"Meteorite strikes. Earthquakes," Galvar said. "Just a fraction of unimaginable disasters the world has suffered."

"We better get moving and meet Jordon along the route," Vynce urged. "I hope they haven't had any problems with hunters."

"I need to be at the location of the final battle." Hediye had a promise to fulfill.

Galvar looked at her. "What are you not telling me?"

"I told you, I know things." She could not reveal the truth...not yet. "Piiric trusted me."

"The Indithian Army is gathered on Morpar's western dunes as we speak, but I have a mission to oversee—to save the human race of this world," Galvar told her. "When we meet up with our travelers, I will have a soldier escort you to the palace. Until then, you remain with us."

Hediye had a mission as well, but keeping her agenda private, she simply nodded. "Understood."

"I never thought to ask, being witches, are you shape-shifters?" Galvar asked. "We have a good distance to cover."

"We carry talismans of transformation." Suna displayed a pure white, square metal amulet that had raised profiles of three animals: a leopard, a falcon, and a draquagor. "Creatures of land, air, and sea."

Vynce took a closer look. "I do not recognize the sea creature."

"The draquagor is a shark-like reptilian," she enlightened him.

"Interesting. Where—"

"Lead the way," Hediye interrupted Vynce's inquiry

in an attempt to avoid further questioning about the talisman...about her.

Vynce's brow lowered as she pulled the talisman from his line of vision.

Hediye observed an exchange between the two men, knowing her sudden reaction had raised their suspicions. "If you're ready, we'll keep up."

Shape-shifting, Hediye and Suna took the forms of pure white falcons and followed Galvar and Vynce into flight. Moving in a northern direction, they had only flewn a short distance when they deceptively dove into a stoop, and without warning, altered their course.

Hediye heard a piercing cry as the nightwalkers became aware of the sudden maneuver, but with a preset cloaking spell, she and Suna vanished from sight. Now, invisible to the eyes of their pursuers, they distanced themselves and raced toward Morpar Palace, not slowing their speed until crossing the outer perimeter of the palace grounds.

Remaining cloaked, they zeroed in on the army situated on the western dunes. Circling once, they aimed for the gound and touched down mere feet from the hierarchy positioned on the front line. Shedding their cover and shifting to human form, they quickly dodged an onrush of immortals who'd been warned of their presence by a young, dark-haired woman.

"We come peacefully," Hediye yelled out. "Please, let me speak." Her eyes caught Tomes's gaze, intuitively knowing that he was the dir cyohr. Looking into his eyes, she felt a sudden surge...Piiric's spirit.

"Hediye," Tomes spoke her name, appearing somewhat dumbstruck.

"Yes." She held his gaze. "Piiric said you would know me."

"I finally see what he's been blocking," Tomes mumbled. "I don't see everything, but I see enough to understand the connection between you and him."

Hediye and Piiric's relationship had crossed worlds; they'd shared a love and passion for one another that was unparalleled. But knowing he was now merged with another person, she wasn't sure what to expect.

At that moment, Galvar and Vynce touched ground behind Hediye and Suna, and upon taking human form, Galvar immediately grabbed Suna's arm. "That was some stunt you pulled."

"Commander Mikhail, who are these two women?" Regent Fehre demanded an explanation.

"Witches, from Earth," Galvar told him. "I should not have—"

"I can help with the battle," Hediye blurted. "The dir cyohr knows."

All eyes turned to Tomes for a response.

"Do you know these witches?" the regent asked.

"Piiric knew her." Tomes's stare was transfixed on Hediye.

"How did you know the location of the Palace?" Vynce asked Hediye.

"I have been here before, with Piiric, prior to the reign of Gaun." Hediye swept her hair back, tilted her head, and pointed out a small metallic dot behind her left ear.

"Piiric marked you for calling?" Regent Fehre stepped toward the women. "I do not recall you, but I had been driven from Morpar during the uprising of Gaun, along with all other Indithians who did not support that overthrow."

"Gaun's uprising," Hediye acknowledged. "Just one of many signs leading to this end time apocalypse."

"The crossmarker...it was made for you," Tomes saw more of Piiric's memories.

"I didn't want to give up my world, and he had duties here, in the Eleventh Dimension. With the crossmarker, I knew to meet him when he crossed to Earth," Hediye explained. "It was Piiric's wish that I be here now, for this battle. He set all of this in place...for a reason."

Fehre's brow furrowed, considering her words. "It is your decision, Dir Cyohr," he told Tomes. "Do we dare trust her?"

"She's telling the truth." Tomes had not diverted his line of sight since laying eyes on her. "Piiric is still blocking memories from his time with her, but I've seen enough to know she had his complete trust. As she said, I believe he *did* set this in place."

Hearing those words, Galvar released Suna and stepped back.

"With that being the case, you are free to stay." Regent Fehre ordered the soldiers surrounding them to return to their positions.

"If things are settled here, Vynce and I should get back to our mission," Galvar said.

Fehre nodded. "Go. See to the human relocation. We have this in hand."

As the two nightwalkers departed, a woman stepped alongside Tomes and drew his attention to her. The manner in which she touched him told Hediye she was most likely his companion...his lover.

"Are you alright, Tomes?" the woman whispered while looking directly at Hediye.

She is jealous, staking her claim. Hediye sized up the golden-locked harlot, barraged by her own storm of jealousy. Blond hair, blue eyes, and dressed a little too girly for her taste, this woman was her complete opposite.

Looking at the dir cyohr, he did not have Piiric's face, but she felt Piiric's spirit within him, an energy that stirred intense, lingering emotions.

"I am Angelique, the dir cyohr's sister." The dark-haired woman who'd sensed their arrival stepped toward her.

Hediye took quick note of her protective male companion. "I am Hediye. This is my sister, Suna," she responded.

Suna greeted her with a silent nod.

"You claim you can help with the battle," Regent Fehre said. "How?"

"Piiric instructed me to never reveal my commission." Hediye gave him no information. "I will know when the time is right to act."

Lavor scowled. "A commission you refuse to disclose? We are to simply trust the word of a stranger—a witch—without question?"

"Trust Piiric," Tomes told him.

The regent's gaze bore into Hediye. "Be forewarned, this battle *will* claim lives. We, Indithians, fight for our world. Is your promise to Piiric worth that great a risk, for a world not your own?"

"I would face any danger for Piiric," Hediye declared. "My sister and I, we understand that we're putting our lives in jeopardy, but I will not let Piiric down."

Tomes stepped away from Kara and moved toward Hediye.

Despite death, or altered forms, you will always come to me if you're able. She did not say the words aloud.

"Tomes?" Kara started to reach for him, but Angelique drew her back.

"Give them a minute," Angelique told her. "Remember, this is Piiric's past, not Tomes's."

Hediye reached out and cupped Tomes's hands. "Piiric." She searched his eyes. "Please, come to me. This may be our last chance."

His spirit was fading, and she knew that soon he

would be fully merged with the dir cyohr.

Tomes's eyes closed. "Hediye," he said, and reopened them. Then, pulling her into his arms, he placed a soft kiss on her plump lips.

"Piiric." Tears filled her eyes when she heard his voice.

"The time has come." He ran his thumb over a blue stone adorning her middle finger.

She couldn't stop tears from flowing. "This is the end for you and me, isn't it?"

He wiped her tears away. "Live your life, Hediye," he whispered in her ear. "It is time to revisit the past. Nordriss needs you."

"What!" Lavor started to advance, but Regent Fehre reined him back.

"This is Piiric speaking," Fehre cautioned him.

Tomes closed his eyes again, and upon reopening them, immediately released Hediye, aware of everything that had just occurred. "You knew Nordriss in the past," he stated. "You knew him well."

"Yes," Hediye admitted.

"Why would Piiric say that Nordriss needs you?" Lavor wanted an explanation. "I am not comfortable with this. He is our enemy."

"Calm yourself, Constable." The regent raised a hand.

Hediye knew the men wanted answers, but all she could think of at that moment was the feel of Piiric's kiss. Rubbing her arms as a chill swept over her, she yearned for his touch to warm her, but she had to accept that he was gone. It wouldn't be easy, but she would find a way to carry on without him, forevermore to lack a part of her soul.

* * * *

Jordon halted the travelers as two patrolling soldiers landed in the road before them.

"We just spotted the Delghorlins arriving in Morpar," one alerted.

"That's good news for us. At least we know we won't be crossing their path," Jordon said.

Staca stood next to him. "One less thing to worry about, and we are over halfway there."

"Let's hope luck stays with us." Jordon sent the soldiers back to their patrol. "With the Delghorlin uprising, all of Morpar is at risk, and there are no soldiers to spare. We are lucky to have the fifty men the constable sent. Even that small number could tip the scales in our enemy's favor."

"The Indithian Army is strong."

Jordon wondered how many soldiers would die before dawn...how much blood would spill on Morpar's western dunes. But knowing Staca feared for Lavor, he kept his thoughts to himself. "Like I said, we've been lucky so far, but the longer we're out here, the risk of detection grows. We need to move faster."

"We all know the urgency, but we cannot ask more from these people than they are capable of giving. They are exhausted." She reached for his arm. "Look at them. A few minutes of rest would help them."

"And danger grows with each rest we take. But you're right. They can only take so much." Jordon stopped and turned around. "Take a short rest," he called out, watching as Plameth hustled to-and-fro, attended to as many people as possible while instructing the travelers to hydrate.

"You should say something to encourage them," Staca persuaded him.

"It couldn't hurt." Jordon raised his hands and gained the peoples' attention. "I know how hard this is for you, but we are well over halfway to our destination."

"We should not be stopping," a young man said. "Knowing the danger, we should keep moving."

"You are stronger than others traveling with you," Staca told the man. "Consider those around you who lack your youth and endurance."

Just then, Bren rushed toward Jordon and Staca from the rear of the train where he'd been patrolling. "We have been detected!" His urgent call claimed full attention.

"How many?" Jordon inquired.

"From what I can tell, less than ten," Bren answered.

Springing into action, Jordon had the soldiers herd the people into a tight circle. Then, quickly barking out several orders, he positioned half of the daywalkers along the train's perimeter while the rest morphed and either took to the sky or bounded into the wall of darkness. He was intent on turning the tables on this small gang of rogues, making the hunters the hunted.

"Listen to me." Jordon's voice rang out over the rising panic. "Put out all but two torches," he instructed, observing Staca who moved through the group, urging the people to remain calm. "Keep your eyes open," he called out to the surrounding guards.

As time slowed around him, he caught sight of a tan wolf lunging from the darkness—a rogue hunter. Rushing to intercept the assailant, they collided mid-air, and the wolf shifted to human form, ravenous with hunger.

Jordon faced the hunter. "These people are protected. I give you once chance to leave with your life."

Screams echoed as the wolf lunged again, forcing Jordon to behead him.

"Another," Torq alerted as a second nightwalker dove into the midst of the panicked crowd and tore into a woman's shoulder. "Stop him!"

Several soldiers managed to pry the monster off his prey, but not before serious damage was done.

Plameth rushed to assess the woman's condition. "She cannot be saved."

Torq bent next to the woman, holding her hand. "I'm sorry," he whispered.

"She's gone." Jordon saw her body fall lax.

The soldiers patrolling the air and the outskirts returned. With only one life lost, they had successfully fended off attack.

"Two got away," one Indithian informed.

"Not good news." Jordon knew the hunters would continue to pursue. This was only the beginning.

"We have another problem." A daywalker approached Torq. "We lost Donian. The last I saw him, one of the nightwalkers had taken him down into a ravine."

"Show me," Torq demanded. "We will catch up with you," he told Jordon.

"Be careful." Jordon didn't attempt to stop him. Looking over the crowd of people, he had his own concerns. "We have to keep moving."

Leading the train onward, the next half-hour passed with no further attacks. Remaining on high alert, the soldiers quickly surrounded Torq and his guide upon their return.

"It's OK." Jordon waved the soldiers down when the two immortals shifted to their human forms. "You didn't find him?" Jordon observed the sorrowful expression plaguing his comrade's face.

Torq cleared his throat. "He was a friend."

"His death won't be in vain. We will get these refugees to the portal."

"I could spot you a mile away," Torq told Jordon. "There is too much light."

Jordon halted the train, seeing that two burning torches had become six. "There is too much light," he called out. "Keep only two burning. You. And you." He pointed out two individuals. "We need to stay as low-key as possible."

Jordon understood their fears. Without light, visibility was slim to none for the humans, and in their situation, utter darkness would not only escalate anxiety, but it would slow down travel.

"The threat of more attacks is high, so keep the group tight, and stay alert." He scanned the group. "Also, as we grow closer to Morpar Palace, we will be forced to detour off the road and into a remote tract of woods in order to avoid contact with Delghorlin uprisers and the end time battle. That territory, as some of you know, was devastated by meteorites. It may be a rough passage, but I'll do my best to lead you safely through."

Plameth, assisting an ailing woman, spoke out. "We will do whatever you say, Jordon. Lead on."

Moving forward, Jordon glanced back at Staca who meandered amid the crowd, offering encouragement to the weary individuals. "Lavor's a lucky man."

"Yes." Torq joined him in the lead. "It sure is a long trek on foot from Jach Lagon Canyon to Morpar." His white hair glowed like a beacon in the darkness. "A real eye-opener for us shape-shifters who depend too much on our abilities."

"Living on Earth, I've done my share of groundwork."

"Earth. I suppose it is a much different place."

"In some ways, and the same in others." Jordon peered into the dark sea of obscurity before him. "I thought Galvar would have joined us by now. I wonder what's holding him up. With hunters nipping at our heels, he can't get here soon enough."

18

Andras called out to his armed men. "Shift and form a pack. It's time for action."

"The Dremlons are not shifters," Nordriss informed him. "They have to proceed on foot."

Andras hadn't considered that handicap, but they were close enough to move in on foot without losing too much time.

"You've used the black cryal crystal since crossing over the army." Andras observed the sorcerer's renewed energy...an extraordinary vigor.

Nordriss's eyes swirled a mixture of colors as they slowly turned black. "I am ready."

Andras nodded. "Move out," he yelled.

Clad in full armor, the Dremlon zombies—large forms with yellow glowing eyes—shook the ground as they marched in steady unison. The Örök Vér loped in wolf form along the fringe of the magnificent force, confident in their association.

Soon, drawing near the palace, Andras halted the

legion before descending. Looking over his clan, who'd shifted back to human form, he knew many of them would lose their lives in the hours to come. "Delghorlins, you will continue from here by air," he instructed. "With blackthorn traps hidden along the palace boundary, that is safest."

"More lay within the grounds," Xylor warned, "so watch yourselves."

"What is their number?" One immortal asked.

Andras looked to Xylor for the answer.

"Two Thousand," Xylor stated.

"They may have us outnumbered, but we have Delghorlin strength, a thousand giants, and Nordriss on our side." Andras pointed out his side's advantages. "We will overpower them."

"By air, you can guide us in our charge," Nordriss told Andras. "I suspect their forces are gathered on the dunes, facing northward."

"Yes." Andras confirmed.

"The Delghorlins will attack from the south while you and I lead the Dremlons on a head-on charge from the north—the direction they're expecting. However, this army of dark zombies, that is something they don't know is coming. There lies our real advantage."

Nordriss leaned close to Andras, his eyes now a stormy combination of achromatic hues. "Do not forget our pact, Andras," he whispered in a deep, fixed tone.

"Xylor has shown me the entrance to the temple. One way or another, the Eye of Ephog will be yours."

"I am sure you have weighed all options. As I see it, if the dir cyohr cannot be captured alive, he must die by no other means but the Clyth. If his life is taken in any other way, Piiric's chamber will be lost forever, and with it, the Eye."

"My clan understands that the dir cyohr is my mark, and mine alone," Andras assured him. "I have made that absolutely clear."

Tomes was Andras's primary target. His sole mission was to seize the Body, no matter the cost.

"Good." Nordriss held a stern stare. "There is no room for error."

Lehndra turned her head in short, quick turns, mimicking the movements of a bird. Andras, sharing her detection of an outside presence, motioned to Meical who stood across from him.

Meical shot into action, flushing a spy from hiding—a spotted owl that leapt to a narrow escape at the last possible second.

"Let him go!" Andras stopped Meical from initiating pursuit. "Take the clan and follow him. Nordriss and I won't be far behind with the Dremlons."

Andras sought Jozsef's position, hoping he could trust him, and wishing they had a moment to talk before separating. But there was no time to spare.

As the Delghorlins traded flesh for feathers and leapt into flight with fierce energy, Nordriss roared a command, and the Dremlon army assailed from the woods. Cracks and thuds of triggered traps whooshed through the air as the giants stormed the grounds, aimed for the western dunes.

Andras, catching sight of a second unexpected arrival, rushed the on-comer, but suddenly slowed his gait when the individual claimed human form. "Umorius. What brings you here now? We just initiated attack."

Matching their gait, Umorius was visibly astonished by the sight of the Dremlon army. "Two witches are here, in the Eleventh Dimension. They crossed over with Galvar and Vynce. One claims a past relationship with Piiric. I thought you should know."

Nordriss suddenly halted movement and shot a frightful stare at Umorius. "Hediye?"

"Yes." Umorius held a puzzled expression. "She is with a sister called Suna. After a meeting they had with Galvar and Vynce, I saw Suna with a bag that held ten amber stones...stones that had belonged to Boldor."

"I hope this won't be trouble." Andras looked at Nordriss and saw red flash in the sorcerer's eyes.

Nordriss didn't respond as he resumed his stride, this time moving with a fierce determination. Andras kept pace, wondering what his intense reaction meant.

"There's one other thing." Umorius followed. "Galvar has set into place a plan for human relocation from here to Earth. They are crossing over the survivors tonight."

"Trying to save what's left of our human race...to later repopulate," Andras said.

"Humans," Umorius belittled. "What wasted effort."

"Am I the only nightwalker who understands the importance of humans in our world?" Andras snapped. "Without food we die. And daywalkers would not make easy prey."

Umorius lowered his gaze. "I was spotted leaving the Order," he informed Andras. "I have a feeling Galvar has grown suspicious of me and set a spy."

"In that case, your place is now here, fighting alongside your brethren," Andras told him. "The Great Battle...this is history in the making."

* * * *

Tomes glanced to his right at Pierson and Patricia who paced back and forth along the front line. His gaze then trailed to Angelique, sharing her unease as she sensed something coming. "They're here."

Commotion arose from the far reaches of the dunes. The Delghorlins had struck from behind.

"It has begun!" Lavor called out.

"Pierson." The beast turned in response to Tomes's call. "Cover the back."

Pierson hesitated as if undecided, but he was quickly spurred forth by sounds of violent upheaval. He and Patricia darted away and disappeared into the darkness embedding the lattermost passel.

"God help us." Tomes's sight froze on an unholy sight coming into view from the north—a profusion of large, armed figures drifting in their direction from the dark, hazy distance. He took in a deep breath and exhaled, alarmed by the frightful appearance of the opposing army.

"During the Great Battle, a powerful evil will arise," Lavor quoted prophecy.

"Nordriss's power." Regent Fehre stood aghast. "There is no telling what lies beneath that armor."

Lavor gripped his sword. "We will find out soon enough."

"Their eyes," Angelique mumbled. "They glow."

Lavor stood ready to charge. "That will make them easier to pinpoint."

"They're triggering the blackthorn traps," Corin said. "But it's not slowing those giants down."

In the dim distance, Tomes's vision zeroed in on a figure boldly advancing in close accompaniment of two immortals. *Long hair and cloak—Nordriss.*

Corin looked at Tomes. "That must be Nordriss."

"Yeah. That's him." Tomes knew the sorcerer from Piiric's memories. Then, getting a flood of new images, he cut his eyes to Hediye who returned his stare.

"Umorius. He is with Andras. I cannot believe he has betrayed us." Lavor growled. "With Xylor, that makes two snakes tonight."

"Spies hiding among us." Fehre sighed. "There is no end to treachery and deceit."

"Andras will be after the Body...at any cost," Lavor

reminded Tomes.

"And I'll protect it at all costs," Tomes declared.

"It's time." Regent Fehre faced Tomes, then knelt. "Full allegiance to thee!" he cried out.

The army lowered in a timely wave with each man pressing a fist to their center chest, and in mass unison pledged: "FULL ALLEGIANCE TO THEE!"

"Prepare to charge!" The regent waved his sword above his head. "We await your command, Dir Cyohr."

Tomes raised his arm, holding up three fingers symbolizing the trinity. "For Morpar. For the Eleventh Dimension. With fate on our side, victory be ours!" He called out a battle cry.

Morpar's flags billowed as the army returned his last three words in a spirited roar: "VICTORY BE OURS!"

Giving the signal to charge, the army raged forward in a deafening roar. Many daywalkers shifted to animal forms, but others, including Tomes and those who charged at his side, chose to remain in human form.

The onward surge of their charge quickened the dark army's approach, shaking the earth as the two armies collided amid a swell of red dust.

Total carnage ensued. Animal ripped into animal. Clanging blades lacerated flesh and lopped heads from shoulders. Fallen nightwalkers disintegrated to ashes while daywalkers meeting dispersal dissipated amid flashes of light.

Lavor, fighting alongside Tomes, targeted one of Nordriss's dark figures. "Let us see what we fight." He assailed the warrior, and with Tomes's aid, took him down and decapitated him.

"No disintegration. No dispersal," Tomes said.

"I do not believe they are immortals." Lavor yanked the giant's head from a heavy helmet, revealing an alien creature with gray skin, sunken eyes, and pointed teeth.

"With their size, we're lucky they don't match our

speed. But their strength...it takes two of us to take down one of them."

"But it can be done." Lavor dropped the head. "Their armor is strong, but not impenetrable." He blocked a down-swinging strike from an assailing zombie.

Tomes executed a quick maneuver and dodged a zombie's blade, then ducked as a pitch-black wolf leapt over him and tore into the monster.

Angelique. He psychically heard her warning.

Finishing the giant off, he whirled and call out to the Indithiain Army. "They are mortal!"

Whirling back as another immortal targeted him, this time, the fight was his alone. One-on-one with the nightwalker, Andras. He recognized the Delghorlin leader's face from their encounter in the forest near the quarries, and he knew what the devil was after—the Body. "It'll be my life before you get your hands on the Body."

"Sobeit." Andras stood undaunted.

Tomes, prepared for Andras to make a move, was thrown when Nordriss suddenly intervened.

"This is my fight," Andras reminded the sorcerer.

The hem of Nordriss's full-length cloak—soiled a rusty hue—ruffled in the wind. "Surrender the Heart to me. I will face the dir cyohr."

Andras refused to concede to the predominant power. "That was never part of the deal."

Standing transfixed by the sorcerer's fearsome glare, Andras expelled a roar as Pierson lunged past Tomes and tackled the Delghorlin leader, forcing him backward and into the great throng of immortals.

Nordriss faced Tomes and outstretched his hands, enveloping them in a sphere of golden light that illuminated their surroundings. "The mighty dir cyohr—Piiric—he resides within you."

Tomes stared into Nordriss's raw umber irises that

swirled with red, seeing something he never expected. "No. It can't be." He was taken aback by a message the fading spirit dwelling within him managed to communicate. "I know who you really are."

"I thought you might sense me...Piiric." Nordriss sneered.

"Gaun." Tomes identified him. "How?"

"I possess this body the same way you possess your host."

"Piiric is with me, but I am not possessed."

"He resides within you." Gaun, in Nordriss's body, took several steps to his right. "I call that possession."

"You've deceived the Delghorlins. Andras has no idea who you really are—an Indithian warlord intent on obtaining the Clyth, and with its power, control of the Eleventh Dimension."

The environment inside their field of energy was queerly clear, with the sounds of battle outside their circle, distant and muffled.

"The Clyth belongs to me." Gaun's words rode on a growl.

"Granted to you by a very dark demon—a power you chose to use to annihilate all other species but your own. There has not been so much death in the Eleventh Dimension since that time."

"Death walks with war."

"It certainly walks with you." Tomes watched Gaun's every move. "How did you manage to possess such a powerful sorcerer as Nordriss?"

"I walked the Plane of Death, searching for a way to return, and I found a gap, a tear in the dark reaches of Raining Void—a black abyss most spirits dare not enter. Passing back into the physical world, I entered Nordriss's dreams, a vulnerable place, especially for one troubled by matters that followed him from the waking world. It was there, in his dreams, that he let his defenses down.

He stood at the Range of Koll, overlooking the distant sea. Turning, he sensed me, but I was already in motion, giving him no time to react with magic. I hurled him from the cliff and into the dark abyss below, where he remains."

"Be forewarned, I will do all I can to help him reclaim himself."

Tomes glanced to his right, through the transparent force field encasing him, and saw Corin signaling Lavor, both fighting to reach his position. Then, looking to his left in what felt like slow motion, but was no more than a second, he caught sight of Angelique teamed with Kara against Jax, the girls superbly holding their own.

Pierson. He took in a sharp breath when the beast bounded into view, combating a team of four: Andras, Meical, another immortal that appeared to be chattering like a manic hyena, and Jozsef, the sight of the latter somewhat disconcerting, being Corin's double.

Meical's white hair blew chaotically about his face as he skillfully cut air with his daggers, narrowly missing Pierson with each strike.

Thank God. Tomes released his breath when Patricia suddenly leaped from the horde and planted herself at Pierson's side.

"I will not give up the Body," Tomes declared. "You will never again possess the power of the Clyth."

"Do you have the power to stop me?"

With outstretched arms Tomes called out: "Gheallo habrith," generating a blast of energy that struck Gaun mid-body and knocked him several steps backward.

Gaun quickly regained his bearings. "You are not strong enough."

Tomes then felt Piiric's faint presence and

concentrated on his inner voice. Guided by Piiric, he called out an incantation that broke Gaun's energy field, freeing him from confinement.

"Tomes. Look out!" Corin narrowly reached him in time to fend off Andras's strike.

Hearing a thunderous roar, Tomes whirled, catching sight of Meical laying a blade deep into Pierson's spine. "No...."

Patricia bellowed as Pierson fell, and the nightwalkers scrambled to escape her wrath.

"Andras. You've been deceived," Tomes told the Delghorlin leader who crossed blades with Corin. "This sorcerer you've allied with is not Nordriss, but Gaun."

"That's not possible," Andras rejected his claim. "I've seen his power, things only a sorcerer could do."

At that moment, Lavor reached Corin, adding another immortal to the standoff.

"This *is* Gaun. He has taken possession of Nordriss's body...his spirit...his powers, similar to my merge with Piiric. Only they will never fully merge." Tomes shared Piiric's understanding. "Nordriss has been caged, but he will never stop trying to rise, with the two spirits forever remaining in a constant state of struggle."

"Gaun?" Lavor uttered in bewilderment.

"The sorcerer did not make it easy, fighting to regain control at every turn." Gaun glared at Tomes from twenty feet away, conjuring another field of energy that encircled all five of them in a circle of light. "But when I broke through his memories and obtained his knowledge, I discovered that I could use his power against him, preventing him from crawling back to the surface."

"A spell? A charm?" Tomes knew it had to be one or the other. "Nordriss may be caged, but I sense him within you."

"A speck, trapped in obscurity, where he will

remain." Gaun's eyes narrowed into a scowl. "He will never rise again."

Andras confronted Gaun. "Your goal is the same as mine. You want the Clyth to seize control of the Eleventh Dimension." He clasped the Heart. "To make that wish reality, you need both halves of the Clyth, and you have neither."

Gaun returned his stare. "The night is young."

"You played me." Andras clenched his fists so tightly that his talons pierced his palms.

"Following the signs of prophecy, I waited for the great dark power to resurface," Gaun told him, "counting on those opposing the dir cyohr to seek out the aid of the last sorcerer."

"And I came right to you." Andras snarled. "Our agreement meant nothing. By making our pact, you could keep the Heart close while using me to go after the Body. You never wanted the Eye of Ephog. Did you lie about its power as well?"

"The Eye can indeed see the future, but nothing useful in the long life of immortals. It can only see seven days forward." Gaun conjured their signed alliance and disintegrated it in Andras's presence. "I have but one goal, a perfect Indithian world."

"Under your total control, all species die but your own." Lavor's contempt of the warlord rode on his words. "Indithians already hold the power here. Why must other species be wiped out?"

"Nightwalkers are predators with a detrimental weakness. Humans are plagued with mortality. Daywalkers are the perfect creation," Gaun said. "It would be a world of perfect immortals."

"Your insane conception of a perfect world will never come to fruition," Lavor declared. "The dir cyohr will stop you."

Corin and Lavor claimed positions on either side of

Tomes, holding protective stances, ready for a charge. But to their surprise, Gaun rushed Andras, sending the nightwalker airborne with a conjured bolt of energy that hurled him into the force field enclosing them. Falling to the ground, completely immobilized, the Delghorlin leader was unable to stop Gaun from claiming the Heart.

Tomes fired a strong burst of energy at Gaun, but the impact wasn't strong enough to stop the warlord. *I need more power.*

He needed Piiric to rise from the depths and help him one last time. It was the only way to defeat Gaun—sorcerer against sorcerer.

"Piiric." Standing amid the chaos, Tomes invoked the deity. "I can't do this without you. You have to rise one...last...time." He closed his eyes. "I give you full control. Rise and save the Eleventh Dimension." Experiencing a feeling of falling from a great height, he reopened his eyes, no longer Tomes, but Piiric.

Gaun, in possession of the Heart, aimed for Tomes, intent to kill. Discharging a rage of energy as he assailed, he was suddenly halted by a conjured shield that blocked his attack. "Piiric. So, you have surfaced. But this time, we are both sorcerers. Whatever magic you perform, I can now match."

"I defeated you once, Gaun, and I will again. Then, as prophecy states, the dir cyohr will claim the great dark power. And with the Clyth in his hands, no evil will dare oppose him."

"The Clyth belongs to me." Gaun indicated himself by thrusting his fingertips against his chest. "Granted to *me* by the dark one. No one has a right to the Clyth's power but me."

"Who was the dark one?" Piiric asked. "What was his name?"

"A name I will never say." Gaun's eyes narrowed.

"You will not stop me, Piiric. I have one half of the Clyth, and I will have the other."

"I will never let that happen." Piiric clutched the pouch holding the Body. "Such a dangerous power must be contained."

"It will be mine again, and when I have it, this time, I will succeed. There is only one greater power—the Lucent Stone—and I know it was taken by a demon when you fell through the door to the Plane of Death. Without that power, you will not stop me."

Piiric opened the pouch at his side and pulled out the Body. "The Clyth will never again be yours." He pressed the charm between his palms and a dark, vaporous cloud materialized and cloaked his hands. In a blink, the fog dissipated, and with it, the Body vanished.

Infuriated, Gaun cursed and charged Piiric, but Piiric turned the tables on the warlord, uttering three quick words that bound him in a radiant metallic energy. Gaun fought to break free, but Piiric held superior power.

"You do not consider what I became after death, more than a sorcerer—a deity." Piiric circled him. "You thought you could win this battle?"

"The dir cyohr, he is not a deity." Gaun continued to fight restraint.

"He is me. I am him," Piiric told him. "When we are fully merged, he will be no ordinary immortal."

"He could not stand against me on his own, forced to call upon you," Gaun pointed out. "When you are gone, he will have no superior power over me."

"I was meant to rise one last time for a purpose...for this moment." Piiric looked to his right. "Hediye. Suna."

Two figures suddenly unwrapped from a veil of

invisibility.

"What is this?" Gaun glared.

Upon command, a black spider that was used as a means of communication between Piiric and the witches scurried down Piiric's arm and across the ground to Suna, who bent to meet the arachnid. With an amber stone resting in her palm, she watched as the spider melted into the gem.

Hediye quickly removed a ring from her hand and handed it to Piiric, its stone magically changing color, size, and shape the moment it left her finger.

"The Lucent Stone." Gaun recognized the lustrous black, white, and gold cabochon that showcased a perfect lengthwise division of the three colors.

"Becoming deity, I crossed from the Plane of Death to Zarmeva, and I reclaimed the stone," Piiric informed him. "I then placed it in safe hands."

"No." Gaun roared, still bound in Piiric's field of energy. "You could not have known I was possessing Nordriss...that you would need the Lucent Stone."

"No, I did not know that you would be the evil power prophesied to appear during the Great Battle. I was merely preparing for whatever was to come, armed with the most powerful charm known in this world, a power born of Zarmeva, that will now stop you a second time."

Piiric raised his arms and cited an incantation that opened a portal. A whirlwind of white fire filled the vortex, and three spirit guardians emerged with flaming staffs. Looking at Piiric, they understood the message he conveyed, and turned their fiery staffs on Gaun. Encapsulated in plasma, the warlord's host body levitated, arching as his spirit was exorcised, freeing Nordriss from possession. A faint cry grew to a thunderous roar as a current of fire enwrapped Gaun's spirit, ensuring no chance of escape.

Piiric moved toward the guardians. "Take him to Zarmeva. We cannot trust the Plane of Death to hold him."

"How did he get past the guardians of the portal?" One spirit spoke, and his cavernous voice resonated.

"He found a way of escape through a gap in the depths of Raining Void."

"We will see to his confinement." Another guardian said as each spirit bent his head at Piiric in respect.

The three guardians then cast Gaun into the vortex and followed their prisoner into the blazing passage. The moment they disappeared among the flames, the portal closed.

Nordriss, who had regained consciousness, pushed himself up to a sitting position. Glancing down at his right hand, his fingers fell open, revealing the Heart.

19

Seeing that the battle still raged, Corin spotted Angelique teamed with Kara in the mayhem, watching as Jozsef blocked an oncoming strike that might have ended her life—a close call that caused his heart to stop as the scene around him slowed to a crawl. Then, catching their synchronous stares, he knew both Angelique and his brother had experienced his moment of fear.

"Lower the force field," Lavor called to Piiric, who quickly cast a spell that shattered the transparent circle of energy confining them.

"The giants." Piiric rushed toward Nordriss who rose to his feet. "You must stop that dark army."

Nordriss shouted a command that ceased the zombies' motion. He then waved his hand before him in a curved pass, and a window opened. "Return to Dremlon," his words echoed.

The window expanded, and the surviving Dremlons entered the portal, returning to their hive. But despite the giants' withdrawal from the battlefield, the Delghorlins refused to give up the fight.

"Regent Fehre!" Lavor rushed into the battle zone, aimed for the regent, but he wasn't fast enough to prevent Meical's dagger from piercing the ruler's side.

Corin followed his charge, seeing Meical dive into the midst of havoc.

Lavor motioned to Corin. "Take care of the regent."

The constable turned to pursue Meical, only to be diverted by another enemy. "Xylor." He targeted the nightwalker. "It will be a pleasure taking your head, snake."

Unable to escape the one-on-one confrontation, Xylor made the first strike, but his wield of the sword was no match for Lavor's skill, and the constable initiated a clever maneuver that decapitated the spy.

Corin, bending next to Fehre, assessed the regent's injury. "Can you walk?"

"I can." Fehre held pressure against his wound, releasing a groan as Corin pulled him up and onto his feet.

Angelique rushed toward them at the same moment Patricia lunged from the chaos, blocking them from attack.

"Let's move him to a safer position," Corin pointed out an area along the sidelines.

Regent Fehre groaned with each excruciating movement.

"This will do." Corin leaned him against a large rock.

"He's in a lot of pain." Angelique said.

"Those nytum daggers. The cut is deep, but nothing compared to the neck injury Galvar suffered." Corin partially healed the wound. "I'm sorry, Regent Fehre, there's nothing more I can do. It's going to take time."

"I know. I will recover soon enough." Fehre scanned the scene. "Go. The fight is not over."

Corin, eyeing Andras, left Angelique with the regent and quickly took a defensive position at Piiric's side.

"We have unfinished business." Andras halted with a defying stance. The hate in his expression told his malicious intent. "This was my fight long before it was Gaun's." He shape-shifted into his form of origin—Var. "I've seen my death by your hand. If you live, I will die."

"Be warned." Nordriss stepped between Piiric and Var. "I will protect the dir cyohr. What power have you against me?"

"I fight for my life." Andras stood his ground. "One of us must die."

"Your actions stem from fear of death. Yet, should you fight the dir cyohr—a wizard—without the Clyth, it *will* be your life lost," Nordriss told him. "Today, you lose the fight and win no world, but you can walk away with your life." The wizard's eyes shifted color. "Let there be no more death today."

Andras growled and reluctantly ordered his men to cease fighting. He glared at Piiric. "This isn't the end, Dir Cyohr." He stormed away.

Corin spotted Jozsef and called out his name. He saw that Andras whirled back in response.

"This is your chance to break free." Corin reached out to his brother. "I offer family."

"Jozsef has family," Andras jetted the words at Corin.

Jozsef stood in a moment of indecision before facing Andras. "I'm not going with you."

Andras held a blank expression. "Where is your loyalty? You said I had nothing to worry about."

"Please understand. I've never felt I belonged," Jozsef told him.

"Something I've always known," Meical spouted, producing a cackle from Jitters. "Cut him loose, Andras."

"Quiet," Andras warned Meical.

"You've kept so much from me. Who you really are. My brother's existence." Jozsef did not shy from eye contact with his maker. "In five hundred years, I never really knew you."

Andras hesitated, then reluctantly turned away, letting him go.

Lehndra hissed, peering side-to-side with her head turning in short, quick motions. She then charged Jozsef, but her action was halted by Andras who barked an order to desist.

"Shift and depart!" he called out to his clan, leading them into flight and disappearing into the distant darkness.

Corin closed the gap between him and Jozsef. "You stayed."

"We've been robbed of time," Jozsef said. "Forgive me for what I've put you through."

"Andras's influence is strong." Corin laid a hand on his shoulder. "I knew there was still hope when I saw you save Angelique's life."

"I know what she means to you."

Corin pulled him into a hug. "Score, Jozsef—"

"Worthy of the shield," Jozsef finished. "But this time, we both win."

The sight of Hediye inching toward Piiric captured Corin's attention, knowing they had unfinished business.

"Our last moment," Hediye whispered to Piiric. "One last touch."

Piiric pressed his lips to hers. "Guard the power." He placed the Lucent Stone on her finger. "Goodbye, Hediye." He lowered his head, and when he straightened, he had returned consciousness to Tomes.

Tomes released Hediye and stumbled back.

"Goodbye, Piiric," Hediye spoke under her breath,

then moved past Tomes, toward Nordriss.

"Hediye." The wizard appeared bewitched. "You have returned after all these years."

"Piiric came to me in death, as a deity, and entrusted the Lucent Stone to me. We had no idea Gaun had possessed you. Being the last sorcerer in this world, he figured you'd play a large role in the latter days. His hope was that my presence might sway you back to the side of good. The fact that you were possessed by Gaun was unexpected, but thankfully he's been exorcised."

"There has been too much suffering." Nordriss tenderly pressed a palm against the side of her face. "Forgive a jealous fool. When you chose Piiric, I was so angry. And that anger is what allowed Gaun to take control."

She reached for his hand. "All of that is in the past...forgiven."

Corin stepped toward Tomes. "You're back to yourself?"

Tomes nodded, then catching sight of Kara, aimed for the woman he loved. "What happened with Hediye, I—"

"It was Piiric, not you," she said. "I understand that."

He exhaled a breath of relief and wrapped her in his arms.

"I will never get used to this." Angelique's gaze shifted back-and-forth between Corin and Jozsef. "You two really are identical."

"Mirror images," Tomes agreed. "If not for the clothes, no one would be able to tell you apart."

"I will always know the difference." Angelique smiled at Corin. She then turned and scanned the battlefield where Indithian soldiers healed injuries and awaited orders. "I can't believe it's over."

Tomes caught a stir of dust riding on the wind as he

moved to her side. "So many lives have been lost tonight. And with our enemies still out there, it will never be over."

* * * *

Corin stood in front of Pierson and Patricia whose injuries had rapidly healed. "Nordriss. Is there anything you can do for these two? They are under a spell cast by one of Andras's henchmen—a curse that turns them into the beasts you see now and then back to human form at first light."

Nordriss walked toward them. "Carhalli."

Pierson snorted and stomped the ground in response.

"I recognize her power at work here." Nordriss brushed a twisted section of hair from his right field of vision. "I have summoned Carhalli before...made my own trade. She is not a power of light."

"But you can help them?" Corin interpreted his words as favorable. "Break their curse?"

Nordriss extended his hands before him and closed his eyes. Delivering a spell, a portal materialized, and a figure emerged from a passage engulfed in white flames. A ghostly form, the supreme being was a beautiful and fearsome sight to behold.

"Nordriss." She knew him. "Why do you summon me?"

"I ask that you free these two from their curse," he requested. "A curse placed by you."

"I remember." Carhalli's gown flowed around her form in a rippling sway. "What do you offer in exchange for this favor?"

Nordriss showed no fear of the demon. "What items of power I possess reside in my Kingdom of Shudrorah."

She glared at the sorcerer. "There is no favor without exchange."

"I have something." Suna displayed the ten amber stones.

"Suna." Hediye reached for her. "You can't give those up."

Suna leaned toward her. "Trust me," she whispered.

Hediye released her sister's arm, and Suna presented her offering.

Carhalli examined the stones. "There is a familiar power here." The demon's gaze rose to meet Suna's. "Keep them. They are attached to you." She caught Suna's hand. "A witch, and yet more. You have connections with one of high standing in Zarmeva."

"Yes," Suna admitted.

"Without exchange, I will free the cursed." The demon's semi-transparent form drifted toward Pierson and Patricia and she cast a misty energy over them. "Those not born of the accursed, be exorcised."

With that command, Pierson and Patricia transmuted to human form, free of their curse.

"They need something to cover up with." Angelique solicited several articles of clothing and tossed them to Pierson and Patricia who stood naked.

Carhalli moved closer to Pierson. "You are no longer immortal, but I have cleansed your body of disease."

"My cancer? You, you mean it's—" Pierson stumbled with his question.

"All affliction and disease have been washed away." Carhalli said. "Make good use of your mortal years." She turned back to Suna. "You may call again." Then, drifting back into the sea of white fire, she closed the portal behind her.

"I can't believe the curse is broken." Patricia fell into Pierson's arms. "We are not immortal, but we're free."

"Knowing I was dying drove me to extremes."

Pierson held her tight. "Now that I'm cured, we have many happy years ahead of us. And as she said, I intend to make the most of them."

"You were desperate to live." Corin understood Pierson's motive for his risky manner of seeking immortality. Now, he had the chance to grow old with the woman he loved.

"It is time I return to my kingdom and begin the process of correcting the damage stamped on Shudrorah by Gaun." Nordriss's expressions were much more animate since being freed from Gaun's possession. "This, I believe, belongs with you." He handed the Heart of the Clyth to Tomes. "The Eleventh Dimension is in your hands, Dir Cyohr. Recovery will be long, but I have faith that we will rise to new heights. And you know where to find me should any problems arise."

Tomes gripped both charms. "The Heart and the Body. The Clyth. It is a huge responsibility."

"You have inherited a world." Regent Fehre managed to stand. "Now, *you* are ruler of Morpar."

Lavor turned and faced the infantry. In a loud voice he bellowed: "All hail the dir cyohr, King Tomes of Morpar, Savior of the Eleventh Dimension."

A great roar rolled o'er the dunes: "ALL HAIL THE DIR CYOHR. KING TOMES OF MORPAR. SAVIOR OF THE ELEVENTH DIMENSION."

Watching as Tomes raised his hands, displaying the symbol of the trinity, Corin felt Angelique's pride and amazement. Her brother was a king.

Tomes looked at Corin. "This will take some getting used to—being king. But I think I'm up for the task." His lip curled upward.

Corin laughed, focusing on an object in the backdrop. "I can't believe it." He stepped past Tomes.

"What is it?" Tomes turned.

Corin aimed for his trampled Stetson, scooped it up, and dusted it off.

Tomes narrowed his eyes. "There's something strange about that hat."

"It's lucky." Corin combed his fingers through his hair and flipped it on.

"Nordriss." Hediye clasped the sorcerer's hand. "I want to stay with you, here, in the Eleventh Dimension."

Nordriss pulled her aside and spoke in a hushed voice. "You will never love me the way you loved Piiric."

"Choosing between you and Piiric was not easy," she admitted. "I loved you both."

"But you chose him." Nordriss said as a fact, without anger.

Overhearing, Corin now understood the link binding Nordriss, Piiric, and Hediye. Two sorcerers in love with the same woman. A situation that could topple kingdoms...and did.

"Piiric is gone, and we deserve the chance to see where the love we do share can lead us," Hediye told him. "We need each other. Especially now. Say you'll let me stay. That you'll have me."

Nordriss buried his fingers in her two-toned strands and bent to meet her vivid, blue stare. "I want nothing more."

Regent Fehre hobbled toward Nordriss. "What about the Lucent stone?"

"Piiric was right about keeping the powers separated." He lifted Hediye's hand and viewed the stone. "There is no safer place than Shudrorah."

Corin stood with Angelique, watching as Nordriss, Hediye, and Suna departed through a window, to the Kingdom of Shudrorah.

Lavor rotated. "I will take a company of soldiers and see to the human relocation."

"I would take no more than a quarter of the force. I do not trust the Delghorlins." The regent pressed a hand against his side. "We need the majority here. To protect Morpar."

Tomes agreed, and Lavor quickly enlisted a small battalion to the assignment.

"You must be worried about your family. Rest assured that they are in the best of company. Jordon is the most capable, not to mention tenacious, person I know," Corin told the constable, with his declaration seconded by Tomes.

"They have had trouble." Lavor communicated what he'd sensed.

"Your connection with Staca." Corin understood. "How close do you think they are to the portal?"

"On foot, it is a ten-hour excursion from Jach Lagon Canyon to Morpar, and that is without rest, which the humans will need. Every minute they are out there, the danger of starving nightwalkers overrunning them grows." Lavor signaled to his company to prepare for flight. "At least you have Earth to return to, something we cannot allow of our own nightwalkers in these dire times. There would be no control."

"It would be carnage." Corin couldn't imagine such a happening on Earth. "But thankfully they can't pass through the Passage of Dimensions without shalym discs. Otherwise, Earth would be in real trouble right now. And the Örök Vér are trouble enough."

"With Regent Fehre injured, I'm needed here," Tomes told Lavor. "But I'll meet you at the portal for the relocation."

"I will come along," Corin volunteered. "Angelique, you should stay here with Tomes and Kara."

Angelique refused to separate, as he'd expected she would.

Jozsef relocated to Angelique's side. "I go where you

go," he told Corin.

Corin looked into his brother's face, a mirror copy of his own, and wondered how he would ever explain him when they returned to Hixton. Even living a secluded, private life, it was likely that someone would eventually see them together.

A long-lost, identical twin.

They'd have to come up with a believable story, because the truth could certainly never be told.

20

Corin followed Angelique into a sudden stoop, avoiding an attacker's onrush as numerous starving nightwalkers ambushed them in mid-air.

Forced to the ground, he saw that the hunters were vastly outnumbered, but too desperate for food to react with any rationality.

"To your right." Corin telepathically warned Angelique as they touched earth.

Shifting to human form, battle erupted, claiming several lives before the nightwalkers withdrew.

"Galvar." Corin strode toward his friend who appeared with a small group of men a moment before the nightwalkers fled.

"I am certainly glad to see reinforcements," Galvar expressed relief. "These attacks are shrinking our numbers fast."

"How close are the people?" Corin asked.

"Just ahead." Galvar pointed out their position. "We are trying to intercept the nightwalkers before they can get close enough to strike, but they are unpredictable. "We are moving as fast as the people can manage, but it is not fast enough with starving nightwalkers stalking us."

Lavor immediately placed his company of soldiers on guard duty. "I figured it was bad, but I never imagined so many rogues, so soon."

"The soldiers you brought gives us a fighting chance," Galvar told him. "I was beginning to have my doubts."

"I wish the number was greater, but Morpar cannot be left unprotected," Lavor said.

"We should join the commute. Give Jordon some good news." Galvar led the way.

Landing, Angelique watched as Lavor reunite with Staca. "He can breathe easy now."

"Not quite yet." Corin looked upward at several nightwalkers diving toward the train, pursued by Indithian soldiers. "Getting these people safely to the portal isn't going to be a fast or easy feat. Those hunters aren't going to stop trying to reach these people. They've lost all sense of reason. With poor odds of survival, risk means nothing to them."

"I'm so glad to see you guys." Jordon clasped Corin's arm and pulled him against his shoulder. "I was getting worried." He kept the train moving. "Your brother?" He eyed Jozsef.

"He is with us now," Corin assured him.

"The battle is over?" Jordon assumed by their presence there. "What happened with Nordriss?"

"It was discovered that he was possessed...by Gaun. Piiric exorcised him. And without Nordriss or the Clyth, Andras didn't stand much of a chance."

"Andras is dead?"

"No. When he knew he couldn't win, he gave up the fight," Corin clarified.

"You'll have to fill me in on the details later," Jordon said.

Lavor joined their huddle. "Where is Bren?" He visually raked the scene.

Staca clutched his arm. "Patrolling...in the back."

Lavor glanced in that direction, where the travelers faded into darkness. "We should strengthen the ground patrol. Then, in the air, form two lines of defense."

"Yes. We should have enough men to set up two barriers." Galvar darted away with Lavor to set the plan into action.

Angelique veered toward Staca. "The people look so tired."

"They are traumatized and exhausted." Staca leaned close to her, nearly touching. "But we cannot slow down."

"How long till we reach the portal from here?" Angelique asked.

"Two to three more long and deadly hours." Jordon made a 180° turn and scanned the fold. "But we'll make it." His gaze stopped on Jozsef. "Unbelievable. With the same hair and clothes, I wouldn't be able to tell you two apart."

"Where is Vynce?" Corin asked Jordon. "I expected to see him with Galvar."

"He and several others are a short distance ahead, flushing out any attempts of ambush. A dangerous task with nightwalker numbers growing by the minute." Jordon stayed alert. "But being shinobi, he's well trained...a superb fighter. He'll know when it's time to fall back."

Several screams ripped through the air as a nightwalker materialized within the crowd. Having slipped in as mist, he rushed toward a man, but failed in his attempt when he was intercepted, and his life terminated by pursuing soldiers.

"Keep your eyes open," Jordon yelled. "We cannot let that happen again."

Staca tugged Angelique's arm. "Help me calm the people."

Corin looked at Jozsef. "We should join the patrol."

"Go." Jordon kept a steady pace. "Galvar's instructed me to keep the train moving."

Angelique looked at Corin. "Be careful," she communicated mentally.

After a lingering second, Corin broke their locked gaze and hurried away with Jozsef, catching sight of another hunter attempting to slip through their barrier in the form of mist. Luckily, the rogue had no chance to materialize, and fled.

"You could probably use one of these." Corin offered Jozsef a Traxl-1. "It'll calm your hunger."

Jozsef took the pill. "I'm not sure we can hold out two...three more hours. They're coming at us from every direction."

"We have to. For their sake." He nodded toward the people. "Do you think Andras is up there?"

"I'm assuming he's returned to Earth to plot some future revenge," Jozsef figured.

"He'll never stop trying, will he?"

"No. He doesn't like to lose."

Two hours passed as they steadfastly fought back constant assailment, relieved when they finally reached Morpar's West Bowman Woods, a point giving rise to hope of reaching their intended destination.

Corin and Jozsef maneuvered to the front line when the train came to a sudden standstill, seeing that Vynce had fallen back from his patrol. Lavor and Galvar then appeared, inquiring on the delay.

"We have run into trouble ahead. Rogue's lying in wait ready to ambush," Vynce reported. "I think we should exit the road here and cut through the woods," he proposed.

"It is the shortest route. A straight line to the portal." Jordon supported Vynce's suggestion.

Lavor was hesitant. "We would be facing areas of dense terrain, when not crossing simmering craters."

"I see no other option." Vynce's face was drawn with worry. "The rogue nightwalkers now easily match our numbers. With them stalking us along the road, this is our best chance.

"We won't have long till they realize what we've done and pursue," Lavor said. "We will need plenty of soldiers to encircle the people while moving through the woods."

All eyes fell on Galvar for a decision.

"They will pursue no matter what we do. We will exit here." Galvar had little choice.

"I will tighten the patrol and bring the inner line to the ground." Lavor darted away.

Looking at the road ahead, steam drifting from nearby craters blanketed their path, exuding an ominous feel that lent to dread. Adding to the eeriness, a low-toned caw sporadically sounded from the distant, unseen depths. It evolved to a higher pitch, then a shriek, and with the next second...silence. Corin concluded that some exotic bird, very likely the last of its kind, had just become a light snack for a quick-handed nightwalker.

Seeking Angelique's position, Corin linked with her through thought. "We are about to exit the road. Stay close to Staca."

His attention was then drawn to Galvar, who climbed atop a massive, fallen oak, and spoke out to the people. Torq, the supporters' leader, stood at his side.

"There is danger ahead. We have decided to abandon the road and plot a course through West Bowman Woods," Galvar informed them. "It may be difficult, but it will shorten our route."

"Are we going to make it?" A woman asked the question everyone was thinking.

"We will give our lives to get you there," Torq promised. "We are very close to the portal."

Within minutes they entered the woods that quickly transitioned from a dense canopy to charred remnants as they circled a crater.

Dead silence. Corin was unnerved by the unnatural calm.

"Hurry. Get to the next line of woods." Jordon, with Torq's assistance, rushed the skittish group through the exposed area and into another thick canopy.

The practice of hopping from pocket-to-pocket of scattered woods continued for at least thirty minutes, giving Corin a good sense of how the forest had looked before the meteorites marred the area.

"Wolves." Howls too close for comfort struck his ear. His breath caught, knowing it was nightwalkers closing in on them, looking for any chance to assail.

"We are in for real trouble." Galvar swept past Corin and Jozsef, aimed for Jordon, who'd just led the group into another clearing.

Corin scanned their dark surroundings as he and Jozsef followed.

"They're not going to make this easy," Jordon said as they approached.

"We have to get around this crater. Fast." Torq was on edge.

Passing through the clearing, Corin paused before entering the next pocket of woods and searched the aggregation of people for Angelique, spotting her in the inner crowd. Then, detecting movement beyond the train, on the opposite side of the crater they'd just circled, his eyes widened in horror at the sight of rogues, too many to count, pouring from the distant tree line in human and animal forms...in fast pursuit.

Corin rushed toward Bren, who covered the back of the train, to help ensure that everyone made it into the woods. "I have never seen anything like this."

Bren gaped on the sight. "Nothing will stop them now."

Just then, Lavor, who'd been overseeing the air patrol, landed in the clearing with a group of soldiers. "Run!" he shouted. "You are almost at the portal."

Bren whirled and alerted the people. "The rogues are attacking from behind! Run!"

The urgency in his voice ignited a frantic surge as the people bolted forward in panic.

Corin looked at Jozsef who'd fallen back with him. "There are too many to hold back."

A child fell and Jozsef scooped her up and placed her back with her mother. "Keep going." He looked back at Corin. "This is chaos."

Corin's anxiety escalated. "In case this doesn't play out well, I need to be with Angelique."

Engineering through the host of people, they spotted her coming toward them, and Corin latched onto her hand. "If we don't make it out of this alive, I love you always," he communicated psychically as she reversed course and matched their pace.

"Move! Keep moving!" Galvar trumpeted from the sideline.

"Corin!" Angelique suddenly halted as a nightwalker leapt from an overhanging branch, latched onto a man, and dragged the poor soul into the dark, misty outskirts.

"It's too late for him. He's lost." Corin scooped up a torch the man had dropped, glad to see the flame was still burning. "The people need light to find their way." He urged her into movement.

"The rogues are slipping through!" Galvar's voice

boomed again.

Corin, spotting another hunter, passed the torch to Angelique and intercepted the immortal's attack, scarcely saving a woman's life.

"Look out!" Jozsef jumped to his brother's defense when several more hunters leapt from the shadows."

Corin glanced up through the thinning canopy at a surreal scene—a battle raging mid-air above them—a nightmare. Hearing several screams, he knew they had lost more lives to the hunters, but being overrun, it was impossible to protect them all. All they could do was keep running.

Reaching the end of the woods, Corin feared this was the end for the people as they barreled into the open, completely vulnerable to attack.

"Wait." Angelique came to an abrupt stop, looking dead ahead. "Tomes."

A moment later, Tomes appeared, leading a charging army, along with Pierson and Patricia who dove into the swarm of bloodthirsty hunters.

Corin took a deep breath. "I've never been so happy to see your brother."

Tomes rushed toward them and pulled Angelique into a hug. "I felt your anxiety and knew you were in trouble."

"You got here just in the nick of time." Corin slapped his shoulder, eyeing Galvar, Jordon, Vynce, and Lavor who congregated around them.

"The Passage is no more than ten minutes ahead," Jordon said. "We shouldn't delay."

Continuing on to the portal, Corin was relieved when they reached their destination.

"I should cross over and let the Order know it is time for relocation." Galvar reached for his shalym disc and attempted to open the portal. "Something is wrong. The Passage...it is not opening."

"What?" Jordon stepped toward him. "What could be the problem?"

"I am somewhat familiar with the controls." Lavor took Galvar's disc and walked up to a cubed pillar. He placed the disc into a perfectly fitted groove that triggered a hood release, exposing the inner mechanisms.

Looking over Lavor's shoulder, Corin thought the controls seemed rather simple. For a portal that crossed worlds, he'd imagined something much more high-tech.

"I see the problem," Lavor said. "It is missing a charge."

"What do you mean...missing?" Galvar sought clarification.

"It has been removed." Lavor scoured the controls. "Wait. There's something here." He reached. "Caught between the panels." He pulled out a circular object. "A shalym disc." He examined his find. "The bail has been broken." Lavor caught Galvar's stare. "This is no ordinary disc."

Galvar took a closer look. "Marked with suns...this is Regent Fehre's disc. It is the only one of its kind."

"You can't be accusing Regent Fehre of—" Tomes's sentence was cut short.

"Sabotage," Jordon finished his thought. "The regent...where is he?"

"He's at the palace ruins," Tomes answered, "recovering."

Jordon stressed the urgency of finding him. "Without that charge, the portal is useless."

"Constable." Tomes turned to Lavor who was visibly unsettled by what appeared to be rightfully placed blame. "Being head of the army, this is your assignment."

"I will find him." Without delay, Lavor employed

several soldiers and set a course for the palace ruins.

Torq scanned the crowd where Staca and several other immortals healed the mortals' injuries under Plameth's instruction. "This relocation is their last hope. Without the Passage of Dimensions...."

"We will get them to Earth," Galvar declared. "Meanwhile, being in the company of the dir cyohr will give them reassurance, as well as knowing that an army is standing guard."

Tomes took several steps to his left, then spun back. "What would be the regent's motive for this sabotage?"

"It may not be what we are thinking. It is possible that he disabled the Passage as a safeguard to prevent nightwalkers from crossing into other worlds should they manage to obtain discs." Vynce offered a plausible explanation.

"That does make sense," Corin said.

Galvar shook his head. "Lavor would have known. No, there is more to it." He glanced over the multitude of weary travelers. "For their sake, I hope we find that charge." His line of vision shifted to Tomes. "They know something is wrong, and they need reassurance...from you."

Tomes motioned to Torq. "Being leader of the supporters, you should stand with me."

The two faced the crowd, and the people grew silent in anticipation of their message.

"There is a problem with the Passage?" A man called out. "What will happen to us now?"

"It's true. There is a delay. But we are working to fix it," Tomes assured the people.

Corin watched in awe as Tomes continued to deliver additional words of encouragement in an effort to ease their fears, instilling calm in the midst of chaos. He marveled at his miraculous transformation...that it could be real—a boy he'd watched grow to a man, blessed with such a phenomenal destiny.

Angelique gripped Corin's arm. "I hope they find that part. We can't lose these people."

Corin pulled her into a walk, pacing a short tract as they waited for Lavor's return. Time crawled as they remained in motion, anticipating the outcome.

"He's back," Jordon alerted.

Hurrying toward Lavor, Corin was disappointed to learn that Fehre had not been found. But Lavor had not returned alone, escorting the regent's assistant, Engll, along with Kara who was shocked to have learned of the traitorous act.

"Where is Regent Fehre?" Galvar demanded a response from Engll.

"Engll is not forthcoming with answers." Lavor held a tight grip on Engll's arm. "When I could not locate the regent, Engll took me to where he was last seen...resting in the ruins. That's where I noticed this." He pointed out a chain draping Engll's neck. "I believe it held Regent Fehre's disc."

Galvar stormed toward Engll and took a closer look. "Yes. It is his."

"Your plan was to implicate the regent?" Tomes stepped forward. "Or were you not aware that you lost the disc when removing the charge from the controls?"

"What are you accusing me of? I have done nothing...nothing wrong," Engll's voice broke.

Corin glared at the man, angered by the attempt he made to play ignorant, knowing it was pretense.

"Where is the charge?" Galvar's tone was threatening. "And what have you done with Regent Fehre?"

Engll's gaze rose with a defiant glare, and his disposition suddenly changed, as if a second personality had risen to the surface—a wretched one.

"We need that charge." Torq pushed past Bren,

aimed for Engll.

Tomes reined him back. "Look at your people. They're watching, and they're scared."

Corin scanned frightened faces in the torchlight.

Torq nodded. "I will calm them." He aimed for the people.

"I will come too. They have come to know me." Staca went with them.

Galvar yanked Engll close. "Why are you doing this?"

Engll's brows contracted into a menacing glower. "To kill all of you...nightwalker."

"Wipe out the nightwalkers?" Tomes stood next to Galvar. "What is your motive?"

Engll glanced past the immortals, settling his stare on Bren who stood in the backdrop. "I had a wife and son once." He looked at Lavor who still restrained him. "Until nightwalkers killed them."

"So, this is revenge." Galvar said. "Punish them all for the crimes of one lineage?"

"None of their kind are to be trusted. Something I regret having done and have paid dearly for...during Gaun's uprising. At that time, I had taken my family and left Morpar, working with other rebel Indithians, forming allies with nightwalker clans. That is where I went wrong, becoming too trusting with the blood feeders. Learning too late that savages will always be savages." Engll shot a glare at Galvar. "Yet you hold positions in the Indithian Army, remaining a continual threat to not only Morpar, but to the world."

"How does stopping the humans from crossing to Earth have anything to do with your revenge on nightwalkers?" Corin didn't understand his reasoning. "Without the Passage, we can't cross them over, and the rogue numbers are growing by the minute."

"I have seized an opportunity." Engll was vague with

his response.

"What opportunity?" Galvar stood tall. Feet parted. Muscles flexed.

Corin could tell the commander was growing impatient.

"The apocalypse," Engll answered. "The perfect chance to free this world from hunters...nightwalkers. With no Traxl-l and lack of food, it would not take long for them to turn on each other."

Jordon's body stiffened. His eyes narrowed. "They will turn on us too...daywalkers. And every other species that manages to survive this apocalypse. That will happen regardless of human presence. So why not allow us to relocate these people to Earth? Why condemn them to die? Letting us save them will not affect your plan."

"Yes. It would. In time." Engll showed no emotion. "Some nightwalkers will manage to survive...that is foreseeable. And if the human population is saved and later brought back, those nightwalkers would once again arise. Terminating our human race would prevent that from ever happening."

"We stand with friends who are nightwalkers, who have fought at our side, and you propose outright genocide of their kind, as well as the humans?" Tomes was outraged.

"The loss of both species could be blamed on the apocalypse. The rest of the world need never know," Engll said. "Using the apocalypse as a cover, we could prevent this from staining our history the way Gaun's uprising did."

"You are no better than Gaun." Lavor's words held disgust. "Sacrificing all other species but your own."

"I never supported that warlord who killed even his own kind." Engll appeared perturbed by the comparison. "This is different. I did not cause this apocalypse. Why is it so wrong to take advantage of it the way the Örök Vér just did with their attempt to seize control? You must see, this is our chance to rid our world of their kind...for good."

"Who here, besides yourself, do you propose will turn a blade on me?" Galvar's jaw tightened.

Engll met Galvar's stern stare with hatred.

Lavor leaned toward Engll. "Galvar is right. None here will take part in your inane plan."

Engll did not back down. "Then our world, our kind, or a safe future for your own family mean nothing to you, Constable. One day you will come to sorely regret the choice you have made today."

"Your plan is not only inane, but shortsighted." Jordon shifted his weight from right to left. "Too many of us have discs. Daywalkers and nightwalkers."

"Without portals the discs are useless." Engll's lips stretched as if confident he'd covered all bases. "As I have proven, they can easily be disabled, and soon, all of them will be. I have sent a squad to see to the task."

Jordon clenched his fists. "You'll never shut them all down permanently, just as you won't stop Traxl-1 from eventually reaching nightwalker survivors. Regent Fehre told me that Traxl-1 is being produced as we speak. In weeks there will be enough quantity to distribute. With that being the case, killing the humans would do nothing toward rendering the nightwalkers extinct."

Engll's lips drew into a sneer. "Without Mirillow Traxl, there is no Traxl-1."

Corin didn't like the sound of Engll's words, fearing what they meant.

"I have seen to that as well," Engll said. "Regent Fehre ordered his immediate execution." The daywalker flinched as Galvar spun on his heels in a stir of dust.

Corin could see that the commander fought to hold back his inner monster, understanding his temptation to rip Engll's head right off his shoulders.

"Regent Fehre gave no such order. It was all you. He stood in your way." Galvar's fists tightened. "I presume he is dead...by your hand."

It was apparent what Engll had done, all in the name of "revenge."

Jordon cut his eyes at Galvar. "Whoever Engll sent to kill Traxl, they believe the order came from the regent."

"We have to find him first," Vynce said.

Engll tried to jerk away from Lavor, failing to break the constable's grip. "When Traxl is dead, there will be no more miracle pills to save the bloodfeeders. If time allowed, Traxl-1 could possibly be reproduced, but for the nightwalkers, that wouldn't be soon enough."

Galvar looked at Lavor. "We need to move fast. Traxl first, then the portals."

"I'll take a squad and head for the Xallon Lowland Territory...try to warn him," Jordon volunteered.

"It is too late to intercept my squad," Engll said, with satisfaction in his achievement. "They deployed over an hour ago. Six of our fastest men. Trained sentry. You cannot catch them."

"But we can." Tomes informed him. "I don't have the ability to cross people from one world to another, but I can transport from place to place within worlds. When Piiric returned control to me after the battle, a rush of knowledge flooded me. I believe, at that moment, we fully merged."

Galvar took in an audible breath. "Then we can warn Traxl and reach the portals ahead of Engll's squad."

"If you're able to do that, why can't we just cross the people to another portal?" Corin proposed.

"We don't know the dangers waiting at the other

locations; besides, we don't need to do that. I can tell you where the charge is." Tomes stepped toward Engll. "I am a sorcerer. And I now have full control of my powers."

"What are you going to do to me?" Engll fought Lavor's hold. Fear showed in his wide-eyed stare as Tomes moved closer.

"I'll give you one last chance to cooperate. Tell us where the charge is," Tomes demanded.

"I will never give it to you." Engll snarled.

"Then you leave me no choice but to take the last several hours of your memory. Memories you will not get back." Tomes gripped Engll's head in his hands.

"Take them all. Every memory. It is worth the cause." Engll remained defiant.

"Lucky for you, I can't take more than twelve hours." Tomes maintained a steady tone.

Galvar stepped back. "Let us hope that will be enough."

Tomes shut his eyes and whispered a short spell. Concentrating, his palms emitted a faint, mystic haze that blanketed his hands. Several second passed before he opened his eyes and released Engll. He looked at Lavor, then rotated. "He killed Regent Fehre...caught the regent vulnerable while he was resting."

Lavor grabbed a handful of Engll's hair and yanked his head back. "He trusted you."

"His memory is gone. He won't remember killing him," Tomes reminded the constable.

"What about the charge?" Galvar asked. "Did you see what he did with it?"

"It's beneath the palace ruins," Tomes divulged. "Several meters inside the mouth of a tunnel."

Galvar straightened. "I am familiar with the tunnels. Which direction did he go?"

"South. It's hidden along the wall of the first bend,

on the right side, in a gap concealed by an optical illusion." Tomes revealed what he'd seen. "The gap is at shoulder height, a narrow space, just wide enough to fit an arm into. The charge is there."

"I know the way." Galvar prepared to depart.

"I am coming with you," Vynce followed, and the two immortals shifted and leapt into flight, disappearing into the darkness of night.

"What has happened?" Engll grasped his head. "How did I get here?"

"You sabotaged the portal...ordered Mirillow Traxl to be killed," Tomes told him. "Things you won't remember since I've taken your last twelve hours of memory."

Lavor passed Engll off to several soldiers, ordering that they escort him to the palace ruins. "Keep him under continuous watch."

Tomes signaled Torq who hurried over. "Mirillow Traxl is in trouble."

"I heard." Torq stood with elbows bent, his hands resting on his hips.

Tomes drew the immortals into a huddle. "I am going with Jordon to warn him, then, to take care of the situation with the portals. Galvar will be back soon with the charge."

"Get to the Xallon Lowland Territory...to Traxl. We will see to the relocation." Lavor stood between Jordon and Corin. "I will ready some men to accompany you. You will need guards for each portal." He broke from the huddle and darted away.

"I've relayed once how to use the crossmarker, but just so there's no confusion: Place a pin behind each individual's ear and hold the crossmarker against the end of the pin. Say: Compitum Erebus Evoco Percur Insero Earth." Tomes reviewed the process. "The pin will melt into the body, marking them for recalling."

Corin repeated the instructions. "I'm sure Galvar will remember."

Within minutes Lavor returned with a small company of soldiers

"Tomes." Angelique rushed toward her brother. "Be careful."

Tomes hugged her, then reached for Kara. "Don't look so worried." He leaned in for a kiss. "I'll see you soon." Releasing her hand, he took several steps backward and opened a window to the Xallon Lowland Territory. "Look after them." He tossed Corin a nod.

Corin nodded back, settling his gaze on the watery view of the distant land, watching as his two friends led a company of men through the window.

21

With the words "Compitum Erebus Evoco Percur Insero Earth," Galvar watched as a pin he held behind a woman's ear melted into her body, leaving a tiny metallic dot at the insertion point.

"Join the others." Galvar motioned toward a group that was tagged and prepared to pass through the Passage of Dimensions. He then turned his attention to the next person in line.

Lavor stood next to Galvar. "I admit, I was a little worried earlier." His right foot was propped on a large rock.

"We all were." Galvar quickly tagged the individual standing in front of him, doing his best to maintain a timely pace.

Within the hour, the refugees had all been crossed over to Earth. Gathered on the back grounds of the Order of the Clythguard compound, they listened as Galvar gave instructions.

"One day you will hear a calling to return. It may be

months...even years. I cannot guarantee when. But the Order is here to guide you...teach you the way of life here, on Earth. Just remember, no matter where you end up, at the time of recalling, you must return. No matter how settled you become here, this world is only a temporary home. When the time is right, we must return to our own world," Galvar made clear.

"There is a lot to cover, and we will have a full orientation later, but right now, you have to understand that we live here in secret. This world is much different from our own."

Vynce stepped forward. "Those living here do not know that other worlds exist, so we have to keep who we are secret."

"Earth humans appear the same as you, but there are differences in their anatomy, so do not seek medical attention outside of the Order." Galvar reviewed the differences. Also, watch out for the Örök Vér—those we just fought in the Great Battle. They are a Delghorlin clan whose leader is from our world, so be cautious of any outside immortals." He went over several more things, then turned control over to the council.

"It is a little chaotic at present, but this will work," Vynce assured him as they stepped away from the people.

Galvar looked over the group. "There will be more...as they are found."

A council member stood with them. "It will not be easy maintaining a low profile with this many people."

"It will be a challenge," Galvar said. "But the future of their existence in the Eleventh Dimension now lies in our hands. Think of this assignment as the most priceless treasure you will ever guard."

Pierson approached the three immortals. "Should you decide to broaden your operation, you might consider Black River Falls."

Galvar rubbed his chin as if considering the idea. "You, being sheriff, would certainly be beneficial." He faced Pierson. "You have done so much for us already."

Corin, Angelique, Patricia, Kara, and Staca joined the close-knit congregation.

"You and Patricia saved our butts more than once," Corin said.

"It was..." Pierson paused as if searching for an appropriate response, "an experience."

"One hell of an experience for us all," Corin said.

At that moment, the council member excused himself and darted away, having matters to attend to.

"I imagine you and Patricia are eager to get home," Galvar told Pierson. "I have a car you can take," he offered.

"We will take that offer." Pierson thanked him. "I suppose you will be returning to the Eleventh Dimension."

"Yes," Galvar said. "There is a lot to put in order, and it will take time."

"The most critical situation right now is the hit on Traxl." Vynce brushed a gloved hand across the top of his head.

"Jordon and Tomes will find him." Corin was confident.

"It is nearly sunrise." Vynce nodded toward the eastern sky. "We nightwalkers will have to take cover here, at the Order, for the day."

"Take this." Galvar handed his shalym disc to Staca who'd crossed to Earth to help with the relocation, having earned the trust of the people. "I imagine Lavor is waiting for you at the portal. I will get it back when I see you tonight. Vynce and other clythguards have discs."

"With the sun coming up, the rogues will be taking shelter, so you should be safe," Vynce told her.

"We will see you later." Galvar spotted Torq among the people and called out to him. "All nightwalkers must get inside, so you are in charge of the people till nightfall. Find me if there are any problems."

Torq waved in acknowledgement, and Galvar ushered his friends, along with the clythguard, into the building. There was nothing more to be done till next nightfall.

* * * *

"What is bothering you?" Corin walked along a windowless corridor with Jozsef.

"You are very close with Tomes. And not just because of Angelique."

"Yes. We have become close friends."

"Like brothers. I can feel it."

"I do consider him a brother. Family." Corin wasn't sure what Jozsef was trying to get across. "Where are you going with this conversation?"

"The Tree of Lelkek." Jozsef came to a standstill. "Tomes possesses the power to call my soul back from purgatory."

"How do you know your soul is even there? None of us know what becomes of our souls when we are changed."

"I went home about a year ago. The first time in all these years." Jozsef grabbed Corin's arm. "I saw myself in the tree. I couldn't believe it, but my soul, it is there."

Corin backed against the wall, absorbing Jozsef's claim.

"After we were changed, our ancestors must have summoned our souls from beyond, calling us back to where we belong, with them in von Vadim purgatory. You know how strong magic was in our family. Being táltosok, Father said our line was special...why the von

Vadims were set apart in our own purgatory." Jozsef paused for a response. "You believe me, don't you? That I saw myself there?"

"Yes, I believe you, because I saw myself there five hundred years ago, before leaving Hungary," Corin revealed. "I scrambled back when I saw my face appear alongside the face of our uncle. I'd convinced myself it couldn't be real. How could it be real? But now, you've seen yourself in the tree as well." Corin stared at the opposite wall. "I'll never forget the feeling I had, like my soul was drawing me in."

"I had the same feeling."

"Tomes knows about the Tree of Lelkek, but I told him that if my soul was somehow there, that I could never reclaim it."

"I don't believe that's true. I think our souls can be called back. With the Clyth." Jozsef was too worked up to stand still.

"Imagine it. What it would be like to have your soul back. What it might do for us. Would we be more powerful? More human?"

"As far as I know, it's never been done." Corin contemplated the thought. "I'm not sure the Clyth can resurrect souls?"

"It gives its wearer the power to steal the life force of mortals and immortals. I'm banking that it will."

"You will be very disappointed if it doesn't work."

"We have to try. Will you ask him? Being like a brother, he will do it...for you."

Corin hesitated for several seconds, then agreed. "I should get back to Angelique. Rest, Jozsef, night will be here before you know it."

* * * *

At the ruins of Morpar Palace, Tomes and Jordon

emerged from a portal. Lavor, who'd caught sight of their return, immediately approached and dropped onto one knee before Tomes.

"Please stand up." Tomes gestured. "There's no need for that."

It felt strange having people kneel before him. Almost laughable.

"You had best get used to it," Jordon told him. "This is a different world. A different way of life."

"What news do you bring?" Lavor inquired.

"Mirillow Traxl is aware of the threat against his life and is well-guarded?" Jordon announced. "As well as the portals."

Lavor stood with his back to the wind, his brown hair blowing away from his face. "What news do you have of the Traxl-1 supply?"

Jordon sighed. "It's going to take time. The Xallon Lowland Territory was hit hard. Traxl is working under tough conditions as fast as he's able. He has a team in place, but it will be weeks before any large amounts are distributed, and months to cover all regions."

Lavor shook his head. "I hope we can hold out that long. The nightwalkers...it will be a nightmare."

"Of the portals, four are inoperable. Not from Engll's men, but damage from the end time disasters." Tomes had never seen such devastation as what he'd just seen in some of the other regions. "We left soldiers at each of the operable portals."

"With not only the threat of sabotage, but the issue with the nightwalkers, it's imperative we keep the working portals under constant guard. We should send more soldiers to set up camps at each portal," Jordon suggested. "Discs could end up in the wrong hands, and we can't allow any rogues to slip through the Passage."

Lavor nodded. "I will see what men we can spare when I get back."

"Where are you going?" Tomes asked.

"To the portal," Lavor told him. "Bren is there with a company of men, waiting for Galvar, Vynce, whoever returns from Earth. They had to remain there for the day."

"We'll come with you," Tomes said, and changed form.

Reaching the portal just after sunset, Galvar, Vynce, Corin, Angelique, Jozsef, and Kara arrived minutes later.

"I hope all went well," Galvar said.

"Traxl is aware of the threat, and the portals are being guarded," Jordon told him.

Tomes greeted his friends and then reached for Kara. He pulled her into his arms. She was his future...a nightwalker. How would the Eleventh Dimension respond to a mixed union between nightwalker and daywalker? He mulled over the words of prophecy, somehow recalling every word describing the chosen one—a son of man, an outlander who will possess strong blood and an inherent wisdom and understanding. Resurrected from loss, he will be a great peacemaker. And though born of day, and a light of life, he will walk with the night, where a part of him forever dwells.

I will walk with the night. Kara. Angelique. Corin.

The people closest to him, who followed him into a post-apocalyptic alien world and risked their lives for him.

"This is just the beginning of rogue aggression." Galvar's black eyes scanned the circle of immortals, reeling Tomes back from his thoughts. "However, unlike the humans, we are able to withstand their attacks."

Lavor stood alongside Bren. "I want you to keep a company of soldiers here and continue guarding the portal," he told his son. "Ensure no one opens the Passage that is not authorized to do so."

Tomes caught Bren's expression, seeing that he was honored by the task, figuring that this was the most responsibility he'd ever had. His gaze then shifted to Jozsef.

What is it about you that bothers me? He averted his eyes when Jozsef looked in his direction.

The nightwalker had been too close to Andras, but being Corin's brother, he would give him the benefit of the doubt.

"We should get back to the palace ruins and continue with the cleanup efforts." Tomes shape-shifted into a red-tailed hawk, a form he'd assumed before, and with his comrades, set a course for the palace ruins.

Looking down on what remained of the magnificent structure, reality struck him. His surreal reality. This was now his home. His destiny would bind him here for an indefinite time to come. But it felt right. This was where he belonged.

* * * *

"Strange looking at the field now." Corin walked with Tomes along the edge of the western dunes. "I've seen a few wars, but never a war among immortals. This was a first for me. And you. But we survived." He suddenly came to a standstill and faced Tomes. "I have a favor to ask."

"After all we've been through together, you know you can ask anything."

"Do you remember me telling you about the Tree of Lelkek?"

"I remember. The tree that holds the souls of your family. Von Vadim purgatory."

Corin nodded. "I told you how I saw my face in the tree five hundred years ago. Well, now Jozsef tells me that he saw himself in the tree a year ago."

Tomes's brow rose. "So, your souls must be there."

"Jozsef's theory is that our ancestors somehow reclaimed our souls, and he believes that the Clyth may be able to resurrect them...call them back from the tree."

"You want to go there. To the tree. Test his theory." Tomes understood. "If the Clyth can draw forth a life force, maybe it can draw forth a soul. But the trick would then be transferring the soul from the Clyth to the body."

"I told him to be prepared for disappointment." Corin had doubt. "And I would like to keep this from Angelique."

"But it could work, since the souls are there, in the tree, never having crossed over into death." Tomes was intrigued by the prospect. "There is perfectly good reason to believe that it would work. But why keep it from Angel?"

"She has lost her soul...because of me. What right do I have to get mine back when she can never regain hers? Knowing the person she is, if she knew it was possible for me to redeem my soul, she would never let me walk away from the opportunity."

"But you will...walk away?"

"Even if this did work, there is no guarantee of the outcome. How it might change me. I won't take that chance. I have Angelique."

"You choose her over your soul?" Tomes greatly admired his friend. "But you want this for Jozsef?"

"He's lost so much, having lived under Andras's oppression for so long."

Tomes held a silent pause. "Okay. If he's willing to take the chance, I'm willing to see what the Clyth can do." He resumed a slow gait.

"Once the Clyth holds the soul, how will you transfer the soul to its former body?"

"When the Clyth takes a life force from a nightwalker they disintegrate. Daywalkers disperse. So it's impossible to ever rejoin body and soul. But in this case, we have a body. We have a soul. I believe I can use the power of the Clyth concurrently with a spell of transference to draw the soul out and return it directly to Jozsef. Sorcerer instinct tells me it will work, but there are no guarantees. Jozsef will need to understand that."

"I know he will take the risk, and I hope, for his sake, that it works."

"I have to admit, I'm curious. And I'd like to see that tree. What do you say we take a quick trip back to Earth?"

"I wasn't expecting to go tonight, not with everything that's happening here?"

"We wouldn't be long. Lavor can manage for a couple of hours. Don't forget, once we've crossed, I can open a portal to wherever we want to go."

"I won't leave Angelique."

"I'm sure Angel would like to check on the estate...the farm...Dusk and Dawn. We could manage to slip through a portal to the tree."

In agreement, they located Angelique and Kara inside the ruins.

"Staca needs us here." Angelique told Corin.

Tomes saw that the constable's wife was emotional.

"This was her and Lavor's quarters. She is salvaging what's left of their belongings," Angelique explained. "With Lavor on duty, she needs support. I don't want to leave her alone. But you should go and check on things back home."

Corin refused. "I won't leave you here, Angelique."

"Kara is with me. And it's quiet right now." She downplayed the danger. "Go. Check on Dusk and Dawn. I've been worried about them. I'll be right here when you get back."

Tomes looked at Corin. "What do you think? We shouldn't be gone long. Two...three hours tops. And I'd really like to check up on that hired hand while no one's around at night."

"OK. We'll make it a quick trip," Corin reluctantly agreed.

Collecting Jozsef, the three immortals departed Morpar Palace ruins, aimed for the portal. Upon arriving, they found Bren and his company of soldiers guarding the Passage.

"Stand." Tomes motioned for the soldiers to rise from kneeling. "I have some things to attend to on Earth," he informed Bren while removing his disc and activating the Passage. "We will be back soon."

The three immortals passed through the wormhole, entering Earth on the back lawn of von Vadim Estate. Making a quick sweep of both the estate and Jaffler Farm, they quickly moved on to their intended destination—von Vadim Castle in Hungary.

"Wow," Tomes remarked. "This place is certainly impressive. A real castle."

"It's been a very long time." Corin stared at his childhood home.

"We should get out of sight. We wouldn't want the owner to catch us on his property." Jozsef aimed for a wooded area.

Corin called him back. "The owner won't mind." He knew they had nothing to worry about. "*I* am the owner."

"What?" Jozsef expressed surprise. "When?"

"I bought it ten years ago," Corin clued him in, "a few years after the last mortal von Vadim passed away."

"You said you hadn't been here in five hundred years," Jozsef recalled.

"I haven't. I employed an agent to purchase it when it became available, and to see to its upkeep since," Corin explained.

"I should have known." Jozsef gazed on his dimly lit ancestral home for a long, silent moment. "It is not entirely the same."

"No. There have been renovations." Corin stood next to him.

"I want to see it." Jozsef moved toward the entrance.

"Wait," Corin stopped him. "I have a caretaker. He and his family live here. We shouldn't disturb them tonight."

"We should get to the tree," Tomes said. "We don't have a lot of time."

Taking wolf form, Corin, Tomes, and Jozsef entered the woods beyond the grounds. Corin led the way, moving deeper into dense terrain, guided by his night vision. The great wood had changed from what it once was, but it was also still familiar, and he knew when he had reached the sacred territory—an area that had not changed over the years—an area that always remained the same. Here, every tree was as he remembered. Every twist. Every turn. Even the heavy atmosphere that he attributed to the area being protected by magic, which was a necessary precaution in order to keep the tree safe from discovery by the outside world.

Corin suddenly stopped and took back human form. "There." He pointed. "The Tree of Lelkek. Looking the same now as it did five hundred years ago."

The old, disfigured oak moved.

"Did you see that?" Tomes's voice rose in volume and intensity. "The tree...it moved. That wasn't the wind."

"They know we're here." Corin inched toward the

tree's large base, stopping when a cold breeze struck him. Peering upward, the tree's magnificent, twisting limbs repositioned and a face appeared. "Father."

The image slid along a downward-sloping limb that was mottled with algae and laden with resurrection fern.

Jozsef grabbed Corin's arm and whispered, "I didn't see him before. I only saw myself."

"Jozsef," the entity spoke, having overheard. "I was here but could not reveal myself. You were not alone. There was a spy."

"I was followed?" Jozsef expressed surprise. "I recall feeling a presence, but I figured it was just the tree...the souls."

Corin shot a look of concern at Jozsef. "Who could have followed you?"

"Andras," Jozsef answered. "It had to be Andras."

"Then he knows about the tree." Corin feared the Delghorlin leader would be real trouble yet again. "He probably saw your face appear to you."

The spirit of Count Ramone von Vadim drew closer, gliding along a branch that snaked toward Tomes, the limb magically materializing as it expanded, twisting and turning in an unnatural manner.

Corin quickly maneuvered to Tomes's side, standing so close that their shoulders touched.

Tomes took in a quick breath. "Unbelievable. And I thought I'd seen everything."

"He's no danger." Corin vouched for Tomes. "He is here to help us."

"My sons place enormous trust in you to have disclosed our secret." The count held a fixed stare on Tomes.

"Your secret is safe with me," Tomes swore. "Corin is now my family."

"It is true," Corin confirmed. "I am joined with his

sister, Angelique. We are all immortals. It is a long story."

The count shifted his focus from Tomes to Corin. "Centuries have passed, and you are unchanged. You and Jozsef...still young men. Both of you still living your earthly life," he paused. "My sons. Immortals."

"Jozsef and I are nightwalkers," Corin told him. "Changed five hundred years ago."

"Nightwalkers," the count repeated. His face momentarily contorted as if he might be losing his connection to the physical world, but he quickly regained balance. "At least your souls are safe."

"So, our souls, they are here, in the tree?" Corin sought affirmation.

The limbs encasing Corin and Tomes slowly withdrew and merged back into one limb.

"Yes. They are here," the count answered. "But they are not whole. The life force that is meant to accompany a soul into death is missing."

"Because we are still living," Corin surmised. "But I don't understand how our souls are here, in the tree. When Jozsef and I were changed, made immortal, our souls were taken by the Angel of Death. So, how could they come to be here?"

"You already know the answer, Corin. You stand here now, talking to ancestors hundreds of years long passed, just as I did when I was living." Count von Vadim's voice was haunting. "Feel the power at work around you. Our bloodline is special."

Jozsef moved closer to the apparition of his father. "Why? Why are we so special?"

"We were chosen." The count's features momentarily distorted again as the limb hosting his spirit curved toward Jozsef. "It is as it is, and shall be, till the last of our line."

"But Jozsef and I are now the last," Corin informed

him. "With no children to follow, the line will end with us."

"Our line? At its end?" The count appeared disturbed by the news.

"Tell him why we've come," Tomes whispered to Corin. "We shouldn't stay away from the Eleventh Dimension—from Angelique and Kara—too much longer."

"Why have you come?" The count overheard.

"We may have a way to reclaim Jozsef's soul," Corin told his father.

The count's stare locked on Corin. "That is not possible."

"It is very possible. With this." Tomes showcased the Heart and Body of the Clyth. "A charm having great power."

"I have to try," Jozsef told the count. "What about your soul, Corin?" He faced his brother. "It's Angelique, isn't it?"

"Yes. I cannot take a chance on anything changing between us." He would always put her first. "But I want this for you."

"Corin, we've been gone from the Eleventh Dimension too long. Let's get on with this," Tomes urged.

Corin laid a hand on Tomes's shoulder and gave a firm squeeze. He looked at Jozsef. "Are you ready?"

Jozsef nodded the go ahead.

"Good luck." Corin stepped back.

Following instinct, Tomes connected the two charms, forming the Clyth as a whole. Then, claiming a wide stance, he held the charm before him, and with a bowed head, mumbled several foreign words. Suddenly straightening, his eyes widened, and he spoke clearly, calling forth the soul of Jozsef von Vadim to be reunited with its earthly body.

The Clyth emitted a bright light, engulfing the area in a brilliant glow as he called out the command a second time.

The glow waned as several lingering seconds passed.

"Nothing's hap—" Jozsef was silenced by an unexpected bolt of energy that ejected from the charm that struck the tree and rent its base.

The count's face contorted, then withdrew on a lingering wail as hazy blue light escaped the tree. The fissure widened, affording Corin a glimpse of another realm of existence, a place much brighter and more peaceful than he had imaged.

"Someone is there." Corin straightened as a ghostly form approached, interrupting the flood of blue light as it crawled through the opening in an inhuman manner, its expressionless face eerily identical to his own.

Corin backed up as the entity neared, the soul never ceasing in motion as it targeted Jozsef and entered his body.

In dim silence, Corin shared Jozsef's experience, feeling his complete fulfillment. It had worked.

Jozsef slowly turned and faced Corin. "You felt that?"

Corin nodded. "It worked. You have your soul. How do you feel?"

"There are no words...." Jozsef appeared somewhat dazed. "It is just as I remember. No, it is more."

"Corin." Tomes laid a hand on his back. "Your soul, it is there for the taking. Are you sure you don't want to reclaim it?"

Corin thought of Angelique. "I can't take that chance. And remember, Angelique is to never know about this."

"I understand." Tomes separated the charms. "But not knowing how this will affect Jozsef, this secret might not be so easy to keep."

Corin didn't respond, transfixed by the sight of the gap in the tree magically closing on its own, regenerating new wood, new bark, as it repaired itself. Within seconds, the Tree of Lelkek was once again whole, and the rift exposing von Vadim purgatory was no more.

In the silent aftermath, the face of the count reappeared. "I never thought it possible for a soul to leave purgatory."

"What exactly is von Vadim purgatory?" Corin wanted to know more. "Is it another realm?"

"As you would think of heaven and hell, that is our purgatory. The tree is our doorway, and once we enter this life, we are forever bound here."

"How do you know when someone comes to the tree, like we have today?" So many questions bounced around Corin's mind.

"We, von Vadims, are all tied to the tree, and it calls to us. It knows." The count's response was short...vague.

It knows. Corin pondered those words.

22

Andras stood amid an army of starving rogue nightwalkers, an unruly horde united in one endeavor, and that was to feed. He refused to leave the Eleventh Dimension knowing that the dir cyohr was still alive and would eventually end his life. He feared the power of the Clyth, but all hope was not yet lost, because there was still a way to cut down the dir cyohr. He intended to strike where Tomes was most vulnerable, that being the two women the dir cyohr loved most in any world—Angelique and Kara.

"Are you sure you want to do this?" Meical scanned the ungovernable, make-do army. "The Morpar Army is strong."

"They lost numbers during the battle," Andras reminded him. "This army is driven by hunger."

Meical rested his hands on his sheathed daggers. "Making a dangerous army."

"For now, the promise of Traxl-1 will keep them in my control."

"There's no way of knowing for certain how much we'll find. But any amount will start pandemonium. They'll kill each other over it." Meical pulled his daggers and inspected the blades.

"I know they are not reliable, but I need an army, a number to rival Morpar. A number I'm certain we've surpassed. And my plan will work. We'll go in disguise...hide among the rogues. We'll take advantage of the mass chaos that's sure to ensue. It will all work to our advantage."

"They'll believe it's just the rogues attacking."

"The Clyth is a real threat now, and the dir cyohr is powerful. Even in disguise we have to move quickly. We have to get in, grab our targets, and get out. If all goes well, he'll never suspect what we're up to until it's too late." Andras took pleasure in treachery.

Calling the Delghorlin clan together, Andras briefed them on his plan, explaining the importance of remaining in disguise. He then ordered the clan to rally the masses into flight, with the great army of immortals darkening the sky as they set a course for the ruins of Morpar Palace.

Drawing near their destination, trumpets sounded out a warning of invasion and outermost guards met their charge, but the rogue army was unstoppable and quickly swept through the first onrush of opposition. Indithian soldiers attempted to encircle the ruins with a second barricade, but they were too late to prevent the rogue army from reaching Morpar's innermost sanction, where the hungry nightwalkers dove mindlessly into the opposing force, driven by the promise of Traxl-1 awaiting within.

Taking human form, Andras looked to his right at Meical who wore the face of a stranger. *Always loyal. You've never let me down.* His thoughts then shifted to Jozsef, troubled by his absence, and betrayal.

"The army is out of control." Meical gripped a dagger in each hand. "It's just as I figured. They're so desperate for food that they're turning on each other. They'll kill anything in their path."

"They are definitely serving their purpose of not only giving us cover, but weakening the enemy."

A deafening uproar drew Andras's attention to the entrance of the palace ruins, where rogues crammed the space, the horde climbing over each other in a mad rush. There was no doubt, Traxl-1 had been found.

"We'd best avoid that madness." Andras scanned their surroundings in search of their targets, spotting a number of his clan members fighting amid the chaos.

"Look out!" Meical blocked an assailing Indithian soldier, stopping him in his tracks, and quickly taking him out.

Andras's expression tensed. "We need to find our marks, before we're discovered." He alerted Meical to Lavor's close proximity, watching as the constable met up with Jordon Black less than ten feet away from them.

Hiding amid the crowd, Andras tuned in on their conversation, making an interesting discovery—the girls were there, in the Eleventh Dimension, but the dir cyohr, Corin, and Jozsef had crossed over to Earth.

"The dir cyohr...he's not here." Meical had also heard.

"This changes things." Andras's mouth twisted in wicked anticipation. "No sorcerer. No Clyth. We have them outnumbered. We can take the kingdom."

"Jordon. He's going after him." Meical continued to eavesdrop.

"We'll have to make the most of the little time we have." Andras glared at Lavor. "To topple the army, we must take out their pillar of strength."

"Taking out the constable won't be easy, and don't

forget about Galvar."

"Galvar. Yes, he could be a problem."

"We do have them outnumbered, but at present, we have no control over the rogues."

"The Indithian Army has their hands full with the rogues. We may never get a chance like this again."

Meical spotted Lehndra. "Lehndra." He gestured with a nod. "I'll have her spread the word."

Andras and Meical made a swift dash to her position and filled her in on the change of plans.

"We will take this opportunity to seize the kingdom," Meical told her. "Spread the word."

Lehndra darted away, and Andras scanned the great throng of immortals that were in violent warfare around him. "We need several Delghorlins." He set his sights back on Lavor. "We have to eliminate him."

"I'll see what I can do." Meical disappeared among the horde, returning minutes later with four of his comrades.

The six nightwalkers moved into positions to assail Lavor, but a moment before making their strike, a sudden outcry alerted the constable of their sneak attack.

"Protect the constable!" An Indithian soldier had cried.

A growl rose in Andras's throat when Galvar and Vynce appeared—two clythguard nightwalkers he knew to be powerful fighters and trusted superiors by the Indithian soldiers.

"They are not rogues." Galvar's voice rode above the clamor and commotion. "It must be the Delghorlins."

Quickly scanning the scene around him, Andras saw that Meical was right, there was little chance of regaining control of the rogue army. He cursed. But he refused to leave empty-handed. "Our cover is blown. Find the girls!" His order rolled on a roar.

"There." Meical pinpointed their initial targets, both girls trailing two soldiers who appeared to be escorting a prisoner away from the ruins.

Andras glared in their direction. "Slow the constable and those two clythguards down," he told Meical, "and I'll see to this."

Shifting to vapor, Andras rushed to intercept the girls, the two soldiers, and the prisoner. "What have we here?" he said upon reclaiming his form in their direct path. "One of your own in chains?"

Umorius suddenly appeared behind him. "The regent's assistant."

Andras smirked. "The regent's assistant?" he repeated. "Now a prisoner?"

"Crimes against other species," Angelique bravely spoke out.

"Against nightwalkers." Engll shot the word at him. "I only regret that I failed."

Andras remained focused on Angelique, a highly attractive Delghorlin, both in beauty and bravery. "Blood of my own."

One of the Indithian soldiers charged Andras, but Umorius intercepted his onrush and slayed him. "Try anything, and you will join him," he warned the other guard.

A rise in upheaval drew Andras's attention back to his clan members who were scarcely holding back the enemy. He glimpsed the constable—an unstoppable warrior—the Indithian wielding a sword with great skill.

You have pledged life and loyalty to the dir cyohr, and to the kingdom, and you will fight to the death.

Andras's breath momentarily stopped when the constable's sword pierce Meical's side.

"Retreat!" Andras's thundering order echoed as he stormed several steps forward. "Delghorlins, retreat!"

Glaring at Lavor as Meical changed form and escaped, the steely look in the Indithian's eyes showed a fierce determination, and Andras knew they had to move fast.

"Get the girls." Andras turned and motioned to Umorius, releasing a growl when the second guard made a bold move to intervene.

Engll ducked and rolled to avoid a blade that passed inches from his neck, only to be caught by Umorius's second swing that brought about a flash of light...his dispersal.

"Stop them!" Andras rushed after Angelique and Kara who took advantage of the opportunity to shift and leap into flight.

Angered by their escape, he snatched up a sword and finished off the guard. "After them," he told Umorius. "Remember, we need them alive."

Meical took form next to Andras. "I saw what happened." He clutched his side.

"It's time to go." Andras spun on his heels and called for his clan to retreat, and he and Meical shifted and took flight.

Catching up with Umorius just as he dove into a wooded area in pursuit of the girls, the Delghorlins managed to surround their prey at the edge of a smoking crater.

"We should hurry. The Indithians won't be far behind." Meical took the opportunity to heal his wound.

"These two lovelies are just what I need to sway negotiations in my favor." Andras stepped toward Angelique and Kara. "I'm betting that the dir cyohr will give his life for you two."

Angelique struggled against restraint. "If you're after the Clyth, Tomes will never give it up, not even for us."

Andras bent close enough to feel her breath on his

face. "I won't be asking for the Clyth. I will be asking for his life. To save my own."

A number of rogue nightwalkers continued to pour into the space, having heeded Andras's call for retreat. He knew that these were the lucky ones that had managed to obtain Traxl-l, temporarily satiating their hunger, leaving the unfortunate lingerers to their doom. More lives had been lost—the bulk of the casualties being rogues—but Andras was content with the outcome. He may not have seized Morpar, but he got his hostages, setting the core of his plot—leverage needed to use against the dir cyohr. And with this small triumph, everything was falling pleasantly into place.

* * * *

At the Tree of Lelkek, Corin absorbed some distressing news, having just learnt that the future of the tree did not look promising. He and Jozsef were the last of the von Vadim line, and without new souls, the tree would eventually die.

"The tree requires a soul every hundred years." Count Ramone von Vadim's spectral face slid to-and-fro along a twisted limb, as if pacing, something Corin often did when agitated. "When that time comes, we will be separated forever if a soul is not produced. This tree is our only connection to the physical world."

"Being nightwalkers, Jozsef and I can't produce offspring to continue the line, but there must be something else we can do. Some magic...ritual." Corin was ready to do whatever it took to save the tree.

"At least we have some time to find a solution," Jozsef said.

"You may not be the last," the count revealed. "There may yet be hope."

"We're not the last?" Jozsef looked perplexed.

Another face then appeared in the tree alongside the count, a woman that seemed familiar to Corin, yet he could not place the connection.

"I am Neena." Her gaze settled on Corin. "My son saw me to purgatory forty years ago, yet he is not here now."

"Yes." Corin recognized her name. "I've followed our line closely. I recall your death. An accidental shooting by your son. The firearm went off while he was cleaning it. At least that is what was claimed."

"Ócsa." Neena spoke his name. "It is true. It was an accident."

"He was the last von Vadim, or so I thought. He passed away fifteen years ago from illness. Only in his forties." Corin thought back. "I purchased the castle from his widow five years after his death." His brow furrowed. "Why isn't he with you in purgatory?"

"At some point, no one is left to perform the Ritual of Passage," the count explained. "But it can still be done. His soul can be drawn back from where it now resides and placed where it belongs. That would renew the tree for another hundred years."

"It's been fifteen years." Jozsef was skeptical. "Can we call his soul back after all that time?"

"He is of von Vadim blood. The Tree of Lelkek will claim his soul. But the ritual must be performed." The count stressed the latter. "Fifteen years is but a drop in a sea of eternity."

"You said that Jozsef and I may not be the last. Is there another living von Vadim?" Corin sought clarification.

"Ócsa fathered a son two years before he died, but upon birth, the child was sent with his mother, an American," Neena disclosed. "His name is Táltos."

Corin tensed. "I wasn't aware of a son. The estate was not left to him."

"Táltos was conceived out of adultery. As it was, Ócsa's wife never bore a child, but she knew about Táltos. I must presume she schemed to cut Táltos out of his inheritance."

"I'd say that's a safe assumption. Like I said, I purchased the castle from her." Corin recalled the transaction. "I acted through a middleman to protect my identity."

"It's only been ten years since she sold the castle," Tomes said. "If we can locate her, she may know where to find Táltos."

Neena's face gently swayed as if blown by a soft wind. "She was very bitter over the child. Do not count on her cooperation."

"I'm confused." Jozsef's eyebrows drew downward. "How do you know all of this, since it has all occurred since your death?"

"When I died, Ócsa visited the tree often. He confided in me. He told me about his life...about his son. When he stopped coming, I knew something was wrong." Neena's face faded and then reappeared. "The last we spoke, his illness had rapidly progressed, and fearing his time was growing short, he had planned to reunite with his son and the boy's mother."

"When he died, other than his wife, there was no one left to perform his passage." Corin thought the situation very tragic, wondering if it were possible that his family line had been cursed at some point. "She must have known about the tree, but chose not to help him, being bitter over the affair," he figured. "If only he had found his son."

"That is what you must do. You must find Táltos." Count Ramone stressed the importance to his sons. "Also, it is your duty to exhume Ócsa and perform the Ritual of Passage."

"With Neena's passage being the last, forty years

ago, the tree doesn't require a soul for another sixty years," Tomes pointed out. "But I understand that he belongs with his family."

"Ócsa has been cheated. It must be made right," the count made clear. "With the Ritual of Passage, each time a soul is given, one hundred years is reset. With Ócsa, the sixty remaining years will become one hundred years again."

"Giving us time to try to resurrect the von Vadim lineage...through Táltos." Corin thought about his ancestors, those preceding him who'd been lost to war and disease. "You must know, father, that I walked away from the Art. But today.... Today, I am back."

"You are not the first to have been led astray," the count informed him. "However, they all returned once mortality reared its ugly head. When that time came, they knew where we belonged in the afterlife."

Since Táltos was taken away as an infant, he may not know anything about our family," Jozsef pointed out. "What if he doesn't accept it?"

"You know the importance," the count told him. "I leave that task in the hands of my sons."

Tomes gripped Corin's shoulder. "I hate to rush you, but we have to go. We've been away from the Eleventh Dimension too long."

Corin thought of Angelique. "You're right. We need to get back." He looked into his father's haunting eyes. "We have to go. There are others depending on us right now."

"Do not forget your duties here," the count reminded him. "The tree must live."

"We will return soon," Corin assured him.

While Jozsef said goodbye to his father, Tomes positioned his shalym disc in the palm of his hand and opened the portal to the Eleventh Dimension.

"Amazing that doesn't hurt," Corin's face scrunched

up at the thought.

"I'm ready." Jozsef joined them.

Corin took one last look at the tree, then entered the portal and crossed through the Passage to the Eleventh Dimension. "Jordon." He was surprised to be met by his friend upon emerging Morpar's portal. "What are you doing here?"

"I was just about to cross to Earth to find you. Where have you been?" Jordon's voice held distress.

"Has something happened?" Tomes asked.

"Andras is still here. He led the rogues in an attack on Morpar," Jordon reported.

Corin cut his eyes at Tomes. "Angelique."

"I know." Tomes returned his stare. "She's in trouble."

Bren swiftly approached. "Two of my men just returned from the palace. The enemy has fled."

"This is my fault," Tomes said. "I should never have left Morpar unprotected. Andras is after me, and he'll stop at nothing to see me dead."

"We all assumed he had returned to Earth," Jozsef told Tomes. "None of us ever thought he'd try anything again so soon."

"We need to get to the palace." Corin felt Angelique's distress. "Something is still wrong."

"Wait." Tomes opened a window. "This is faster."

"I must remain here, guarding the Passage of Dimensions." Bren wished them luck.

With no further delay, Corin, Tomes, Jozsef, and Jordon passed through the portal to the ruins of Morpar Palace.

"Galvar." Jordon spotted him.

Galvar rushed toward them. "You know what happened?" He looked at Tomes, then Corin. "The Delghorlins."

Jordon gestured toward Lavor who approached.

"You've got some nasty cuts there."

"He fought with the strength of ten men." Vynce also appeared, healing his own wounds.

"We have staved off another attack, but not without more loss of life." Lavor looked around. "And our Traxl-1 supply...that is now gone."

"Angelique? Where is she?" Corin felt her anxiety.

Galvar's head lowered. "She and Kara. They were targeted by Andras. They were forced into flight, and the Delghorlins went after them. We are not sure—"

"Angelique is alive. That much I know." Corin clenched his fists. "I have to find her."

Galvar pressed a hand on his shoulder. "We did pursue them, but the rogues, they hindered our efforts."

"We will get them back," Jordon assured Corin. "It's clear what Andras is doing...most likely planning to use them to get to Tomes."

Corin felt a strong sense of déjà vu as memories of Angelique's kidnapping six months earlier flooded back. "Boldor all over again."

Tomes caught Corin's stare. "Andras knows I'll do anything to save Angelique and Kara."

Corin turned and stared into the distant darkness. *Hold on, Angelique. After everything we've been though, I cannot lose you now.*

23

Tomes stood at the gates of the Kingdom of Shudrorah, given welcome passage by the guardian gargoyles. Crossing a moat of fire, he was met by Nordriss and Hediye on a wide terrace.

"What has brought you so soon?" Nordriss's eyes transitioned from rich green to unnaturally metallic silver.

"Morpar was attacked again. Andras has Angelique and Kara. I thought you—"

"You are in a tough position, caught between those you love and a world depending on you. Come inside. Hediye will locate them." Nordriss led him through an inner bailey to the keep.

Inside, Hediye hustled toward a basin filled with what Tomes presumed to be water and proceeded to sprinkle several powders into the krater, producing a rising mist. "They went south. I see mountains."

Nordriss nodded. "Zarchia." He looked at Tomes. "I will accompany you until this is settled."

"I will get Suna." Hediye aimed for a large doorway that towered to a height of at least twenty feet.

"Hediye," Nordriss urged her back. "I would feel better if you and Suna remained in Shudrorah."

"You, better than anyone, know how capable we are." Hediye stood her ground. "We will come." Her highlighted strands whipped as she spun and exited the room.

Tomes wasn't sure whether the look on Nordriss's face showed his amusement or irritation at Hediye's feisty comeback, but when she returned a moment later with her sister, he gave no further objections.

"First, we need to set a plan into place." He opened a window to the ruins of Morpar Palace, and they passed through, arriving amid a state of commotion.

"What is happening?" Tomes observed a captive being restrained by Lavor and Jordon, with Corin, Jozsef, and others encircling them.

"I bring a message. From Andras." The captive showed no fear.

"You have some nerve coming back here, Umorius," Jordon spoke through clenched teeth.

Lavor gave the spy an intimidating glare. "I can fault you for many things, Umorius, but never courage."

"The girls? What has Andras done with them?" Corin confronted Umorius, demanding an answer.

"They are in Zarchia." Nordriss approached Umorius who tensed in his presence. "I make you nervous. I do not expect Andras planned on my return."

Umorius shifted his defiant stare to Tomes. "He knows you will never surrender the Clyth, so instead, he demands your life in exchange for theirs. Surrender yourself at Zarchia Point next nightfall, or they will die."

Corin cursed, and with fangs and talons extended,

he stormed toward Umorius, but Galvar blocked his charge.

"We need him alive." Galvar held him back. "Control your monster. You know what happens once fully consumed."

Corin rotated on his heels with a growl and looked at Tomes. "I can't feel her anymore."

"Morvormanite runs to Zarchia. He must have her underground," Lavor presumed.

Tomes stepped in front of Umorius. "Tell Andras he can expect us." He leaned close. "And the girls better be alive and well."

"They are." Umorius was not intimidated. "For the time being. And if you want them to stay that way, you will come alone."

Tomes stepped back. "Lavor. Jordon. Let him go." He held Umorius's stare. "You'd best hurry if you want to beat sunrise."

"Remember, come alone, or they die." Umorius whipped a sharp glance at Nordriss, then transformed and took flight, disappearing into the hazy abyss.

Corin paced to control his rage. "Where is Zarchia Point?"

"It is south of here," Lavor answered. "The center mountain in a range entering Zarchia. The perfect location for an ambush."

"Precisely why he chose it," Galvar said. "With morvormanite running through the area, it will be impossible to detect them. He also has the peace of mind in knowing that should we attempt a rescue, the morvormanite would block our powers...even the sorcerers' powers."

"I can't do this again." Corin never broke a stride.

Seeing that he couldn't stand still, tormented by the thought of what might happen to Angelique, Tomes stopped him. "I thought the end time battle would be the hardest thing I'd face as the dir cyohr. I was wrong."

Corin groaned. "These devils know right where to hit us."

Jordon secured a strap that tied back his hair. "They find out what means most to you, and they use it to their advantage." His gaze locked with Corin's. "Their mistake—they underestimate you."

"Their obsessions lead them to make foolish choices," Galvar added. "Forcing a sorcerer's hand. Foolish. In the end, he will likely bring about his own death."

"What about the tunnels? Could we use them to our advantage?" Lavor asked.

Galvar shook his head. "Following the earthquake, the south tunnel was flooded," he informed him. "However, we might be able to enter from another point, before reaching Zarchia, beyond the area of flooding."

"Leave that to me," Vynce volunteered. "I will take a squad and find a way in."

"Be careful," Jozsef cautioned. "You can count on Andras covering the bases. He will have every point of entry leading into Zarchia Point guarded."

"Let us hope he missed one," Vynce said.

"Once underground, with your powers blocked and having no ability to shape-shift, it will be risky," Nordriss told Vynce.

Hediye and Suna stood alongside the sorcerer, their pale, porcelain faces clearly visible in the dim surroundings.

"How long will it take us to reach Zarchia?" Corin wished he knew more about the territory.

"Less than an hour." Galvar leaned against a waist-high boulder. "Andras will be holed up in the caverns. Hopefully, you will be able to draw them out."

Corin looked at Nordriss. "Umorius tensed up when he saw you. They will be cautious."

"Yes. A second sorcerer is not in their favor." Galvar straightened, drawing attention to his tall frame.

Tomes stepped in front of Nordriss. "There is something we need to settle...the reason I needed you here." He handed him the Heart and Body of the Clyth. "I have to save Angel and Kara, and that may mean my life. With that being the case, I am depending on you to protect the Clyth."

Nordriss took the charms.

"You cannot give up your life," Lavor protested. "You are king of the Eleventh Dimension. Our world is depending on you."

Nordriss agreed with Lavor. "You cannot go. But I can. As 'you.'" He shape-shifted into Tomes's form. "Using my powers would give my identity away, but there are spells."

"It could work." Corin supported the idea. "I would do it, but being tied to Andras, he would sense me."

"It is a good plan," Lavor said. "But the loss of either sorcerer would be detrimental to the Eleventh Dimension...affecting an entire world. I should go. If I die, it affects only a few."

"There are spells to protect whoever goes." Nordriss took back his own form." As long as you remain outside of the caverns."

"Spells." Tomes looked at Nordriss. "A spell of invisibility. That's how we'll do it. No one will go in my place, but you'll be right there with me, invisible to the eyes of the enemy."

"They will sense our presence," Lavor pointed out a flaw in his plan.

"With other immortals present, they may not, but it would be nice to mask our presence upon arrival, when they will be on high alert," Nordriss told Lavor. "There is a spell that can conceal our presence for a short time; however, it is not the most reliable of spells."

"You can conceal our presence from other immortals?" Corin was surprised.

"It is not a strong spell, but it can be beneficial, if cast by the right individual." Nordriss glanced at Hediye.

"Would it conceal me and Jozsef from Andras?" Corin asked. "You know our connection to him."

"I would not chance that strong of a connection." Nordriss wasn't favorable of testing the power of the spell at such a critical time. "The point is to lessen our risk."

"I know you're worried, Corin, but this time, it's on my shoulders," Tomes told him. "We have a good plan. A risky plan...but cunning."

* * * *

Next nightfall, Corin, Jozsef, Galvar, and Vynce emerged from the dark recesses of the ruins to a gathered army.

"Finally." Tomes hurried toward the four immortals, followed by Nordriss, Hediye, and Suna. "Your squad is ready," he addressed Vynce.

"Good." Vynce adjusted his gloves. "I had best get moving. Find that entry into the south tunnel."

Galvar caught his arm. "Be careful."

"I will see you soon," Vynce assured him.

Corin thought of nothing but Angelique as he stared in the direction of the soldiers, catching sight of Lavor's approach.

"I have separated the army into two battalions," the constable apprised the nightwalkers who had just surfaced. "One half will remain here and guard Morpar under the charge of Bren; the other half will go with us.

Held at a distance, the Delghorlins won't detect them."

"Are we ready to go?" Galvar asked.

"Upon the dir cyohr's command," Lavor answered.

Departing a few minutes later, the battalion reached the northern outskirts of Zarchia less than an hour later.

"An amazing sight," Suna remarked on the mountains' jagged formations, searching for peaks that were concealed by a streaming aurora of colors. "It reminds me of Earth's aurora borealis."

Corin could hardly appreciate the view, too consumed by worry.

"For those of us continuing on to Zarchia Point, we should cast the spell of invisibility now, before moving in any closer," Nordriss suggested to the others.

Galvar reminded Tomes of the morvormanite. "Do everything you can to draw them outside. We will not be able to follow you into the caverns and remain invisible."

"There is something you should know about Zarchia Point," Nordriss told Tomes. "There is a small space within the caves that is free of morvormanite. It is said to be located near the outer edge, and by first rights, can be found."

"By first rights?" Tomes said. "What does that mean?"

"It is part of a riddle." Nordriss quoted the veiled rhyme.

By first rights come freedom
By boundaries come power
Through this passage of time
To a point you must cower

Past a shallow reflection
A weeping curtain reveals

The only path forward
Marked by a great seal

Lured forth by a guide
Past a dragon long bound
With a touch and a whisper
Your freedom is found."

Nordriss pressed two fingers against Tomes's temple. "Remember it."

Corin stared into Tomes's face, seeing his mouth draw to his left, figuring that he was pondered the riddle that had just been injected into his mind.

"The caverns will be an interconnecting maze. Take every right turn." Nordriss handed Tomes a small, brown bottle, no more than two inches long. "If you find yourself in trouble, throw this down with force. The impact will generate a chemical reaction and ignite a blinding flash that will temporarily blind the nightwalkers, giving you a means of escape. Lingering fumes will then continue to burn their eyes and interfere with their vision for a short time."

Tomes gripped the bottle and thanked Nordriss. "Piiric used this in the past. I know what to do." He slipped the bottle into the pouch he had used to carry the Heart and Body, the charms that were now in Nordriss's care.

"If you are forced into the caverns, follow the clues, and find that escape." Nordriss tossed back his gray cloak, displacing his dark dreadlocks that draped his shoulders. "Then open a window and return to Morpar. We will know to find you there."

Jozsef stood next to Corin. "We can't get too close or Andras will sense us."

"I know." Corin scowled. He would have to watch from a distance. But not too distant.

"Constable, you are needed here, in control of the army," Nordriss told Lavor.

"I should be protecting the dir cyohr." Lavor objected.

"With Nordriss, Jordon, and myself, he will not be alone," Galvar reminded him.

Lavor reluctantly accepted his position. "About the battalion, what will be our signal to move in, should it come to that?"

"In this case, the signal we used in Sloe Forest—three consecutive eagle cries—will not work. It would not be heard at this distance." Galvar looked to the others for suggestions.

Nordriss stepped past Hediye, to Suna. "You hold our solution. The stones."

"One of my biraz falcıları." Suna reached for the stones and chose an arachnid. Calling it forth, she sent the spider to Tomes, where it climbed up his body and claimed a hiding place beneath his clothing.

Tomes shuddered. "I would never get used to this."

"As long as you remain outside of the caves, Suna will know what is happening." Nordriss's eyes slowly changed color. "Hediye." He reached for her hands. "You and Suna will stay with the constable and keep him informed of what is happening."

She gave no argument. "We will know if and when to act."

"We part here then." The hem of Nordriss's cloak ruffled as he spun around and gazed on the highest mountain, its peak hidden in the misty aurora. "Zarchia Point"

"I'm coming with you to a closer position," Corin informed Nordriss. He looked at Tomes. "Angelique is up there."

Tomes understood. "Just don't get too close."

"Tomes." Corin held his stare. "Be careful."

Corin reminded himself that Tomes was no longer the mortal man he'd protected six months earlier. Now, he was a sorcerer, the dir cyohr, an immortal possessing powers far superior to his own. But he was not immune to morvormanite, and without his powers, he could be killed.

Corin turned and caught Nordriss. "Tomes and I have been in this position before," he whispered. "Stay close to him. He *will* give his life to save Angelique and Kara."

"I will do everything I can," Nordriss assured him.

"Nordriss." Galvar drew the sorcerer's attention. "How about that spell of invisibility?"

"I will cast it." Hediye drew Nordriss, Galvar, Jordon, Corin, and Jozsef together and executed the spell, followed by a second spell to conceal their presence. "The spell of invisibility is tried-and-true; however, as you are aware, the spell to hide your presence is not reliable, and will gradually wear off."

"How long do you think it will last?" Galvar asked.

"Maybe an hour," Nordriss answered.

"Then we had better get moving." Tomes said.

"You can't see us, Tomes, but we will be right there with you," Jordon assured him.

Corin shifted and followed Tomes into flight, aimed for Zarchia Point. He kept him in his sights until eyeing an impressive canyon at the base of their destination, an open space surrounded by soaring rock columns.

I can't chance getting any closer.

He dropped back and claimed a position on a ledge that afforded him a clear view of Tomes in the canyon below.

I know you're here, Jozsef.

Looking around, he could not see his brother, but he had heard him following and caught a faint detection of his presence that was barely discernable. Something

Andras likely would have detected, spell or not.

You were right, Nordriss. With strong connections, the spell is not dependable.

Turning his gaze upward, he was close to the rolling bands of colors, a beautiful yet eerie display. His line of vision then shifted and settled on two Delghorlins hiding on a nearby ledge.

They can't see me, he reminded himself while scanning the walls of rock surrounding the canyon, catching sight of other Delghorlins lying in wait.

This doesn't look good.

He zeroed in on Tomes's position.

Watch yourself down there, my friend. Andras is ready to move in for the kill.

* * * *

Standing before a tall, narrow opening of a ground-level cave, Tomes summoned his adversary. "Andras, I am here. Show yourself!"

Meical appeared in the mouth of cave. "We prefer to conduct business inside, sorcerer."

"Tell Andras that is not going to happen. Not until I see Angel and Kara, alive and well." Tomes needed to know that they were safe.

Andras appeared next to Meical and passed Kara off to him. Gripping Angelique's arm, he glared at Tomes. "You know what I want—you, in exchange for the women—one life for two."

"No, Tomes. Don't give yourself up," Angelique yelled, receiving a firm strike from Andras.

Tomes stormed closer to the cave in a flash of anger. "Keep your hands off of her!"

Seeing Angelique at the mercy of Andras brought back images of Boldor.

"I am here. Now, let them go," Tomes demanded,

catching Kara's vibrant, blue stare as Meical withdrew several steps, keeping her well within the safety of the cave.

"When you come inside, we will let them go. Not before." Andras had the upper hand. "Knowing your power, sorcerer, we would be foolish to exit this cave. Within these caverns of morvormanite, you have no power."

"If I enter the cave, what assurance do I have that you will honor our agreement, and let them go?" Tomes knew better than to trust him.

"That is a chance you will have to take. Throw down your sword, give yourself up, and the girls go free. Those are the terms." Andras suddenly paused, tipped his head, and scanned the canyon. "Jozsef is near," he spoke under his breath to Meical.

"He didn't come alone," Meical answered.

Andras cut his eyes back at Tomes. "Umorius informed me that Nordriss was with you when he delivered my message. I know he is here." He called for his men to sweep the area, and a number of immortals emerged from hiding amid the surrounding rock. "The witches' spell. They are likely invisible. Be thorough."

"I won't let my brother give himself up for me." Angelique fought Andras's hold, forcing him to drag her to Meical's safe position.

"Don't hurt her!" Tomes saw what was happening.

Andras peered back outside. "Nordriss," he yelled, "show yourself!" His eyes narrowed. "Try anything and these two die."

Nordriss uncloaked from his veil of invisibility, startling several immortals standing near him. "Back away," he warned, then turned his focus to Andras. "Let them go. You will not win."

"Your powers can't reach me inside these caverns." Andras remained firm in his endeavor. "If I lose...you lose." He lifted a blade to Angelique's throat.

Tomes raised a hand. "Wait. The solution is a simultaneous exchange? I step in as they step out." He threw down his sword.

Andras narrowed his eyes again, considering the demand. "I will release only one. Choose. Who gets their freedom?"

"What!" Andras's cruelty enraged Tomes. "You can't ask me to choose one over the other. The agreement was both in exchange for me."

"Agreements change." Andras sneered.

Tomes glared at Andras, fighting to control his temper.

"You want me dead, and I want you dead," Andras said.

In a state of indecision, Tomes whirled around, turning his back to Andras. Glancing at Nordriss, he patted the pouch at his side, knowing that once inside, there was still hope. But that knowledge made this decision none the easier.

"I'm here," a voice struck Tomes's ear in a barely audible whisper.

Corin. Tomes did not verbally acknowledge him, keeping his presence hidden. *I know what I have to do.* The sound of his friend's voice had brought him to a decision.

Forgive me, Kara.

Tomes spun back and faced Andras. "Release my sister, Angel." He moved toward the cave.

"Wait." Nordriss cast a spell that placed a swirling barrier of energy between Tomes and the mouth of the cave, stopping him in his tracks.

The immortals encircling them scrambled back, fearing his power.

"This may mean your life." Nordriss took several long strides to reach him. "Once inside, there is nothing

I can do to help you."

"With the riddle, I have a chance."

Nordriss said nothing more and lowered the barrier.

"I've warned you, try anything, and they die," Andras reminded the sorcerers.

Tomes advanced to the mouth of the cave. "I step inside when Angel steps out."

Andras stepped forward with Angelique. "On the count of three." He counted and shoved her outside the moment Tomes entered the cave.

"No, Tomes." Angelique doubled back in an attempt to stop him, but as she reentered the cave, someone grabbed her from behind and pulled her back out.

"Corin. Jordon." Tomes was able to see both immortals since their spell of invisibility had broken upon entering the cave. He had counted on Corin to intervene, but Jordon, though not surprising, was unanticipated.

Now trapped inside, he whirled when Kara cried out, catching sight of Meical dragging her away.

Hold on, Kara. He maneuvered past advancing Delghorlins and rogues, guided by her cries that reverberated throughout the cavern. Passing into an adjacent cave—a large, open space dimly lit by torchlight—he came face-to-face with Meical.

"Back off," Meical warned.

Tomes gave the area a quick once-over, taking note of three passageways branching to deeper recesses— one directly ahead of him, and the other two located along the right side of the cave.

"You have me, now let her go," Tomes demanded, turning to face his pursuer—Andras.

"It's okay, Meical," Andras motioned to him. "You can release her." He stepped closer. "He is no threat now."

Meical shoved Kara toward Tomes. "Say your

goodbyes."

"Are you okay?" Tomes pulled her into his arms.

"I'm not hurt." She clung to him.

"Something's about to happen," he whispered in her ear and inconspicuously slipped a hand into the pouch at his side. "Cover your eyes, and don't open them until I say to. Get ready to run."

"Stop him!" Andras ordered. "He's up to something."

Before Meical could reach him, Tomes raised the small bottle and threw it down in one swift motion, generating a brilliant flash of light that blinded the nightwalkers.

"Keep your eyes shut." He grabbed Kara's hand, snatched up a torch, and fled through the nearest passage to their right.

Unable to see, Kara stumbled and fell, opening her eyes. "My eyes. They burn. Everything is blurry."

"It's a chemical reaction." He helped her up and hastened her forward. "At least you were spared the flash that has the others temporarily blinded. But it won't last long."

"How do we get out of here?"

"By first rights...no time to explain."

Taking every right turn they came to, the underground system was proving to be a complex labyrinth.

"The ceiling is getting lower." He led her into a cave chamber riddled with dripstones of various forms. "To a point you must cower," he quoted a line from the riddle, stooping to keep from hitting his head on stalactites that hung from the ceiling. "Watch your footing. Flowstone and stalagmites are everywhere."

Pausing, Tomes scanned the cave, seeing no way out other than where they'd entered. "We can't backtrack with the Örök Vér pursing. There has to be another way out."

Moving through the cave, Kara slipped and fell several feet down, into a shallow body of water.

"Are you hurt?" Tomes reached for her hand, catching his reflection in the pool. "Past a shallow reflection."

Kara tried to stand. "My ankle. I can't put any weight on it."

Tomes laid the torch aside and climbed down to her position. He assessed her injury. "We have no powers in here to heal it. Can you keep going?"

"It's going to slow me down, but I'll make it."

Tomes helped her out of the pool and retrieved their torch. "This pool is another clue solved. We are on the right track."

"Clue?"

"There is said to be a small space located within these caverns that is free of morvormanite. Nordriss gave me a riddle that leads to that space." He visually scoured the cave. "The next clue is a weeping curtain." *A weeping curtain reveals*. "There." He pointed. "That has to be it." He aimed for a drape of stalactites that presented a stunning formation several feet in front of them. "A weeping curtain reveals." Circling behind the curtain, he found an exit. "This is our way out."

"Strange that it's several feet off the ground."

Tomes observed a carving above the pass-through—the Circle of the Morpar Kingdom. "The only path forward, marked by a great seal."

He helped Kara through the opening, entering a circular cave that contained entrances to six continuing passageways.

"My vision is clearing." Kara let go of his hand.

"That means the Delghorlins has too. Andras won't be far behind."

"Six tunnels. Which way do we go?"

"We go this way." Tomes pointed to the first passage on the right. "Always the first right."

Following the widening tunnel, Kara suddenly stopped. "Listen. That sounds like wind. I think it's coming through gaps in the rock."

"That tells us we're near the edge of the mountain, right where we need to be."

"What is the next clue?"

"Lured forth by a guide, past a dragon long bound."

Kara slowed down. "This tunnel branches into four passages."

"Take the first right," Tomes reminded her.

Following that course until reaching another set of branching tunnels, Tomes was impressed by the intricate course of entangled pathways.

"How is that ankle." He saw that Kara was struggling and stopped to check her injury. "It's worse."

"We have to keep moving. I'll make it."

Continuing, they soon emerged into an array of spectacular rock columns, an interwoven space formed by the merging of numerous tunnels.

"Stay close." Tomes caught the sound of movement in the cavern. "We're not alone. Someone else is here."

"Dir Cyohr." A voice reverberated. "The chemical was a nasty trick. Only delaying your death."

"It's Andras," Kara's voice trembled. "He's found us."

Tomes visually searched their dark surroundings, but it was impossible to pinpoint his location amid the grand web of rock formations and tunnel openings. "Show yourself." He caught sight of the enemy's silhouettes as they endeavored to encircle them.

"This is as far as you go." A dark form stepped from behind a column, gripping the handle of a sword.

Meical appeared next to him with deadly daggers drawn, ready to strike, but before they had a chance to assail, an unexpected arrival halted their action.

"What's happening." Kara stumbled back.

A slew of immortals had surfaced from a tunnel behind Andras and Meical, and in attack mode, assailed the Örök Vér.

"Indithian soldiers," Andras alerted, and released a devilish roar as he and Meical dove into combat.

Tomes caught sight of a familiar face. "It's Vynce and his men."

"Run," Vynce yelled. "More of the enemy are coming. A lot more."

"What about you?" Tomes watched as the expert fighter took down an opponent with a skillful maneuver.

"Our job is to get you out alive. We will be right behind you," Vynce assured him. "Go!"

"That's our tunnel." Tomes ushered Kara toward the passageway they needed to take—the first right—but with her injured ankle, her pace of movement was slow.

"Hold this." He handed her the torch. "I'm going to carry you." He scooped her off her feet and darted into the passage.

Not far ahead, the tunnel transitioned into a cave that could only be entered through the skeletal mouth of a long-dead dragon.

"The next clue." Tomes slowed his pace and lowered Kara back onto her feet. "The dragon long bound."

He ran his hand along the partially embedded skeletal remains. "A real dragon."

"How did it get in here?"

"That wall," he motioned directly ahead. "You can tell it was formed by a collapse." He looked up at the soaring roof of the cave. "This was once a large space."

"I don't see any tunnels. The collapse might have blocked it."

"No. It's here. 'Past a dragon long bound' is a clue,

proving that the dragon skeleton was already here when the riddle was written." Tomes walked the cave. "This is it." He discovered their passage next to the dragon's head, concealed by a large rock formation that deceived the eyes.

Hearing someone's fast approach, Tomes rushed toward Kara, glad to see that it was Vynce and several of his men.

"They are right behind us," Vynce alerted. "Keep moving."

Tomes scooped Kara up again and darted into the tunnel.

"I hope this leads somewhere," Vynce said.

"I'm following a riddle that is said to lead to a space that is free of morvormanite," Tomes told him. "We are almost there."

"We had better find it...fast." Vynce observed Kara's injury. "How bad is it?"

"I can't run," Kara answered. "I'm slowing you down."

"We're close." The last clue from the riddle kept replaying in Tomes's mind. *With a touch and a whisper.*

"I hear the sound of wind again," Kara said. "I feel it."

The soft brush of wind against Tomes's skin brought him to an immediate stop. *A touch and a whisper.*

"Wait." He backtracked several steps. "Look at the walls." He pointed out the ordinary color.

Vynce ran a hand over the rock. "No morvormanite."

"It's definitely a small space." Tomes put Kara down. "But it's all we need."

"They found the tunnel." Kara gasped at the sight of their Delghorlin pursuers' swift approach.

"There are too many to hold off," Vynce said.

Now able to utilize their powers, Tomes quickly

conjured a shield that enclosed his party, blocking Andras's charge. "It's time to go." He opened a window to Morpar and ushered Kara and the soldiers through the portal to safety.

"He is not happy." Vynce stared at Andras.

"No." Tomes met the Örök Vér leader's glare, feeling his hatred. "Let's get out of here." He turned with Vynce and passed through the portal.

The fight was over...for now.

* * * *

At Zarchia Point, Corin, Angelique, Jozsef, Galvar, Jordon, and Nordriss stood aghast at the sight of immortals pouring out of the caverns.

"We will never stop that horde," Corin said.

"We can slow them down." Nordriss cast several bolts of energy at the cave entrance, triggering a collapse.

Jordon made a 360° turn. "We're surrounded, and the effects of the fumes appear to be wearing off."

Nordriss quickly encased them within a protective field of energy—a shield of transparent, golden light.

Looking out at the enemy, Corin saw several familiar faces—Lehndra, Jax, and Jitters, the latter uttering a nervous cackle. "Jax." He narrowed his eyes. "You'll one day pay. In the worst way."

Seconds later, Lavor stormed onto the scene with his battalion, sending the Örök Vér and rogues on the run.

"Perfect timing, Constable," Jordon said, the moment Nordriss lowered the shield.

"We moved in when we saw the exchange." Lavor looked at Angelique. "At least you are safe."

"The dir cyohr has the riddle. I trust that he will find his way to freedom." Nordriss stepped toward Hediye, then opened a window to Morpar. "All we can do now is wait."

Crossing over to the ruins of Morpar Palace, Corin stood with Angelique, staring south, in the direction of Zarchia.

"He's not dead," she said. "I would know, morvormanite or not."

Sitting down near the palace entrance, time crawled as they waited for any sign that Tomes had made it. Minutes felt like an eternity.

"Are you okay?" Jordon approached.

"How long has it been?" Angelique asked.

Jordon sat down with them. "I figure half an hour."

"Wait." Angelique sat up and looked at Corin. She smiled. "Tomes."

"Look." Jordon got back up. "A portal."

Rushing toward the portal, Corin saw that Kara and several soldiers had passed through.

"Where is Tomes?" Angelique asked Kara.

"He's coming." Kara looked back through the portal.

"You're hurt." Angelique helped her.

A minute later, Tomes and Vynce passed through the window to a roaring cheer, and the army dropped onto one knee before their king crying: "ALL HAIL THE DIR CYOHR. KING TOMES OF MORPAR. SAVIOR OF THE ELEVENTH DIMENSION."

Vynce stepped toward Galvar. "I cannot say that I was careful, but I am back."

Galvar laughed and pulled him to his shoulder.

"Another victory won." Nordriss stood between Hediye and Suna.

"Hopefully we won't have any more battles for some time to come," Tomes told him. "But with Andras still living, this won't be our last fight."

"Knowing you have a destiny to fulfill, I trusted you would survive; however, there is always a small chance to alter one's destiny and change their fate."

"Something Andras is desperate to do," Tomes said. "Let's hope his window of opportunity is now closed." He offered Nordriss a handshake. "It's good to know I have you as an ally."

Nordriss shook his hand. "You are always welcome in Shudrorah, King Tomes of Morpar."

With that farewell, the sorcerer opened a window to his kingdom.

"King Tomes," Suna addressed him. "You still have one of my biraz falcıları." She bent down with an amber gem and called the arachnid to her.

Tomes jumped when the spider sprang from his shirt and crawled down his body. "I forgot it was there."

"You know where to find us." Nordriss tossed a wave of his hand, and he, Hediye, and Suna departed.

Turning, Tomes's gaze fell on Corin. "I cannot believe it."

"What?" Corin was focused on reshaping his Stetson.

"Is there anything that thing won't survive?" Tomes laughed. "I swear, it must possess magical properties."

Corin cast a swaggering grin that accentuated the dimple indenting his left cheek. "Anything's possible." He brushed back his wavy, blond mop, tipped his head, and slid his hat on.

EPILOGUE

Von Vadim Estate
Hixton, Wisconsin

Corin stood with Jozsef on the lanai. "It has been one hell of a journey. So many changes. Tomes's immortal calling. And you, regaining your soul." He gazed toward the woods that rang with distant howls.

"Tomes mentioned he would be returning to the Eleventh Dimension following the ceremony."

"He *is* king." Corin chuckled at the sound of his own words. "Hard as that is to fathom."

"I suppose Kara will be going back with him."

Corin nodded. "Nothing is going to separate those two now. I wouldn't be surprised if we're all attending another union soon."

Jozsef bumped his shoulder. "But tonight, it's all about you and Angelique."

Corin's upper lip curved into a wide smile. "I have a surprise for her. Following the ceremony, I plan to take her to Hungary. I want her to know our ancestral home...to know the man I once was. And I want you to come with us. As a family."

"What about your estate here?"

"I've made arrangements with Jordon," Corin told him. "He's going to stay awhile. Look after things."

"Seems you have it all worked out."

"So, you'll come?"

Jozsef nodded. "We have five hundred years of lost time to make up for."

"Good." Corin straightened and adjusted his collar. "How do I look?"

"Like you're worth a million bucks. Which you are. Many times over."

Corin's attention was drawn to Jordon and Tomes who approached the outside door.

Jordon tapped his watch. "It's 11:45. Time to get out there."

Aiming for the gazebo, Jordon suddenly stopped. "Someone's here." He spotted two figures at the side of the house.

"Pierson. Patricia. I'm glad you made it," Corin welcomed them.

"From now on, it's Allen." Pierson shook each man's hand.

"You should know, Allen, that I'll be sticking around Hixton for a while. Staying at the estate," Jordon informed Pierson. "I might even consider lending my expertise to that small force of yours. You know my credentials."

Pierson rolled his eyes. "Ego and all."

Jordon slapped his shoulder. "In all seriousness, Sheriff, I'm glad to see you looking so well."

"Thank you, Marshal. And I'm glad to see you looking...older." Pierson displayed a half-grin.

Moving toward the gazebo, they passed through an

aisle formed by rows of white chairs draped in blue roses.

"This is beautiful," Patricia said, and she and Pierson slipped into their seats.

Corin turned his sights on the gazebo that was bathed in soft, pearlescent lighting and adorned with white orchids and blue roses. He walked toward Galvar who stood in the structure's center, ready to perform the ceremony, and took his place.

Glancing over the small congregation, he felt blessed to have such trusted friends. He looked into the face of each guest: Lavor, Staca, Bren, Pierson, Patricia, Jordon, Vynce, Kara, and of course the three men standing with him, Galvar, Tomes, and Jozsef.

"It is time." Galvar signaled Tomes who was ready for his cue and darted away.

Melodic tones of wolves howling their distant symphony, blending with typical night sounds, rode on a light breeze. In anxious anticipation, Corin soaked in the magical atmosphere, elated in the surreal moment.

Watching for Angelique's entrance as a traditional bride, he caught sight of Dusk and Dawn in the backdrop, an indication that she was about to appear, for the servals had scarcely left her side since she'd returned home.

Angelique.

His breath caught when she appeared, dressed in a long, white satin gown adorned with silver lace. Escorted by Tomes, she was a vision of perfection.

As she neared, he outstretched his hand, captivated by her hazel gaze that held a sprinkle of golden flecks. "I'll take it from here," he told Tomes, who kissed his sister's cheek and stepped next to Jozsef.

"Stunning," Corin leaned down and whispered. "You take my breath away."

"I hope not, because you have vows." She smiled.

Corin kissed her hand. "From this moment on you will forever be Angelique von Vadim. There is no backing out now."

"I never would." She interlocked her fingers with his. "We have been through a lot together in six months. We survived Boldor. We survived Tomes's immortal calling that carried us into an apocalyptic world."

"Hey." Tomes squirmed under the scrutiny of onlookers. "Don't make this about me."

"Don't worry, King Tomes, we won't." Corin's response prompted their guests to laugh. "I honestly don't know how that crown fits." He communicated the latter telepathically to Angelique.

Looking into Corin's eyes, Angelique continued. "What I'm trying to say is that we can face anything, as long as we face it together. You, Corin, are my immortal calling. Now and always...eternally mine."

"It is the midnight hour." Galvar reached for a small silver box lying atop a stand on his left and requested that Corin and Angelique face him. "Before we begin." He handed the box to Angelique. "A gift from Tomes."

Angelique tossed her brother a questioning glance and then opened the box. *A shalym disc.*

With no words spoken aloud, Tomes's message rang loud and clear. "Even when we're worlds apart, I'll only be a crosswalk away."

A powerful charm.
A forbidden love.
A deadly rivalry.
Corin & Angelique
After the Fall of Night
S.L. CLAYTOR